New York Dai...

BROADWAY
BUTTERFLY

BROADWAY BUTTERFLY

A THRILLER

Manhattan, 1923. Dot King, one of the most beautiful women in the city, is found murdered. As the daughter of working-class immigrants, with no visible means of income, it's hard to explain how the glamorous gal-about-town could afford her fashionable Midtown apart...

greatest unsolved crimes of the century, and is written in the style of a fictional mystery, told through 4 points of view: (1)Julia Harpman, a reporter at the New York Daily News, and the lead crime reporter in New York at a time when most...

the case. Set in the roaring 20s, in the wake of the global pandemic of the Spanish flu, and against the backdrop of a presidential election campaign in which the attorney general tries to ... for Republican incumbent W...

SARA DIVELLO

THOMAS & MERCER

Published by Thomas & Mercer, Seattle

www.apub.com

Amazon, the Amazon logo, and Thomas & Mercer are trademarks of Amazon.com, Inc., or its affiliates.

ISBN-13: 9781662510137 (hardcover)
ISBN-13: 9781662510151 (paperback)
ISBN-13: 9781662510144 (digital)

Cover design by Richard Ljoenes Design LLC
Cover image: © Daniela Iga / Shutterstock; © Sudha Peravali / ArcAngel

Printed in the United States of America

First edition

BROADWAY
BUTTERFLY

Author's Note

Broadway Butterfly chronicles a true crime that gripped the nation in 1923. I carefully researched this case for several years, interviewing professors, police officers, and other subject-matter experts, while amassing over fifteen hundred distinct pieces of research. My intention in writing this book is to honor the truth of this story and the (very) real people involved.

An essential part of the telling of this story required incorporating the racism, sexism, ethnic prejudice, socioeconomic power dynamics, and corruption of the time, including the offensive attitudes and language of the time. These in no way reflect my own beliefs or moral values.

1923

Chapter 1

There was never a good day for a murder, but reading about one was a very good way to pass the morning commute, Ella Bradford decided, as she turned page 4 of the *New York Daily News*. Like most of the city, she'd been following the Pettit-Wells trial, in which a ruffian innkeeper had been shot—by his mistress, the DA alleged; by himself, the defense insisted—and Ella found herself thinking the distinctly un-Christian thought, *That man probably deserved it.*

While nobody wanted to find themselves at the business end of a shotgun, maybe the hard-drinking wastrel who'd found himself in exactly that undesirable spot had earned his way there. Ella folded the paper, careful not to get ink on the folks sitting on either side of her, just as the train screeched into the 59th Street station, which sent everyone aboard careening into their neighbor. The passengers rose—there were plenty of seats this time of day, one of the benefits of working for a scandalous flapper who kept scandalous hours—and crushed toward the doors. Ella let the white lady next to her go ahead, even though she didn't have to and the white lady didn't seem to notice. New York wasn't segregated, which still seemed strange, even after three years.

Back when she'd first moved up north, the city had overwhelmed her—how big, how many people, how fast, even the number of exits at each subway stop. But now, Ella hurried up the stairs, just as quick and confident as everyone else, in her factory-made wool coat with the fine fur collar, which she'd gotten brand-new at Ohrbach's on 14th Street. She sure had come a long way since she'd sat in the "colored waiting room," to board the "colored car" back in Jacksonville, with no idea what life would be like once she got here, a thousand miles and a world away.

As she crossed Central Park West and cut down 7th Avenue toward Miss Dottie's, she couldn't help but feel like things had finally fallen into place. Even though it was hard to hand her baby, James Junior, who they called "June" for short, over for day boarding each morning, she was thankful to have a job—let alone a good one in Midtown—and to be able to send money back home.

She stopped off for eggs to make that soufflé Mr. Marshall loved so much before he went away for another month. She plunked the money on the counter. It gave her a small thrill, knowing there was ten times that in her purse. Miss Dottie gave her the whole house allowance as soon as she got it from Mr. Marshall. Nobody trusted the help like that—especially if they were Negro. But Miss Dottie trusted her with *all* the money, just like she trusted her with all her secrets.

Ella tucked her chin deeper into her collar as she hurried the last two blocks. She still wasn't used to the cold—how it cut straight through a body, right down to the bone. She tried to remember just how miserable those summers back home were, when Jacksonville grew so hot and clingy that she'd lie just-so at night so as not to stick to herself. The bed she'd shared with her sister had been closest to the window, but there was never much hope for a breeze. But now, sweltering and summer and home felt very far away.

Miss Dottie's building on fashionable West 57th was just a few doors down from Carnegie Hall and across from the Calvary Baptist Church. It boasted a marble lobby, an elevator attended round the clock by an operator, and a dress shop run by a Frenchwoman on the second floor.

Ella hurried inside. "Feels like snow," she said to Womba, the day-time elevator operator.

"Sure does," Womba agreed. She closed the grate, shifted the lever toward "Up," then leaned in too close. "John Thomas said Miss Dottie come in round about midnight with Mr. Marshall, and he never left." She smiled like she'd just won a round.

Ella stiffened. She didn't care for Womba's overfamiliar tone or the news itself. John Thomas, who worked the building's night shift, would do better to keep watch over the lobby and run the elevator instead of keep watch over Miss Dottie and run his mouth. Of course, he wouldn't have anything to run his mouth about if Miss Dottie and Mr. Marshall behaved themselves.

Mr. Marshall never stayed the night, which allowed them all to preserve some sense of respectability. But now that was spoiled, and John Thomas and Womba were already talking about it. Ella didn't want Miss Dottie's reputation—what was left of it, anyhow—ruined. And she didn't want her own stained by association. You were only as good as the house you worked in. Respectability was hard to come by, and to be respectable was everything.

Ella lifted her chin, half a mind to preach a piece on how gossip wasn't Christian. But she didn't want to seem like she was putting on airs or taking the white lady's side. Then again, it was Miss Dottie—*her* white lady. Ella stared straight ahead. "I reckon a person oughtta be able to do as she likes without it being everybody's news."

Womba straightened up. "Well then!" she said.

Thick silence filled the cramped space until they reached the fifth floor, where Womba jerked the car to a stop and yanked the brass grille open. "Y'all have a good day, now," she said, sickly sweet.

Ella lifted her chin. "You too, now," she said, just as prissy, and stepped out.

Whatever Womba grumbled next was lost as the elevator slid away. Ella fished the key out of her handbag and sighed. Miss Dottie was generous to a fault and as close to a friend as a boss could be, but sometimes Ella wished the woman would just live quiet and not draw attention.

Every morning, she crept in so as not to wake Miss Dottie, who always slept late. But now, irritated by the gossip, and to give Mr. Marshall a chance to get some clothes on, she slammed the door hard. She looked down and frowned. Two of Miss Dottie's spring coats lay dumped on the floor. They were cotton, too light for this weather.

Ella bent down, but at the last second didn't pick them up for reasons she couldn't account for. The fine hairs on the back of her neck prickled. No matter how drunk she got or how late she came in, Miss Dottie *never* left clothes on the floor. If you'd been born poor, you were cursed to be neat, Miss Dottie said.

Ella straightened. "Miss Dottie?" she called. No reply. Womba's gossip must've been wrong—Miss Dottie was probably just over at Guimares's again, Ella reasoned, where she wound up most nights. It was like he'd put some sort of love spell on her that lured her into his bed, where she wouldn't see truth, wouldn't listen to reason.

Ella sighed. "Lord, give me patience." Now she'd have to sneak Miss Dottie fresh street clothes and face Womba's smug smile.

Ella stepped over the coats to go put the eggs in the icebox, but stopped short. The place didn't feel right, didn't smell right. She pulled the strap of her purse closer. "Miss Dottie?"

Silence.

One of the french doors to the bedroom was open. Some of the panes were smashed out. Glass shards were scattered on the floor, and among them, the bedroom telephone—its cord stretched out beyond it into the dim bedroom, as though the machine itself had grown legs and tried to escape, only to be brought up short, tethered by its own leash.

A shiver cut through her. This was all wrong. The open door, which Miss Dottie always kept closed so Ella's arrival wouldn't wake her. The broken glass. The out-of-place phone. Every room had its own extension. There was no reason for the phone to be so far from the fancy little table next to Miss Dottie's bed.

A high-pitched whine sounded in Ella's ears. She looked around the small living room again. "Mr. Marshall?" she called, hoping against hope he'd answer, that everything was all right. But the sick wave in her belly knew it wasn't.

"Miss Dottie?" Ella called louder, craning to see into the still-dark bedroom. Maybe the broken glass was a clumsy drunken accident. Miss Dottie could've run into the door when she came in last night. Or maybe she'd had another one of her parties, and there'd be some drunk, no-good man passed out in the bed. Lord, that was all she needed—having to shoo some unknown white man out of here.

But what if it wasn't?

Ella set the eggs down and forced herself to walk over. Tentatively, she pushed the door all the way open and stepped into the bedroom. Her eyes adjusted to the dim light, and she gasped. The room was catawampus. Drawers yanked open. Clothes dragged out. Jewelry boxes dumped upside down. *They'd been robbed!*

But then she saw the body on the brass bed, and her heart near stopped. It was Miss Dottie, crumpled up and broken, like a doll that had been roughed up and thrown away. Her face was half-hidden under a pillow.

Ella ran to her. "Miss Dottie!"

Silence. Thick, unnatural silence. And the smell—*Lord, the smell!*—a cloying stench of hospitals.

The covers were rumpled. Miss Dottie's pale right arm hung limp over the edge. Her left arm was twisted up behind her like a chicken in a roasting pan, legs sprawled midkick. Her yellow silk nightgown with the black lace was rucked up to her hips. She'd fought hard to get free of whoever'd done this.

The ringing in Ella's ears shrieked like a teakettle whistle. The chemical odor made her stomach heave. The room started to spin. Slowly, she reached out and touched Miss Dottie's foot. It was cold—terrible cold.

She wanted to turn and run, but she sucked in her breath, held it, and forced herself a few steps closer to Miss Dottie's face. It was frozen in that same awful stillness. Her eyes were closed. Ella reached out and put a hand gently on her chest. It was warm. Hope flared. Maybe she was just out cold drunk. *Wouldn't be the first time.*

Ella grabbed her shoulders and shook her. "Miss Dottie!"

No reply—just a loose-boned deadweight.

She shook her harder as hysteria bubbled up. "Wake up, you hear?! Please! *Please!*" Still nothing—just that terrible hush.

Ella knew then—knew for sure. Miss Dottie was gone.

Her heart galloped so hard it hurt. She let go of the pale shoulders she'd rubbed with lemon juice to get rid of freckles, lotioned, and dressed a thousand times. The black, lacy straps had fallen half-down.

The tingling in Ella's scalp tightened, pulling on the back of her head like some bully yanking her hair. Suddenly, she was *sure* there were eyes on her. She frantically looked around the dark, ransacked room. The bathroom door was halfway open. *Could the killer be in there?* A wail rose in her throat. It sounded like a trapped animal.

Ella turned and ran. Her hip slammed into the doorframe, which brought her up short. The glass panes rattled.

She near flew back to the elevator, pushed the call button. "Womba? Womba! Help!" She pounded on the closed doors.

She punched the button harder, again and again. But the motor didn't whir. What if Womba had gone on a break? Out for lunch? Was mad at her sass? Ella glanced at the door to the emergency stairs—anything to escape. But the stairs were only for fire—dark and old. She'd never used them before. Nobody did.

Desperate, she looked around the tiny hall, toward the front apartment. What if the killer was still in the building, working his way through?

She punched the call button again and again—frantic now. *"Womba!"*

Silence. The lift wasn't coming. Nobody was.

She ran back inside and slammed the door like the hounds of hell were on her heels. She twisted the lock. The skin behind her ears gripped so hard it hurt. What to do? *What to do?* She couldn't think.

She looked down. Lord almighty, she'd stepped on Miss Dottie's coats. She jumped to the side. Standing on a dead woman's coats couldn't be good. And why had the killer brought them from the bedroom closet only to leave them dumped on the hall floor? She stumbled back to the living room.

The bedroom phone in the doorway made her shiver. Whoever'd done this had moved the phone out of Miss Dottie's reach, but hadn't yanked it clear out of the wall. Somehow that was worse—the cruel, careful placement.

She edged around it.

The living room phone was still where it oughtta be, on the side table. She clicked the lever, desperate for a connection. "Operator! Give me the police! There's been a murder!"

Chapter 2

"All rise!" the bailiff called. Julia Harpman stood with the rest of the assembled crowd as the judge swept from the room, his black robe billowing ominously behind him. Reflexively, she patted her head, then thigh, an instinctive female inspection to make sure her riotous curls were still tucked under the blue cloche hat and her skirt hadn't shifted immodestly. As one of only a few women in the courtroom—and the only one who wasn't on trial, testifying, or there to gawk—it was imperative to keep up professional appearances.

The Pettit-Wells murder trial had reached closing arguments. It would soon be up to the jury to decide the fate of Miss Billie Wells, the scorned mistress who stood accused of shooting her violent, hard-drinking, loose-spending, live-in lover, "Roadhouse Jim" Pettit. The trial had looked fairly bleak for the accused until Mrs. Pettit, Roadhouse Jim's estranged wife, had stepped forward to testify in support of her husband's mistress.

From the start, the case had every ingredient to make sensational, front-page news—a mistress, a bad man, and a murder. But the wife-mistress alliance was a twist nobody had seen coming, and the public and press had seized on it with equal glee. Julia had carefully hewed her coverage to capture each scintillating detail, and when the case reached its sure-to-be searing verdict, she'd be there to report on it for the *Daily News*. Just as she always did.

As the rare female reporter—and the even rarer woman on the hard-hitting crime beat—Julia had found the solidarity of mistress and wife, defendant and widow, particularly interesting. The few other women at her paper, and in the newspaper field as a whole, covered cooking, astrology, fashion, and advice for the lovelorn. Julia had started her career on the "ladies pages" in her hometown of Memphis, then worked hard to transcend them and gain entrée to all-male desks, first heading to Knoxville to cut her teeth covering the courts, then heading to the Big Apple to test her mettle on the crime beat in the biggest, most glamorous, and most competitive city in the country. Since then, she'd become the lead crime reporter at the paper, and one of the best in the whole city. And yet the pressure was always on to prove she deserved to be there and had the chutzpah to stay. That pressure would not end with this story or the next. The necessity to arrive earlier, stay later, and work twice as hard (and get paid half as much), simply for the privilege to be allowed to be there, trailed her like a constant shadow.

But it also meant she found herself with the power to shape the narrative of the news, not only by *which* stories she covered but also by *how* she covered them. So when, like this case, the accused was a woman and the *Brooklyn Daily Times* headlines had crowed, State Flays Wells Woman at Start of Murder Trial, Julia had ensured *her* paper's headline trumpeted, Innkeeper's Wife Aids Miss Wells; Calls "Roadhouse Jim" a Wastrel.

Facts were facts. But the storyteller steered the narrative and the narrative steered public perception. It was an invisible power. And Julia was the rare woman to wield it.

"Recess! Fifteen minutes!" the bailiff called.

While the rest of the packed courtroom streamed toward the lobby and restrooms, Julia headed toward the pressroom, grabbed an open phone, and waited while the operator connected her to Philip Payne, the city-desk editor at the *News.* "It's me," she said when Philip came on the line. "Did I miss anything?"

"Well, it's been a busy day for the good ladies of the society pages," Philip said with only a hint of amusement. The guy was half-deaf, near-sighted, and quick to spot a good story. He was also unflagging in his quest for front-page dominance, which had whipped the fledgling *News* into a force to be reckoned with. "The Stotesburys are hosting some European royal family while they winter in Palm Beach, and rumor has it they're going to hold a lunch for President Harding next week."

"Exciting week for the Stotesburys," Julia said, rolling her eyes. The Stotesburys were pillars of high society and, consequently, of the society pages. Wintering in Palm Beach and spending their remaining time in a 147-room Georgian mansion outside Philadelphia known as Whitemarsh Hall that boasted three floors aboveground, three below, and a staff of seventy full-time gardeners just to maintain the estate, they were a living illustration of opulence. And then there was the fashion: custom-made clothes from Paris and extravagant jewels.

Julia had never been interested in those stories, but the Stotesburys were hot news for the society pages. Every detail would be devoured by the *Daily News*'s female readers, who would aspire to ape the styles set by society ladies as best they could on far-more-meager incomes. "Anyway," Julia said, "I guess Harding's got to line up the big donors before he announces whether or not he's going to run for reelection."

"The real question is, who the heck's going to support the most scandal-ridden president in recent memory running *again*? You'd have to be crazy. And they'd have to be even crazier to announce he's running *now*," Philip replied.

Julia had to agree. The head of the Veterans Bureau was facing congressional inquiry for misappropriating funds, and the attorney general had barely survived the special investigation around Teapot Dome. Harding's so-called Ohio Gang, the band of good old boys from his home state that he'd appointed to cabinet positions, could slaughter his chances before he even threw his hat in the ring again.

"Perhaps a tour of the Stotesburys' private zoo will break the tension," Julia joked. "I wonder if they already have an ass in residence or if they prefer exotic animals."

Philip snorted. "A zoo can always use a second ass."

Julia had learned the prevalence and power of the society pages early on. After she and her brothers left the house, their mother, Josephine—Josie to her friends, and nearly everyone was her friend or hoped to be—had built a career for herself presiding over Memphis's *News Scimitar*'s society pages until her passing a few years back.

Julia knew the only thing more unusual than a newswoman was a newswoman whose mother was also a newswoman. But Josie's lifelong devotion to writing, first as a novelist-by-night when her children were young and later in newspapers, had shown Julia what was possible, carving a trail through the nearly impenetrable world of working men and bringing her daughter with her.

When Julia was eight, Josie had brought her as an official guest to the Tennessee Woman's Press and Authors' Club meeting in Nashville. Julia could still remember the pink and white sweet peas that had decorated the tables, the feel of the skirt her mother had gotten her for the occasion, the look of pride on her father's face as he saw them off at the train station. But most of all, she remembered her sense of awe that her mother had taken her two hundred miles to Nashville, where she'd gotten to sit in a room of forty women, all of whom were professional writers, and that *her mother* was one of them. Anything had seemed possible after that. Now, twenty years later, she was living that possibility every day. She was a newspaperwoman, and of most immediate importance, she had a developing story and an editor waiting.

"*Listen*," Philip said, "more pertinent to us, Hellinger just got a tip that some Broadway butterfly offed herself over on West 57th. Apparently, he'd met her a few times. Says she was one of the prettiest girls in New York—some sort of model or something."

"Of course he did," Julia said, shaking her head. Mark Hellinger was a baby reporter and the newest addition to the city desk. Fresh off working at some stage-industry rag, he now covered the theater beat for the *News* and seemed to know every Broadway bum and sugar baby the city boasted.

"Well, as soon as the verdict comes in, hurry up and get back here. Should be quick and easy, but I need your touch on it: *Good-Time Girl Crumbles under Pressures of Big City Life!* Tug the heartstrings. Sob-sister stuff. You know the drill."

Julia did, indeed, know the drill. She wasn't surprised Hellinger knew this girl who'd taken her own life, or that the girl had done it. The city could be a harsh place, especially for women.

"I'll take care of it," Julia promised. Under her pen, she would honor the girl's life and write her as a full-fledged person, even as she tugged the requisite reader heartstrings. "I better go."

"Wait!" Philip said urgently. "What's my star crime reporter predict for Miss Wells?"

"Acquittal," she said.

"Yeah?" Philip asked, notably perkier. "I got a little pool going. Maybe I'll increase my wager."

"Right. It's all about your wager. Who cares if a murder was committed and a woman's life hangs in the balance?" Julia countered. Gallows humor and a thick skin were requirements on the crime beat.

"Is that sarcasm, or do we have a bad connection?" Philip joked. "Just hurry up and get back here, will ya?"

"Absolutely," Julia promised. "I wouldn't want to miss a single riveting detail of the Stotesburys' next dinner party."

"See? That's why I need the infamous Harpman nose for the news—you've got to work your magic and dig up the next doozy," Philip returned.

Julia snorted through her apparently infamous nose and hung up.

She and Philip had come a long way since the day she'd shown up clutching a folder of clippings and having been flatly refused at the first few papers she'd gone to. Philip, at the helm of the newly launched *News* and determined to grow it, had looked her dead in the eye and told her if she could get the scoop on a church scandal whose preacher was causing a schism, he'd consider giving her a job.

He hadn't mentioned that his top two reporters had tried and failed to get that same story.

Julia, who'd arrived in New York with sixty-three dollars, one suitcase, a borrowed squirrel coat, and a heart full of dreams between her and failure, had returned hours later with the story about the preacher . . . as well as another story about secret communist meetings being held in that very same church.

Philip had hired her on the spot.

Covering this Broadway butterfly's death meant she'd miss dinner with her husband, Westbrook, but he would understand. Between his job covering sports and whatever else the *United News* threw at him and hers covering crime, it was a rare night the newlyweds, married just seven months, had the luxury of a meal together, but that small sacrifice was well worth it for life as a newspaper duo. Westbrook, more than anyone, would understand. Which was one of the many reasons she considered herself the luckiest girl in the world.

She rushed back down the hall toward the courtroom. Juries were unpredictable, but she was confident they would acquit the sweetly smiling, indefatigable Miss Wells, despite the DA's argument that it would be physically impossible for a man to shoot himself with a shotgun that was four inches longer from muzzle to trigger than his arm.

Male jurors—and of course, all jurors were male—didn't want to believe women were capable of murder. It threatened their sense of safety and world order, where only *they* were capable of passion, violence, and retribution. A wife *and* a mistress teaming up against their man struck inordinate fear in men who were as comfortably settled with their ideas about women's roles as wives and mothers as they were with their pipes and newspapers after a day of toil.

Julia yanked open the courtroom door, wondering just how many women surrounded by laundry, stacks of dishes, and children in need of attention, and all too often, themselves victims of violence and hardship, would have to cluck reassuringly that *of course* Miss Wells hadn't done it . . . all while a certainty roiling deep in their marrow that she probably *had*.

Julia made her way past rows of gum-chomping newspapermen, her colleagues and competitors from every paper in the city, and the usual assortment of curious spectators. A brittle, keyed-up excitement zinged through the air as the gallery waited to see how the DA would close, what impassioned plea for justice he would make, how he'd try to remind the jurors of poor "Roadhouse Jim," and how the man's small but murderous mistress must've been the one to pull the trigger.

Every living creature seeks survival first and foremost. A cornered animal will attack. Women, Julia had learned from ten years on the beat, were no different. Women mostly committed homicide out of sheer desperation to protect themselves and their children. Men, on the other hand, were more apt to murder for lust, rage, revenge, greed . . . or simply because they could.

Chapter 3

Late-afternoon bleariness spilled into police headquarters, where it spread like a bloodstain. Inspector John D. Coughlin, commander of the Detectives Division, adjusted his glasses, which had dug indentations into the bridge of his nose, and squinted at the impossibly high stack of reports. Daylight saving wasn't for another month, which meant darkness fell early, crime was up, and his entire staff was overworked. He had twelve hundred men under him, but with Manhattan as big as it was, they were still always stretched too thin.

One of his lines rang, and he reached for it wearily. "Coughlin."

"George LeBrun from the medical examiner's office for you, sir," the pleasant voice of the operator announced.

"Put him through," Coughlin said, as a flicker of warning stirred. He talked to the ME's office all the time, but LeBrun, the towering French-Danish secretary to the chief ME, never called.

LeBrun came on the line. "I got a very strange call about a suicide from our favorite gumshoe, Frank Houghtalin."

Coughlin lifted his head, smelling blood in the air. "What'd *he* want?" Houghtalin didn't deign to work for run-of-the-mill clients. The so-called fixer specialized in well-heeled circles. If he called, it was because some bigwig had gotten himself on the flypaper. Usually, it was some misdemeanor or infraction that only bogged down the system.

It benefited all parties if it quietly went away. Coughlin had helped do just that a few times.

But Houghtalin usually called the local precinct for such requests, not the ME's office. If Houghtalin was reaching out to the ME's office, it meant a bigwig was somehow involved with a dead body. And if the bigwig had bothered to hire Houghtalin, the best fixer in the city, he wanted it handled fast and quiet and was willing to shell out big bucks to make it happen. That pegged this as a high-stakes ordeal.

"He was asking about reports on West 57th. I checked the log, and sure enough, a patrolman called in a woman's suicide this morning. The patrolman said nothing looked suspicious. But after Houghtalin's call, I figured I'd better go over myself. And well, something doesn't look right. You'd better come over right away—144 West 57th."

Coughlin froze. He had an encyclopedic knowledge of the city's crimes and their locations. Mention of an address triggered an unsolicited roll call of every crime committed there.

West 57th Street.

Robbery-murder, 1913. Canadian milliner found on his bed in a boardinghouse. Hands bound behind his back, gas tubing and a towel stuffed in his mouth. Never solved.

The 1919 debacle when Arnold Rothstein, the biggest mobster in New York, shot two patrolmen during a raid on his gambling place but later walked because the nineteen witnesses whose bail he'd paid wouldn't testify against him. Nothing ever stuck to Rothstein—

"Coughlin! Can you hear me?" LeBrun said.

Coughlin shook his head to clear it, hoping the dull ache pounding behind his eyes would clear too. "On my way."

He sensed this would delay him getting home to the Bronx. He called Mamie to tell her not to wait on him for dinner. His sister, younger by two years, ran as tight a ship at home as he did at work.

She was brisk and efficient and ran the household in a ceaselessly punctual manner, managing her husband, Samuel; their son, William;

and their father, a retired beat cop. Mamie didn't appreciate tardiness, and John D. Coughlin was nothing if not punctual and efficient.

◆ ◆ ◆

Back when Coughlin started on the force in 1896, this stretch of West 57th had been *the* one to live on for New York's richest families. Then city ordinances shaved ten feet off sidewalks to fit more cars, forcing mansion dwellers to roll back their private stoops and yards—which offended the Rockefellers and Roosevelts so bad they packed up their servants and the family silver and hightailed it to more accommodating streets. The fancy brownstones they left behind got chopped into apartments.

Now jazz babies in furs and impractical shoes strolled the still plenty-wide sidewalks, wasting money on frilly stuff at frilly stores like Henri Bendel. Then they'd "recover" at one of the beauty parlors that had cropped up like weeds on every block.

Number 144 looked like every other brownstone on the street— glass-windowed lobby with some sort of dress shop above, topped with three floors of residential apartments.

Inside, a giant archway connected the lobby to the adjoining one at 146 next door.

A female elevator operator stood waiting. Women, it seemed, were doing everything these days. "Five, please," Coughlin said, stepping into the car.

She followed him in. "Yes, sir."

He flashed his badge and opened his notebook. "Name?"

"Juanita Marable, sir." When his pen stalled at that jumble, she added, "They call me Womba."

Womba, he noted. "You work last night?"

"No, sir. John Thomas works seven to seven."

"Notice anything unusual this morning? Seen anyone who isn't a resident?"

Womba halted the elevator at the fifth floor. "No, sir. It's been a slow day. Nobody but residents in or out until Ella called the police."

He nodded. "We'll have some questions before you leave today."

"Yes, sir." If she was curious as to why, she kept it to herself. She opened the accordion grate and let him out.

Coughlin assessed the hall: empty—only two apartments, one at the front of the building, door closed, and one to the rear, door open. LeBrun's measured voice came from within the rear.

Coughlin approached, examining the walls, the door, the door-frame. There was no sign of forced entry—no chipped paint or splintered wood; the Yale lock looked new and untampered with. If she hadn't taken her own life, the victim had either let her killer in or the killer had a key. That was the thing people didn't want to think about: murders generally were committed by people the victims knew—most knew their attackers well.

The tiny entryway held a stone stand with two umbrellas—one larger, a men's umbrella. A torn scrap of medical gauze dangled from it. He made a mental note to collect the gauze as evidence.

He stepped into a small living room, and a dopey-eyed patrolman jumped up. "Kelleher," he said by way of introduction. "The body's on the bed." He jerked his thumb at a set of french doors. It was clear the guy thought his talents were wasted guarding a dame who'd offed herself. Coughlin scowled, and his notoriously frosty gaze made the kid straighten up. Some young bucks these days didn't appreciate having to pay their dues. Perhaps an assignment to some sleepy, far-flung outpost in Queens mediating sheep-grazing disputes would set him right.

Coughlin waited an additional beat until the kid started to squirm, and then turned to begin mentally cataloging the room: a sideboard held a stash of prewar booze nobody could get these days, a giant vase of hothouse flowers that probably cost what he made in a week, and both a radio *and* a phonograph. Based on the lacy shawl, girly slippers, and stacks of women's magazines by the couch, no man lived here. He was also sure that no girl earning an honest living could afford all this. Whoever she was, she was kept.

He quickly memorized the names of the magazines and which musicians were featured on the twelve-inch shiny black records, also noting the quantity and position of every item in the room. People often marveled at his ability to do this—and have perfect recall later. But he was more surprised when they couldn't. Then again, almost everyone disappointed him somehow.

He continued to study the room. Even the most seemingly insignificant detail had to be cataloged. To the left, the french doors had three glass panes knocked out, the shards scattered on the floor toward him, indicating the breaking force had come from within. A telephone sat by the doorjamb, oddly out of place, while a side table just feet away displayed another telephone.

To the right was a cubbyhole kitchen, where LeBrun talked quietly with a colored woman. She was tall and lanky, her dress hanging loosely in the style these days. Her hair was swept back neatly. She wiped her eyes and looked at him, and he suddenly knew why the Frenchman had stationed himself near her instead of the patrolman. She was very young and very scared, but remarkably pretty with a certain grace.

LeBrun hurried over to Coughlin. "That's Ella Bradford, the girl's maid," he said, leading the way through the french doors. "She found the victim."

The bedroom had been ransacked, drawers pulled out and half-empty, articles of clothing strewn about. There were boxes partly packed, as though someone had just moved in . . . or was moving out. Coughlin didn't have to look to know that anything of value was already gone.

"Dot King was twenty-seven and a model," LeBrun said, looking at his notes. "Reading between the lines, I'd say she was also somewhat of a scandalous flapper."

The somewhat scandalous flapper in question lay dead on a brass bed. There were about three hundred homicides a year in New York City, so Coughlin estimated he'd seen more than eight thousand victims in the course of his career. Every body told a story; he approached to learn hers.

Immediately, it was clear this was no suicide. The bent legs tangled in the sheets said she'd put up a fight. The right fingers curled inward said she'd been holding something or clawing her attacker. Crumpled gauze—which looked to be the same as the shred in the umbrella stand, Coughlin noted—lay beside her mouth. There was an empty glass bottle—about the size of a deck of cards—label-side down, by her shin. Near her knee, half-hidden under a fold in the sheet, lay a men's mustache comb. It had probably fallen out of the killer's jacket during the tussle. That the items had been left behind told him the killer was sloppy or new to the sport.

He bent closer to the bottle and sniffed. "Chloroform," he said.

LeBrun's face said he already knew.

Coughlin withdrew a bleached-white, perfectly pressed kerchief from his pocket—Mamie's laundry skills were second to none—and carefully lifted the bottle so as not to disrupt the collection of fingerprints later. The portion of the label containing the medicine's name, and below it, the serial and batch numbers, had been scratched off. Although the execution of the crime was slapdash, the removal of this identifying information indicated the killer had taken care to plot and cover his tracks—and at a hundred milliliters, it was also an unusually large size. Like many potentially deadly medicines, it was usually sold in very small vials.

Coughlin examined it from all sides. This wasn't adding up. He carefully replaced it at the precise angle he'd found it, refolded the handkerchief along its previous lines, replaced it in his pocket, and continued his examination.

Her left arm was twisted back in a hammerlock hold. But unlike the classic wrestling maneuver designed to incur submission, the victim's arm had been wrenched so violently her fingertips nearly grazed the base of her skull. That would've dislocated her shoulder. The victim had been in extreme pain before she died.

Yet even in death, she was one of the most beautiful women Coughlin had ever seen, with the face of a Gibson Girl and a cap of blonde curls. Her lips were full and slightly parted. They were the sort of lips most men longed to kiss. But now they were lifeless and bruises had formed around them.

This attack had been personal. Violent. Fueled by anger. Dot King's killer had brutally wrestled her down and held the chloroform-soaked gauze over her nose and mouth while she fought for her life. Perhaps he'd even enjoyed the struggle.

Coughlin's fingers flexed. The murderer was a man—no woman was strong enough to have done this. This man was a bully, and he hated bullies. He would find this man and make him pay for what he'd done.

"Every minute she lies there, we're losing valuable evidence. Plus, Houghtalin and whoever he's working for have now had all day to get ahead on this, all thanks to that goddamn idiot patrolman who called *this*"—Coughlin gestured around the room—"in as a suicide. A suicide! This!"

LeBrun shrugged. "It's unfortunate."

"It's *incompetent*," Coughlin corrected. "But here's what I don't get: *This* is a robbery." He gestured around the room. "But *this*"—he pointed to the woman's lifeless body—"is personal. And what the hell's that phone doing stretched out the door when there's another extension in the living room? There's much more than meets the eye. Leave it for the fingerprint men."

He led the way back to the kitchenette, where Ella Bradford perched on a stool in the farthest corner. Coughlin cleared his throat, never much good with emotions or women. "You live here?"

"No, sir. I live up in Harlem with my husband and our little boy." Her voice was soft, but he caught a hint of shy pride at the mention of her family.

"Where's her roommate?"

The maid crumpled a white hankie nervously. "Miss Dottie lives alone."

"*All alone?* No female friend to keep her company?" He shook his head. This new trend of women living alone was wholly unnatural and, as this mess proved, unsafe.

"She did, but Miss Hilda moved out two weeks ago. She's a showgirl over at the Music Box."

Coughlin raised a brow. If Miss Hilda the showgirl had stayed, Dot King might still be alive . . . or maybe he'd have a double homicide on his hands. The chance and fickleness of life, and death, could set a soul crazy if you let it.

He added the name to his list, jotting it down, though he did not need to. Trying to remember was never a problem. No, his problem was trying to forget.

"Did she have any admirers? Anyone sore at her?"

The maid looked uncomfortable, and he wasn't sure whether it was the question or the fact that they were feet away from her slain employer. Still, she answered right away. "Yes, sir—she's sweet on a man named Albert Guimares. He's very cruel. Beats her black and blue. She's got bruises from him more days than not."

Coughlin made note. He was unsurprised. Violent men weren't known to change their stripes. They'd bring this guy in tonight for some questions. "When did she last see him?"

Tears pooled in her eyes. "Yesterday morning, he dropped her off so she could go to the chiropodist before—" She stopped abruptly, looked away. "He called her last night, and they got into a terrible fight."

"About what?" Coughlin asked. *A violent guy and a terrible fight the night before she turned up dead.* Most murderers were brutes, and their motives were primitive: jealousy, money, sex, greed, rage. Guimares seemed to fit the bill.

Mrs. Bradford shook her head. "I don't know, but he screamed so loud, I could hear him through the phone clear across the room. He wanted her to do something, and she wouldn't—said she wasn't ever gonna do it. But he wouldn't let up—he never did, you know." This last bit was said with a bitter resignation. "She cried herself sick when she hung up."

Coughlin bet the maid had at least *some idea* about what Guimares wanted. "We'll come back to that," he said briskly. "What do you remember from the moment you walked in?"

She looked toward the door. "I knew something was wrong as soon as I saw the two coats on the floor. They're too light for this weather, and Miss Dottie never threw clothes around anyhow."

He turned automatically to see whether he'd somehow stepped over two coats, even though he never missed anything. The floor was empty. "What coats?"

She glanced nervously toward the patrolman. "Miss Dottie's mama had her boys take them when they took the rest."

"Took the rest?" A lightning bolt of disbelief sliced through him. The girl's family had come in? And *taken* things? He swung toward the patrolman, who shot to his feet. "You let evidence leave a goddamn crime scene?"

"I-it was a suicide. She came this afternoon. Why shouldn't a mother? It's a comfort to women . . ." The patrolman trailed off.

In two steps, Coughlin grabbed him by the collar, leaned in, nose to nose. "Only an *idiot* would think *this* was a suicide!"

Coughlin shoved his rage down to his gullet and this half-wit toward the door. "Get out," he said in a stone-cold voice he knew was worse than yelling. "Stand outside like a goddamn doorman and don't let anyone in except residents. Think you can handle *that?*"

The patrolman nodded miserably, slithered away, and went to pull the door closed behind him.

"Don't touch that!" Coughlin exploded. "We still need fingerprints!"

The patrolman ran.

Coughlin realized with a sinking, impotent fury that his crime scene was hopelessly compromised. Any hope of getting fingerprints was probably gone. A prickly surge of resentment spread down his neck like heat rash. He spun, and Ella Bradford shrank into herself like he might come for her next. He closed his eyes, took a breath to gather himself, and got back to the business of getting information. "Was Miss King afraid of anyone else or just this Guimares guy?"

Even as he asked, it didn't sit right: the incongruity of chloroform—a sedative—and a violent lover who beat her. But every avenue had to be pursued.

Before Ella Bradford could answer, a shrill voice, cloaked in an Irish brogue, shrieked, "You there!" Coughlin turned to see a gray-haired woman in a black dress, trailed by two young men—early twenties— who looked defiant and embarrassed by turn. The woman pointed at him accusingly. "I want me daughter's body released! I have final arrangements to make, though Lord Jesus only knows what can be done since a suicide can't be buried in a Catholic cemetery."

The woman seemed more irate that her daughter had deprived her of a Catholic burial than grief-stricken that the girl was dead. "Mrs. King?" he asked, though it couldn't be anyone else.

It was, somehow, the wrong thing to say. The woman swelled angrily like a fighting bird shirring its feathers. "I am Mrs. Catherine *Keenan*, and I demand you release Anna's body to me!"

He looked around. "Who the hell's Anna?"

"Me daughter's rightful name's Anna Keenan. She started calling herself 'Dot King' when she moved out, like what we gave her wasn't good enough." She wiped her nose on the wrist of her glove. "She was always puttin' on airs."

"Miss Dottie didn't put on airs." Ella Bradford spoke up, quiet but determined. "She did her best to make her way."

"You stay out of this!" The older woman sneered. "I told 'er this Broadway lifestyle would lead to nothin' but trouble and the money she was takin' was no good. But she wouldn't listen with this one and that dancer tramp eggin' her on."

Ella Bradford looked horrified. "Ma'am, I *never*—"

The ruckus brought LeBrun hurrying in from the bedroom. "Madame, I'm from the medical examiner's office, and I'm afraid we won't be able to release your daughter's body—" he began in his apologetic, French way.

"We're investigating this as a possible murder," Coughlin cut in.

That stopped the Irishwoman cold. "*Murder?* Why—what're ye on about? Your man said this mornin' she overdosed herself on chloroform. She's terrible moody and suffered indigestion, didn't she?" She turned to her boys as though this somehow explained everything.

Coughlin scowled. He'd never seen anyone—let alone a woman—so pompous at a crime scene. If she wasn't going to act like a grieving mother, he wasn't going to treat her like one. Why, the girl's maid was more upset than her own kin. He pointed at the couch. "Take a seat."

The old Irishwoman looked as though to refuse, but the taller, older-looking son took her arm, and she reluctantly stomped over and plunked down. "As though I haven't been through enough!" she huffed.

Coughlin clenched his jaw. "We need information, lady. Information is what catches killers. Do you know anyone who might've had a grudge against"—he hesitated, unsure whether to refer to the victim as Anna Keenan or Dot King—"your daughter?"

"Albert Guimares!" The mother spat the name like it dirtied her mouth. "He's a terrible man—so cruel to me daughter. She lived in constant fear of him. I told 'er he was no good, but she wouldn't think of leaving him, and she's the one payin' his bills, y'know. He's nothin' but a cheap Broadway gigolo." This was the new slang for the lowest kind of rat—the kind who lived off women.

"Anyone else who might've had a grudge against your daughter?"

"Are ye daft? *I just told ye* Guimares is your man! Look no further than that sundodger. You should see all she gave him—diamond cuff links, rings, furs. He's a parasite livin' off me daughter." The mother jerked her head pointedly at Ella Bradford and lowered her grating voice half a degree. "And he's Negro, you know."

The maid's face tightened. "Albert Guimares is Puerto Rican, ma'am, not Negro."

"I'm tellin' ye, he's dusky—" the mother said crossly, like it didn't much matter since he wasn't white.

Coughlin cut her off. "That's enough!"

"Well then! Me daughter lyin' dead in the next room, and this is how he talks to me!" The mother flared indignantly, looking toward her sons once more. The boys looked uncertainly at Coughlin and back to their mother.

"Are ye just gonna stand there?" she prattled on.

"Mother!" the older son, slender and wiry, warned, even as the younger one, shorter and barrel-chested, took a half step forward and braced his legs, ready for a fight.

"Sit down, boy," Coughlin ordered tersely, rising to his full height. LeBrun, just as tall if not as broad, moved in closer, and the kid shrank back, defeated. Coughlin turned to the maid, the only reasonable one in the room. "Where can I find this Guimares?"

"He lives over at the Hotel Embassy," Ella Bradford said. "Broadway and 70th."

At the address, Coughlin tried to stanch the flow of crime statistics flooding his brain.

Last month, his detectives had arrested six men hiding out at the swanky hotel with $75,000 of stolen bonds. It was the same corner where the infamous Elwell murder had taken place, the gambler found locked in his town house, shot in the head while reading his mail . . .

"Well? Aren't ye going to go arrest him?" the mother demanded.

He knew everyone was waiting, watching, would soon give him curious looks. And that curiosity would quickly turn to discomfort, or worse, pity. Normal folks tolerated him when they had use for him, but that didn't mean they tolerated his peculiarities. His inability to forget addresses was a weakness. And people hated weakness.

August 1920: suicide / attempted double murder in a dentist's office . . .

"Coughlin?" LeBrun prompted.

A hint of bright-yellow fabric—the exact same shade as the victim's negligée—under the couch caught his eye. It was enough to stop the runaway train of thoughts. He walked over, yanked it out, and found himself holding a balled-up pair of men's silk pajamas. It was clear they were meant to coordinate with the victim's, which was both pitiful and enviable. Coughlin had never had a matching set of pajamas with anyone. He shoved the mushy, unwelcome thought aside and turned to more practical matters. "What the . . . ?"

The maid blushed and looked down. LeBrun, a Frenchman to his core, raised an appreciative eyebrow. "Very nice," he said. "At least $35."

Coughlin snorted. People found silly ways to waste money. He'd seen men's pajamas advertised for $1.44 at Bloomingdales and silk could be had for less than $10. "Guimares's, I guess?"

The mother lifted her chin and looked away, daring him to try to make her talk. The boys stayed stubbornly mute.

Finally, Ella Bradford spoke. "They're Mr. Marshall's."

The Keenans rounded on her like attack dogs. "How *dare* you!" the mother hissed at the same time the younger son snarled, "Shut up!"

Nobody would meet his eyes, but Coughlin wasn't surprised. Broadway girls always had more than one guy. "Who's Marshall, and where can we find him?"

"Well . . . uh . . . Marshall isn't his real name," Ella Bradford said.

"OK, well, what's his *real name*?" Coughlin demanded.

The maid reluctantly met his gaze. "Nobody except Miss Dottie knew."

Chapter 4

5:30 p.m. Palm Beach. Blakely Cottage.

It was a quiet, sun-splashed afternoon. Golden light danced through the palm trees, casting shifting shadows on the bed. Frances stretched as she woke from her nap. Slipping into crisp, fresh sheets for a nap in the warmth of the Florida afternoon was a delight she would never cease to enjoy. They were well into the social season, and she'd never felt more rested, which was very good indeed—one ought to be at one's very best when planning a party for the president of the United States.

They'd last hosted President Harding two years ago, when he'd come to tea at Whitemarsh Hall, her father's country estate outside Philadelphia, as the first notable guest at the then-new house.

Her stepsister, Louise, occasionally hosted him as well, along with his secretary of war and General Pershing, in Washington. Louise was the rare woman who played poker, and was quite good at it. The president had once challenged her to a two-man, cold hand, winner names his stakes.

Louise, a consummate storyteller, later admitted she'd taken the bet "with reservations," as Harding was a notorious lothario. But she'd won, and named a set of White House china as her prize. Harding almost certainly wouldn't have named a china set as *his* prize had he bested her shapely stepsister but, true to his word, had made sure some of President Harrison's gold corn-and-wheat set was delivered to her the next day.

Frances hoped to have her own, albeit less scandalous, story to tell about hosting Harding soon.

Frances loved wintering in Palm Beach: the weather, the light, the balmy breezes, the warmth of the ocean, more inviting even in winter than coastal Maine would be in August, when they'd be at their cottage in Dark Harbor for the summer season.

She rang for Emily to draw her bath—no other maid ever got the temperature so precisely right—and then help her into her dinner dress, the final outfit of the day. Emily, who'd come to work for them straight from Paris, was indispensable. Whether it was dressing her hair or making sure the upstairs maids who tidied the bedrooms and changed the sheets twice daily kept on schedule, everything ran seamlessly under her watch. In the hierarchy of servants, the French enjoyed a well-earned reputation as the best, followed by the British and Swedish, which was why everyone in society only ever hired from those pools.

After her bath, as Emily brushed her hair and twisted it up into a loose bun, Frances noticed how many more strands of gray were appearing. She told herself this was dignified—the natural order of things. The First Lady, Mrs. Harding, was entirely gray. All respectable women allowed their hair to gray. Society counted on women of her position to uphold and guide life as they knew it. A newspaper article had recently referred to Frances and three of her friends as women so powerful, a single word could stop even the most ambitious social climber. At dinner that night, Jack had raised a glass and joked that perhaps he could put that powerful word of hers to work in boardroom negotiations, and everyone had chuckled and toasted. She'd shaken her head and smiled, modestly dismissing the foolishness of it all. But she couldn't deny the recognition was gratifying, and later she'd surreptitiously clipped the piece out and stashed it in the recesses of her writing desk, bolstered by its presence.

Frances felt acutely the weight of her social standing, standing she'd been born into and then sought to live up to. Her social position had been secured through her father's extraordinary success, which had made him the wealthiest man in Pennsylvania. She'd then married into a respected Philadelphia society family. And if they were not as wealthy, well, who was? It was impolite to speak of such matters, anyway. Since attaining the coveted role of "wife," she'd gotten to work carrying out its duties: bearing two healthy, beautiful children; volunteering with various charities; and carefully honing her skills as a hostess, presiding over the most elegant, enviable events. All of which added up to according her the position and power that had been noted in the papers.

A younger hostess simply wouldn't possess the poise to be a pillar of society, let alone assist in stabilizing a presidency as besieged by scandal as Harding's. It would take the whole family and every bit of their social influence to pull Harding out of the muck and secure his reelection, and she would play her part.

Harding's reelection had to be secured at any cost—*literally*.

"Madame?" Emily asked, stepping back.

Frances appraised the work from all angles. "Just a bit higher at the back, *s'il vous plaît*."

As the maid began adjusting, Frances watched their reflections in the mirror. She would turn forty-two in November. She was no longer a young woman. She accepted this with graceful acquiescence. Whatever beauty and charm she'd possessed had faded into comfortable, stately middle age, and it was her duty to keep her graying head held high and continue reigning socially with the poise and elegance befitting her station.

She told herself that this was what her mother would've looked like had she had the opportunity to reach this age. But she would never know. She'd lived her whole life with the burden that her mother had died bringing her into this world, leaving her and her sister, Edith, four years old at the time, motherless, and that their father had been heartbroken over it for the next three decades, before he finally remarried. Frances's stepmother, Eva, was warm and kind, but Frances would've given anything for her mother to see the women she and Edith had become. Every year that Frances lived beyond thirty-one, the age her mother had died, felt like a gift. She had the perfect family—a husband who was her best chum, children she would get to watch grow and eventually marry—and she had her social position.

Her wedding announcement, the pinnacle of every society lady's existence, which had been featured in the *Philadelphia Inquirer* and every other paper of note up and down the East Coast, had referred to her as "tall and stately," noting her "clear pink-and-white complexion" and her skill in overseeing her father's estates as a "most charming hostess."

Tall, stately, charming: everyone knew these were attributes applied kindly when one could not note a bride's beauty. To be certain, they were attributes highly valued by her social set. But that didn't mean that her tender, feminine heart hadn't smarted from the careful wording.

"Et voilà, madame." Emily stood back and, at Frances's approval, placed the emerald necklace Frances had selected for the evening around her neck; traded her dressing gown for her evening gown, fastening the innumerable seed-pearl buttons down her back; buckled her shoes; and took the newspapers out to her sunporch.

Frances thanked Emily, settled herself in the lengthening afternoon shadows with a newspaper, and, luxuriating in the quiet solitude for a few minutes, scanned the headlines for news of President Harding's potential candidacy for reelection. She noted that he was in Saint Augustine and, according to the article, in the best health. It was good he was well, and even better that the reporters had, for the moment at least, stopped harping about the seemingly endless parade of scandals—allegations of selling naval lands in Teapot Dome, fixing sugar prices, and then of course all the whispers of the president's infidelity. These were regrettable, of course, but the family would still support his anticipated bid for reelection. And Harding would need their support—indeed every bit of support he could gather from both corporations and society—which surely was what he intended to speak to her father about next week. President Harding, Attorney General Daugherty, and a few other top advisers were heading down the coast to

Palm Beach in the next few days before the family hosted his luncheon, which was considered the most enviable social event of the season. Even that dreadful Representative Keller and his vicious accusations couldn't dim the excitement. Her father, one of J.P. Morgan's partners, assured her that Keller's antitrust accusations were poppycock and nothing would come of them.

But in spite of his reassurances that J.P. Morgan and Co. was a strong, upstanding business and that nothing and no one could possibly hurt them, every time she read about it, something tightened in her chest. Perhaps it was a glimmer of danger, or perhaps, as her father insisted, it was nothing at all. She tried to focus instead on party preparations.

She and Eva were terribly busy overseeing it all. In addition to the usual goal for financial backing, the politicos hoped to ensure a less clearly defined sort of support in terms of social influence, which the campaign desperately needed.

Should her father decide to extend it, the Stotesbury name had the power to help steady any ship, even one as shaky as Harding's presidency. In this way, politics was an unexpectedly delicate business, Frances mused. And like all business, she was glad the men managed it, so she could attend to more interesting matters, such as charity work, the children, and social engagements. The intricacies of orchestrating a flawless event—every careful, thoughtful, intricate detail—were just as complex.

She only hoped the demands of the day wouldn't unduly tax her father, as host. His advancing age worried her, and she wondered how many years he had left. She hoped his delight in his grandchildren would keep him young. Family was, after all, everything.

Tonight, before bed, she would telephone Jack, back home in Philadelphia for business, with highlights of their day. She smiled, thinking of him. How lucky she was to have found love and friendship in her marriage, how proud she was to support his professional and social ascension. And how so much hinged on this presidential visit.

Harding's reelection could erase those ugly rumors about her father's firm *and* catapult Jack's career and social standing immeasurably beyond Edith's smug husband, Sydney, which would be quietly satisfying. It could not be easy to marry a woman whose family's wealth so dramatically outpaced your own, no matter your efforts or success. But that could soon change, and she relished the opportunity for Jack to shine at the Harding reception.

Frances took a deep breath, pushed the paper away, and hurried downstairs, the pressure to make this a success bearing down. It was a feat that had to be accomplished at any cost. And she would see to it that it did.

Chapter 5

8:15 p.m. Manhattan. Hotel Embassy.

Coughlin pushed through the revolving doors and marched down three shallow steps to a modern black-and-white-tiled lobby. The symmetry of the geometric pattern—small squares forming larger squares, with rows of squares around them—was pleasing. It was orderly, precise, logical. This was how facts added up in a case—each one lining up with the next to build to an inevitable conclusion. Follow the trail, gather evidence, catch the crook: one, two, three. Repeat.

He was here to question the prime suspect in the case, the violent, hotheaded Broadway parasite Guimares. But discovery of the yellow silk pajamas had led to the revelation that Dot King had maintained a second lover, who was also necessarily a suspect: the alias-wielding Mr. Marshall. Additional questioning of the mother and the maid had revealed that Marshall was older, perhaps around sixty, and that he lavished the girl with gifts of jewels, fur, and cash. The mother argued he was merely a good "friend" to her daughter. Over the course of his career, Coughlin had learned there was no limit to willful blindness. But for everyone else, you didn't have to be a genius to see how the arrangement worked.

The mother had talked loudly and overconfidently—declaring she knew Marshall well, then later admitting she'd really only seen him once in his chauffeured car.

Ella Bradford was clearheaded and earnest. She'd said Marshall had taken the girl out to dinner last night, which established the man's presence at the crime scene within hours of the murder. Coughlin's interest in interviewing this "friend" of the dead girl had ratcheted up with every detail.

The mother had sniffed at his interest in Marshall, grumbling that Ella Bradford was a bad influence on her daughter, who'd chosen to confide in only the maid, while barring *her own mother* from the apartment altogether. Ella had lifted her chin and looked away. The only thing the malcontent mother had agreed with Ella Bradford on was that Albert Guimares must be the killer.

He had a feeling Mrs. Bradford, while she didn't say much, knew more. But for now, he had to get to Guimares, while the rest of his men fanned out through the Broadway underworld to find this "Marshall," whoever he was, and question him before he skipped town.

He marched past the usual assortment of the rich and fashionable lounging on furniture that looked more stylish than comfortable, to the reception desk. His men, O'Donnell and O'Roarke, flanked him.

O'Roarke whistled low under his breath. "Boy, ya sure don't live here on a detective's salary," he said, taking in the crystal chandeliers.

"No," Coughlin agreed dryly, "you gotta be a criminal."

A few guests looked over curiously when he announced they were police. The desk clerk looked nonplussed.

Coughlin took both reactions in stride. "What's Albert Guimares's room number?"

The clerk didn't ask what it was regarding. "Guimares . . ." He flicked through the card file. "Suite 904."

The ninth floor, Coughlin noted—too high to even consider taking the stairs.

A redheaded elevator operator who looked like he hadn't started shaving yet leaped eagerly into action as they approached. "Police," Coughlin said, flashing his badge. "Whaddya know about the guy in 904?"

"Oh, *that* guy!" the operator said. "Typical gigolo—real flashy. He wants everyone to think he's a high roller—heavy sugar, if you know what I mean."

The fellas smirked at that, and it was all the encouragement the kid needed. "Wait till you see him—he's got the biggest fur coat you've ever seen, plus more jewelry than a cheap dame. He's always flashin' fancy watches, big rings, diamond cuff links. And he won't let five minutes go by without tellin' you he's got a showy car and his own chauffeur."

"Oh yeah?"

"Mind you, I ain't buyin' it. He's a rat for sure. But it seems to work for the ladies. The guy never sleeps alone—I'm always taking him up with some broad or other late at night."

"So not just one blonde?" Coughlin asked.

"Nope," the kid said, relishing his role as informant. "More like a parade. He's got at least two regulars, both blondes. One's been around for a while—they say she's one of the prettiest girls in New York. The other's newer—real tall."

The fancy new elevator slid to a smooth halt. Coughlin hammered on number 904 with a sizable fist, rattling the door in its frame.

Inside, footsteps hurried, dishes clinked, papers crumpled.

Coughlin knocked again. Back in his days as a builder's apprentice fresh out of New York City Public School 74, his fists had wielded hammers and plasterboard, and often jammed boards into place by sheer might. He was lucky then–Police Commissioner Roosevelt had put the call out for able-bodied men to join the force and that his size and strength had made him a good candidate. After years as a patrolman, he'd made detective. It was better to wear a suit and investigate crooks—even in a never-ending, often-losing battle—than wear overalls while slapping plaster on laths all day.

He banged on the door one last time, annoyed it hadn't already been answered. "Police! Open up!"

The lock on the other side snicked and the door swung inward, revealing a man of average height, slender build, and light-brown skin.

Decked out in a pinstripe suit and dripping jewelry, he looked exactly like what Mrs. Keenan and the elevator kid had described: a Broadway gigolo.

"Albert Guimares?" Coughlin asked, knowing full well it was.

"Yeah?" the gigolo said smoothly.

"Inspector Coughlin, head of the New York City Police Detectives Unit. Mind if we come in?" He shouldered his way past. The plush suite reeked of stale air and cigarette smoke. A coffee table was piled high with newspapers, half-empty glasses, and overflowing ashtrays.

"Sure," Guimares said, as though they'd waited for his permission. He quickly shoved his hands in his pockets. Coughlin scanned for a weapon, but the guy's pants were too tight to hide a knife or pistol.

Guimares had jet-black hair slicked back with too much Brilliantine and a tiny, close-cropped mustache. It looked like he spent a lot of time in front of a mirror . . . the kind of guy who'd carry a little pocket comb everywhere—unless he'd dropped it last night in the struggle to chloroform Dot King.

"Lived here long?" Coughlin asked, walking toward the coffee table. Piles of newspapers were spread out. It seemed Guimares had copies of every rag in the city. What story had he been looking for?

"Long enough."

"Where were you last night?" Two large windows looked east toward Central Park. Daylight was long gone, and the streetlights were on.

Guimares regarded him warily. "Out. Why?"

Coughlin ignored that. "Out with who? What time did you get home?"

Guimares moved a step away, still keeping both hands in his pockets. "I had dinner with some friends, then came back here and went to sleep around midnight. Alone. You can ask my roommate when he gets back," he added, nodding to a closed door across the room.

The offer annoyed Coughlin. Of course they'd question the damn roommate—he didn't need Guimares's invitation—but if this guy was offering his roommate up, it was just as likely they'd coordinated their stories as it was to be a real alibi. "This roommate got a name?"

Guimares hesitated briefly, then shrugged. "Sure. Edmund McBryan."

Coughlin noted it. "So you came home, saw McBryan the roommate, and went to bed."

Guimares nodded. "That's right."

Coughlin pointed to the gigolo's pockets. "What's with your hands?"

"Nothin'," Guimares said, shoving his hands deeper in his too-tight slacks.

Coughlin took a step closer. "Lemme see 'em."

Guimares's eyes darted right and left, but there was no running. He wouldn't even make it to the door. Finally, he dragged his right hand from his pocket while trying to shrug his cuff lower.

It didn't work. Coughlin twisted it toward the light. The back of Guimares's hand bore red scratches and what looked like a full set of teeth marks in the fleshy triangle between his thumb and forefinger—injuries perfectly in line with holding some chloroform-soaked gauze over a victim's mouth as she fought to get free. Coughlin narrowed his eyes. Criminals were so predictable. "Well, well, well. How'd this happen? Were you attacked after you came home and went to sleep—*alone*?"

Guimares jerked his hand away and yanked his sleeve down. He moved to the far side of the coffee table and opened a fancy gold cigarette case. "It's nothin'."

O'Roarke stepped forward. "The inspector asked you a question: *How'd it happen?*"

Guimares removed a smoke and lit it, taking his time. He shook out the match and scowled. "Misunderstanding with a friend."

What a weasel. Coughlin narrowed his eyes. "Friend, huh? With friends like that, who needs enemies?"

Guimares shrugged like it was no concern of his.

Coughlin was undaunted. The guy had no real alibi and injuries in line with the method of the murder. This was gonna end one way: his. He'd get to the bottom of it. It was only a matter of how long it took and how hard Guimares was gonna make it on himself. "Anyone see this alleged *misunderstanding*?"

"Sure."

"We'll need their names," Coughlin said; the volley was taking on a faster pace.

Guimares narrowed his eyes. "Why's that?"

Coughlin was tempted to tell the rat he didn't owe him an explanation. But he didn't want to lose the upper hand. "O'Roarke's real interested."

O'Roarke stepped forward and lifted his big barrel chest, towering over the suspect. "Yeah, *real* interested."

Guimares's eyes darted toward the bedroom. "Sure. I'll, uh, write 'em down for you."

Coughlin stepped into his line of sight. "Did this 'misunderstanding' occur before or after your dinner with friends?"

"Uh, after."

Coughlin stared him down. "You said you had dinner and went straight home."

Guimares hesitated. "Well, I didn't mention it before because it didn't seem worth mentioning."

Coughlin decided to get right down to it. "Did you see Dot King last night?"

"No," Guimares said, not missing a beat.

"Well, when *did* you see her last?"

"Yesterday, late morning. We spent the past few days at a hotel, and then I dropped her off at the chiropodist. Haven't heard from her since."

"I'll take the name of the hotel along with those witnesses," Coughlin said, wondering why the couple allegedly stayed at a hotel when Guimares lived at this one, and she had her fancy little jewel-box apartment. None of this felt right. He also wondered how Guimares would feel if this guy knew his girlfriend had gone straight from the chiropodist and into the arms of her other, older lover. "D'you know where she went or who she saw after that?"

Guimares shrugged, sitting down and taking another drag. "Who knows? Dot knows lots of people and goes lots of places—"

Coughlin cut him off. "So you don't know who Miss King was with or where she went last night?"

Guimares was getting shiftier. "I just told you, *I don't*. Say, what's this all about, anyway? What do you care about Dot?"

Coughlin narrowed his eyes, zeroing in on Guimares like an animal on its prey. "Oh, I care a lot. In fact, I'm gonna make it my business to spend a lot of my time on Dot King. It may interest you to know that your sweetheart was killed late last night."

Guimares's eyes widened. It was exactly the sort of gaze he'd give if he wanted to look innocent. Or, a small part of Coughlin countered, if he actually *was* innocent. "*What?*"

"Murdered," Coughlin said steadily.

"That can't be true!" Guimares protested. It was *almost* convincing.

"Oh, but it is," Coughlin insisted, playing right along. "Found dead in her bed and a fortune of jewelry and furs gone missing." He paused to let that sink in, before delivering a final punch. "Looks like someone who knows her well did it. I wonder who that could be."

They stared each other down. Guimares held his gaze with what looked like Herculean effort, before his eyes skittered toward the front door. The fellas caught it. O'Donnell stepped left. O'Roarke fanned out to the right. They stood their ground in case the rat tried to run. Guimares looked back and forth between them and slumped as he admitted defeat, his lean frame in the too-tight suit deflating.

"Mind if we take a look around?" Coughlin jerked his head toward the bedroom door, and his men wordlessly spread out and began to search. Guimares was just the type to leave a sack of jewels lying around, thinking he was so much smarter than anyone else. "How long you known her?"

Guimares's eyes followed the search. "I . . . I guess about a year and a half?" He didn't sound like he much cared.

"How'd you meet?"

Guimares shrugged. "I dunno—we move in the same circles."

Coughlin crossed his arms. "Oh yeah? What circles are those?"

"Broadway circles." Guimares's smug tone might as well have said, *Cops don't make enough sugar to run in Broadway circles or meet girls like Dot King.*

"You got a job? Or are you one of those gigolo types?" Coughlin asked.

Guimares scowled. "I'm a stockbroker, and I'll have you know I do very well at it. So don't come in here assuming things you got no idea about. I've given Dot King more jewels and gifts than a cop could ever imagine."

Coughlin ignored the cheap shot. "Buy any chloroform lately?"

Guimares's brows shot up. "No. Why?"

"Hey! I got something over here!" O'Roarke hollered.

And there it was. Sometimes it was almost too easy. Coughlin didn't take his eyes off Guimares. "Bring it out."

O'Roarke emerged holding an automatic pistol and a side of cartridges in his handkerchief to preserve fingerprints. "Look here, fellas. I saw this on the bureau over there. Seems we have a violation of the Sullivan Act."

It wasn't what he'd hoped for—Dot King hadn't been murdered by gunshot. But it was enough to take this smug bastard downtown, where, on his turf, Coughlin would do what he did best: extract information. And he'd bet his bottom dollar that illegal possession of a gun was the least of this guy's crimes. "You're gonna accompany us down to headquarters, wise guy."

Guimares paused, his reluctance clear. But there was only one way this would go, and Guimares seemed to know it.

"Sure," he said evenly, lifting his chin. "I got nothin' to hide. Can I get my coat?" The gigolo sprang up and lunged toward the hall closet.

Reflexively, Coughlin yanked him back. Four and a half years ago, he'd taken a bullet that could've cost him his life while trying to apprehend two hold-up men. Guimares could have another revolver stashed in the closet. Heck, he could have a stash of automatic rifles in there. "Not so fast," he said, nodding to O'Roarke. "Get the man his coat."

O'Roarke yanked the closet door open. There was one item: a knee-length fur coat, with a giant collar flaring out past the shoulders. The detective patted it down for weapons, then tossed it at Guimares. "You serious?"

Guimares ignored him, shrugging it on. Together with his bejeweled rings and the huge gold chain of his pocket watch, the guy looked like a caricature, preening as he smoothed down his tiny, oily-looking mustache.

Coughlin grabbed Guimares's fur-swathed elbow and escorted him out the door, glad they got the weasel before he skipped town. Twenty-seven years on the force told him he had his man.

The mother, the maid, and the elevator kid were right: Guimares was a Broadway parasite. By all accounts, he'd been frequently violent to the victim. He was shifty and clearly hiding something. His injuries were consistent with a victim putting up a fight against being asphyxiated. Plus, the guy had no solid alibi.

But they still had to track down the mysterious Mr. Marshall. Coughlin's motto was *leave no stone unturned*.

Coughlin pressed the elevator button. If he was a betting man—as he was known to be from time to time—it was hard to imagine some elderly sugar papa had snuffed the girl out, when all signs pointed to Guimares. But then again, investigations were like races: sometimes the dark horse surprised you.

Chapter 6

After closing arguments, the judge had solemnly warned the jurors to disregard Miss Wells's gender as he sent them off to decide her fate. Julia could've told him to save his breath. She was sure, beyond a shadow of a doubt, that the twelve men would acquit Jim Pettit's mistress and possible murderer. Four hours later, she was proven right: not guilty.

Julia rushed back to the converted five-story warehouse that the *New York Daily News* called home, and the smell of ink, paper, and cigarette smoke greeted her. With its pale stone front, Italianate cornices, and ornate moldings above every window, the building looked much the same as any of the lofts around it. But inside, the floor vibrated as the printing machines in the basement hummed to life, ready to churn out copies of the nation's largest morning daily. It felt like home.

She ignored the archaic birdcage elevator and ran up the stairs to the second floor, which housed the editorial department. She waved to the bench of copy boys waiting to run stories up to the linotype operators, who would then cast lines of metal type in preparation for printing.

"Julia!" Hellinger waved as she hurried into the narrow, long room toward the far end that served as the city desk. "Julia! We got a hot one!"

She hung her coat on the nearest coat-tree, slid into her seat at the battered desk adjacent to his, and cranked a blank sheet of paper in. "Hold your horses. Gotta finish this hot one first."

"Hurry!" Hellinger urged. "You won't believe what I got."

Her fingers were already hurriedly typing the recap—Miss Wells quietly smiling as she was set free, the crowd rushing to congratulate her, the confident, celebratory remarks from her lawyers. She ripped the sheet out of the typewriter with a *zzzzip*, held it aloft, and shouted, "Copy boy!"

One of the boys leaped from the bench, ran over to grab it, and sprinted toward the door.

There was no time to celebrate. Julia turned to Hellinger, who was drumming his fingers to oh-so-subtly convey his impatience. "OK, shoot," she said, realizing belatedly it was a poor choice of words, having just come from a murder-by-shotgun trial. "What's the story with the model?"

He twirled his fedora on a finger. "She was known along the roaring forties as the 'Broadway Butterfly.'"

The hairs on the back of Julia's neck rose, tingling in the prescient way that heralded a big story. *The Broadway Butterfly.* It was a title that would immediately hook readers, not only conveying the effervescence of a social butterfly but also homing in on that section of the city as ablaze with electric lights as it was with its heady culture of glamour: *Broadway.* There was nothing else like it in the world.

"Did you hear I'd met her?" Hellinger asked.

"I did," Julia observed dryly. "It seems Manhattan is no match for you." Even in a city of millions, it stood to reason that Hellinger had crossed paths with the dead model—he not only covered the theater beat but made it his business to know as many of the city's beauties as possible.

"I also finagled access to the crime scene, and it turns out, this was no suicide. A small fortune of jewelry is missing, and some weird chloroform bottle, in a size nobody's ever seen before, was found next to the body," Hellinger said, ignoring the gibe.

Julia raised her brows. "Impressive finagling. Spill the beans."

He passed her his notes and quickly filled her in, concluding with Inspector Coughlin's arrest of Guimares and the citywide manhunt for Dot King's other lover.

"So the patrolman who was first on the scene completely bungled it," he added. "From what I heard, Coughlin hit the roof when he realized it had been called in as a suicide, and then charged out of there to go make arrests."

Julia's pen raced across the paper. "What do you know about the victim herself?"

Hellinger passed her a photograph. Like every paper, the *News* kept stacks of photos of everyone notable in the city. "I pulled this. As you can see, Dot King was a real doll, and *quite* the gal about town. She had at least two lovers—Guimares, this flashy gigolo, and an elderly sugar daddy who kept her decked out in jewels and furs."

Julia studied the picture of the beautiful model shrugging gracefully in a white fur coat: lips painted in an exaggerated bow shape, perfectly waved hair chopped into a bob, wrists and fingers bedecked with bracelets and rings. The girl stared, unsmiling, directly into the camera, which made it now seem she stared directly at Julia. Julia, who always felt awkward in front of any camera, looked away from the model's frank, unabashed gaze.

"I'd see her around at the swankiest cabarets, always dressed to the nines. And I heard when she had parties, the Brevoort sent each course by taxi plus a waiter to serve cocktails," Hellinger said, consulting his notes. "Seems she had no shortage of admirers—I heard about a famous aviator in Atlantic City, a race car driver, a nationally known golfer, and the headwaiter of the Tent before it burned down, among others. Rumor has it, she even lived with the headwaiter and he introduced her to smoking hop and also served up black eyes and split lips, but she gave as good as she got."

"It's never 'as good as you get' if you're female," Julia corrected, protectiveness surging for this girl, who was at once brave and beautiful, the petted darling of luxury, and the victim of male violence.

Hellinger put his hands up. "I'm just passing along what I heard—and trust me, I heard plenty. I also heard she could be melancholy. She started worrying about getting bumped off a few months ago. Got so nervous, she even had her will drawn up with a special clause about something 'unforeseen' happening to her. Poor kid."

"Yes, well, it seems the 'poor kid' was right. Maybe next time a woman says she's worried she's in danger, someone in her life will listen. You know, *before* it happens," Julia said more sharply than she meant to.

"Hey, I listen!" Hellinger protested.

Julia rolled her eyes and silently counted her blessings—yet again—that she'd met and married Westbrook Pegler. Peg—she'd picked up the habit of using his newsroom nickname—was the rare fellow who really *did* listen. She'd always thought that was part of what made him such a good newspaperman . . . and a good husband. She thought of calling him, just to say hello, just to hear his voice, but a quick glance at the clock changed her mind. She had to stay focused on getting this story. It was the one thing she could do for this girl whose voice had been silenced. "Did you talk to Coughlin?"

"Figured I'd leave that to you," Hellinger said.

Julia nodded. Coughlin had been promoted to chief inspector shortly before she'd arrived in New York, making him the head of nearly every investigation she'd covered, and therefore her go-to source for updates and quotes. He was notoriously brusque but mostly decent to reporters. He seemed to understand that they, like him, had a job to do: he caught crooks and they reported on it.

Over the years, they'd developed a mutual respect, which was the most that could be hoped for between policeman and reporter, and which had probably grown out of the fact that both of their jobs required long, strange hours and a level of dedication that bordered on obsession. But even considering that was the norm, they were outliers, working round the clock, the first to arrive and the last to leave, always pushing for more.

She appreciated that when he found his hands tied by city politics, Coughlin was known to let reporters "eavesdrop" on calls where he loudly repeated key information. Most of all, she appreciated that he accepted her as a newspaperman—same as all the rest, in spite of her gender. That was rare.

Julia stood. "OK, if we want to make the morning edition, we gotta work fast. Since Coughlin already arrested Guimares, go straight for Marshall."

Hellinger held up a finger. "Just one problem: nobody knows who he is. 'Marshall' is a pseudonym."

Julia froze. A pseudonym-wielding mystery man was the sizzle that took a story from the crime beat to the front page, and the front page was the difference between cases that got solved and cases that fell by the wayside. It was also, a small, calculating voice within her whispered, the sizzle that kept her employed and could propel her to a promotion as an assistant editor. Her fate was aligned with a dead woman's; such was the singular life of a crime reporter.

Julia pulled on her gloves. "Well, get a move on and figure out who he is before someone else does!"

"Oh, sure," Hellinger said. "I got a list of fake people's addresses and phone numbers right here. Should I call first? Or just show up unannounced?"

"I'd say head straight over—it'll be faster," Julia volleyed back, not missing a beat.

"Ha ha," Hellinger said mirthlessly. "Seriously. If the cops can't find him, what makes ya think we can?"

"Because *we* have *your* contacts," Julia reminded him.

Hellinger rolled his eyes. "Guess I can forget about sleep."

Julia was of the rare breed who didn't need much sleep. "What we should be asking is, *Why's* he creeping around Manhattan with an alias, and *how* can we get to him? If Coughlin found his pajamas at the crime scene, he must've been there often. I bet the building staff knows something."

Chapter 7

It was late by the time the police finally let Ella leave Miss Dottie's. She was so wrung out and desperate to pick up June, she decided to splurge on a taxi, knowing full well it might be more trouble than it was worth.

John Thomas, the nighttime elevator operator, took her down. They nodded but didn't speak—it felt like ears were listening, even though it was just the two of them.

She pushed through the lobby door and hurried out into the cold night air, where yet another policeman who'd been in the tiny apartment all day now stood guard. He nodded as she passed. Ella kept her eyes down and hurried by.

At the curb, she lifted a gloved hand. The need to be home, to hold her little Junebug, ached in her chest. A few cabs passed by, and she told herself they already had calls. But taxi after taxi sped past, even though she was dressed just as nice as any white lady, even in *the brand-new coat*. She looked down at the sidewalk, humiliated that the patrolman who'd been with her all evening now watched her get denied.

The day had passed strange and slow. She'd tried to make herself small and stay out of the way, which wasn't easy in a tiny apartment crammed with policemen, fingerprint men, crime scene photographers, medical examiners, reporters, and of course, the Keenans, who seemed to take up the most room of all. Lord, she was tired—tired down to her bones—and just wanted to get home.

Another cab passed and she deflated a bit more.

So many policemen had asked the same questions over and over that she couldn't swear to her own name anymore. She hadn't eaten since breakfast, hadn't had a moment away from the fuss and fear, and the cloying chemical smell of chloroform. And now, a full day that felt like a lifetime later, she was out in the cold and no cabs would stop.

She pulled her coat tighter as the wind bit at her legs. A choking sob threatened to rise, and she fought it down. She would not cry on the sidewalk. Finally—*finally*—a taxi pulled over and she got in. Vanilla pipe smoke wafted toward her. "Oh, thank you! I'm at 127th between—"

He cut her off. "I don't go to Harlem."

"Please," she said, desperate and low. "I'll pay extra."

"I don't go to Harlem," he repeated, staring straight ahead, and all she could see was the set of his jaw and that he needed a shave. She realized that, at this hour, with her head down, he probably hadn't realized the color of her skin.

She climbed back out, ashamed like it was somehow her fault, careful not to blink so the tears wouldn't squeeze out, careful not to look at the patrolman as she raised her arm again.

The police whistle blew sharply. The sound cut through the cold night and she stopped short. *What had she done wrong?*

The whistle shrilled again, the patrolman suddenly at the curb. The cab jerked to a halt and backed up. The driver leaned over to the passenger window. "Can I help you, Officer?"

The patrolman opened the back door. "Ma'am?"

"For *me*?" she asked, stunned.

"Today's been hard enough," he said, jerking his head back toward the building.

"Thank you," she finally managed.

He shut the door and leaned in the front window. "You take this lady home and make it snappy. I got your medallion number, and when I see her tomorrow, I don't wanna hear you took the scenic route or gave her any guff, or you ain't gonna have a medallion no more, got it?"

"Yessir," the cabbie muttered.

He grumbled the whole way uptown, and every so often glared back at her, but she sat tall and stared out the window. And when they arrived, she paid in full, plus a good tip so he wouldn't have any other reason not to go to Harlem next time.

She nearly flew up the stairs and rapped quickly at Bea's door. She wanted to get her baby and get home.

Bea yanked the door open. "It's day boardin', not overnight," she said by way of greeting, as she handed June, sound asleep, over.

Ella closed her eyes, holding the warm, solid weight of him to her chest. She had her little Junebug. Something within her eased.

Bea stuck out her hand. "You's late. That'll be another nickel."

Ella stiffened. She could've offered her day up by way of explanation, but she would've sooner hung herself on the cross than ask Bea for charity. She shifted the baby to one arm and dug for the coin with her free hand—a whole extra day's board—then started to leave.

"Think you's too good for Harlem puttin' on airs, takin' taxis, wearin' them fine, white-lady coats," Bea muttered.

It was the final straw. Ella turned back, and Bea lifted her chin defiantly. They stayed like that a long minute, as the words hung between them. Nobody would deny Bea deserved to get spoken out. But it was late and Ella didn't have any fight left in her. What would she say anyhow? That she'd found her white lady murdered? That the police had called her down to the criminal courts for more questions tomorrow? No. Bea had a big mouth. All of Harlem would know by dawn. So Ella kept quiet, let the silence pull tight between them like a clothesline, then gave the door a good hard slam behind her.

Sheer fury propelled her back outside, where she stomped down the sidewalk, and up the stairs of her own building. She was out of breath when she reached the third floor, shifting June, near eighteen pounds now, so she could wrestle her key in the door. Once she finally had him down for the night—chubby arms flung out, tiny rosebud lips parted, eyelashes longer than any boy had a right to—Ella ran a bath and scrubbed herself near raw.

As she waited for James to come home from the late shift—Negro staff always had to stay even later for cleanup—worries chased circles in her head.

Miss Dottie had been *murdered*!

It was impossible but true.

She kept the lamp on, even though electricity was up over a penny a kilowatt, to try to keep away the memory of finding Miss Dottie. Ella rubbed her palms on her flannel nightgown to try to make her hands forget the cold of Miss Dottie's feet.

And Mrs. Keenan—bitter old bat—with her unkind words about her own daughter. And Inspector Coughlin as he pulled Mr. Marshall's pajamas out from where she'd hidden them under the couch. Ella cringed, remembering those frosty eyes as they came to rest on her. Lord almighty, she'd near fainted right then and there.

Ella paced. She shouldn't have hidden them. She'd wanted to protect Miss Dottie from that mother of hers, with her sharp eyes and sharper tongue, but she'd also wanted to protect Mr. Marshall. The pajamas weren't the only things she'd kept hidden. There were other secrets, shocking and shameful, that she hadn't revealed. She hadn't wanted to dishonor Miss Dottie's memory or embarrass Mr. Marshall by publicly revealing things most private. But in protecting them, Ella realized she was also protecting Guimares, and she couldn't have that.

Mr. Marshall hadn't done it. This, she knew. He didn't have it in him. He was kind and good and he *loved* Miss Dottie. She'd challenge anyone to find another white man who paid for a maid's medical care plus extra for her lying-in when June had come along. She hadn't even asked (and never would). One day, there was just an envelope with a note and more money than she'd ever had. There just wasn't white folk like that.

It was Guimares who'd gone and killed Miss Dottie, that was for sure. The man was just plain *mean*—his sneering, the way he cut Miss Dottie down, even on the so-called good days. And then there were the things they never spoke of . . . the other kind of secrets women keep.

The first few times, back when Ella had just started, Miss Dottie had called and said she was ailing, and Ella had best not come to work that day lest she catch it.

Of course, it hadn't taken long to guess the truth. Ella had first seen the bruises after another "sickly" spell while she fastened what must've been a hundred tiny seed-pearl buttons no girl could reach herself. Regular folk didn't buy such dresses.

Ella's hands had stilled. By then, the splotches had mellowed into yellow-green, and Miss Dottie had blabbered some foolishness about how she'd tripped. Ella had accepted the lie—what else was there to do?—and said, real careful, "I know how that goes," which could've meant a number of things, then kept on with the buttons.

It was understood then, in that moment that passed between them. There'd been no more calls about sickly spells after that, and there'd been no other secrets either. They never spoke directly of it. But from then on, Ella dabbed cold cream on the bruises and dusted them with face powder. And if she had to, she'd swipe some of Miss Hilda's grease paint. Miss Hilda never ran short on makeup or bad behavior. The months she'd lived in the apartment had been rocky at best. True, she was a mother too—at only nineteen, she had a three-year-old girl she'd left with her parents back in Baltimore while she tried to make it on Broadway—but motherhood hadn't settled her any. She lived hard and fast, constantly out at cabarets, wearing Miss Dottie's dresses and jewelry without asking, and hosting parties at the apartment while Miss Dottie was away, inviting people Miss Dottie hated.

It had been a relief when Miss Hilda had moved out two weeks ago, though the good Lord knew it wasn't like Miss Dottie lived a quiet church-girl life. Between juggling Guimares and Mr. Marshall and the recent "endeavors" that Miss Dottie counted toward building her "sugar cushion," there had been more than enough excitement at 144 West 57th Street.

On the days when the damage from Guimares's fists couldn't be covered (as split lips can't), Miss Dottie would stay home while Ella did what needed to be done—even if it meant she had to deposit very, *very* large sums of cash into the accounts Miss Dottie kept at three different banks.

Ella sighed. She'd seen too many women try to make bad men good. And now he'd gone and killed her, just as he'd threatened, left her dead and crumpled up in the bed for Ella to find, like trash. A jagged sob bubbled up just as Ella heard James's key.

In the split second before he saw her, he looked so tired that she tried to shove the sob down. It didn't work. "What's wrong? What happened?" he asked.

The whole story poured out then. And James listened, worry carved plain on his brow. Ella realized it was the first time she'd ever seen him scared. Which scared her worse. She hadn't thought past the fact that Miss Dottie had been killed, but now the truth settled into her bones: she was smack-dab in the middle of a white-lady murder and already called down to the police station for more questions tomorrow.

She didn't want to burden him, or shame him that he couldn't protect her. But everyone heard tell of what could happen to Negroes down at the police station. Everyone knew to never let yourself alone with a white man. *Never let the door close.* And now she had to go down to the police station alone with a whole lot of white men. They had no idea all she knew, all Miss Dottie had told her. She started to tell James but stopped. "I don't know what to do," she said instead.

It fresh broke her heart to see him *helpless*—her wise, strong, respectable husband who always wore a suit. He was eleven years older than her, and already a widower when they'd married. James *always* knew what to do. "Just tell 'em what they ask and come straight home," he said.

She couldn't bear it, couldn't bear to see him brought low, couldn't bear that she was the one to do it. She'd bear the burden alone. "Don't worry—I'll be all right," she said, sharper than she meant to, anxious to end it.

They went to bed with the hardest things left unsaid. When she closed her eyes, she saw Miss Dottie crumpled on that bed, her beautiful face empty with the curious blankness of death, nightgown hiked nearly up to her hips, legs frozen like she'd tried to run . . . or kick. Miss Dottie had fought hard, this Ella knew for sure.

Ella stared at the ceiling. What would the police ask her? What did they already know about who Miss Dottie was, what she'd gotten into? The questions buzzed in endless circles, but one stopped her cold.

The letters. Lord almighty. What about those letters? They were, after all, what had driven Guimares into the screaming rage Ella heard through the phone from across the room. When Inspector Coughlin asked what the fight was about, Ella said she didn't know. But she did. She knew *exactly* what that fight was about and what Guimares wanted Miss Dottie to do.

Chapter 8

Julia approached the elderly doorman who stood sentry in Dot King's deserted lobby. Hellinger had provided his name. "Excuse me, Mr. Thomas? I'm from the *Daily News*. Do you have a few minutes to speak about Dot King?"

He looked past her to the door. "The police already been here. I told 'em all I know."

Julia reached for her pen. "And may I ask what you told them, sir?"

"I don't know as I should say," John Thomas said.

Julia nodded. "I understand, but I should also tell you I've also been on the crime beat for a good number of years, and the more this case stays in the news, the likelier it is they'll find the killer. And if not, well, it'll end up unsolved and collecting dust like ninety percent of murder cases in the city." She let that hang. "I won't print anything you don't want me to. You have my word on that."

Mr. Thomas, seemed to consider, the dark brown skin of his forehead furrowing into well-worn creases. It occurred to Julia he might ask her to leave. She tried to think of what she could say to persuade him or which sources she could go to next in the event he did.

"All right then. I'll do it for Miss Dottie—she was good to all us who work here. Generous—and not everyone is, if you take my meanin'. Like I told the police, Mr. Marshall and Mr. Wilson called around 7:30 to take her out to dinner. Now, Miss Dottie got plenty of gentleman callers and these two been here before—they respectable, older club men, and white of course, so I didn't think much of it. They came back about midnight, and I took 'em up. Miss Dottie was in high spirits. Seemed like they'd had a nice time."

"So all three came in together at midnight?"

John Thomas nodded. "Yes, ma'am."

"Did anyone else come in after that?" she asked.

"Just the newlywed couple on the fourth floor, round about 1:00 a.m."

She nodded, pen poised. "And what time did the men leave?"

"Mr. Wilson—the younger man, Mr. Marshall's secretary—left about twenty minutes later."

All three home at 12. Wilson left 12:20, Julia wrote. "And Mr. Marshall?"

John Thomas looked away, cleared his throat. "Mr. Marshall never left. Not on my shift anyway, and I'm on till 7:00 a.m."

Julia froze. If nobody else had come in after Marshall and Wilson, and Marshall had stayed . . . The hairs on the back of her neck rose. "You're sure he didn't come down?"

"Yes, ma'am. Sure as I'm standing here. I never took Mr. Marshall back down last night. I told the police that too."

She looked around the lobby. "But since Ella Bradford didn't find him in there, he must've left at some point. Are there any other exits?"

He gestured toward a large archway that led into an adjoining lobby. "There's emergency stairs. They old and dark and ain't nobody ever uses 'em, but they do go from the fifth floor down to the second; then a hallway cuts across to number 146. Then one more flight takes you out to the street."

"Maybe he took the stairs to be a bit more discreet?" Julia ventured.

"Mr. Marshall been callin' on Miss Dottie for a year or two now, and I *always* take him up and down in the elevator," John Thomas insisted. "Nobody ever takes those stairs, near as I can tell."

"But he *could*?" Julia pressed.

John Thomas looked her straight in the eye. "Miss, *nobody* uses those stairs. They for emergencies, see? You can't even get *in* that street door. It's got a spring lock on it. And Mr. Marshall . . . well, he even older 'n me. Folk his age not lookin' to walk down rickety stairs in the dark."

"I see," she said. "What about Albert Guimares? Do you know him?"

John Thomas frowned. "Stay away from him, miss. He's no good."

Julia nodded. She'd known some no-good men and reported on many more. Nearly every case she covered involved a no-good man who felt that the world or a woman had wronged him somehow. But no matter what he'd done, she'd yet to meet a no-good man who thought of himself as the villain. Everyone, Julia had learned, found a way to paint themselves as the heroes in their own stories.

She turned the conversation back to Marshall. "Did you ever leave the elevator—even just for a few minutes, when Mr. Marshall could've taken it down himself?"

"No, ma'am. I *never* leave my post," he said, lifting his chin.

"I'm sorry," she began. "I didn't mean—"

"And even if I *had*—which I didn't—I got the key. Can't operate the elevator without the key." He pulled a small bronze key from his jacket pocket.

Julia nodded. This certainly didn't bode well for Marshall. Since Hellinger hadn't mentioned that Ella Bradford had found the murderer standing over Dot King's body holding a rag soaked in chloroform, the man had clearly left at some point. Had he sneaked down the emergency stairs? Or was John Thomas mistaken? Maybe too afraid to tell now? Nobody would want to admit having left their post the night someone turned up murdered. "Would you mind showing me the emergency exit?" she asked.

Mr. Thomas led the way outside and a few paces down the sidewalk. He pointed to a slab of metal where the two buildings joined.

Without any sort of handle, pull, or latch, she'd walked right past it. "And could I possibly take a peek at the stairs?" she asked.

He nodded. "I'll take you up in the elevator—like I said, you can't get in from out here. Spring lock's on the inside."

Back inside, he locked the front door and took her up. On the fifth floor, he pointed to a plain door down the hall. "The stairs are through there. You go ahead and take them down. I'll be in the lobby." He was a man of his word; he didn't leave his post unsecured.

Julia stood alone in the silent hallway. It was hard to believe someone had killed a woman here less than twenty-four hours ago. A woman nearly the same age as Julia herself, a woman with hopes and dreams, plans and promises, with tasks left undone and conversations left unspoken, now just a cadaver to be sliced open, and organs weighed and analyzed at the medical examiner's office. The frailty of life, and the power to end it, was nearly impossible to comprehend. Julia crept quietly toward the rear unit's door. The brass doorknob gleamed. She looked around again, made sure she was still alone, and tried the knob.

It didn't budge. She tried again, twisting it back and forth a little more aggressively, but it was definitely locked. Disappointed but, she realized, also relieved, she headed for the emergency stairs. Unlike the lobby and the elevator, which had been renovated, the stairwell was neglected. Brown paint had been haphazardly slopped on the walls. The stairs themselves were narrow, steep, and dimly lit by only one bare bulb. She could hardly see to the first turn.

She stepped forward and the old floor creaked. She leaned over the railing and peered down the center of the narrow spiral. She couldn't see anything in the gloom. A flutter of anxiety shimmied through her. She told herself to brace up. She'd faced far more menacing obstacles while on the job. She'd been followed, received letters detailing violent threats, even had her life threatened. She'd spent a night in a drafty, grubby shack, listening as a suspected murderer paced restlessly in the next room. And yet she hadn't backed down and wouldn't back down now.

Holding the rail tightly, she began to feel her way down into the inky darkness, one creaky, narrow step at a time.

On the second floor, as John Thomas had said, the stairs fed into a narrow, low-ceilinged hallway that led to the adjoining building. One light at the end was all that lit the way. There, she went down one more flight of equally rickety stairs, opened the spring-locked door, and found herself back out on the sidewalk.

The door slammed behind her.

Unless the door was somehow propped open or someone opened it from the inside, there was no way back in. She looked up and down the street, ten years on the beat making it second nature to check for being watched. But West 57th was empty at this hour. Only a taxi puttered by.

John Thomas was waiting back in the lobby. The overhead lights shone on his closely shorn white hair. Julia suddenly realized that his testimony pointing to Mr. Marshall at the scene of the crime, and possibly as the killer, put John Thomas in a vulnerable position. While covering courts and crime, Julia had seen best friends viciously turn on each other when faced with the prospect of prison. What would a man such as Marshall—a white, wealthy "club man," as John Thomas said, be prepared to do and say to secure his freedom? And what could Mr. Thomas—a doorman and of presumably rather humble means—do to protect himself?

"Thank you very much," she said. "If you think of anything else, just let me know."

He nodded. "Yes, ma'am. But there's nothin' else to tell."

She nodded. "Well, you take care, all right? People say and do a lot of crazy things when they find themselves wrapped up in a murder."

He raised his graying eyebrows, forehead folding into well-worn creases. "Maybe so," he said. "But you can't change the truth."

"No, you can't," Julia agreed. She didn't have the heart to say that she'd seen too many men try.

Chapter 9

The interrogation room was small, furnished with only an old, battered table and two stiff-backed chairs. Coughlin rubbed his forehead, tired down to his bones. A large dome light hung overhead. It was too bright by design—a tactic to cow suspects—but it was starting to get to him too.

Hunger gnawed in equal strength with the desire for a stiff drink. Coughlin didn't believe in so-called rubber-hose methods. So while some of his colleagues resorted to bastinadoes, which in spite of inflicting extreme pain, left no visible marks on the soles of the suspects' feet, or blackjacks on the men they were less concerned about bruising, Coughlin prided himself on being able to extract information without brute force. One way or another, crooks always talked. And sleep deprivation usually helped. Guimares would crack soon.

Guimares had seemed such a promising suspect just a few hours earlier—a violent gigolo with no real alibi, scratches and bite marks on his hand, and the girl's mother and maid both witnesses to his brutality to the victim. But that had all slid sideways when the nighttime elevator operator insisted Marshall—not Guimares—was the last person he'd taken up to Dot King's apartment. Even more damning was that the elevator operator never saw Marshall leave.

Still, there was *something* Guimares was hiding, and Coughlin didn't have time for the runaround. He was racing the clock to wrap up the interrogation, then find this Marshall character and question him.

The gigolo was twenty-seven but arrogant as all get-out. He looked tired but had held up frustratingly well under hours of questioning, while he smoked and brooded and glared resentfully. He kept his right hand, with its red scratches and bite marks, out of sight and still had the gall to insist he'd never laid a hand on Dot King and had been in his hotel asleep during the murder.

But twenty-seven years on the force—the same number of years this little creep had been alive—had honed Coughlin's ability to sniff out liars. And Guimares was definitely a liar. Coughlin just had to figure out *what* he was lying about.

Coughlin closed his eyes and mentally returned to the scene of the crime. The door had been unharmed, the Yale lock pristine, no splintered or dented doorframe. "You got a key to her apartment?" he asked.

"Not anymore. I returned it a week ago," Guimares said, blowing a thin stream of smoke upward.

Coughlin leaned back and the chair creaked in protest. "Oh yeah? You two get into a fight?"

"Nope. I just didn't need it. I only visit if she's there, and if she's there, she can let me in." Guimares made an effort to seem blasé. It fell flat.

Coughlin closed his eyes and clicked through his mental images of the crime scene: shattered panes in the french doors, the ransacked room, the disheveled bed, the victim stilled midfight, the bruises around her mouth, the lacy, skimpy negligee, the unusually large bottle of chloroform, the mustache comb by her knee. He opened his eyes and pinned Guimares with his gaze. "You carry a pocket comb?"

Something flickered across Guimares's face—fear? Guilt? Frantically trying to remember the last time he'd seen his little comb? "Nope."

"I suppose that mustache of yours grooms itself?" Coughlin prodded.

Guimares snorted. "Is that a real question, Detective? You care about my groomin'? You sweet on me or somethin'?"

"I'm interested in the comb we found at the crime scene and the fingerprints we're gonna pull off it," Coughlin said. He didn't so much as blink, trying to make the gigolo squirm.

"Well, I guess you'll just have to wait and see," Guimares said, and blew another stream of smoke out in such a way it felt like a challenge.

"Oh, you'll be the first guy I call," Coughlin promised. "Your girl's in the morgue, and a fortune of jewelry is missing." He flipped through the insurance policy Ella Bradford had given him. It seemed Dot King had no secrets from her maid. "A four-and-a-half-carat diamond. Two-carat sapphire. A whole yard of pearls. I know a chump like you ain't pullin' down that kind of sugar. Where'd she get all that loot?"

Guimares scowled. "I make good money."

"Yeah?" Coughlin prodded. "What's your racket?"

"No racket," Guimares corrected. "I'm in stocks. In case you haven't heard, the market's really good right now."

"Not *that* good," Coughlin cut in. "We both know she had a sugar daddy. What's his name?"

Guimares tapped the ash off his cigarette. "Who knows?"

"Well, *I* wanna know," Coughlin said. "He must have quite a sugar barrel to pay for that apartment, a full-time maid, fur coats, and all that jewelry. In fact, there's some diamond cuff links on this list that match the description of the ones you got on right now."

Guimares scowled and tried to shimmy his sleeves lower. But the flashy gems wouldn't be covered.

Coughlin twisted the knife relentlessly. "We don't meet too many kept men in here. What's it like pawin' through some dame's crumbs like a street dog?"

"I spent more on Dot than anyone—at least sixty or seventy grand last year, easy!" Guimares ground out tightly.

"Sure you did," Coughlin said.

"I *did*!" Guimares snapped, the anger seeming to energize him. "Not that a flatfoot like you can even imagine that much money."

Coughlin ignored the jab. He finally had Guimares right where he wanted him: hotheaded and talking. This was when suspects started to get sloppy, say things they hadn't meant to, reveal the truth. He just had to keep going. Adrenaline pumped through his veins. He leaned across the table, uncomfortably close, where he could see the beads of sweat forming on the gigolo's brow. "Who'd she have on the side?"

Guimares, hardened in the way that guys who'd been in the game their whole lives were, flicked his ash on the floor. "Some prize fool by the name of Marshall—old and don't ask too many questions."

So Guimares knew about the older man who shared the girl's bed and favors—her rich angel, whose generosity, according to the mother and the maid, Guimares also benefited from in the form of gifts of cash and jewelry she'd passed along, including the very cuff links the gigolo currently wore and had failed to hide. Coughlin pressed on. "Maybe she loved the old fella. Dames love jewelry and the guys who give it to 'em."

"Chumps," Guimares said dismissively. "Broadway girls can get whatever they want if they're pretty enough. And Dot was the prettiest girl in New York. She had a line of guys around the block, throwin' gifts at her like lemon drops. Meant nothin'."

Coughlin shrugged like he wasn't convinced. "Well, the only lemon I seen in that fancy little jewel-box apartment was *his* silk pajamas."

Guimares only shrugged. *Christ, these Broadway types had no morals.*

"I wouldn't want anyone's pajamas at my girl's place except mine." Coughlin waited an intentional, sanity-testing beat. "Although he probably didn't wear 'em for long."

Guimares's jaw twitched.

"Can you imagine what she did for him?" Coughlin gave an appreciative whistle. "Jesus, when I think of the seven ways to Sunday he must've screwed her. You know girls like that'll do anything for their sugar daddies."

Guimares jumped up. "It meant nothing!"

"She tell you that, did she?" Coughlin prodded.

The gigolo caught himself, smoothed his mustache, and sat back down. "We never talked about that sorta thing. I didn't wanna hear."

Coughlin tapped a finger on the table. "Look, pal. Your girl's been murdered and you don't seem too cut up about it. Her mother and her maid swear you must've done it. They say you beat her so bad she had black eyes and fat lips half the time. It don't look good for you. So unless you wanna rot the rest of your miserable life away, locked up in the Tombs, you better start talkin'. Let's start with the sugar papa's real name."

Guimares smoked, refusing to look at him. "Don't know and don't care."

"You *don't* wanna go to the Tombs," Coughlin said, lowering his voice. "You ain't gonna last long. They don't like gigolos. You go over the 'Bridge of Sighs,' pal, and you ain't comin' back. Not the same, anyway."

Guimares stared, mutinous, defiant. "I didn't do it!"

Coughlin raised a brow. "Here's how I see it: it burned you up some old guy kept and had her. Everyone says you're good for it. And you got no alibi. Which makes you my top suspect."

Guimares's eyes slid away. "I got an alibi, you just don't like it."

Coughlin changed tactics. "You ever bought chloroform?"

"I told you back at the hotel: *no*," Guimares said firmly.

"Well, I found a bottle of it next to the victim. It's gonna be easy to trace," Coughlin said, the lie coming easily. "So if you got something to say, you better share it now. 'Cause if I waste my time, only to track it back to you, I'm not gonna be happy. Understand?"

"I don't know nothin' about it," Guimares insisted, unblinking.

So it was gonna be like this, then. Coughlin grabbed his papers and made for the door.

"You just gonna leave me here?" Guimares bleated.

"You got any useful information for me?" Coughlin demanded.

"I told you, I don't know nothin'!"

Coughlin slammed the door and let that be his answer. He was a firm believer that a snitch in time saved nine months of investigating, but he'd gotten as far as he could tonight. A night in jail jogged most men's memories. Guimares ought to be more talkative tomorrow.

Coughlin would use the time to think about how the mystery man, Marshall, fit into the picture. It didn't look good for the bigwig that he was the last person to be seen with Dot King or that John Thomas had never seen him leave. But Guimares made more sense as a murderer—he was full of passion and anger. And yet death by chloroform wasn't a crime of passion. It required planning.

Coughlin stepped outside, finally ready to head home to the Bronx, to the dinner plate, long cold now, Mamie always left in the icebox for him. It had been like this since they were kids. Even though he was two years older and twice her size, Mamie had always appointed herself his caretaker. Sure, he looked out for her as any big brother should—made sure the boys kept a respectful distance, even Samuel until they were properly married—but she was the one who looked out for them all. She'd fussed over him when they were kids, stayed up late worrying until he got home when he was assigned to the rough-and-tumble tenderloin district, and even now made sure he was well fed and looked after. She did the same for their father, and Samuel, and once William had come along and made her a proper mother, him too.

Mamie lived in a house of men and ran it with an efficiency and briskness he admired.

He took a deep breath. The night air was clear and crisp, but all he could smell was trouble.

Chapter 10

June's wail jolted Ella awake. She was surprised to realize she'd slept at all. She lifted him out of his crib and kissed his head. James swung his legs over the edge of the bed, worry a yoke on his shoulders.

Ella went through the morning routine: washing up, making coffee, scrambling eggs, buttering bread, laying it to fry. June pounded his chubby little hands on his high chair tray and cooed.

"You need to eat, honey," James said. "You're already a string bean."

She shook her head. "Not hungry." All she could see was Miss Dottie dead on that bed.

On his way out, James stopped in the doorway, handsome in his suit, but fear etched in his eyes. "Be safe now, y'hear? You know how it is. Just tell 'em what they wanna hear and hurry home to us."

She closed the door. Yes, of course she knew how it was. But maybe James was wrong—maybe it was different up here. Hadn't that white patrolman hailed her cab last night? Hadn't the big, gruff inspector seemed all right? She drew a deep breath.

She took June over to Bea's and kept it to herself that today would be the last. There'd be no money to day board unless she got another job.

She took the subway to Canal Street, and walked the last piece along Elm, just the same as when she and James got married over at the Municipal Building. It had been cool that morning, nearly two years past, and James's hand had been warm and sure through her cotton gloves.

They'd waited in line for a marriage license, he'd paid the two-dollar fee, and then they'd waited in line again to say their words. She'd teased that if he'd asked her sooner, he could've saved half his money, since the fee had just doubled. He'd said he figured he still got a bargain, and looked at her in such a way she got a shiver.

The "chapel" hadn't been much to speak of. The small room with tile floors and just one little window had smelled of stale air and lye soap. The few potted palms, a kindness, were wilted. But when James, so proud of the diamond, slid the ring on her finger, it felt like she could've jumped at the sun.

She'd been so proud to send the news back home, knew how her mama would've shown half of LaVille that letter. But there'd be no letter home about this. There'd also be no money to send, now that she was out of a job.

From the outside, the police headquarters looked more like a fancy hotel. Ella looked up past the giant pillars, the gods and goddesses, shields, horses, eagles, and Lord only knew what else carved into the white stone that stretched six stories high and took up an entire city block; the giant gold dome atop the tower glinted in the sun.

Inside was a maze. Some people looked important and some looked scared, but everyone was in a hurry. She looked for the policeman who'd hailed her the cab but didn't see him. She found her way to the Homicide Bureau, where Womba and Miss Hilda sat on opposite sides of an empty waiting room, looking just as edgy and out of place as she felt.

Miss Hilda, who had more makeup slopped on than any respectable lady ever wore, let alone when called down to police headquarters about the murder of her friend, saw her first and perked up, all excited. She patted the chair next to her. "Billie! Over here!"

Ella startled at the use of her nickname. It felt all kinds of wrong to be called something so personal in a police station. But then, everything about this felt all kinds of wrong.

"Billie! Over here!" Womba called, not to be outdone.

Ella hesitated. It felt like she ought to sit with Womba, since they were the only two Negro women wrapped up in all this, but Womba's snotty "Y'all have a good day" was still fresh in her mind. Plus, she knew Miss Hilda better, having spent all day, every day with the girl. Heck, she'd even helped her dress and washed her underwear. Maids were privy to more of a girl's secrets than their mothers or their men.

Ella had, in fact, seen the showgirl in her birthday suit more times than she could count. But since Miss Hilda's costume over at the Music Box wasn't much more than a few sequins, so had plenty folk. Miss Hilda wasn't what they called shy.

"Sit there." A white policeman behind a desk pointed toward Womba.

Womba puffed up like she'd won, shot Miss Hilda a smug "so there" look, and squeezed Ella's arm when she took the next chair, which was probably supposed to be some sort of sorry. Ella gave a half nod, even though she was still put off. They were here now and in it together.

Miss Hilda crossed her arms over her bosom, which couldn't ever be mistaken for small, and scowled. Then she tapped her heel real sassy, just to let the patrolman know she wasn't pleased.

"*You.*"

The disgusted Irish sneer could belong to only one person. Ella turned. Sure enough, Mrs. Keenan stood in the doorway, but her ice was aimed at Hilda. The old woman took in Miss Hilda's skirt and heels—too short and too high—and looked like she'd bitten a raw onion. "Broadway filth." Mrs. Keenan's gaze swept the room. "All of ye, then—I shoulda known."

Hilda rolled her eyes and snapped her gum. "Old bat," she muttered.

"Like a cow with its cud," Mrs. Keenan retorted. "Come on, boys!" She made a show to lift her skirts like she didn't want to get dirt or bad morals on her, turned sharp on her heel, and stomped as far away as the room let. Her boys trailed after her like obedient ducklings but couldn't stop themselves from a quick look back at Miss Hilda. No red-blooded man could help but look twice at Miss Hilda.

"Lord almighty!" Womba said with a delighted sort of pity. And Ella knew she'd tell everyone just how mean Miss Dottie's mama was.

Then they waited. The clock ticked slowly on the wall. It felt like each tick-tick-tick ratcheted up the tension in the room a little more. Miss Hilda smacked her gum, recrossed her legs, and sighed loud and often to let everyone know how she felt. But it was Mrs. Keenan who acted like she'd been made to carry the Lord's cross. She glared and muttered, and Ella caught snippets about "Broadway tramps puttin' on airs."

Ella stiffened. It wasn't airs to want a better life, to dress nice, put yourself forward, or change your name if yours didn't fit. After all, she hadn't been born Ella Bradford.

She shook her head as she remembered all Miss Dottie had done for the Keenans: the money for rent, her brother's car, the seaside cottage she'd arranged for her mother this summer. There'd been no complaints then. *So just who was the filth with no morals?*

Miss Hilda looked over and raised her brows, plucked and penciled, her expression asking, *How much we gonna tell 'em?* Miss Hilda didn't know all Ella knew, but she knew more than anyone else since she'd lived there.

Ella nodded: *Tell them.* Two would be better than one. Plus, the police might listen more to a white woman.

"Ella Bradford!"

The shout of her name startled her to her feet, and she hurried to follow the policeman to a large private office.

"Captain, this is the girl's maid. Coughlin said she should be first." He closed the door and was gone. Ella looked around nervously. She heard her mama's voice: *Never let yourself alone with a white man, and never close the door.*

The dark-haired man barely glanced up when she sat. He tamped down a stack of papers and cleared his throat loudly. "I'm Captain Carey, head of homicide. State your name and address."

"Ella Bradford—" she began.

"But you also go by Billie?" he cut in.

"Yes, sir, to friends and family," she said.

He looked at her sharply, as if he'd caught her using an alias.

"Billie's my nickname," she clarified. "Like some ladies called Elizabeth go by Betty?"

He heaved a sigh like why'd it all have to be so hard and reluctantly made a note. "You worked for Anna Keenan?"

She noticed right off he used Miss Dottie's given name instead of the one she'd chosen. It didn't sit right to dishonor the dead, but she nodded anyhow. Life had taught her it was usually best to keep quiet and be agreeable. "Yes, sir."

He crossed his arms like they was gonna have a serious chat now. "OK, Billie, how long did you work for the Keenan girl?" he asked.

When Miss Dottie'd called her Billie, it'd felt familiar, kindly. When this policeman did, it felt like he'd shoved his way in somewhere he didn't belong. "I guess about a year and a half now, and sir, I want to tell you about—" she began.

He lifted a finger, stopped her. "I'll ask the questions."

"Yes, sir."

"That's a fancy coat you got there."

She knew what he meant by that and started to sweat. Her hand fluttered to her neck and fussed with the monkey-hair trim. "Thank you, sir."

Those dark eyes bored into her, and she didn't like how it made her feel guilty. "Where'd you get it?"

"M-Miss Dottie gave it to me two weeks ago."

"*Gave* it to you?" His eyebrows shot up.

She swallowed hard, wondered whether he thought Miss Dottie would only give the help rags. "Miss Dottie was generous to everyone, sir. She was very kind."

He held her gaze for a long beat, then shook his head and made another note. "So as her maid, you what? Fixed her hair? Picked up after her?" At her nod, he went on. "Seems she had quite a collection of expensive things . . . furs and jewels. You must've gotten to know them pretty well."

She swallowed, edgy at where he was headed. "Yes, sir. I-I took care of Miss Dottie and the house. Did whatever she asked."

The captain looked back at his notes, whistled appreciatively. "A four-and-a-half-carat diamond? I'm sure a girl like you had never seen something like *that* before."

That much was true. But she took what he really meant by it, and fear stabbed her. Just like a spider, he was at work on a web. What could she say? How could she stop him? She tried to remember what she'd come to say. "Sir, yesterday, I told Inspector Coughlin about Albert Guimares—"

The captain lifted a finger, cut her off again. "We're not done with the jewels. You must've mentioned them at some point, maybe around your neighborhood, to your husband or his friends."

She felt her cheeks burn but held his gaze. If she looked down, she'd look guilty. "No, sir. I kept Miss Dottie's business to myself. I know my place and I keep to it."

He half-smiled at that. "Oh, I don't mean it's your fault, Billie. I'm just saying it'd be hard not to mention jewels that size. In fact, it'd be damn near *impossible*."

She didn't dare tell him he was wrong.

"Well?" he prodded.

She couldn't get enough air. She looked around, desperate. How was she here at the police station? How was Miss Dottie dead? She'd come to tell the police more.

Truth was, Miss Dottie had run with some dangerous and powerful men. And then in January, she'd gone and made her decision—said she had to think of the future, and had her will done up in case the worst happened. And now the worst had.

And all the policeman could talk about was her jewels.

"I kept Miss Dottie's business to myself, sir."

He put his pen and notebook away and heaved a big sigh like she'd let him down. He planted his elbows on the desk, leaned closer. "Billie, this robbery is a classic flat-worker job," he said. "Now, flat workers are a certain kind of thief who steal clothes and jewels for their women friends. And flat workers are always colored. You understand?"

Sweet Jesus. He is gonna try to pin this on James! Pure panic slashed through her. Her heart thundered and her breath came short, but she tried to keep her voice calm and steady. "Sir, I swear I didn't—"

He lifted a hand, and she stopped short. He opened a drawer in his desk, the wood scraping in a high-pitched squeal that sent a shiver down her spine. "Can you read and write?"

She felt her cheeks burn hotter. "Yes, sir."

He pushed paper and pen toward her, tapped his finger on it. "Write down the names of every colored man you know and where we can find 'em."

Her stomach did a sick little flip. She stared, frozen, horrified. She wished she could disappear, go home, right on back to Jacksonville, curl up and rest her head on her mama's lap. She wouldn't even have to tell her what had happened. Her mama would tuck the patchwork quilt her granny had hand-stitched out of old squares of calico around her.

Ella ached for home so hard it hurt. Instead, she was trapped in this room with this white policeman who scowled at her like *she* was a thief or a murderer. She stared down at the paper—white and blank as it waited for the names he'd told her to write. A panicked sob swelled up in her chest and burned to be let out.

"Well?" he prompted, knocking sharply on the desk. "Go on."

Everyone knew what could happen to Negro men at the hands of white men who figured they'd done something wrong. And never mind down at the police station—everyone heard tell of the "third degree." If she gave over the names—none of whom had ever even met Miss Dottie—to the police lookin' for a fella who'd gone and killed a white woman, it'd be just about the worst thing she could do. If this were back home, she might as well help tie the noose. If she gave him innocent men's names, how could she live with herself?

But if she didn't give him the names, she might as well tie the noose around her own neck. She was twenty-three—a grown woman, a wife and a mother who went to church and kept a respectable home. But she was also *alone* at the police headquarters, with a white policeman—the one they called *captain*—who said she had information he needed. She was only a maid here. And if she didn't give him what he wanted, what would he do to her? Hurt her? Beat her? Throw her in jail? She thought of her sweet little Junebug. Who would take care of him?

"I—" She wanted to tell him about Guimares, his threat to toss Miss Dottie, his plan to ruin Mr. Marshall.

"The names," he ground out, and where he was stern before, now there was a threat. She didn't want to think about what came next.

She picked up the pen. Swallowed down another sob that threatened to choke her. She closed her eyes, and thought again of June, his round cheeks, chubby little arms reaching for her . . .

Sick to her stomach at the betrayal of their friends, she wrote the list—all good, innocent, church-goin' deacons and elders, all with good jobs—and prayed each man's innocence would carry him through. James had been right: the less you tell police, the better. Just say what they wanted and get on home. She wrote the final name and couldn't stop the tear that landed on the page. She wiped it away with the tip of her glove. It smeared the ink. She pushed the paper back to the captain as hot shame poured over her.

Never let yourself alone with a white man. Never let the door close.

Chapter 11

"Whaddya mean, no leads?" Coughlin demanded. The morning was not off to a good start. After checking all the overnight arrests for the usual assortment of minor crimes, it was time to get down to business. The first order of the day was the King case. There'd been lots of mumbled excuses, but Mystery Man Marshall remained at large. "He's an old man who likes showgirls. Somebody knows something! Find out who he is and bring him in! And you two! Find out what the hell is going on with that chloroform bottle!"

The detectives thus dispatched, Coughlin consulted the list of interviewees: first up was Hilda Ferguson, the victim's roommate who'd moved out two weeks ago. Arthur Carey, his colleague of twenty years and head of the homicide squad, was handling the witnesses he'd already questioned at the scene: the maid, the mother, and the daytime elevator operator. Carey didn't have his finesse for information, but he was a solid cop. They had a shared trust built up over decades on the force . . . as well as frustrations with the system and an intolerance for incompetence.

A rookie by the name of Sullivan inched closer. "Say, Inspector, need help with interrogations?"

"I'll do it," O'Roarke cut in.

Coughlin was immediately suspicious. Offers of extra help were few and far between. Despite all his men, in a city the size of New York, the number of crimes far outstripped the number of detectives, which usually left them all scrambling.

"Fine—you take the maid, and I'll take the roommate," Sullivan replied.

"Captain Carey's questioning the maid right now," O'Roarke said smugly. "I'll take the roommate. *You* take her ma."

The rookie shuddered. "That old biddy's voice strips paint off the walls."

Coughlin cracked a smile. Nobody could deny that. "All right, simmer down, you mugs. Sullivan, make yourself useful and get the roommate. We'll start with her."

"Yes, sir!" The kid beamed a smile the size of Brooklyn.

A moment later, he returned with a dame in tow who cleared up all the confusion. She had a figure that'd stop traffic, and a smirk that said she knew it.

It was the middle of the morning at police headquarters, but this girl looked like she'd just tumbled out of bed and the bed had held a bacchanalian orgy.

She sauntered up to his desk and cocked a hip. Sullivan rushed to pull out her chair. She sank slowly into the seat, then flicked her eyes up to reward him with a smile that reduced the rookie to a simpering schoolboy.

The showgirl didn't seem to feel any pressure to rush as she lifted her shoulders and shimmied her fur wrap down. She appeared to enjoy the audience.

Girls like this called furs, jewels, cars, trips, and even apartments "service stripes," prizes to be wheedled out of unsuspecting suckers. When the fur finally reached her elbows, she turned the full force of her big blue eyes on him. She held him in her sights for an endless second, and then her lips, painted fire-engine red, drew back in the small smile of a victor.

Coughlin cleared his throat. "Name and age?"

"Hilda Ferguson, nineteen."

He blinked. This creature was *nineteen*? "Do you work?"

"I do the hula shimmy," she said.

"That's a *job*?" Coughlin didn't bother to hide his skepticism.

"I'm a dancer in the Music Box Revue," Hilda explained in a tone meant to convey she shouldn't have to.

He noted it. "And you lived with Dot King?"

"Yeah. Until two weeks ago." The girl's eyes filled with tears, but she looked away, drew a shaky breath, and got herself under control before she looked back. "Now I got my own place at 327 West 56th," she said, a note of pride creeping into her voice.

The address triggered the usual response. *1921: Attempted suicide, some guy took a swan dive off the fire escape, holding—but not using—a gun . . .*

Coughlin stemmed a flood of crimes by forcing himself to focus on the fact that it was two blocks from Dot King's. It shouldn't be more than a five-minute walk, even for a dame wearing such impractical shoes. It was a relief Dot King hadn't been murdered in Five Points or Hell's Kitchen, where the list of crimes at each address would distract him for hours.

"Why'd you leave?"

Her eyes swam with tears again. She took a deep breath and shook her head, as though to clear away whatever thoughts weighed on her before answering. "Dottie was likable enough when she was sober, but she became unmanageable when she drank. Which was often, lemme tell ya. She'd get moody and melancholy. I . . . I just couldn't take it anymore."

"Whaddya mean, 'unmanageable'?" he asked. Of course, he knew what an unmanageable drunk was. Even if his time on the force hadn't brought him to thousands of crime scenes where nasty drunks had done awful things, any kid raised in an Irish ghetto knew. But it was usually the men.

"Listen," the girl said, "I don't pretend I'm the president of the church temperance union. I get sozzled and have my fun. But Dottie didn't know when to say no, and then she'd get belligerent. And if she was in one of her moods, you better watch out—one time she kicked the glass out of a taxi window."

"Any hard feelings?" he asked.

Hilda Ferguson opened the metal clasp of her comically small bag, withdrew a cigarette case, took one out, struck a match, and lit up. She shook out the match and tossed it in the ashtray he purposely kept closest to witnesses. Her fingernails were painted the same fire-engine red as her lips. "Nope."

Coughlin doubted it was that simple but let it go for now. "How'd you meet?"

She shrugged again. "Around. I needed a place to stay last summer, so I sublet hers while she was in Atlantic City. Then she came back, and we lived together. It was pretty small for the two of us, but she often went down the shore, and I'd have the place to myself."

Coughlin kept his expression neutral. Atlantic City was the elbow of the drug trail between New York and Philadelphia. "Yeah? What brought her there?"

"The sea air?" she deadpanned.

"Miss Ferguson, I don't have much time. If this interview takes too long, you'll have to wait until I'm free again, and that could be *a very, very long while*. Understand?"

She rolled her eyes. "Fine. I dunno. She said she summered there."

"First of all, it ain't summer. Second, nobody but society people 'summer' anywhere," Coughlin said. "So let's have it. What was she really doing in Atlantic City?"

"All's I *know* is Dot went down there all the time," Hilda said stubbornly. "She was there all last week, and she went back again this past weekend with Guimares."

"It's so cold out, you got a fur coat on, but she went to the beach twice in the last two weeks?"

Hilda snorted. "She's got a free room at the Ritz anytime she wants it. What's not to like?"

Coughlin frowned. There was lots not to like about Atlantic City, but at the top of his list was that it was a thriving hub for trafficking both booze and drugs. And Nucky Johnson, who was known to unofficially run the town, owned the Ritz and ran his illicit businesses out of it. Coughlin would immediately dispatch his men to the shore and see what they could dig up. Nucky wasn't his problem, but Dot King was. "Who'd she go with last week?" he asked.

"Nobody," Hilda informed him breezily. "She went alone."

"All alone?" Coughlin asked. "No female friend to travel with?" Girls like this, reckless girls, who traveled alone, lived alone, and drove cars only led to trouble . . . trouble that, he was quick to tell anyone, later landed on his lap. Second, and he never told anyone this part, his discomfort with, and suspicion of, this brash, bold new breed made him feel old and stodgy.

Hilda shrugged. "Dot never had many female friends, and she lost the few she did have on account of her wild life the last year. We were all sick of hearing her boast about her conquests."

"What about men in her life?" he asked.

Hilda lifted a shoulder. "Just Marshall and Guimares and the occasional fella she picked up in cabarets."

Coughlin narrowed his eyes at the moral code of these girls. "Do you have any information about Marshall? Any idea who he is?" he asked, zeroing in.

The showgirl took a drag on her cigarette and tilted her head back, exposing the pale expanse of her throat. She blew the smoke upward in a thin stream and watched as it dissipated. "Nah. She kept him to herself. Never brought him around or let any of us meet him. But when she was drunk, she'd often take one of his mushy love letters from her bosom and read it to us."

Coughlin's interest in finding the girl's sugar daddy doubled. He found that men were wont to say a lot of foolish things they later regretted when passions passed and cooler heads prevailed. If Marshall had committed his tomfoolery to paper and the victim had a habit of saving and sharing his missives, it could be a recipe for trouble . . . especially since they already knew this alias-wielding sugar daddy cared very deeply about keeping his identity secret. Blackmail was a common game in sinister Broadway circles.

One thing was clear: they needed to find Marshall. He leaned in. "Miss King's mother claims she can identify him if we bring him in. Says she and the family were on good terms with him."

Hilda rolled her eyes. "She's a liar and a money-grubber. She never even saw him. Dottie knew better than to try to visit those hyenas without bringing money and gifts. All they ever did was bleed her dry."

"Can anyone identify this guy?" Coughlin asked.

"Ella Bradford was there when he came to call. But honestly, I don't even think Dot knew his real identity, or really cared. He was too wise for her. Shortly after they met, he told her he'd give her a year to make good. But instead she went from bad to worse. She hid everything from him—her wild parties and her wild ways. But he was onto her. It was only a matter of time before he left her." Hilda leaned forward to stub out her cigarette.

Coughlin didn't like these odds. Nobody knew this guy's real name, and only one person besides Dot King could identify him in a lineup.

Whoever Marshall was, he was smart. Which made Ella Bradford uniquely valuable, and uniquely vulnerable if Marshall was the sort of guy to tie up loose ends. Coughlin made a note to provide police protection for her.

"You think Marshall could be a gangster?"

"Nah. He's just some old sugar daddy. They just want pretty girls." She rubbed her fingertips together to signal money. "It's a job, see?"

He didn't need to ask what the job entailed. "Can you tell me anything else?"

"Nope. Dottie never confided in me. The only person she trusted was Ella Bradford, and Ella's the most closemouthed person I've ever met." Hilda lit another cigarette. "I paid half her wages, and she never told me nothin'."

Coughlin made note of it. He'd had a feeling that Ella Bradford would be a key witness, not only because she'd worked for the victim but because she'd been so distraught, which indicated that they'd been close. He'd see if Carey had gotten anything further from her. "What about Guimares?" he prompted.

The showgirl rolled her eyes. "We never understood why Dottie put up with him. She thought she'd be the happiest woman in the world if only he'd marry her. Well, my dear, lemme tell ya: I married a Spaniard just like him when I was sixteen, and trust me, they just get worse."

Chapter 12

11:00 a.m. Manhattan. West 69th Street.

MODEL MYSTERIOUSLY SLAIN

ACQUITTED: MISS. BILLIE WELLS

The headlines from Julia's articles dominated the front page and spilled to the coveted page-three spot. These cases—Miss Wells acquitted of murder and Dot King found dead, one quest for justice concluding as another began—were the steady pulse of the crime beat, the rhythm of newspaper life.

And the most urgent task on the new case was to find this Marshall and ascertain when the man of mystery had left Dot King's love nest. From what Julia had gleaned, the entire case hung on it. John Thomas's account didn't just pin Marshall as the last-known person to see Dot King alive—it pointed to him as the *murderer*.

Westbrook poured her coffee and clinked her cup across the two-person table in their tiny kitchen. "Cheers to my front-page wife," he said.

"Aww, thanks, precious!" Julia said, the Tennessee creeping out with her pet name for him.

After a quick breakfast, they headed out to work together. He kissed her on the cheek and headed downtown, and she caught the el uptown to pay a call on Dot King's mother. The northern boundary of the Upper West Side, where it abutted Harlem, wasn't considered as fashionable as Julia's West 69th Street address. But as gentrification pushed north to keep up with the city's burgeoning population, 101st Street now boasted buildings, that, according to advertisements, had live-in servants' quarters. That was Manhattan: always growing, expanding, getting fancier.

At Julia's knock, the door was yanked open by a gray-haired woman in a black dress. "Yes?"

"Mrs. Keenan? I'm—"

"Go away!" The woman tried to close the door.

Julia wedged her shoe across the doorsill. "I'm so sorry for your loss, ma'am. But every paper in the city is writing about your daughter. So wouldn't you rather talk to a girl reporter, instead of a pack of newsmen who don't know the first thing about women?"

The mother scowled. "Newspaper girl, are ya?"

"Yes, ma'am," Julia said. "Just like my mother."

"Five minutes, no more," the woman said, already stomping away.

Julia scurried after her host. Compared to some of the things she'd done to get interviews, like trekking eight miles through a blizzard with snow up over her knees to speak to a woman who'd been jailed as a spy, this was a relatively warm welcome. She took a seat, though it wasn't offered, in a large, airy parlor, and a deep silence settled around them.

"Are you here all alone?" Julia asked. Where were her loved ones? Julia had been taught the importance of sitting shiva from a young age. Her mother, Josie, had always been the first to show up with food and Julia in tow to keep loved ones company as they grieved a loss. To do so was a mitzvah, a kindness, and also a duty and an honor. A mother whose child had died would never be left alone. There should be more food than the family could possibly eat, neighbors and family offering condolences and company, and a general sort of bustle to try to fill the aching loneliness every death imparted. Julia felt this absence as keenly as she felt the absence of any trace of sorrow in the woman herself.

"Me grandchildren are at school, and me daughter Helen's at me laundry," Mrs. Keenan said, briskly flicking at her skirt.

"You *own* the laundry?" Julia couldn't keep the surprise from her voice.

The woman leveled an assessing gaze at her. "*You're* a reporter?"

Julia flushed. While it was rare to be a woman on the city desk, let alone a crime reporter, it was even rarer that this woman—older and an immigrant—owned a business. But it was clear the topic was not a welcome one. Julia took out her notebook and began. "What kind of questions did the police ask, ma'am?"

"Wanted to know about Anna, her life, friends. I said she'd always been willful—married a decent-enough fellow from upstate when she was seventeen, but she couldn't be satisfied with a quiet life. He caught her red-handed with another fella, so she had to move home." Mrs. Keenan heaved a sigh. "She got work as a model. But Lord almighty, the riffraff she went around with."

"Albert Guimares?" Julia prompted.

The mother sniffed with disgust. "A parasite livin' off me daughter."

"I see," Julia said. She'd counted at least nine rooms in this swanky apartment, in this fancy building, in this newly stylish neighborhood. Even with her own business, perhaps Guimares wasn't the only parasite living off sugar-daddy Marshall. "And what's Mr. Marshall like?"

Mrs. Keenan's face softened slightly. "He's been a very kind friend to Anna. He came with her one night when she dropped somethin' off. He's very distinguished—European manners, ye might say. He lives up in Boston, but I expect to hear from him tomorrow."

"I see," Julia murmured, looking down at her notes. "Friend" was, of course, euphemistic. "Are you aware that John Thomas, the elevator operator, says Marshall is the last-known person to be with your daughter?"

The Irish woman startled. "What're you sayin'?"

"Um . . . that maybe he could've . . . ?" Julia let the rest fill itself in.

"*Marshall?* Oh no, not him."

"How can you be so sure?" Julia pressed. "He's—"

"I'm sure," the mother cut in firmly.

Julia glanced around and then quickly away from the gilt-framed mirror hung on the opposite wall. In Jewish homes, mirrors were covered after a death, and mourners even ripped their clothes to demonstrate the depth of their grief. This woman's daughter had just been *murdered*, and yet, as Julia searched for and failed to find any signs of grief in either person or place, she had to wonder whether the woman was grieving at all. And what did it mean if she wasn't? Julia looked for anything—eyes red, a voice hoarse from crying—but was met with only stern resignation. She'd interviewed a lot of cold, hard people—criminals weren't known to be a kindhearted lot—but she'd never met anyone quite like this.

"What can you tell me about your daughter, ma'am?"

"There was no reasonin' with Anna and her wild ways," the woman said. It was clear she'd said it many times before, and had, somewhere along the way, convinced herself of it. "After me husband died two years past, me oldest boy, John, took over as man of the house. Anna went and bobbed and bleached her hair—looked like a proper tramp, she did. They quarreled about it, and rather than try to live a good, quiet life, she packed 'er bags and left."

Julia shifted, thinking of how she herself had packed her bags and left her mother's home for Knoxville and an opportunity on the *Journal and Tribune* court beat, where she'd honed her skills before heading north, and the dream of writing feature stories for a daily press in the biggest, most exciting city in the country. The difference was, Julia had had a mother who boosted, supported, and lifted her. Dot, apparently, had not been as fortunate.

"When did you last see her?" Julia asked.

"She just come by Tuesday. Told me she was gonna buy me a bungalow by the sea this summer. Cost $1,000, ye know."

Pride about the expense was the closest thing to affection Julia had seen from this woman. She wanted to build on the positive moment. "That's very generous."

"Me girl was generous," Mrs. Keenan agreed. "She left me everythin' in her will."

"Was she in high spirits? Or low? Or . . . ?"

Mrs. Keenan carelessly dropped her hands, red and chapped, in her lap, and stared off into a corner. "She was happy," she finally said. "Mr. Marshall was finally goin' to Paris to get his divorce so he could marry her. They'd been plannin' it for a year—they were gonna settle in Washington Heights. Put that in your story."

Julia froze as one very plain motive for murder laid itself calmly at her feet. *Marshall was married . . . and had promised to leave his wife.*

Chapter 13

2:00 p.m. Manhattan. Police Headquarters.

Atlantic City, unsigned will, Guimares: bite marks / scratches on hand, who is Marshall, why take the stairs?

A knock on his closed door—which everyone knew meant *not* to bother him—interrupted Coughlin's notes. Carey stuck his head in. "Got a minute?"

Coughlin granted a reluctant wave. He spent a precise one-third of his time examining suspects and snitches, flimflams and felons, gangsters and thugs, getting various and sundry members of the underworld to talk. Nobody could get information like he could. But Carey, head of the homicide squad and a lifer like himself, usually had a few decent leads. "Any news on Marshall?" he asked before Carey even made it to a chair.

"Nope," Carey said. "The guy was careful—I'll give him that—and the victim was vigilant in protecting him."

Coughlin sighed. "Well, we need to find out who this son of a bitch is and haul him in. Good thing George LeBrun wasn't asleep at the wheel when Houghtalin called to fish around for his mystery client. If LeBrun hadn't raised a red flag and called me, this whole thing just might've passed for a suicide."

"LeBrun's a good man," Carey agreed. "What've you found?"

"So far, more questions than answers. John Thomas is sure he didn't take Marshall down or see him leave. Clearly the guy left somehow, so he *must've* taken the stairs. But it doesn't sit right that he took those steep, lousy stairs for the first time ever on the night of the murder. If he's got nothing to hide, why sneak out? But meanwhile, Guimares has a criminal record, is fighting extradition, has a full set of teeth marks and scratches on his hand, and no alibi." Coughlin rubbed his forehead. "This may be the first case in the history of the New York City Police where we have too many suspects."

"I—" Carey began.

"Meanwhile," Coughlin plowed on, "it seems Marshall was quite the letter writer and Dot King took frequent trips to Atlantic City alone—including last week."

Carey's eyebrows shot up. "This time of year? *Alone?*"

"I sent men to look into it," Coughlin said. "So . . . Ella Bradford. At the crime scene, she said she heard Guimares screaming at the victim on the phone. He was trying to force her to do something, but she refused. Any idea what that was about?"

"She didn't say anything about that," Carey said. He slid a piece of paper across the desk, looking pleased. "But I got a valuable lead—a list of every colored man she knows. We're already on it."

Coughlin blinked. Had he missed something? "Just because they know Ella Bradford?" he echoed.

"Everything points to this being a flat-worker robbery gone wrong," Carey said, not bothering to keep an impatient edge from his voice. "From the coats left behind in the hall to the sloppiness of leaving the comb and the bottle behind. And *as you know*, that sort of thief is always colored. So it makes sense to start with the girl who worked there and knew how much this loot was worth."

"I know *thieves*, I know *crimes*, and I know *people*," Coughlin said tightly. "This wasn't a random flat worker—it was personal. You don't snuff a girl out in her bed, in her negligee, if it's not."

"I—" Carey started to say, scowling at him.

Coughlin cut him off. "And that spring-locked door? The emergency stairs? Whoever did this knew her and the place well—not some random guy who happens to know her maid. *Especially*," he added, "when the maid is Ella Bradford. She's married, *with a baby*, and keeps a respectable home."

"Ella Bradford could've told the guy how to get in," Carey argued. "Imagine bein' around all those jewels and furs and cash all day, when you're only a maid?"

"There were no signs of forced entry," Coughlin pointed out tightly. For reasons he didn't understand, this was escalating into a power struggle, and he had no time for it. "And I doubt Dot King would just open her door in the middle of the night for some guy she's never met before. Plus John Thomas said nobody else went up after Marshall."

Carey frowned. "Ella Bradford could've given the guy her key so he could sneak in while the victim was sleeping. As for John Thomas? He could've been in on it too."

Coughlin's irritation rose. He focused on his door, wishing it had remained shut and Carey absent. He didn't want to strain his relationship with his colleague, a partner he'd worked well with for decades, and an invaluable ally within the city's tangled web of interoffice politics. "This case is practically open and shut," he said, giving patience one last try. "Guimares has scratch and bite marks on his hand *and* I've already got him in custody. I'd be ready to call it a day except John Thomas says he never took this guy Marshall back down that night. So the way I see it, we've gotta find out who the hell Marshall is and bring him in, just to run this thing to ground. I've got fifty men out there, but so far nobody's come up with anything. That's where we need to focus . . ."

"I still think this list is worth exploring," Carey said, crossing his arms.

One of Coughlin's lines rang. He snatched it off the hook. "Yeah?"

"Ferdinand Pecora's calling for you, sir," an operator said. Coughlin tensed. Jesus Christ. Just what he didn't need. Pecora was one of twelve assistant district attorneys, but he'd been feeling his oats ever since he'd been promoted to *chief assistant* last year, and had recently become completely unbearable when he took over as the acting DA while the real DA was out with some sort of illness. Coughlin didn't trust Pecora as far as he could throw him—he was too eager, too ambitious, too greedy, too slick. He was the kind of guy who always had an angle, and the angle benefited only himself.

The line clicked and Pecora's voice blared without preamble. "Inspector! I just got an interesting call from Neilson Olcott. Apparently, he's representing 'Mr. Marshall' from this King case, and he and his associate 'Wilson,' who was with him that night, want to come in tomorrow afternoon to share what they know. Do you and Carey want to sit in?"

"Marshall? *My Marshall?*" He sat bolt upright.

"Well, he's *my* Marshall now—" Pecora started.

"Did you get their real names?" Coughlin demanded, trying to wrest control of the conversation.

"No," Pecora said after only the slightest pause.

Coughlin didn't buy it. Until three months ago, Neilson Olcott had worked alongside Pecora as an assistant DA. The two were thick as thieves.

"Let's have 'em come down to headquarters," Coughlin said. "Say, 1:30 or so?"

"Sorry, pal, but one of their conditions for coming in was meeting in my office," the DA said smoothly.

"They have *conditions?*" Coughlin scoffed. Olcott had always been a worm. Apparently, making ten times his salary to sell his soul wasn't enough. Now he was trying to cash in on his former connections to get special treatment, which explained why he'd called Pecora instead of the police.

"Why are you making this so difficult?" Pecora said with a forced calm that instantly annoyed Coughlin more. "They wanna meet at my office, and Olcott said Marshall will only share what he knows if we agree to protect his real identity. He doesn't want to embarrass his family."

"And you *agreed*?" Coughlin didn't bother to hide his outrage. Since when did they accommodate anyone connected to a murder? Too damn bad if it *embarrassed* his family.

"If I didn't, you'd still be chasing some vague description of an older man with gray hair," Pecora shot back.

Coughlin leaped to his feet. "My men have already interviewed every Broadway bum and sugar baby out there and amassed a ton of information in the span of a day. What've *you* done? Answered a phone call from a former colleague?"

"I called as a courtesy," Pecora said testily. "If you can't make it, I'll meet them alone."

Coughlin gritted his teeth. Nothing about the situation sat right. Pecora was giving the two alias-wielding men who were the last-known people to see Dot King alive special allowances? Why? Because they'd hired his old pal and colleague Olcott?

Coughlin would be damned if he'd let a possible murder suspect call the shots. But what could he do? Pecora had already agreed to the terms. This was clearly only the tip of the iceberg. And Coughlin already knew he wasn't going to like the rest.

Coughlin took his glasses off and rubbed the bridge of his nose, where they'd left an indentation. His men must've been closing in on the suspects, which had sent them scurrying to secure that little weasel Olcott.

"We'll be there," he snapped.

"Fine," Pecora said, sounding none too thrilled. "If the press asks, just say Marshall will be coming in sometime in the next few days. Obviously, we don't need any newshounds pounding down our door."

"And *I* don't need you tellin' me what to say!" Coughlin slammed down the phone and turned to Carey. "Goddammit! Pecora cut a deal with Marshall and Wilson to come in tomorrow, but we have to protect their real identities."

"To hell with him," Carey said smoothly. "My list will give us our man."

Coughlin was about to inform Carey his flat-worker theory was bunk when his door flew open and an eager new recruit came running in. "Sir! A girl reporter's here asking about Mr. Marshall."

Coughlin had been wondering how long it would take for Julia Harpman to show up. She was a near-constant pain in the ass. Ever since she'd arrived in New York and covered the Elwell case, which, she was quick to remind her readers every chance she got, *remained unsolved*, she'd been on just about every case he worked.

Girl reporters usually stuck to the society pages, but Miss Harpman, writing first under the title "Investigator" and now her own byline had become his constant shadow. He'd heard she'd gotten married to another reporter last summer, but she'd bucked convention and kept her name . . . and her job. This, like so much female behavior these days, including the antics of the murder victim, was previously unheard of. But that was her business. His business was that she kept up a stream of never-ending, incredibly annoying, and—yes, he admitted—smart questions. Her gentle manner and southern drawl took the edge off, but her line of investigation was always razor sharp.

Coughlin closed his eyes and sighed. Miss Harpman and her legion of fans at the *Daily News* would have a field day with the special considerations for Mystery Man Marshall. He braced himself for articles full of thinly veiled jabs and accusations, which always led to his office fielding dozens of calls, letters, and even crime-obsessed spectators demanding "justice."

As though he didn't have enough on his plate navigating a war on crime and the equally perilous interoffice politics of the justice system. He took a deep breath. He would manage—he always did. Unless Marshall produced something earth-shattering, Guimares would stay in his crosshairs as the prime suspect.

"Tell her I'm busy."

Chapter 14

Coughlin was dodging her, which meant *something* was afoot. Something had come to light that he didn't want the press to know about. She would try to winnow it out later. In the meantime, Julia headed to the medical examiner's office to learn what she could about the autopsy. The guy at the front desk, short, stout, and bespectacled, grimaced when she came in.

"Well, if isn't Julia Harpman, star reporter at the *Daily News*," he said. "To what do we owe the honor?"

Julia liked that he didn't say "girl reporter" like most men. She smiled. "Don't tell me you missed me?"

"A stinker like you? Sure. About as much as I miss having a sharp little rock in my shoe." But he said it with a grin. "You here for George LeBrun?" he asked, already lifting the phone. As the secretary to the medical examiner, LeBrun was a knowledgeable source Julia had spoken to on and off the record many times.

A few moments later, she was waved back to LeBrun's clean, well-ordered office. The tall Frenchman stood when she entered. "Mademoiselle Harpman," he said, taking her hand. "Always a pleasure."

"Monsieur LeBrun, thank you for making time."

"I can guess what brings you to our office," he said with a smile.

Julia removed her gloves, took a seat, and crossed her ankles. "I hear the toxicologist finished his examination of Dot King."

LeBrun nodded, reaching for a folder. "Yes, I have Dr. Gettler's results right here. With them, Dr. Norris estimates the time of death between 5:00 and 7:00 a.m. Gettler also said he'd never seen a brain as soaked with chloroform in his entire career."

Julia took out her notebook and pen. "And how long would the victim have inhaled the chloroform to reach that level of saturation?" she asked, an image flashing in her mind of a beautiful blonde pinned on her bed, a male hand holding the poison-soaked rag over her mouth.

"At least five minutes," LeBrun said.

Julia wrote it down. "I see. And what else is chloroform used for besides murder?"

"It has many uses," the Frenchman answered. "As I'm sure you know, it's commonly used by dentists and doctors as an anesthetic, and it's sold in pharmacies for personal use as a sleep aid. It's also used as a chemical solvent in many industrial and building processes, but that wouldn't interest you."

"A sleep aid . . . Is that why the first patrolman thought it was suicide?" Julia asked. At his nod, she continued: "Does your office intend to open your own investigation for this case?"

Most people didn't know the New York ME's office had the power not only to run their own investigation on any case they saw fit but also to hold their own trial, the results of which were legally binding. Julia could include reference to that possibility in articles should the police—or the ME—need a kick in the pants.

"Not at this time," LeBrun said. "We're supporting the police in their investigation." He leaned forward and lowered his voice. "You know how Dr. Norris is—pathological about not interfering."

Julia nodded. Norris had been appointed by Mayor Hylan five years ago as the city's first ME, after the coroner's office had been abolished. Norris was thus in the precarious position that all "firsts" found themselves in: walking a tightrope of working in new and innovative ways, while also not ruffling any of the old guard's feathers. But Julia also knew that his stoic refusal to "get involved"—his self-imposed pledge to remain neutral and thus not deploy the full powers of his office—frustrated some members of his team, even as it preserved the longevity of their positions.

She hoped it didn't mitigate the likelihood of bringing Dot King's killer to justice. She was on the case to ensure it didn't.

◆ ◆ ◆

Back at the *News*, the city desk bustled as always, a cacophony of ringing phones and overlapping conversations. Press agents lurked, waiting for their chance; reporters rushed out in pursuit of a source, or rushed back in fresh off a tip, everyone always in a hurry. The floor, as usual, was filthy, littered with detritus, ash, cigarette butts, scraps of paper, containers of coffee, and remnants of sandwiches left in a hurry and never disposed of. The old building's army of mice would be scurrying toward the feast later, and the copy boys would reach for their makeshift rubber-band slingshots and paper clips to wage war against the vermin.

Julia took her seat and tucked into writing her story.

> Dot King is followed in death by the same shifting elusive images that danced across her sparkling path in life. The Dashing Dot, who combined in her slender beauty the gay cloak model of a thousand loves and the doleful daughter of Melancholia, was murdered in her bed on the top floor of the apartment building at 144 West 57th Street sometime after midnight Wednesday.

Julia's fingers flew over the keys, and the Broadway Butterfly began to take shape.

Philip, prowling the newsroom in all his editor glory, king of their small universe, wielding a list of possible stories, tips, and ideas, descended on Hellinger, seated at the adjacent desk. "Kid!" he boomed, louder than necessary. "A little birdie told me they're gonna raid a series of speakeasies to tamp down on St. Paddy's Day tomorrow. Rumor has it Rothstein might be involved."

At the name, Julia paused typing to look over.

Hellinger perked up. "Arnold Rothstein? The biggest gangster in New York City?"

The editor didn't miss a beat. "No. Arnold Rothstein the ballet dancer."

Hellinger flushed, but quickly rallied. "I won't let you down, boss." He turned to Julia as Philip moved on. "This could be my big break! Imagine if Rothstein's there."

"Rothstein's too smart for that. And anyway, it'd take more than one speakeasy bust to bring down 'the Brain,'" she said. "He's been arrested before, remember? Big splashy trial over fixing the 1919 World Series? Rothstein allegedly the criminal mastermind behind it all? Never could pin it on him? Ring any bells?"

"That was three and a half years ago," Joe, a grizzled city desk veteran who seemed to be as timeworn and inherent to the space as the walls of the old building themselves, piped up. "The kid was fresh out of di-dees and still in knee britches!"

Julia ignored that. The truth was, Hellinger should've still been in high school three years ago, but he'd been expelled when he was fifteen for organizing a student protest. "Two years ago, he lost $250,000 on one race!"

Hellinger whistled long and low. "*One race?* Imagine havin' that kind of sugar!"

Julia couldn't.

Hellinger leaned in confidentially. "I know one of his guys, you know."

It shouldn't have surprised her. Hellinger seemed to know people everywhere, due in equal part to his endless Broadway connections from his last gig and his seemingly bottomless generosity—giving a buck to every Broadway bum he passed. "Who?"

"Legs Diamond."

"Legs?" Julia didn't know this Legs character and, based on his name, had no interest in changing that fact.

"Yup. Legs is quite a guy. You never know, I may need a source one day."

"Better move fast. With a name like Legs Diamond and friends like Arnold Rothstein, I wouldn't count on his longevity." Having issued that sage advice, which Julia was sure Hellinger would ignore, she turned back to her article about the Broadway Butterfly. What were the police hiding?

Chapter 15

March 17, 11:00 a.m. Manhattan. Police Headquarters.

As he walked the few blocks to the criminal courts, Coughlin's irritation that *he* should have to go to Pecora's office to question a suspect redoubled with every step. By the time he reached the lobby, irritation had grown into resentment. And by the time he got up to the fourth floor, he was in an officially foul mood.

By his own admission, Marshall was the last-known person to see Dot King alive. He wasn't exactly in a position to be making demands—and yet the guy *was*. It was really all Pecora's fault, caving like a chump, agreeing to protect the man's identity, hosting him at the DA's office for a cozy chat, and on St. Patrick's Day, one of the busiest, most raucous days of the year.

Accommodating a goddamn *murder suspect*? What the hell was Pecora thinking?

Coughlin stomped into Pecora's office and slammed the door to announce his arrival.

"Inspector," the chief-assistant-turned-acting-DA said from behind his desk, looking especially full of himself, his ever-present cigar clenched in his teeth. He rose and extended his hand.

The lawyer stood around five foot six, barely clearing Coughlin's shoulder, with light-brown skin and jet-black, wiry hair. He sported a navy-blue pinstripe suit. It looked too expensive for what an assistant

DA could afford. He probably had relatives who were tailors. Italians always did.

Pecora had been born in the old country and had come to New York when he was just a tyke. Everything about him was a little too eager: his grooming too flashy and his English a little too perfect—a tribute, no doubt, to his efforts to become as American as possible as quickly as possible. If they were friends, none of that would matter. Coughlin's parents were immigrants—hell, half of New York was immigrants.

But they weren't friends, so Coughlin cut to the chase. "What time's your pal Olcott gonna show up with the suspects?"

"They're *not*—" Pecora started, then shook his head as though it was hopeless.

A knock came at the door and Carey came in, followed by Pecora's secretary. "Mr. Olcott and his clients are here."

"Where's the stenographer?" Coughlin demanded.

"Oh, I hardly think that's necessary—*they* called *us*," Pecora said, buttoning his too-flashy jacket. "Show 'em in."

"It's standard procedure to have a stenographer present to take down testimony from persons of interest," Coughlin reminded him.

"I *told* you, they're not persons of interest. They're coming in as a courtesy to *help* us!" Pecora shot back.

"What a goddamn joke," Coughlin muttered, turning away. Apparently, not having a stenographer was to be yet another privilege Pecora extended this guy.

He was still fuming when Neilson Olcott drifted in, looking just as wispy and weak as he had during his time at the DA's office. He was followed by four men who looked like his aged uncles. They barely managed to conceal their horror at the outdated, standard-issue metal filing cabinets, battered wooden chairs, and lumpily patched walls in need of a fresh coat of paint.

The swells probably felt some mix of pity for the poor city lawyers, and relief that they could hightail it back to their swanky offices.

Coughlin drew himself up to his full height, pride bleeding into defensiveness, layered with resentment.

Pecora, meanwhile, leaped eagerly forward and pumped Olcott's hand. "Neilson!"

"Ferdinand," Olcott returned, his pale, flaccid cheeks warming slightly. "I knew I could count on you to understand our unique situation."

A client who claims he's innocent—real unique, Coughlin thought, but managed not to say. Saying what was on his mind had landed him in hot water too many times.

"Inspector," Olcott said as he offered an unnervingly limp grip, "it's been a while."

"Seventy-four days," Coughlin corrected, his memory demanding precision. He crushed Olcott's hand as though he could pump some life into him. "I've been on the force twenty-seven *years*—now *that's* a while."

Olcott ignored him and turned back to Pecora. "These are my co-counsels, William Moore and Warren Cunningham, and our clients, John Kearsley Mitchell and his confidential attorney and companion on the night in question, John Jackson."

There were more handshakes all around, Coughlin's reluctant, and a general jostling in the cramped space as additional chairs were brought in. He plunked down in the central seat and flipped through his notebook, loudly crinkling the pages. The others squeezed around him.

"Do you *mind*?" Pecora hissed, leaning too close.

Coughlin brushed his ear where Pecora's breath had tickled moistly. Why should *he* move? Instead, he watched the so-called Marshall and Wilson, who sat woodenly, like Pecora's chairs might get their fancy suits dirty.

After forty-eight hours of mystery that had whipped the newspapers into a frenzy and wasted the time of fifty detectives searching for him, Coughlin was almost disappointed to see that "Marshall" was just a snobby old guy with his wormy lawyer. He was, as expected, gray and balding. Unexpectedly, there was a stony coldness about him. Most men, when facing a room of police and prosecutors, would be tense, revealed by sweaty palms or perspiring brows. Most men would nervously look around, or overcompensate with a gregarious helpfulness.

But somehow, even in the goddamn DA's office, under suspicion about his murdered mistress, this man sat stonily, expressionless, and still commanded the room. He presided with the confidence of a king, a man whose path had been made easy for him by money and name, a man who expected to be accommodated.

Coughlin hated every single bit of the man's arrogance.

"Gentlemen," Olcott said, though he looked only at Pecora. "Thank you for taking the time to meet, and for your understanding and discretion. Mr. Mitchell asked me to set this up so he could share what he knows. As a friend of Miss King's, he'd like to assist in apprehending and bringing her murderer to justice as quickly as possible."

Coughlin narrowed his eyes. His investigation wasn't gonna run on anyone else's timeline. "You want quick? You got nothin' to hide? Then why come in here armed with all these lawyers?"

The stuffed shirts blinked owlishly at each other, as if to see whether anyone had remembered to bring a damn answer. Coughlin wanted to tell them to relax—every minute was billable.

Pecora forced a chuckle. "We appreciate any information your clients have and, of course, understand *their right* to have an attorney present."

"Yeah—*an* attorney—as in *one*," Coughlin grumbled.

Olcott turned away twitchily. "We believe everyone will benefit from this case being wrapped up as quickly and quietly as possible. My client is anxious to get back to his professional and charitable work—he's a patron of *many* charities, including the arts, and employs hundreds of men with families to support. We'd hate to have that work disrupted."

There was general nodding and snuffling of agreement. Coughlin bit his tongue to keep from saying that maybe the patron of various charities *including the arts* should've thought about that before he ran around Manhattan with a blonde mistress half his age who'd just turned up dead.

"Of course," Pecora agreed eagerly, clearly enjoying his role as gate-keeper to the city's legal process. "And as *I* said, we appreciate him coming forward."

Coughlin struggled to restrain himself from rolling his eyes. This was just a little too much bullshit from these goons. *Of course* Pecora was happy to oblige—if the rumors were true, the Italian was a shameless lothario as well. But the detective squad had better things to do—*like solve a murder*. Before the DA could heap on more preening and glad-handing, he jumped in. "All right, let's get down to it. Where do you reside?"

Marshall—it was hard now to think of him as anything else—had the grace to attempt humility. "I keep a small place at 36th and Madison."

Coughlin bit his lip to keep himself from blabbering the flood of crimes associated with the address. There was nothing small about any place on Madison Avenue. And if he wasn't mistaken—*and he was never mistaken about addresses*—John Pierpont Morgan's mansion was across the street. When the founder of J.P. Morgan had died ten years ago, he'd been worth more than $80 million. This guy was his neighbor.

Nobody like that had ever come in for questioning. Coughlin exchanged a look with Carey. They were used to dealing with thugs and gangsters. But whether someone was a ruffian or on the social registry, the job was the job. "When did you last see Dot King alive?"

"I beg your pardon!" Olcott yelped. "You're implying my client saw Miss King dead!"

Coughlin didn't flinch. If anything, Olcott's interruption steeled his resolve to get answers. "When did you last see Miss King alive?" he repeated.

"Ferdinand, are you going to stand for this?" Olcott bleated.

Coughlin turned to Pecora, raised a brow. "Well?"

Pecora looked back and forth between them. "I—"

The upstanding citizen and arts patron in question lifted a hand as though he were signaling for his check. "I'm happy to answer the inspector's questions." His voice was honeyed. It sounded like generations of money and education, good breeding, and careful polishing.

"Proceed," Pecora said like he was the one who'd done everyone a favor.

The suspect calmly folded his hands, his face a mask. "When I last saw Miss King, she was alive and in good spirits. We'd returned from dinner at the Hotel Brevoort. John was with us." He directed a brief nod at "Wilson," his lawyer friend who now had a lawyer of his own. "We arrived at her apartment around midnight and had champagne. And then Jackson must've left about twenty minutes later, isn't that right?"

"Yes, yes, that's right," Jackson piped up eagerly.

"Then I stayed for more champagne," Mitchell continued, "and . . . conversation."

"So you admit to having an affair with Dot King?" Coughlin asked as Pecora shot him a warning glance.

Mitchell's pale cheeks grew slightly pink, but he didn't look away, didn't blink. "Yes."

"What time did you leave?" Coughlin asked.

"I left at ten past two in the morning," Mitchell said like he'd been waiting for the question.

The time caught Coughlin's attention for two reasons: first, because it was awfully convenient, establishing his departure three to five hours before the medical examiner's office had estimated the time of death, and secondly, because of the exact specificity. Most people would've said, "I dunno, around two." Most people didn't keep such exact track of time because they didn't know they'd need an alibi with their exact whereabouts . . . unless of course they *did*. "How?" he asked.

"How?" Mitchell echoed. "Why, Miss King walked me to the door, we embraced, I took the elevator down, and took a taxi home."

Everything came into sharper focus. Coughlin shot another look at Carey, who raised his brows. John Thomas had been adamant that he never took anyone back down that night. "Did you operate the elevator yourself?" Coughlin asked.

The man did not react with so much as a blink. "Of course not. The elevator operator took me down."

The way he said it rubbed Coughlin all wrong—reminding him that this guy didn't do anything for himself. He *expected* to be served. "You sure?" Coughlin pressed.

"Of course I'm sure. The operator—nice fellow—always drives the elevator."

Coughlin noted that the guy failed to refer to John Thomas by name. Likely, he never bothered to remember the name of the "help." Coughlin was also acutely aware that in the world of the wealthy, he was part of the help's class. He'd soon be just some nameless cop. "Hmm. That's strange—he doesn't remember any such thing."

Mitchell's brows drew together ever so slightly, confused but unbothered. "I beg your pardon?"

"*John Thomas* says he didn't take you down," Coughlin said loudly, as though Mitchell were hard of hearing.

The man looked at Olcott. "But of course he did. I even gave him a two-dollar tip."

The exorbitant amount was the second noteworthy thing this guy had said in the last minute. "That's awfully generous."

The older man coolly held his gaze. "I'm very fortunate. I can afford to be generous."

"That's probably half a day's salary for him," Coughlin pointed out. While generosity was usually a trait to be admired, doling out half of a working man's daily wage as a tip felt arrogant. It grated on Coughlin's nerves.

Mitchell shrugged, casting a hand toward his bank of lawyers. "I always tip him. He's a nice fellow."

"A nice fellow who says he never took you back down," Coughlin pressed.

"Why, this is *ridiculous!*" Mitchell protested, looking to the lawyers like they should help.

Coughlin could've told him not to bother—there was no help for no alibi. "*Something's* ridiculous," he agreed. "Take a minute. Think it over. You sure you took the elevator down and gave John Thomas a two-dollar tip?"

"He *just said* he's *quite* sure," Pecora said, louder, like Coughlin was the one hard of hearing.

Coughlin scowled at the DA. Was it his imagination, or was the Sicilian putting on a snooty accent? "Well, John Thomas is also 'quite sure.'"

Pecora flushed. The old lawyers looked indignant. "Perhaps someone took down the elevator boy's testimony wrong?" one elder-uncle offered. "We can imagine how *overworked* your men are."

Coughlin leaned forward, glaring. "Listen, bub, my men shoulder all the work the city throws at 'em and ask for more. They got steel in their veins. And for your information, *I'm* the one who took the *elevator boy's* testimony." He glared around the room, daring any of these stooges to question how "overworked" he was. "And the *elevator boy* wasn't in Dot King's apartment the night she was killed. The *elevator boy* wasn't having an affair with her. The *elevator boy* is also a *man* well into his sixties. And lastly, this *man* has no reason to lie—none of which I can say for your *client.*"

A long silence followed as the tension in the room, which had held at a steady simmer, spiked straight up to a boil.

"This is preposterous!" Olcott spluttered. "I want to remind you gentlemen, my client *volunteered* to come in!"

"Which is *exactly* what I'd do if I was guilty and wanted to look innocent," Coughlin said smoothly.

All the lawyers jumped on that at once.

"All I'm saying," Coughlin said louder, over the din, "is two bucks may be a damn good tip, but it's pretty cheap for a murder alibi."

A real ruckus ensued as all the lawyers started squabbling. Coughlin slouched, staring at his notes. With the case already in the spotlight and the newspapers having a field day over the beautiful murdered model, there was no room for mistakes. These lawyers—and apparently their puppet Pecora—would be breathing down his goddamn neck, going over everything with a fine-tooth comb, trying to uncover details he might have missed.

Of course he'd taken down John Thomas's testimony correctly. He didn't make mistakes. So either John Thomas's memory was faulty, or maybe he'd fallen asleep or gone to take a piss and then been too afraid to admit it when the police turned up.

And yet . . . John Thomas had seemed so steady, so sure. Twenty-seven years on the beat had trained Coughlin to sort truth from lies, and every single bit of that experience, coupled with his gut instinct about people, said John Thomas could be trusted.

His gut also said this rich, arrogant bastard was hiding something. He just wasn't sure what it was yet. *Was it murder?* The guy's baby-soft skin and slack muscles indicated no. But then again, Dot King was a small woman. It wouldn't take a professional wrestler to take her down.

"Well, *perhaps*," Pecora said, "Captain Carey could question him again, just to be sure."

Coughlin wanted to retort that perhaps Carey should question these guys in front of a stenographer *just to be sure*. But comments like that landed him in Idiot Enright's office, where the so-called police commissioner took immense pleasure in dressing him down.

"That's no problem. *Is it, Inspector?*" Pecora pressed.

"No," Coughlin ground out.

Witness testimony often varied. Memory was imperfect, fear a powerful motivator. And the truth was, even if John Thomas's memory was perfect, *and* even if he was willing to stand behind his testimony— two huge *ifs*—they *still* had a problem because this guy and his lawyers had just made it *crystal clear* they were going to stand behind theirs. The sugar daddy's alibi depended on it.

Coughlin shifted, remembering Guimares's hand with its damning bite marks and scratches. The guy was a career criminal, a brute, and he'd bullied and battered Dot King. He fit the profile of a man who escalated from abuse to homicide. But John Thomas had specifically said *this* man never left Dot King's building, and Pecora's bow-and-scrape routine had veered from merely nauseating to downright suspicious. There was no reason to kiss the rich man's ass unless the rich man had given the DA a reason to.

There was also no reason to bribe a DA unless you were guilty.

"Do you ever use chloroform as a sleep aid?" Coughlin asked.

Mitchell's haughty gaze turned to him once more. "No."

Coughlin had, of course, expected the denial. But he wanted to get it on record. Not that there was a stenographer present, nor was anyone else taking notes. "Do you keep it in your household for medical or other uses?"

The man's eyes, a light gray, so pale as to be nearly colorless, combined with the remnants of gray hair around the perimeter of his nearly bald scalp, his pale skin, and his gray suit, seemed unnervingly cold, almost ghostly. "No, Detective." Again, the brief, icy answer.

"I think it's safe to say no one here is a drug user," Pecora observed dryly. "Let's move on, shall we?"

Coughlin shot him a frosty look. The office felt too small with the eight of them. Marshall sat there—stonily unflustered—while Olcott droned on, whining about something; the uncles clucked their support; and Pecora groveled attentively. Coughlin twitched with the effort to not tell them all to shut the hell up and storm out.

Jesus, it was going to be a long day.

Chapter 16

5:00 p.m. Manhattan. Criminal Courts Building.

Julia waited in the pressroom with the rest of the crime reporters. Pecora was late. The pack, about fifteen or so, was getting edgy. But they'd been promised an update on the King case, and nobody was leaving until they got it.

Finally, the door burst open. Ferdinand Pecora strode in, trailed by a truculent Coughlin and stoic Carey. The newspapermen rose and swelled toward them like a riptide.

Pecora, roguishly handsome and a natural politician, bestowed a smile upon the group. "Gentlemen, welcome!"

Julia barely noticed the male generalization. The newspaper world, like the world itself, was run by men. Over twenty-five hundred men belonged to the press union in New York, while the New York Women in Newspaper Club had only thirty-six members. Everywhere except those meetings, Julia considered herself a newspaperman . . . and she knew that everywhere except those meetings that was how she was expected to be.

Pecora raised his hands for silence. "I promised you an update on the King case, and here it is: this afternoon 'Mr. Marshall' and 'Mr. Wilson' came to my office. I questioned them for an hour and a half, and they were perfectly frank in their answers—"

A fizz of disbelief and protests rose.

"How'd you sneak 'em past us?"

"Say, what's with all the secrecy?"

"Well, where are they now?"

"When can we ask them questions?"

"Gentlemen! *Gentlemen!*" Pecora held up his hands. "Neither of these men had anything to do with the crime under investigation."

"You call this an investigation?" someone grumbled.

"These men came forward *voluntarily* and gave frank and honest answers." Pecora raised his voice to be heard above the ruckus. "But it's doubtful any information they supplied will be useful in solving the mystery—they simply don't know anything."

"Well, they surely must know *something*!" Julia pointed out.

"Yeah—like their own names?" George, the fellow from the *Brooklyn Daily Eagle*, shouted above the ruckus, and demands echoed around the room: *Names! Give us their real names!*

"I promised I wouldn't reveal their identities," Pecora said.

The swell of outrage intensified from the pressmen. "Why're you protecting these guys?"

"Good old New York," a man behind Julia muttered. "Everything's for sale—including justice."

At the front, Pecora scowled. "Neither of these men had anything to do with the crime under investigation. I want to solve this as much as anyone. But that means finding the real killer, not pinning it on innocent men."

"Funny how rich guys are always innocent," a reporter next to Julia, who'd been on the beat nearly as long as she'd been alive, muttered around the stub of his cigar.

"How can you be sure they're innocent? You only questioned them for an hour and a half!" Julia shouted over the rumble, determined that Pecora should have to publicly explain himself. "Why, the girl's *mother* has been questioned more than that!"

A chorus of male agreement seconded her demand for answers.

Pecora hesitated a split second. "Mr. Marshall admitted that he knew Miss Keenan very well, and that he frequently called on her at her home. Inspector Coughlin, Captain Carey, and myself don't believe he knew anything about a plot to kill her, so I can't see that any purpose would be served by saying more."

"The *purpose*," Julia called out, undaunted, "is that investigators share this basic information openly with the public and the press, just as they've shared the full names and information supplied by everyone else."

An immediate, searing silence descended.

"Are there any further *questions?*" Pecora asked icily.

"Is it true that Mr. Wilson is Marshall's secretary?" Julia pressed. "If so, what cause did Marshall have to bring his secretary along to his mistress's at midnight?"

"I heard Wilson's his chauffeur!" a reporter from the back piped up.

"No—his confidant!" another said louder.

"Bodyguard!" someone else insisted.

"I heard he's the big fella's masseur!" George shouted to a jeering round of laughter.

"But he admits he was there the night of the murder? That he's the last-known person to see Dot King alive?" a loud fellow at the front asked.

"Or maybe dead!" someone behind Julia added just loud enough for Pecora to hear.

"I'll not say a word about them!" the DA insisted hotly.

"Did he know about Guimares?" Julia asked.

To her surprise, Pecora's dark eyes settled on her, taking the question. "I'm pretty sure he didn't know Guimares. Beyond that, all I'll say is that both Marshall and Wilson made full and frank statements to me about everything they knew."

"Has any real progress been made in the case?" Julia asked.

"As I've said, an exhaustive investigation is underway. Everyone even *remotely* associated with the girl—human jackals, blackmailers, thieves, and all—will be questioned and their stories sifted for bits of evidence. No stone will be left unturned. Why, Captain Carey even questioned John Thomas, the elevator operator, for four more hours," Pecora said.

Julia froze, the hairs on the back of her neck rising. "You questioned her *elevator operator*, but not her *sugar daddy*?!"

Pecora swept an irritated look across the room as though they just didn't get it. "The investigation into Anna Keenan's death is ongoing. That's all for now, fellas." And with that, the DA stomped from the room.

How typical, Julia noted with simmering displeasure, that Pecora insisted on referring to the victim as Anna Keenan, her birth name, instead of her chosen name of Dot King. Yet the DA had no problem with referring to potential persons of interest as "Marshall" and "Wilson." Leave it to a man to think *he* should decide a woman's identity, instead of honoring her as she'd wished to be known.

Julia knew firsthand just how much names mattered. Her father and uncle, Sigmund and Solomon Harpmann, had escaped Jewish ghettos and the systemic antisemitism in Germany, ending up in Memphis, where they'd become tobacco dealers and proceeded to earn their way into the southern community with acts of charitable service. The Harpmanns were different but warmly accepted by their Christian neighbors. When Josie died in 1918, the *News Scimitar*, the newspaper whose society pages she'd presided over, had run a front-page article, with photo, that spilled to page 3 with praise.

Nonetheless, when Julia left Memphis for New York, she'd quietly left the second *n* in *Harpmann* behind as well. She began her life—and work—in Manhattan as the less-German, less-Jewish, less-noticeable *Harpman*. That way, she could reveal her identity on her terms.

But death had robbed that power from Dot King.

Dot King couldn't control how Pecora referred to her. But Julia could control how she referred to Dot. In Julia's hands, the world would know the story of Dot King, and Anna Keenan would stay a ghost buried far in the past Dot had tried to leave behind.

George pushed his hat back. "This whole thing seems fishy."

Julia nodded. "Fishy indeed."

She headed back to the pressroom to write her article. *Of course* it was fishy. And *of course* it was easy to write off the whole system as rotten and hopeless. But this fell squarely within the purview of the fourth estate. The power of the press was rooted in the rallying cries for the exposure and eradication of tyranny. And Julia Harpman intended to do just that.

Chapter 17

March 18, 10:00 a.m. Palm Beach. Blakely Cottage.

Frances, sitting at the delicate Louis XIV writing desk, addressed another envelope and shook out her hand. Sometimes, she mused, wintering in Palm Beach was far more taxing than being home in Philadelphia or even summering in Bar Harbor at the height of the season, which she had previously thought of as the most demanding. The mail—selecting which invitations to accept and which to politely decline, writing to the few friends who wintered abroad—always took hours, this she knew. But preparing to host the presidential party was another matter entirely.

Every moment was meticulously considered: her father and Jack would take President Harding, Attorney General Daugherty, and the other men golfing, while the First Lady and other wives stayed behind with Frances, Eva, and their closest friends (a designation that had incurred more than the usual uptick of interest as word spread). They would begin in El Mirasol's Moorish tea house, followed by a tour of Eva's Great Orange Grove, their zoo, and then the gardens.

Thoughtful details were like good servants—unseen, yet vital to the perfect party—and Frances and her stepmother would devise every single one, down to framed, calligraphed seating charts in the ladies' powder room and the men's restroom, so guests could prepare thoughtful conversation tailored to those at their table. And the *seating*, good heavens, was the most challenging task of all. From feuding friendships to adulterers, the presidential party was no exception. Yet it was the greatest accomplishment of any hostess to make it seem as though it were nothing—*oh, nothing at all.*

When the men returned from golf, lunch and cocktails would be served on El Mirasol's famed loggia and patio, accompanied by their usual orchestra.

Soon, Frances would share each meticulously planned detail with the reporters who called to inquire. Ever since the article had anointed her one of society's four most powerful women, the press's interest in her menus, style, and taste had increased.

Of course, the unofficial agenda, which wouldn't be shared with the press, was to provide Mr. Daugherty with the chance to assuage any doubts about the administration's steadfastness. Even stalwart Republicans were finding it hard to ignore the persistent scandals that continued to crop up with disquieting frequency. And as speculation about Harding's renomination, to be run again by Mr. Daugherty, grew, the politicians had been most eager to set a date for the visit.

Of that, the Palm Beach Colony could be sure.

Despite the guest list waiting for her attention, Frances decided she'd earned a much-deserved break to read the papers on the sunporch. She took the ivory brocade newspaper bag and a cup of tea she'd forgotten to drink out with her. Some fresh air would be just the thing.

The front page was full of rumors that some Republicans thought certain members of the cabinet might be a better choice than Harding, but with the cabinet full of members of Harding's "Ohio Gang," many of whom were engulfed in their own share of scandals and gossip, there wasn't a particularly clear alternative. Attorney General Harry Daugherty, for one, had faced articles of impeachment from that wretched Representative Keller, for not prosecuting supposed violations of antitrust laws and protecting companies that had supported Harding's first run, including J.P. Morgan and Co. Although her father hadn't been named . . . *yet*, as the scandals hurtled closer, Frances was afraid. Her father's confidence that nothing could harm them, along with his Victorian ideals about having unshakable faith in those in power, were starting to seem antiquated, even foolish. She sensed danger in ways she couldn't articulate, but he wouldn't hear of it.

Like every man of his station, he'd personally donated thousands of dollars to Harding's first campaign and, along with his Morgan and Co. partners and closest friends, had also donated untold amounts from their corporate coffers. Furthermore, he'd played an invaluable part in Philadelphia's Republican fundraising.

Of course, they expected a certain *understanding* on policies that affected the financial industry and the companies and industries they invested in in return. That was how the world worked. And what was wrong with it? Companies like J.P. Morgan kept this great nation moving forward and gainfully employed. The bond between donors and politicians consisted of money and mutual understanding. They needed a Republican in office who made that effort possible.

But ideally, the Republican in office would conduct himself with decorum and wouldn't have new indecent accusations hurled at him every day. And if the Harding administration continued failing on that front, her father and his partners might simply put their faith (and finances) in someone else. All of which would be politely conveyed at the upcoming party.

Mutual understanding was the key to every good relationship. Money didn't hurt either. And in the very, *very* best relationships, the lines between the two blurred into one. This was something Frances, raised at her father's knee, understood. They each had a role to play, duties to fulfill. These composed the frame and structure of every professional and social enterprise. Women, while exempted from business of course, were not *altogether* exempt.

When her father had politely suggested she should marry at the age of twenty-eight, and that Jack, recently widowed, would be a most suitable mate, she'd agreed. And as the alliance grew into a loving, respectful, and satisfactory relationship over the last fourteen years, she'd felt lucky.

Most husbands didn't include their wives in matters of office and politics, but she relished being consulted. She loved working behind the scenes to assist Jack, politically, professionally, and personally. The right letter, or phone call, or conversation at a party that led to an invitation, an appointment, a board seat. It was her greatest satisfaction to watch him ascend to even greater heights.

She would do the same for their son and make the perfect match for their daughter. This was her life's work, her avocation—to foster the evolution of empire for their children, their families, for society, and for the good of the country. If only the president could keep himself out of further scandals.

Page 3 was a mix of Sarah Bernhardt—when would that French harlot either die or the gossip-hungry papers get enough of her?—and the mystery of the murdered model in New York, the sheer drama of which was staggering. The twists and turns so sensational, they were practically scripted for cheap thrills. It was fun to read, but really, when would the newspapers stop producing this pabulum—wasted space!

Inside, the clock chimed and she stood. She had to get back to work and finish up before it was time to call Jack. He needed to wrap up his business in Philadelphia and return to Palm Beach to hone his golf game. Jack preferred tennis—a sport in which, he joked, he had occasional flashes of mediocrity.

She wondered if he wasn't good at golf because he wasn't tall. There had been a time before they married when she'd fretted about his height. Even in her most modestly low-heeled shoes, she was still taller than him. She'd once confided these worries to her older sister, Edith.

"Don't be ridiculous," Edith had said. "With thirty looming, you're going to have to choose between your vanity and the chance for marriage and children before you have no choice at all."

Frances's flash of anger had melted to shame, and she'd immediately regretted the decision to confide her tender, girlish concerns. Had their mother still been alive, *she* surely would've understood.

Adding vinegar to Frances's wounds was the fact that while blithely offering marital wisdom, Edith had been married to the suitably tall Sydney Hutchinson. It wasn't fair. But in spite of his height—or lack thereof—Frances had married Jack, and it had been the right decision.

Frances reached for the newspaper bag. The fold wrinkled in protest, and the headline, Slain Girl's Angel Sought, brushed against her knee, leaving a black smudge.

Frances brushed at the smudge fruitlessly. Hopefully, one of the laundresses downstairs would be able to remove the stain in time for her to wear the dress again for lunch at the Everglades Club this week. Each seed-pearl button had to be cut off, the dress hand-washed, then the buttons stitched back on.

Frances sighed. Then again, the laundresses always worked miracles. She had nothing to worry about.

Chapter 18

If Coughlin had hoped that finding and questioning the mysterious Mr. Marshall would crack the Dot King case, he was sorely mistaken. It was Sunday and it was madness. His lines rang off the hook, and his department was flooded with more tips than they could possibly follow up on in a year as every sun-dodging, bathtub gin–swilling shifty character with a hankering for publicity crawled forth with stories, suspicions, and hearsay about the increasingly infamous Miss King and reporters circled like vultures, picking the meat off the bones of the case.

As if he didn't have enough to contend with, the unbearable Mrs. Keenan continued to badger him, insisting Marshall was innocent and he need look no further than the "terrible man" who beat her daughter, while the terrible man in question had lawyered up and then promptly clammed up. Unsurprisingly, Guimares had picked Frederick Goldsmith, famed defender of deadbeat criminals, as his counsel.

Meanwhile, the men he'd dispatched to Atlantic City, after Hilda Ferguson revealed Dot King's frequent and suspiciously solo trips there, continued to scour the shore town for leads. So far, they'd learned that they could add Nucky Johnson, the politician and crime boss who ran all things sinful on the Jersey shore, to Dot King's list of former lovers. Nucky lived at the Ritz, where, according to Hilda, Dot King had had an open invitation and her own suite.

His men had also found a three-year-old prior arrest for disturbing the peace with two shady characters. They'd keep investigating, of course, but Coughlin's gut said that while this was possibly notable and probably titillating, it was unrelated to the girl's actual murder. That was the thing about crime that the public and the press didn't want to admit: scandalous and shocking didn't necessarily mean causal or correlated.

Dot King smoked hop. She had no female friends except Ella Bradford. She horrified and offended those in her circle with her showy taste for furs and jewels, and her fondness for bragging about her male conquests. She was a wild girl who lived a wild life.

This was no innocent, churchgoing country girl who'd been kidnapped or bewitched by the bright lights and big city. She ran with dangerous men, involved in dangerous things.

Being on the beat as long as he had, Coughlin had seen all sorts of girls become all sorts of victims. Nothing shocked him anymore. The same could not be said for the good citizens of New York City—they devoured every scandalous detail Julia Harpman and the other mudslingers served up. The press didn't care about justice. They wanted to sell more of their damn papers, and stirring up public sentiment against the police and DA's office was merely a tolerable by-product.

Pecora's stubborn insistence on protecting the sugar daddy's true identity was fanning the flames. But Coughlin toed the line, continuing to refer to the man by his alias both publicly and privately. The effect was predictable: every newspaper hinted at a cover-up, calling out scandals both real and imagined. Coughlin felt himself in the all-too-familiar pinch between a rock and a hard place.

Carey knocked at exactly the appointed time to debrief, and Coughlin dived right in to the thing that had been weighing on him most heavily. "So this business about the elevator, whether John Thomas took Marshall down the night of the murder."

Carey leaned forward anxiously. "Yes?"

Coughlin frowned, surprised by Carey's intensity. "Well, we need to get it straightened out. Marshall's alibi hangs on it. If John Thomas forgot he took the old dog back down at 2:10, we'll consider him cleared, and then we're back to Guimares, which makes a lot of sense given everything we know about that bastard."

Carey hesitated. "Right, but I—"

Coughlin plowed on. "John Thomas seemed so sure when I talked to him. But it wouldn't be the first time a witness was wrong or recanted." He looked skyward, as witnesses who'd been confused or outright lied flooded his brain. "*Anyway*, what did you find? Are we back to Guimares? Or is Marshall our man?"

Carey held his gaze for a long moment. Finally, he reached some sort of decision and spoke. "I gave him a thorough working-over for more than four hours, but the man proved himself to be irresponsible in his memory."

"Oh?" Coughlin said.

"Plus," Carey said, picking up steam now, "it turns out the poor fellow couldn't even say what age he is. Can't hang a murder alibi on that."

"No," Coughlin agreed, and could not have said why he felt a twinge of disappointment.

Chapter 19

The *Daily News* was three blocks away from Manhattan's famed "Newspaper Row." It seemed fitting. They might not have the real-estate credentials of a Newspaper Row address, but "New York's Picture Paper" was scrappy, and now they were the act to beat.

Julia lifted the hem of her midcalf-length skirt and hurried upstairs, her practical, low-heeled Mary Janes tapping lightly on each step.

She'd spent the day chasing down Dot King's friends in an effort to get a fuller picture of her as an individual, not just as the victim of a man's violence. It was the third day of coverage, and the city couldn't get enough of the case. Every detail about the Broadway Butterfly—from her life to her loves, her fashion to her friends, jewels to juicy scandals—was devoured by their readers. Fortunately, as Julia continued to discover, there was no shortage of details.

Dot King had been a conflicting, confounding, complex jumble of a human. She'd been almost unimaginably generous—there were stories of how she'd literally given the clothes off her back to a girl who'd needed them, running home clad in only her step-ins and coat. Dot King had also loved deeply. When her little dog had died the prior year, she'd spent more on the funeral than most people did for their family members. But she'd also been a hothead with a questionable moral code and a near-mercenary determination to get what she thought she deserved. Hellinger's initial information was correct. Julia had ascertained that before Guimares and Marshall, she'd lived—unmarried—with a cabaret headwaiter, with whom there'd been frequent and fierce quarrels. After one such incident, Dot had cut up his shirts and ties, thrown ink on his Persian carpets, and dumped all his suits and shoes in a bath.

Dramatic arguments weren't the model-turned-sugar-baby's only hobby. She'd loved going out, dancing, hosting parties, and generally leading a gadabout life. She drank hard and lived large. In the past few months, she had worried about getting "bumped off," and she'd even gone so far as to have her will drawn up with the stipulation that if anything unforeseen should befall her, all her possessions would go to her mother. Julia thought of Dot's mother and shuddered.

Dot King loved nice things—fashionable clothes, glittering jewels, opulent fur coats. And perhaps because of her modest background, spared no expense in both allowing her admirers to spoil her and spoiling herself. She was a frequent customer at the salon across the street from her apartment, getting her hair styled, massage treatments, and her feet pampered.

As Julia tried to capture all this in one taut article, she found herself stuck on the press update. Why was Pecora still so willing to protect the identities of the last-known men to see Dot King alive? Why were Carey and Coughlin standing grimly by while the strong-willed Sicilian DA ran roughshod over standards and procedure?

Pecora's confident declaration that the wealthy man and his secretary were innocent, his claim that it was "doubtful any information they supplied will be useful in solving the mystery," after such a brief interrogation seemed premature at best and downright suspicious at worst.

Who the heck was this mysterious millionaire, and why was Pecora so quick to declare he had no connection to the case—especially since Mr. Thomas had been interrogated again at such length, but still hadn't changed his testimony.

Pete, standing at the telegraph desk, interrupted these thoughts. "Get this, fellas! President Harding's gonna run for reelection."

The newsroom's din quieted down a notch.

"Says *who*?" Hellinger demanded.

"Oh, only the attorney general of the United States, a certain Mr. Harry Daugherty, wise guy."

One of the older reporters tipped his chair back, balancing precariously on the rear legs. "I don't care if the Blessed Virgin herself came down and said it. Harding will need a goddamn miracle after all these scandals."

"I don't know—" Hellinger started.

Joe, one of the most senior members of the city desk, who'd spent a lifetime chasing stories and making deadlines, cut him off. "Your people don't believe in the Blessed Virgin, kid. Don't worry about it."

Hellinger flushed.

"Anyway," Pete continued loudly. "It says here the presidential party arrived in Miami, and while Harding was out shooting a round of golf and having lunch with the bigwigs, Daugherty called the gentlemen of the press. Guess they don't have any girl reporters down there—sorry, Harpman!"

Julia shrugged. "There's a reason New York journalism is more respected than the rags down south. Why y'all think I came north? For the pleasure of freezing my tail off six months a year?"

Everyone laughed. Pete raised his hand authoritatively. "*As I was saying*, Daugherty said, and I quote, 'Mr. Harding's renomination and reelection will be the result of demand from the nation and the Republican party.' So I guess he'll run the campaign again, huh?"

"Well, *of course* he'll run the campaign again! Anything to keep himself as the AG!" Julia said. "It's so much easier to get away with bilking the American people when you're the highest lawyer in the land."

"A guy like Daugherty is always gonna land on his feet," Joe protested.

"What are you, a Republican?" Hellinger joked.

"Fellas, please!" Philip said. "Harding would need John the Baptist to be his campaign manager and the baby Jesus as his VP in order to have even a snowball's chance in hell."

"If Daugherty says Harding will run again, then Harding *will* run again," Julia said.

Hellinger leaned in toward Julia. "How ya so sure? You got an inside line?"

She swiveled her chair. Three years ago Hellinger had been writing ad copy for Lane Bryant, which had cornered the market on fashion for "stout or expectant ladies." He certainly wasn't working in news; nor apparently, had he been paying attention to the news. She took it upon herself to educate him, lowering her voice so the others wouldn't hear. "I'm just doing the math. Daugherty was Harding's precampaign manager in '20. And since taking office, Daugherty has remained his most trusted political adviser. Officially, he's the attorney general. But unofficially, he runs *everything*. That's why what he says is such a big deal."

"Maybe he needs to get some new blood in there," Philip suggested, raking a hand through his bristly, untidy hair. He looked around the room over the rim of his glasses, squinting to see if there was any action over at the telegraph desk. "'Cause I ain't seen such a scandal-ridden administration in my entire life."

"Speaking of scandal," Julia said, "I've got a murder to write about." She refocused on her typewriter and the King case. She would chase down every scandalous scoundrel and dig up every secret source to keep this prize of a story on the front page, where everyone in New York would read it—the papers would fly off the stands, the muddleheaded prosecutors would wake up, and this case would finally be solved. And if, in the process, she earned her way to being named the first female assistant editor on the city desk . . . so be it.

A woman had been murdered, and nearly $10,000 in jewels and another $10,000 in furs were missing. Her mother had taught her the power to do something about it lay on the page. As women and as Jews, they were excluded from many rooms and opportunities. But the tools of the fourth estate—the power of the written word, disseminating information to the public, and the freedom of the press—*were* accessible to them.

Julia wouldn't rest until this case was solved. She just had to chase down the story, one day at a time. And chasing down stories ran in her blood.

Chapter 20

It had been three days since Ella had left the apartment. She'd drawn the curtains when she'd gotten home from police headquarters and stayed inside, sick with shame over the list. That awful list.

She'd taken care of June, of course, both the baby and the distraction of him a comfort. But aside from that, she'd paced and prayed, worried about those men, *their friends*, whose names she'd given over. What had happened to them? Did they know it was her?

Could they ever forgive her?

Everyone who'd been told, or heard tell—so all of Harlem, then—must surely hate her. She'd hate anyone who handed James over to the police when he hadn't done no wrong. There was a limit on Christian charity, and this was it. The ones who already thought she was too big for her britches, with her fine, white-lady clothes, fancy Midtown job, and the money it brought, were probably glad she'd gotten her comeuppance with this whole mess, and wasn't it just like a highfalutin' upstart to throw good Negro men under the bus.

She wanted to run away, leave New York, hide inside for the rest of her life. *Except* now she'd been called down to the police headquarters for more questions. Knowing she had to face that captain again, with his fleshy face and thick neck and the way he looked at her like she was already guilty made her stomach sick.

The newspapers made it worse. James brought copies home to her, and it seemed every paper in the city, except *The Age*, the Negro paper, had some scandalous story they'd dug up about Miss Dottie. Some were true and some weren't, but nearly all included her: the maid who'd found her employer dead.

Now, a white lady murdered in her bed was always gonna be news, but with Miss Dottie the way she was, it'd gone and landed on the front page. Ella shuddered. They printed her name (some called her Billie, like they knew her) and address, which kept a steady flow of newspapermen and Harlem gossips outside. The *Daily News* was the only paper who'd run a picture, and it'd been of Womba—probably since one Negro girl was as good as the next to white folk. But for once, Ella figured, white-folk ways worked for her—nobody knew what she looked like or where Womba lived. So when she left to head downtown, none of the reporters looked twice at her. Ella took the subway to Canal Street and hurried past newsies—some looked no older than eight or nine—hawking papers. "Extra, Extra! Read all about Dot King's murder! Police Hide Sugar Papa's Identity!"

She paused and the kid sensed a sucker. "Paper, miss?"

Because he was young and Negro, and everyone else went right on by, she dug in her purse for the coins.

"Thank you, miss!" He beamed up at her with a gap-toothed smile and shoved the pennies in his apron.

Just yesterday, the *Daily News* had run a piece that said the police were questioning everyone remotely associated with Miss Dottie, including blackmailers and thieves, and her blood had run cold. The police couldn't possibly know just how close those "human jackals," as they'd called them, had run . . . or how dangerous they were. She'd tried to tell Captain Carey, but he hadn't let her speak.

James had warned her: "Say the least you can. Police and us don't mix. They don't wanna hear what you know. They wanna hear what they wanna hear."

He was right. And yet she knew things. And if they'd only listen, she could help them get justice for Miss Dottie.

The morning crowds rushed past, and Ella let herself be carried along like a buttonwood leaf down a river.

Today, a different patrolman took her down a different hall.

"What!" a gruff voice barked when the patrolman knocked.

"I got Dot King's maid!" he hollered back, and bolted.

She stood there alone. Here it was, then. She would do what had to be done and survive because she had to. She took a shaky breath and opened the door.

Inspector Coughlin sat behind a square desk. The captain was nowhere to be seen. She took a seat and crossed her ankles. Nobody would say Marie Anderson's daughter wasn't a lady.

The inspector adjusted his glasses—little round ones that perched on his nose, without any arms to hold 'em on. He looked as tired as she felt.

He cleared his throat. "Mrs. Bradford, you met with Captain Carey Friday. That list of his, well, it turned up nothin'. All the men were cleared."

He didn't say he was sorry, but that was too much to expect from a white man anyway. "Yes, sir. Thank you," she said. The guilt that sat heavy didn't go away because she never should've been asked, and those men never should've been questioned, but it eased a bit to know they weren't locked away under some false charges.

"Mrs. Bradford, I know you keep a respectable home and you're not like Miss King. But I understand she . . . confided in you. Any information you have could help put her murderer behind bars."

Well, that was easy enough. She relaxed a bit. "Remember the will and insurance policy I gave you?" she said. "You oughtta know Albert Guimares told her to get that insurance. In fact, he insisted—for $15,000."

The inspector raised his brows—a sum worth killing for. "That's very helpful. Anything else? What about Marshall?"

"Mr. Marshall is a gentleman. He didn't do this," Ella told him, calm and steady. It was true. And also, she was determined to help Mr. Marshall, just like he'd helped her when June was born. Loyalty was everything.

Coughlin's face was unreadable. "You seem pretty sure."

"Yes, sir. You've never seen such a kind man and always so *good* to Miss Dottie. Why, he just about worshipped the ground she walked on. You know, he gave her a $1,000 Liberty bond and $700 in cash when he came for lunch? That's more than anyone could ever need, but he did it, just so she'd know he cared."

The inspector waited like he expected her to say more. When she didn't, he held his hand up like a claw. "I noticed her hand was clenched. I'm thinking maybe her attacker ripped away something she was holding. Any idea what it could've been?"

There were secrets and there were lies, and sometimes the line between the two blurred. James believed it was best to say the least she could, but that wasn't going to get Miss Dottie's killer put away. Then again, she was still shaken by how the captain had treated her and she had to think of June first.

"Well that Liberty bond and cash Mr. Marshall had given her earlier was gone," Ella said, which was the truth, but not the *whole* truth.

"What about—" the inspector began.

Ella realized it was now or never. She took a breath, drew her courage. "There's something I need to tell you."

Chapter 21

Coughlin and Pecora had promised the press an update but hadn't spec-
ified when. After waiting for what felt like an eternity, Julia decided to
risk missing the beginning, should the officials decide to appear the
moment she left, to run downstairs to the ladies' room. This was a risk
none of the men had to weigh. The pressroom had its own restroom.
Technically, she was allowed to use it—like most, it wasn't marked
"Men." But that was because everyone else was male. It also wasn't
marked "toilet for humans." The cubby, scarcely larger than a closet and
separated from the pressroom by only a rickety door, looked dim and
filthy. It had one industrial toilet, the seat always up.

She hurried down the stairs—faster than waiting for the elevator—
grateful it was 1923. It had been only five years since public buildings
were required to have female-access restrooms. Before then, she might
not have had the option.

In stark contrast to the pressroom, the far-cleaner restroom for
secretaries offered partitioned stalls, a cushioned chaise, and a well-lit
vanity table with a ruffled skirt. It was a space men had designed because
they imagined the fairer sex needed to lounge and powder their noses,
though Julia had yet to see any woman lounging or powdering. This
was, after all, the criminal courts.

She'd just finished washing her hands and was heading for the door when a well-dressed blonde ran in and burst into tears.

"Are you all right?" Julia asked automatically, though clearly the woman was anything but.

The woman looked up, startled, and swiped at her eyes with the back of her wrist. "I'm sorry. I didn't see you."

Julia dug in her purse for an extra handkerchief and offered it up. She knew the few women who worked in the building—typists and switchboard operators—and this woman was not one of them. Perhaps she'd come to report a crime then. "Can I help you with something?"

The woman tugged off her gloves, took the handkerchief, and dabbed at her eyes. Julia noticed no mascara stained the material. The woman didn't wear makeup. "No! I mean, no thank you. I just need a moment." She moved to the mirror and tried to gather herself, straightening her hat—a smart little number made of dark-green felt, dressed with a bow in the same material—before offering the handkerchief back.

Julia smiled. "Keep it. Listen, I'm here all the time, and I know how intimidating it can be. If something happened to you . . . if someone"—Julia paused, chose her words carefully—"hurt you, it can help to have a woman friend with you when you go to report it. I'd be happy to—"

"No, no," the woman cut in. "I'm not hurt. I came to report something I heard."

"I see," Julia said, even though she didn't. "Well, is there something else I can help with? I'm a reporter for the *Daily News*."

The woman, around her own age, looked surprised. "You're a reporter?"

Julia was, of course, used to that response, even from women, even from peers. She took the opportunity to reassure the woman as a potential source. "Yes. So if you need to tell someone something . . ."

The woman looked around the still-empty restroom, then leaned closer. "I live in the apartment under that woman who was murdered?

Dot King? And I heard something that night—I thought the police should know."

Now it was Julia's turn to be surprised. "I've been covering that case. What did you hear?"

The woman hesitated briefly, as though weighing whether to share what she knew, then continued. "Well, late Wednesday night, I heard several people walking around up there, and music, conversation, laughter. Eventually, things quieted down, but then a woman screamed. I was concerned because I knew she was also a girl who lived alone, and we girls have to look out for each other. Then I heard pacing—agitated pacing—as though someone was frantically rushing around, maybe searching for something. The footsteps were heavy and loud—they had to be a man's."

Julia leaned closer. "Yes?"

The woman took a deep breath. "I didn't know whether to go up and knock and ask if everything was OK or mind my own business. You know how it is with neighbors; you're not friends, but you see each other. Finally, I went over to the window, which is on an air shaft, and I smelled"—she lowered her voice—"I smelled chloroform."

Julia froze. "What time was this?"

"About 12:30 a.m.," the woman said.

"Are you sure?" Julia asked. "Are you absolutely *sure*?"

The woman nodded. "Yes. Because I looked at the clock, trying to decide if it was too late to go knock on her door, and I finally decided it was."

Julia nodded.

The woman twisted her gloves, avoiding, or perhaps steeped in, memories, regrets, or might-have-beens. "I wish I'd called John Thomas to go up with me and check on her. But I felt foolish. I figured she had a man . . . friend over, and I was too embarrassed to intrude."

It seemed this hadn't been the first time this neighbor had had to decide whether to "intrude" on Dot King. "So you'd heard . . . disturbances before?" Julia asked, choosing the word carefully.

The woman nodded, reluctant, it seemed, to tattle. "Sometimes the other neighbors would complain about her loud parties. But there's also been yelling, arguments, with men. People talk . . . the building staff, you know. I never know what to do. I don't want to meddle in her private life."

Julia nodded, thinking of the allegations of violence the police had shared—how Dot King's mother and maid both claimed Guimares beat the girl black and blue. "Listen, this is very important. The police will want to hear this. I'll go with you."

The woman snorted disgustedly. "I've just come from telling them. They said I'm mistaken, that I made it up so that I might see my name in the papers."

Julia drew back, shocked. "Who—"

The woman made for the door. "I shouldn't have come. It was utterly humiliating. Promise me you won't print any of this!"

"I—"

"I wish I'd never said anything." The woman yanked open the door and was gone.

Julia hurriedly took notes. She would respect the woman's request not to print it. But her witness statement established the use of chloroform at the crime scene when Marshall himself admitted he'd been there.

Two questions stood out: Who, besides the man himself, didn't want Marshall pinned at the crime scene at the time of death, and who was in a powerful enough position to have the police silence the witness who could?

Chapter 22

Scrambling to fit the pieces together, Julia made her way back to the pressroom. Were the authorities systematically silencing and intimidating everyone who contradicted Marshall's testimony? The neighbor demeaned and ignored. John Thomas recalled and reinterrogated for four additional, grueling hours. Someone was weeding out witnesses who went against the millionaire's alibi. But who? And why?

The press briefing was already underway as Julia slipped in.

"We've established the time of death was between 5:00 and 7:00 a.m., based on Ella Bradford's testimony that she found the body cool at the feet, but still warm at the chest," Coughlin announced.

"Has any progress been made in reconciling the conflicting statements between John Thomas and the so-called Mr. Marshall?" Julia asked.

Coughlin frowned. "No."

"So if Marshall says Mr. Thomas took him down in the elevator, and John Thomas insists he didn't, what can be done? Who do you believe?" the reporter from the *Philadelphia Inquirer* asked.

"Thomas has so far proved himself to be irresponsible in his memory and has already provided contradictory stories," Coughlin said.

There was a murmur of disbelief in the room. Surely Marshall had more of a motive to lie about when and how he'd left than John Thomas!

Julia raised her hand. Granted, she hadn't been privy to the rounds of interrogation, but when she'd spoken to John Thomas that first night, he'd been clear. Now his memory was "irresponsible" and "contradictory"?

"So does that throw any suspicion on Thomas?" the *Inquirer* reporter asked without waiting to be called on.

"That's for the police to say," Pecora said. "They examined Mr. Thomas—not I."

This time, Julia didn't wait. She stared straight at Pecora. "But you were the one to question Marshall, and it was you who agreed to protect his identity."

"My office has been involved in questioning Marshall, and we agreed to protect his identity because it doesn't benefit the case to reveal it. However, the investigation and capture of the killer rests entirely with the police," Pecora said.

"So both your offices believe *Marshall*? The girl's married lover, who freely admits he was the last person to see Miss King alive?" the fellow from the *Evening Journal* demanded dubiously.

"There's no reason for Marshall to do it, and in these cases the motive is the thing to look for," Coughlin said. "This murder was committed by a thief. The man who killed this woman went in there to get her jewelry and her fur coats, and he got them."

"I heard Marshall's married to one of Boston's prominent families, lives in a mansion on Beacon Street, and runs one of the largest companies in Massachusetts," a man at the back shouted.

"We're not here to discuss what you *heard*," Coughlin said. "We're here to give updates. The update is: we've petitioned the surrogates court to open Dot King's safe-deposit box. We hope to find information in it that will lead to the apprehension of her killer."

"That'll be all for today," Pecora announced. He nodded to Coughlin, who followed him out of the room.

Julia hurried after them, noting that the guys from the *Philadelphia Inquirer* and the Associated Press exchanged a pointed look and fell in step behind her.

"Inspector! Mr. Pecora! Please!" she called, hurrying to catch up with them. "Given that nearly $20,000 worth of jewelry and furs was stolen from Dot King's apartment, what do you hope to find in her safe-deposit box?"

Pecora shook his head. "There's no predicting."

"Do you expect to find an even larger treasure trove in the bank box? If the $1,000 Liberty bond and $700 cash Marshall gave her the night she was killed are also missing, then maybe—"

Coughlin cut her off. "Dot King didn't care about $700."

The Associated Press reporter snorted derisively. "Well *I* care if anyone wants to throw a few hundred my way."

"Women never know how to hold on to money—or their morals," the fellow from the *Inquirer* added with a smirk.

"*I meant*, it's possible you'll find thousands more—" Julia began, trying to steer the conversation back to the money.

"And *I* meant what I said: *that's all for now*," Pecora said, and stomped off.

Julia turned to Coughlin. "Please—"

Coughlin appraised her with his notoriously frosty gaze. "I have a lot of work to do. Good evening." He marched away, and whether it was his large frame or his rank, everyone got out of the way.

It was well known that when he couldn't speak directly to the press, Coughlin let select reporters loiter in his office while he loudly relayed key facts on the phone. Julia hoped tonight might be such a night and she might be one of the chosen. The chief of detectives was good about that. He didn't exclude her based on her gender.

She tapped tentatively at his door. "Inspector?"

He waved her in. He was, as she'd hoped, on the phone. "What I'm trying to tell you, Henry, is that whatever cash and bonds Marshall gave her the night she died was peanuts to Dot King. Why, between January 25 and February 28 alone, she deposited $9,750.56 in her bank account and withdrew $1,247 . . . and that was just at *one* of her banks! We've already found another."

Julia hovered against the wall, neither guest nor interloper, as she scrambled to comprehend the enormity of Dot King's deposits and withdrawals. And that was just at *one* bank. Coughlin had just said the flapper had accounts at several.

"No other leads we can share at this time," Coughlin said. "But once the court approves the petition from the girl's mother to open the safe-deposit box, you can bet your bottom dollar we'll be there to see what it holds . . . could be anything—a signed copy of the victim's will, cash, bonds, jewels. Who the hell knows?" Coughlin pinned Julia with that gaze of his. "Well, you've always gone ahead and done what you wanted to do anyway. You gotta remember this is an open murder investigation and not some dime-store detective novel."

Julia flushed guiltily but forced herself to hold his stare. He looked as though he were about to say more, but then thought better of it.

"Goodbye, Henry," he said, seemingly into the phone, but she took her cue, nodded her thanks, and left.

Chastised, Julia took the stairs down to the lobby. Of course this was a murder investigation, and yet she also had a job to do. And yes, the coverage of that open investigation involved selling papers. But, she reminded herself, keeping the case in the public spotlight also enhanced its chances of getting solved, unlike the majority of homicides.

Julia went over the staggering sums again. Money was always the bread-crumb trail to a story. Nobody—let alone a *woman!*—made that kind of sugar working on the legal side of things. So what *had* Dot King been doing to pull in that kind of cash?

The Broadway Butterfly had left quite a trail, and Julia would follow every single dollar to find out.

She pushed through the doors and out into the night, turning the case over in her mind. Dot King had been notably clever and most definitely kept, but even Marshall's extraordinary generosity didn't account for the staggering sums Coughlin had referenced. The deposit Coughlin mentioned was nine times the exorbitant amount Marshall had given her. *So who or what was the source of Dot King's real wealth? And what had the girl done in order to get it?*

Julia stopped short in the deserted plaza. Hadn't Dot King had her will drawn up in January? Her will with that very specific clause: "If anything unforeseen should happen to me . . ." What had scared her in January—which Julia now knew was the same month Dot had begun making those unseemly gobs of money she then deposited?

Whatever the Broadway Butterfly had done to rake in that kind of dough was dangerous, that was clear.

Julia glanced around the nearly deserted city hall as a sharp wintry gust cut through her woolen layers. Among the long shadows, a movement caught her eye. A man, hat pulled low, leaned against a pillar, watching her.

She shivered again, and this time it had nothing to do with the cold.

They stared at each other for a long beat. Julia calculated the odds of being able to run back inside before he reached her. Running, however, was always a last-ditch effort. Showing fear was admitting defeat.

She squared her shoulders, pivoted, and began walking quickly back toward the criminal courts. Halfway there, she glanced back to see if he was following her. The plaza was empty, the man gone.

She stopped again, turned slowly in a circle. Had she imagined the whole thing? Had there even been a man? *Had* he been watching her? Or was the intrigue starting to get to her, setting her batty.

Something nefarious lurked beneath the surface of this case. Julia was sure of that. Wherever there were gobs of money, there would also be powerful people who wanted secrets to stay buried.

One thing was certain: Dot King wasn't just some sugar baby. And Julia had a sudden feeling that what she might discover was far more terrifying than murder.

Chapter 23

Julia was determined to talk to Hilda Ferguson and Ella Bradford. If Dot King had been involved in illicit dealings, then surely, the two women she'd spent her days with knew *something*.

For the past few days, whenever Julia had tried to call, Ella Bradford's phone line varied between ringing endlessly and a busy signal. When she had finally answered, she'd politely but firmly said she didn't want to talk to any reporters. The showgirl, on the other hand, had told her to stop by anytime.

Hilda's apartment was less than two blocks from Dot's. Hellinger had told her Hilda was known as "The Body," and when Julia had protested that wasn't much to go on, he'd smirked and said, "Trust me, you'll understand when you see her."

Julia knocked on the appointed door. There was no answer. She knocked again, louder.

The sound of a stumble, something crashing, and a mumbled expletive came from inside.

"Who is it?" a groggy, irritated voice demanded.

"Julia Harpman. We spoke on the phone yesterday?" In her line of work, Julia was used to yelling into closed doors.

Once again, persistence worked. The door was yanked open by a sultry blonde in a silk robe that scarcely reached her knees, and Julia suddenly knew *exactly* what Hellinger meant—*The Body* indeed. Hilda's bobbed curls were in wild disarray—more a glorious, fluffy mop. Her eyes, at half mast, were a bleary mix of little sleep and too much booze, and she sported a full face of makeup that hadn't been washed off before she'd passed out. She looked, frankly, like she'd just emerged from a night that would make a less-jaded soul blush. Somehow, she was still achingly beautiful.

"Yeah?" she demanded, nonplussed.

"Good morning, Miss Ferguson," Julia said brightly. "I'd like—"

"What time is it?" Hilda interrupted.

Julia pulled the cuff of her glove down enough to see her wristwatch—a gift from her mother when she'd headed to Knoxville to work on the court beat. "Just past noon." Hilda simply stared at her. "On *Tuesday*," Julia clarified.

"I know what day it is," the showgirl said, rubbing her forehead unconvincingly. "Ignore the mess. My maid won't be in till later." And with that, Hilda Ferguson turned and padded barefoot into the small studio apartment, her robe fluttering behind her. She plunked down on a red velvet love seat and threw her feet up on a coffee table. Both table and surrounding floor were littered with overflowing ashtrays, plates crusted with food remnants, and a random assortment of clutter Julia dared not analyze too closely.

Julia perched on the only other chair and tried to avert her eyes from Hilda's bare legs and astonishingly small feet. "I'd like to talk to you about Dot."

"I already told the detectives everything I know," Hilda said.

"I'm not a detective," Julia said.

Hilda smirked. "Gee, ya don't say."

"I'm the crime reporter at the *Daily News*," Julia said, noting the momentarily surprised upshoot of Hilda's perfectly penciled-in eyebrows, which quickly dived down into a scowl.

"Well, I'm tired of you people makin' us look bad—diggin' up Dot's past. How would you like it if someone went snoopin' around your private life? You can't just use us to sell papers and look down your snoots at us."

"I don't—" Julia started, resisting the urge to point out that Hilda seemed to be a reader of those very same papers.

"Oh, don't ya?" Hilda cut in. She picked up yesterday's copy and read Julia's article out loud: "Dot King's place in the Gomorrah which is Broadway will be taken by another of her kind. Her murder will be a morsel of gossip to mull over for a long time, but it will not make a single shapely hand hesitate in lifting a cocktail glass to rosy lips, nor will it bring warning to the aged and foolish millionaire suckers for whom there always lie in wait a dozen blackmailers and gold diggers."

Julia flushed. "I took 'Gomorrah' out in the second edition," she said, knowing it wasn't much to offer up. It was a delicate balance, writing sensationally enough to sell the news, because without large distribution, the paper couldn't get advertisers, which is what really kept every paper afloat, while honoring the truth of each story, and remembering these were real people with feelings and families. To execute this tightrope act, under deadline, every single day, was not easy, and sometimes she failed.

Hilda fixed her big blue eyes on Julia for a long, assessing beat before she flicked her gaze down and read on. "Dot King's story is not new. Hers is no tale of an innocent, country maiden led astray in the wild and wicked city. The blonde and supple cloak model set out deliberately to get all she could with the least effort. She played the game of the white way, and it matters little to her crowd that she lost. She was envied by the ladies who emerge from their tiny, stuffy, overheated apartments when the electric lights are turned on and seek their beds only when the sun rises. Dot was at home in the nest of blackmailers who thrive on rich men's folly. And they knew when she acquired her wealthy 'angel'—her 'heavy sugar guy.'"

Hilda tossed the paper aside, crossed her arms mutinously, and leaned back in her chair. "So why would I ever wanna talk to *you*?"

"I'm sorry," Julia said. "Truly, I am. But if I don't write stories in ways that keep people reading—*and buying*—papers, they'll tell me to drop the case and move on to the next." She took a deep breath. "Do you know how many murders there are in New York each year? Over two hundred. Do you know how many are solved? About two. The more I can keep Dot in the news—no matter how I have to do it—the more likely they'll find her killer. The quicker she drops off the page, the quicker her case goes cold, buried next to all the other young female victims whose folders sit, collecting dust."

Hilda narrowed her eyes. "And the more *you* have a job."

Julia forced herself not to flinch. "Well, yes, that too. I've chosen a career where my destiny is tied to crime, but that doesn't mean I don't care about the victims. I *do* care. I'm determined to help get justice for Dot." She picked up the paper Hilda had cast aside. "And if you'd kept reading, you'd see I do just that. And that I call the police and DA out for protecting Mr. Marshall's identity."

Hilda seemed to be calculating. Julia waited, realizing that she'd underestimated the showgirl and probably wasn't the first to have done so.

Finally, Hilda heaved a sigh. "Fine. Whaddya wanna know?"

"I recently learned Dot had several bank accounts," Julia said steadily.

Hilda dug under an expensive-looking gown that lay in a crumpled heap on the couch, retrieved a cigarette case, and removed one. She closed the case with a snick and lit her cigarette. "Quite the little detective, aren't ya?"

"I've gotta be," Julia said simply. "I'm the only woman on the crime beat with a pack of men who'd rather I wasn't. And on top of that, I'm watching the murder of a woman almost the same age as me go unsolved because the muddleheaded authorities are stubbornly fixated on the wrong guy. Or perhaps being *persuaded* to focus on him. Regardless, I've got a job to do, and that's to keep Dot King in the news until they find her killer and send him to prison."

Hilda said nothing. She took a long draw, tipped her head back, and blew the smoke out in a slow, steady stream as the silence between them grew.

The muffled sounds of the street below—a symphony of spluttering motors, the call-and-response *aaaooogah!* of drivers negotiating with each other and pedestrians, the piercing wail of a police siren—rose outside the window. Julia cleared her throat. Truthfully, she did not know whether Coughlin kept Guimares in his sights because or in spite of information. "I've learned that Dot deposited enormous sums in her bank accounts starting in January. Know anything about that?"

Something passed over Hilda's face, and suddenly she wasn't bleary and half in the bag. "I don't know about you, but I don't make a habit of going through my friends' bankbooks."

"Right," Julia agreed. "But since you were living there, I reckon you might've seen something."

Hilda smoked, shook her head. "Sorry. Can't help ya."

"You and I both know that's more sugar than any girl can legally make in a year, let alone a month. I know Marshall was generous, but he wasn't *that* generous. And I've also been thinking about how Dot went to Atlantic City two weeks ago."

Hilda swung her tiny feet to the floor, crossed her legs, and began kicking the top one in an anxious, frenzied beat. "Like I said, I don't know anything about it. She had her friends, and I had mine."

Julia waited. A resistant source was usually a scared source, and scared sources usually had reasons. She let the silence stretch between them.

Finally, Hilda spoke. "You use cold cream?"

The question caught Julia off guard. She touched her forehead self-consciously. "Why, yes, I try to." It would've been more accurate to say rarely, by the time she made it to bed after a long day of deadlines.

"You oughtta," Hilda said. "And if you drink two quarts of water a day, you can drink all the booze you want and never wrinkle.

Wrinkles"—and here the tip of one of Hilda's screaming-red fingernails pointed at Julia's forehead—"age a girl."

Julia bit back a smile, reminding herself that Hilda was only nineteen. "Yes, I'll try that. Thank you. Listen, I know it's scary to talk about these kinds of things when powerful people are involved. So how about I just talk and you nod if I'm right, fair enough?"

Hilda looked wary but nodded.

Julia consulted her notes. "A lot of hooch and other substances go from New York through Atlantic City to Philadelphia. So I figure a girl going down there for a week by herself, plus that huge deposit, could mean Dot was involved in some less-legitimate businesses. And I figure you, as her roommate, might've had an idea what they were. Trust me, I've dealt with drug kingpins and bootleggers before—I've gone into their casinos and I've interviewed their molls—so I understand why you wanna keep your mouth shut. But I have a hunch Dot's trips to the shore were mixed up in something like that. Am I right?"

Hilda looked at the floor, tapped her ash in the tray, nodded almost imperceptibly.

"What I can't figure is who she was doing it for," Julia said. "Raking in that kind of sugar, it must be someone big."

Hilda shook back her mess of blonde curls. "D'you know who owns Dot's building?"

Julia blinked. "Her *building*? No. I haven't searched land titles."

Hilda exhaled smoke, her eyes narrow, wary, watching. "Arnold Rothstein." The name hung between them like the smoke, menacing, gray. "So sometimes, she'd take a vacation—all expenses paid—down to Atlantic City and stay at the Ritz for a week. That's all I know."

It was clearly *not* all Hilda knew.

"Does she always stay at the Ritz?" Julia asked.

Hilda looked like she was doing some fast calculations and arrived at an answer. "Yes—unless she's with a man. Nucky Johnson owns the Ritz and they used to be an item, so even though they're kaput, he still keeps a suite for her."

Nucky Johnson . . . The name echoed in Julia's mind. "Nucky Johnson doesn't just own the Ritz, he owns Atlantic City!"

"So I've heard," Hilda said drolly.

Nucky and Arnold Rothstein? It had been rumored that the two gangsters were in cahoots, moving booze and now narcotics from New York to Philly. Here was proof. But how was Dot King involved?

It was hard to imagine a woman working with gangsters in any capacity other than sexual. But that's exactly what made it brilliant: nobody would ever suspect a woman. Who better to take a prepacked trunk to Atlantic City than a fur coat–wearing, high heel–strutting, bleached-blonde sugar baby who undoubtedly traveled with too much baggage and nobody would suspect of anything other than loose morals? And if the sugar baby had an independent streak, enjoyed nice things, was tired of living at the whims of men, and saw an opportunity for financial self-reliance, the fates may have perfectly aligned.

"When did she start working for Rothstein?" Julia asked.

Hilda shrugged again. "No idea. We weren't close. She never confided in me. She never confided in *anyone* except Billie, and trust me, Billie ain't gonna say nothin'."

Dot had her will drawn up in January. *In the event something unexpected should befall me* . . . Running dope for New York's drug kingpin was just the sort of work that necessitated drawing up a will . . . and also yielded huge cash deposits.

The phone jangled and Hilda straightened anxiously. "Listen, you gotta get out of here. I've already said too much. These guys are dangerous, understand? If I was you, I'd stop sniffin' around and go find yourself another story to write."

Chapter 24

The King case continued to feel like trying to carry water in a sieve. Coughlin stomped toward his office, steeling himself for yet another round of questioning Guimares. They'd just returned from bringing the gigolo and his loudmouth lawyer uptown to the Hotel Embassy, where he'd had to face every single member of the hotel staff who'd worked the night of the murder. Not one person had corroborated Guimares's alibi—nobody had seen him return to the hotel, no elevator operators had taken him up to the ninth floor, no waiters had served him breakfast the next morning, and no receipts for his alleged breakfast could be found. The staff did, however, remember seeing and serving Guimares's roommate, Edmund McBryan, and "McBryan's blonde," and there were receipts for their breakfasts.

The trip had successfully shredded Guimares's alibi. Now, back at headquarters, Coughlin had given orders for the gigolo and his lawyer to be put in an interrogation room. He'd let 'em wait, get 'em on edge, their nerves jangled, before he delivered the second half of a one-two punch that might finally—*finally*—get Guimares to confess. Ella Bradford had given him that shot. He'd been right at the crime scene when he'd sensed she had more to share.

In spite of sugar daddy Marshall's arrogance and entitlement, and Dot King's downstairs neighbor, who'd come to the station claiming she'd heard agitated pacing and smelled chloroform at the time the millionaire placed himself at the scene, Guimares remained their prime suspect.

In an effort to demonstrate transparency and thoroughness, Pecora had foolishly shared important information about the case with the press, including Marshall's alleged departure time. This had made it too easy for attention-seeking thrillists like the downstairs neighbor who wanted to see their names in print to step forward with some wild claim or other. This case was already a circus. Coughlin didn't need any more clowns. He needed real evidence, real information, and those scratches and bite marks on Guimares's hand didn't lie.

Guimares, however, *did* lie . . . over and over and over. He'd coolly insisted against all evidence to the contrary that he *had* been at the hotel, alone, all night, and through breakfast. And since no staff remembered seeing him, he alleged the hotel must have a "staffing problem." Arrogant bastard. Well, he wasn't going to be able to dig himself out of the next bit of evidence Coughlin had.

Coughlin slammed the door to his office. His relief at being alone at last was short-lived. Someone had left a stack of Julia Harpman's articles on his desk. He eyed them beadily. They were sure to make him see red. He accepted that it was a reporter's job to cover his cases. He also understood they had to sell papers to stay in business and that the competition for readers was steep. But he didn't appreciate unnecessary digs at his expense. And lately, there had been quite a few.

He flexed his fingers, tried to resist, but couldn't help it. He grabbed the top one.

KING ANGEL RICH BOSTONIAN, the latest headline trumpeted. A line from the article jumped out accusingly: Marshall secretly visited the district attorney's office and contradicted the elevator operator. Coughlin crumpled it into a ball and tossed it in a perfect arc into the trash.

Yesterday's was worse: Despite his admission of his relationship with the girl, his intimate knowledge of her manner of living and her possible fear of enemies, the identity of Marshall is shielded by officials as though his riches and prominence have the power to command such silence.

Other of the girl's friends, less favored by wealth, are not treated with the same consideration. It was so in the Elwell case.

Goddammit. He'd known it was a huge mistake for Pecora to accept that little weasel Olcott's ridiculous conditions to protect Marshall's identity. Anyone should've been able to see that it was going to look bad for law enforcement. Coughlin took no glory in seeing it come to pass, because he was being singed by association. He wanted to serve Pecora a nice solid punch in the face. Crumple, toss.

Sunday's paper: "Neither of these men had anything to do with the crime under investigation," Assistant District Attorney Pecora said after the men had gone. Because Marshall and Wilson came to the district attorney's office voluntarily, Pecora agreed not to reveal their identity.

Goddammit. Crumple, toss.

The lines were a skipping phonograph in his mind: *Pecora agreed not to reveal their identity. Others, less favored by wealth, are not treated with the same consideration.* A hot wave of anger surged. He'd told that garlic-eater not to give Marshall special treatment. Yet here they were, public favor turning against them, a rising tide of outrage fanned by all these damn articles, a chorus of citizens condemning the differences between how Marshall and Guimares were treated, claims that there were two different systems of justice in New York.

Marshall was a pushover who'd had his ass wiped for him his whole life. Guimares was the lead suspect because of the overwhelmingly damning evidence against him. The gigolo was a career criminal with no alibi and a full set of teeth marks on his hand. He also boasted a history of violence against women. Why didn't the papers and the public focus on *that?*

Coughlin knew exactly why: the public read what the papers printed, and the papers printed what the public would buy. Nobody cared about the dull daily grind of criminal investigation or actual justice. His men, detailed to excavate every skeleton from Dot King's past, had uncovered the intriguing fact that Arnold Rothstein owned her building. Or rather, one of his many holding companies did. But he wouldn't release that fact to the press, because they would seize on it with rabid glee and neglect to mention the fact that it had absolutely nothing to do with her murder.

The girl's murder had been at the hands of a brute with an established criminal record. And now Coughlin was about to corner him with the information Ella Bradford had shared.

Coughlin strode down the hall. It was time.

In the interrogation room, Guimares looked nervous and tired. Goldsmith, paid hourly, was notably more relaxed. Well, not for long.

Coughlin yanked his chair out and sat down. "Wanna tell me about the blackmail plot you cooked up against Marshall?"

Guimares glanced nervously at his lawyer—a question. Goldsmith nodded, an answer.

"What about it?" the gigolo countered.

Coughlin leaned in. Ever since Ella Bradford had said, "There's something I have to tell you," and proceeded to fill him in about the gigolo's plot, he'd waited for just the right moment to drop this bombshell. The moment had come. "How you wanted to extort a hundred grand out of the old fella over his mushy love letters about just how much he enjoyed his peculiar passions, like kissing Dot King's *little pink toes*. A guy like that would do anything to keep that quiet. Should've been a grand slam for you. Except your girl wouldn't go along with it. She wouldn't give you those letters," he said.

Guimares snorted, shook his head. "You got it all wrong. She was all for the idea."

"That's not what I heard," Coughlin said. "I heard you were leanin' on her hard and she still wouldn't give 'em to you. And unlike you, my source has no reason to lie."

Guimares lit a cigarette, shook out the match, and exhaled twin tendrils of smoke. "Well, your *source* is wrong," he said. "Dot was all for it. Sure, we planned to offer him the letters for a payout. But we never got the chance. I figure he's the one who snuffed her out."

Coughlin narrowed his eyes. "Now why would he go and do a thing like that?"

Guimares looked down again. "He found out she saved his letters. He didn't want the risk, so he tossed her."

It was an interesting theory. Coughlin had considered it after Hilda revealed Dot King's fondness for reading the letters to her friends, but he wasn't convinced. A weasel like Guimares would do anything to throw the heat off himself. "The way I see it, *you* snuffed her out because she wouldn't give you the letters. In fact, I figure she was fightin' you on it and that's how your hand got all scratched up and bitten, and why hers was found clenched. She was holdin' the letters and you ripped them outta her hand."

"That's a lie," Guimares said bitterly. "We were in it together, and anyway, we never got the chance. You're dead set on pinnin' this on me, even though I got nothin' to do with it."

"I'm set on finding the killer," Coughlin corrected. "And so far, I think it's you. You wanted to blackmail the old man. She wouldn't go along with it. So you figured you'd cut her out of the deal—permanently."

"I'm tellin' ya, it was him," Guimares insisted stonily.

Coughlin shook his head. "So you planned to blackmail him, but *he's* the one who killed her?"

"That's right," Guimares said, growing calmer and more confident by the minute. "He got wise to her ways."

Coughlin laughed, and the bitter sound held no humor. "So you, a lifelong criminal, are only guilty of *thinkin'* about a crime, while *he*, who nobody's said a bad word about, is a killer. *Riiiiight.* You just wanna throw the heat off yourself."

"There's no heat to throw," Guimares insisted, narrowing his eyes. "Sure, I thought about fleecin' the old goat. Maybe I made some bad decisions, or tried to skim a buck here or there, but I ain't no killer."

"I'm runnin' out of patience. Come clean and it'll go easier on you," Coughlin said, shoving his chair back with a harsh scrape. It was better to tower over suspects. He used every tactic he had.

"My client has been very forthcoming," Goldsmith said, attempting a haughty glare, which wasn't helped by the fact he had to look up at Coughlin.

"Your *client* killed Dot King," Coughlin said unyieldingly. "Like you just heard up at the hotel, from all those employees, nobody saw him the night of the murder—not the doormen, not the bellboys, not the front desk, not the elevator operators, and no waiters at breakfast the next day." Coughlin felt things finally clicking into place. This was the process: methodically ferret out information, question, re-question, check with other sources. Guimares had painted himself into a corner—a corner he couldn't lie his way out of this time—and now faced the inevitable end.

"Now I remember, I took the stairs," Guimares said coolly, his expression carefully blank.

Coughlin snorted. "To the *ninth* floor? In the middle of the night?"

Guimares shrugged. "I like the exercise."

This weasel truly thought he was smarter—so smart he could actually get away with *murder*. "See, how it works is, *all those guys* got no reason to lie, and they're all in agreement. *You*, on the other hand, got a big reason to lie, and are the only one not in agreement. Come clean and it'll help you at the trial," Coughlin said.

"I already came clean. I was home," Guimares repeated.

"Nobody saw you. No waiter served you."

The weasel shrugged. "Maybe they got *eccentric memories* like that John Thomas fellow who can't remember Marshall leaving." And now his tone had taken on an edge of taunting.

Coughlin flexed his fingers, which had been itching to punch this bastard for days. "That's not your concern. We're talking about you and your movements on the night of the murder."

Guimares leaned back, cool as a cucumber. "Well, I already told you a hundred times: I took a taxi back at midnight, went up to my suite, went to bed, and had room-service breakfast the next morning with McBryan and his girl."

Coughlin's anger surged that Guimares would have the balls to change his alibi yet again. "Now you had breakfast *with* McBryan? *And* his girl? How come you didn't mention this before?"

Goldsmith's gaze skittered away. Guimares glared. "I didn't think of it."

Coughlin's irritation rose at the obvious lie, and he shoved it down again. He was known for staying unruffled while the suspects got flustered and tripped up. He straightened. "How'd you pay for this breakfast?"

Guimares crossed his ankle over his knee. "Credit."

Bam—not so smart after all. "See, we combed through every credit bill and there's none for you."

"I must've paid with cash then," Guimares said, sounding awfully carefree for a man facing murder charges.

"There's no cash receipt either," Coughlin said, wondering how Guimares would try to get out of this one now.

Goldsmith, looking suddenly concerned, put a hand on his client's elbow. Guimares shook him off. "Then I'd say the hotel has a *real* problem—theft."

It was galling the gigolo remained so smug. Coughlin resisted the urge to grab him by the lapels and beat the tar out of him. "No, pal, it's *you* who has a real problem."

Goldsmith leaped up. "Is there a reason you're so wholly and unnaturally focused on my client?"

"Sit down, fella," Coughlin ordered, rounding on him.

Guimares smoked resentfully. "You just wanna pin this on me 'cause rich-man *Marshall* paid a handsome sum to get off the flypaper."

Goldsmith sat, crossed his arms, glared up at Coughlin. The intended effect was wasted. The lawyer had a round-cheeked baby face that would always make him look like a high-school kid playing hooky. Staying clean-shaven didn't help. "Lemme ask you something," the kidlike lawyer bleated. "Why're you so fixated on whether my client took the stairs or the elevator up to his hotel, but meanwhile have offered no theory whatsoever as to how he could've possibly sneaked past John Thomas or found any other way into Miss King's building? Your own witness, John Thomas, testified that Marshall was the last man he took up that night—not Mr. Guimares. So unless he flapped his arms and flew in the window, I'd say you're chasing the wrong guy."

Guimares stared with a calm, stony resolve. "Maybe the police don't like dark-skinned guys, and especially not ones who *socialize* with white women."

"I don't like liars who beat women, then chloroform, rob, and kill them," Coughlin shot back.

Guimares shook his head like there was just no reasoning with anyone. "I already told you the truth, Inspector. I can't help it if you don't like it."

"I'm gonna need the name of McBryan's girl who you now claim was at this infamous breakfast."

Guimares crossed his arms. "I'm not dragging her into this."

Coughlin snorted. "So you got a moral code about involving a woman who could help secure your alibi? Funny how that works."

Goldsmith clamped a hand on Guimares's arm. "Inspector, I need a moment with my client."

"I *said* I'm not dragging her into this," Guimares insisted, yanking free from his lawyer.

Coughlin didn't back down. "Lemme guess: she refuses to commit perjury for you."

Guimares shook his head. "It seems you've already made up your mind about me and won't let something like evidence change your mind."

Coughlin leaned closer to Guimares's lying, pretty-boy face. "The evidence all points to you, son. So whether you *wanna* drag her into this or not, we're gonna find out who this girl is and bring her in. And if she says you *weren't* home, same as *the entire hotel staff said*, I'm gonna lock you up and charge you with first-degree murder."

He was halfway to the door when Guimares's voice stopped him dead in his tracks. "I sure hope you find the real guy soon, Detective. It'll be a load off my mind to know Dottie's killer is behind bars."

Coughlin rounded on him. "Oh, I've *already* found him, and he *will* be going to prison. Make no mistake, I *always* get my man."

Chapter 25

March 21, 6:20 p.m. Manhattan. New York Daily News.

Julia had spent the day racing around the city, attending no fewer than three press conferences. She'd tried to ask pointed questions about the strange hundred-milliliter chloroform bottle, a size that had never been sold in stores yet had somehow been found at the crime scene, the downstairs neighbor who claimed to smell the drug when Marshall admitted he was there, whether the conflicting testimonies of John Thomas and Mr. Marshall had been reconciled, whether Marshall's identity would ever be revealed. Every question had been refused.

It seemed the DA and defense attorneys for both suspects had finally come to understand what the rest of New York had known all along—this case was being tried in the court of public opinion—and now each was scrambling to gain the advantage.

They had succeeded only in mudslinging. Guimares's lawyer, sensing the tides were turning against his client, had invited the press to his office to meet the man. The opportunity to hear from the murder suspect directly—and ask him any questions they wanted—had sent the crime-beat corps stampeding uptown . . .

. . . where it had become immediately clear that the gigolo had been well coached. He'd been stripped of his now-infamous giant fur coat and flashy jewels and, though nervous, edgy, and exhausted, had continued to proclaim his innocence loudly and often. He denied Dot supported him, denied he'd ever hit or abused her, and even tried to turn the tables—demanding to know why the press was "picking on" him instead of chasing down Marshall's identity.

It was outrageous, of course, and reeked of the desperation of a cornered man. Julia was sorely tempted to ask where his concern about picking on people had been when he'd beaten and bruised his lover. And while there was merit in the man's claims that Marshall was treated differently by authorities, he was wrong about the press. Every reporter was desperate to discover Marshall's true identity and break the story to their readers.

Pecora, not to be outdone by the legal theatrics, held his own audience later that day, where, to everyone's shock, he'd directly addressed rumors of throwing the case. Julia had frozen, stunned, as the DA had looked around the room and said he knew they all thought he was corrupt . . . and they weren't the only ones. To the disbelief of the entire room, the DA had then *read aloud* multiple letters from the public accusing him of corruption. In her ten years on the beat, Julia had never seen anything like it, and based on the similarly shocked faces of her colleagues and competitors, neither had anyone else.

Afterward, the general agreement among the press was that Pecora had valiantly tried to bluster his way out of the situation, probably hoping that bewailing the public's lack of trust in him would make him look like a stand-up guy.

The plan had backfired. Instead of reassuring anyone of his ethics, it had only made the DA look more guilty. He hadn't helped himself by doubling down on protecting Marshall's true identity. In a last-ditch effort, desperately flailing for any scrap of respectability, Pecora had promised to call the world's most famous sugar daddy and his attorneys back for another round of questioning that weekend under the premise of having received new information about a blackmail plot against the man. But the DA's dog and pony show to try to seem ethical and unbiased was far too little, too late.

Then, just when the day seemed like it couldn't get any stranger, Marshall's lawyer, Neilson Olcott, called his own meeting. But because his client's identity was still being protected by the police, Olcott had to speak on behalf of the millionaire, which only served to remind everyone of how differently the suspects were being treated.

Olcott had then inadvertently made things worse, insisting Marshall was ready to step forward at any time, but Pecora had *chosen* not to question him again thus far. He'd gone on to deny there had been a blackmail plot against his client, which made him look like a liar in view of Pecora's announcement. The haughty lawyer had further expressed his extreme skepticism about the press's desire to see Marshall and Guimares treated the same. "You simply desire to provide the public with a choice morsel of gossip," he'd said, which had caused outrage and denials from the assembled press.

To top it all off, he insisted his client never planned to marry Dot King. When Julia had pointed out that Mrs. Keenan swore Marshall *had* promised her daughter marriage, Olcott had said, "I don't doubt that's what Miss King told her mother. Women in *her* walk of life usually tell their mothers such tales when their mothers protest their manner of living."

In less than half an hour, the lawyer managed to insult the DA, the press, and the victim's mother, plus crank the public's interest in Marshall's identity up to a fever pitch.

And so, despite jockeying, the day had ended much as it had begun for the Dot King case: with the public and the press hating Guimares, loathing Olcott, demanding Marshall step forward, accusing Pecora of corruption, and screaming that there were two systems of justice in New York City.

Back at her desk, her feet aching after the long day, Julia went over her notes. From where she sat, the most important issues were uncovering the origin of the mysterious chloroform bottle, when and how Marshall had left his lover's building the night of the murder, why he'd taken the stairs for the first time if John Thomas was correct in his testimony that the man hadn't taken the elevator, and who the heck Marshall really was.

Julia was determined to pursue answers to each of these questions until there was justice for Dot King.

Chapter 26

El Mirasol had twenty-seven telephone lines with fourteen extensions. Yet Frances was nowhere near any of them when the call came. She was out on the terrace, finalizing the details for the presidential party. Eva had excused herself to go inside for a moment, and Frances wondered as she waited whether having cocktails in the Moorish cloister wouldn't make a more memorable impression. Emily and Mrs. Mac, Eva's social secretary, stood to the side, pens poised, ready for the decision.

"Franny!" Eva waved from the door. "Jack's calling."

Dear, sweet Jack always had a knack for calling at inopportune times. She made her way toward her father's office, unhurried. Gentlemen should always be made to wait. Only overeager ladies rushed. Frances had been unable to reach him last night—the butler had told her he was still out at a business dinner. And while it was unusual that he'd call her midmorning, and at her father's house, it wasn't so out of the ordinary as to be alarming.

"Hello, darling." She sat in her father's guest chair, crossing her ankles left over right and adjusting her skirts to fall just so, as though he could see her. "Any chance you can take an earlier train? You must let me know what time you get in so we can send a car. This is going to be marvelous—golf with the president! Such a tremendous step forward for you . . . for *us.*" She smiled, pleased and proud. Oh, how grand the pictures in the papers would be. Jack's star was truly ascending. She was already mentally composing a sympathetic, modest response to the ladies whose husbands wouldn't be included.

"Frances." Her name on his lips was choked, heavy.

A frisson of nervousness sliced through her. "What is it?" she asked. "Don't say you're delayed. Oh, darling, I've already arranged everything!"

"Franny." He took a laborious breath, and she could feel his tension radiating through the phone. "There's been a terrible mistake."

There could be no mistakes. Not after their hard work and everything that was in play and at stake. Didn't he know how very much hinged on this? His business and social position, Harding's reelection, her father's business prospects, Mr. Daugherty's legislation . . . *everything*. She was about to say just that. But then she remembered that a wise woman was like a great ship—steady even in rough waters—and softened her voice into a more soothing, maternal tone. "What is it, darling?"

"I can't go into details over the phone."

"What's going on?" she demanded, growing impatient. Of course she knew he meant someone could be listening in—servants on either end, the operator who'd connected the call.

"Jesus Christ! I can't say over the phone," he snapped. "Something has happened. It's all a terrible mistake. But it's going to be in the papers tomorrow."

Her heart suddenly felt as though it had plummeted down to her toes. "What do you mean?" There was a long pause, and her imagination ran riot as to what on earth it could be. He'd just been appointed to the board of directors of some bank or other in Philadelphia. It had been announced in the papers. Had they asked him to step down? *But why?* Or, her mind spun frantically, perhaps an allegation of fraud? Had horrid Representative Keller turned his vicious attentions to private citizens? Or could it be bankruptcy?

Each terrifying possibility seemed more unthinkable than the last.

"Wha-what mistake?" she asked, and hated that her voice shook.

He said nothing for a long moment. Then—the worst: a broken sort of sob. She'd never heard him utter anything of the sort. It made her toes clench in her new shoes.

Her fingers closed tighter on the earpiece. His heaving gasps kept coming across the line, and she forced herself to sound confident— someone had to. "Whatever it is, we can fix it. Father will help us," she said. In her desire to brace up, to sound calm and fearless, she momentarily lapsed in their unspoken agreement to never invoke calling on her father's support. Jack was proud. They had agreed.

Not that, she admitted, swallowing hard, they'd ever really had to face anything too trying. They'd never actually needed her father's help for anything beyond a few well-placed phone calls for certain introductions or invitations.

The line went silent, and she took his silence as resentment. Still, the reach of her father's power, influence, and ability to sway any particular outcome to his liking seemed unlimited. *Unlimited and comforting.*

"It may come to that," Jack finally said bitterly. "I'd hoped to avert the situation altogether. It's all just ridiculous. A terrible misunderstanding. I've been doing everything I can to manage it, but you know these newshounds—they'll print any filthy lies they can get their hands on to sell their damn papers. They don't care about human decency. They don't care about hurting innocent people. I've done everything I can to protect you and the children, but I never thought it would come to this." His voice held a terrifying finality that Frances had never heard before in anyone.

Human decency? Hurting innocent people? What on earth . . . ?

"Jack, tell me what's happened!" she demanded, her voice growing shrill. "Is this about playing golf with Mr. Harding?"

"Jesus Christ—this isn't about golf. Cancel the damn golf! Cancel the whole presidential visit!"

"Cancel the . . ." Frances trailed off, shocked. "Have you gone mad?"

"Reporters will probably show up in the next few hours," he replied. "They're going to ask all sorts of ugly questions. The lawyers advised that you say you have no idea what they're talking about. That everything they're implying is ridiculous. That you trust me implicitly."

Lawyers? Ugly questions? Trust him? The words knocked around her brain like snooker balls, trailing unerringly toward pockets of possibilities she was too terrified to follow. She still couldn't comprehend canceling the president's visit—not after all they'd done and all it could mean. "What are you talking about? What—what have you done?"

"I really can't say anything more—not now. But you mustn't read any papers tomorrow—promise me. And when the reporters descend on you today like the flock of ghastly vultures they are, just be poised and show them you're completely undisturbed by their presence. We must have a united front. Then prepare to come home as quickly as possible. Ready the children and close up the house. Don't call me or anyone else until then. And Franny? You must tell no one about this."

The line went dead. And for the first time in her life, Frances was truly afraid.

Chapter 27

The crowd of newspapermen huddled on the sidewalk in the chilly damp, waiting for Mr. Marshall to emerge from the promised round of questioning in Pecora's office. A group of gray-haired men, presumably the mysterious millionaire and his fleet of lawyers, had arrived at a few minutes after 1:00 p.m. and hurried inside under police escort. It had been almost three hours and there was still no sign of them.

Julia shifted from one foot to the other. The cold bit through her stockings. She eyed the men and wished, for perhaps the millionth time, that women could also wear slacks and comfortable shoes.

"Here they come!" someone shouted. The doors flew open and three gray-haired men in expensive-looking suits appeared, flanked by policemen. One of them had to be Marshall, but there was no way to tell which one.

The mob of the press surged forward, bellowing questions at the group: "Did you intend to marry Dot King?"

"Were you going to divorce your wife?"

"What did Pecora and Coughlin ask?"

The police blew whistles—shrill, staccato tweets—fighting to clear a path through the crowd.

The three men, heads down and silent, were jostled through the crowd and into a taxi, which took off like a lightning bolt.

Julia sprinted to the next cab. "Follow that car!" she shouted. "Five bucks if you stay with him!"

The driver peeled out. "Five bucks?! You on the level?"

"It's on the level, all right," she promised. "There's a murder suspect in there!" She glanced behind them. The other reporters were pouring into the remaining cabs, but she was in the lead.

The chase was underway. The driver gunned it to keep Marshall's car in sight, then immediately jammed the brakes to narrowly avoid hitting a pedestrian, swerved, and accelerated again.

Marshall's cab sped uptown, made a last-minute left on Prince Street, and tore ahead across Mercer, Greene, and Wooster. A delivery truck lumbered into the intersection, and her cab screeched to a halt mere inches from Marshall's.

"Careful!" Julia warned, palms sweating. Her memory ran, unbidden, to another taxi two years ago, and the terrible collision that had landed her in the hospital for months, unsure if she would ever walk again.

Westbrook, whom she had met six months before that while covering the famous Elwell murder, had come to see her every single day, keeping her company, bringing her souvenir baseballs from games he had covered. He had also proposed every single day, but she'd refused, insisting she had to know whether she'd be able to walk again first. She'd fallen in love with him, over the course of those chats, and those many terrifying months. But she still had a visceral terror of hospitals, and of car accidents. There was no time to dwell on it. Marshall's car lurched forward again and made a sharp right onto 6th Avenue. It accelerated, and the space yawned between them. Julia saw her story disappearing in tandem with the cab.

"Come on! We can't lose them!" she urged.

"I gotcha," the cabbie promised, pressing the gas pedal relentlessly. They picked up speed. The blocks sped past in a blur.

Julia's breath shortened. Her heart pounded. She didn't want to stop, didn't want to forfeit the front-page story. But it was all too fast. Her body couldn't withstand another crash. Her spine still ached from the last one.

At the last second, Marshall's car screeched right on 14th Street. Her driver managed the same, and she tried not to panic as her shoulder slammed into the door. They flew past Union Square, tourists leaping out of the way, a vendor nearly losing his apple cart. Julia's stomach clenched in tight, terrified knots.

Ahead, Marshall's car turned left again on Union Square East, then left on 35th Street, and started back across town.

Julia clutched the seat for dear life. "Where on earth is he going?"

"Got me!" the driver said, white-knuckling the steering wheel.

Ignoring traffic, they sped down 7th Avenue, swung over to 5th, and back toward 36th Street.

Luck, once again, was on her side, as traffic parted. "We're gaining on them! Faster!"

As soon as she said it, a truck pulled out from the cross street. Marshall's car slammed to a stop, but it was too late.

It felt nightmarishly slow as her cab rammed into the rear flank of Marshall's taxi.

Julia's cabbie glanced back at her. "You OK?"

Julia scanned herself and exhaled. "Yes."

Marshall's driver leaned out the window. "What the hell you doin'?"

"*Me?* You gotta be jokin'!" Julia's driver hurled back, grinding the gears and reversing.

The cars idled in a standoff as the drivers threw threats and insults. Julia twisted around, craning left and right to get a lay of the land. More taxis bearing reporters were pulling up behind them, while uninvolved motorists blared their horns at the delay. It was now or never.

Julia opened her door. She would try to run over and get a comment from Marshall or the men with him. Apparently, she wasn't the only one who had this idea. Newspapermen began pouring out of their cabs toward their common quarry.

Seeing the newspaper pack approaching, someone issued an order, and the car jerked to life and drove away.

"It's afoot now!" Julia's driver shouted. She slammed her door and they took off in hot pursuit.

The chase zigzagged across and uptown, until finally, in Times Square, the passengers and two policemen scrambled out and ran down toward the subway station.

Julia's cabbie screeched to a stop behind the getaway car. "Wait here!" Julia ordered as she leaped out and pursued the fleeing men.

Cabs were already pulling up behind hers, newspapermen piling out. Julia darted down the station stairwell, her low-heeled pumps treacherously skimming each step.

At the bottom, Marshall and the men pushed through a revolving door and ran onward. The detectives braced the door with their bodies. Julia squeezed to the side to avoid being crushed as an accordion of reporters piled up.

"Let us in!" Julia demanded. "This is a public space!"

"Get lost," one detective retorted.

"Don't talk to her like that!" the fellow at the *Evening Journal* ordered. "Put your shoulders into it, fellas!"

The newsmen began shoving at the grate of the revolving turnstile. The detectives on the other side held strong, resisting, as Marshall and his lawyers disappeared into the crowd.

"C'mon, fellas! We can do it!" one of the newsmen called, and the rest began ramming their shoulders to break through. One husky reporter at the front slammed the revolving door with all his might, and the two detectives went sprawling.

The newsmen funneled through, leaping over the felled detectives like they were hurdles. Julia hiked her skirt up and followed suit, charging into the fray of commuters. It was every man for himself.

"Hey!" the detectives shouted, scrambling up and giving chase.

As she dodged and weaved her way through the station, on the hunt for their fedora-and-suit-clad quarries, Julia pictured the triumphant headline: Marshall Caught by Daily News!

All around them, the chaos of Times Square surged. The station felt like a warren of underground halls and stairwells with various trains arriving and departing, crowds milling about, travelers running to their track.

In the melee of men in suits and hats, it was hard to keep track of her particular businessmen.

Ahead, but impossible to get to, she saw Marshall and the men board a train.

"Wait!" she cried, shoving forward. But it was too late. The doors closed and the subway disappeared into the inky blackness of the tunnel.

Chapter 28

Every second since Jack called had seemed to pass as though the hands of the grandfather clock were weighted with sandbags. Tick. Tock. Tick. Tock. Frances paced from room to room, ratcheting herself into near hysteria. What on earth could've happened? *What "mistake"?*

Tick. Tock.

She hadn't shared the strange, terrifying call with Eva or her father. She hadn't begun the impossibly overwhelming work of canceling an event of this scale—the food, flowers, orchestra, and most horrifying of all, notifying the guests.

She told herself she didn't want to sound an alarm unnecessarily, that Jack was probably being ridiculous. But deep down, she also knew she was ashamed. She couldn't bear to imagine the disappointment on her father's face or Eva's forced cheerfulness as they learned of whatever Jack had done—whether he now faced bankruptcy, losing the business, being kicked out of a club, or some other mortifying possibility. Her father had always been a model of Quaker morality, a pillar of Philadelphia modesty. His professional and personal conduct commanded the utmost respect. She felt the hot licks of shame that her husband had failed to do the same.

She'd told Eva she had a headache. A chauffeur had driven her the few blocks back to their cottage. There, the children playing outside under the supervision of their governess had waved excitedly. She'd sent them to the beach and begun to pace.

Tick. Tock.

She was too nervous to eat. She stared, transfixed, at the clock and attempted to stem a parade of horrifying possibilities, like having to ask her father for money or Jack being asked to resign from a board, while Edith's husband, Sydney, continued to excel professionally and sat on multiple boards.

And yet with each passing hour that no reporters appeared, a glimmer of hope grew that perhaps Jack had been wrong. Perhaps he'd overestimated the severity of whatever situation was afoot. As the minutes slogged by, she listed all the reasons why he *had* to be wrong.

Tick. Tock.

The doorbell rang, and the tiny glimmer of hope fizzled and died. Her hands began to shake. This was it. The time had come. She could swear she actually felt her heart galloping in her chest. She made her way from the sitting room to the foyer, where the butler was carefully hiding his curiosity. "Reporters, madam?"

"Thank you." She took a shuddering breath and stepped outside, closing the door firmly behind her. It was time to face the firing squad. She just wanted to get it over with. A wild, hysterical thought popped up: she could've told the butler to send them away, that she wasn't accepting callers, or was out for the day. But to do so was unthinkable. Her world was structured on doing what was expected. She would never thwart that duty.

Plus, she had to know what the dreaded thing was.

Two young men stood in suits that, she could not help but notice, were cheaply made. One was tall and gangly; the other barely reached his shoulder. Each held his own notebook, looking at her with blatant curiosity. "Frances Stotesbury Mitchell?"

"Married to John Kearsley Mitchell?" the shorter one added.

"Yes?" she said, and had the feeling she was sealing a fate she couldn't anticipate with that simple admission.

The taller one cleared his throat. "Good afternoon, ma'am. We're, uh, we'd like your comment on your husband, Mr. Mitchell, being identified as the Mr. Marshall in the Dot King murder case up in New York."

The sky slid out of focus. The sun became too bright. Her entire body ceased functioning. Surely, it must've. She could neither speak nor move. She had died and this was hell.

"Mrs. Mitchell?" he asked timidly. "Are you aware that your husband is alleged to be the Mr. Marshall in the Dot King slaying in New York?"

She stared at them, dumbstruck, as the words sifted through her brain. Dot King slaying . . . the murdered model . . . in New York . . . a mysterious millionaire sugar daddy . . . Jack? *Her* Jack?

Frances's mind flailed. She could not remember a single word Jack had told her to say. In the torturous hours since he'd called, she'd imagined many terrible outcomes, but not *this*. It was impossible.

A warm breeze blew a strand of hair into her eye, and she automatically brushed it away—only then realizing she actually *could* still move. She blinked, then blinked again. Tried to pull the world back into focus. She was still on her doorstep.

The young men were staring. She pressed herself back against the doorframe, feeling its scratchy texture with her fingertip. *This was real.*

The taller fellow glanced around nervously. "Uh . . . ma'am? A reporter for the *New York Evening Journal* found him out by tracing records of telephone calls Mr. Mitchell placed to Dot King. But when confronted by this reporter at his home in Philadelphia—uh, *your home*, ma'am—Mr. Mitchell claimed it's untrue. So . . . do you believe him or the report, ma'am?"

He claimed it's untrue. He claimed it's untrue. He claimed it's untrue! The words echoed over and over in her head. She hadn't died and gone to hell. She hadn't fallen asleep or been hit over the head. She wasn't hallucinating or insane. She swallowed dryly.

Jack's words came back to her in a rush: *terrible mistake . . . ghastly newshounds*. These reporters had come to ask her if she believed her husband, and that was horrifying, but the young man had just confirmed exactly what Jack had told her: it was untrue!

She drew breath into her body. *Of course* these ludicrous charges were untrue—just as this boy had said. Imagine giving a person such a scare—over a ludicrous lie!

Relief made her weak. She was Frances Butcher Stotesbury Mitchell. She was the daughter of E.T. Stotesbury. She was the wife of John Kearsley Mitchell III. She was a member of Philadelphia society and the Palm Beach Colony and deemed one of the four most powerful women in the social set. She had to teach these whippersnappers it was wrong to go around spreading filthy, outrageous lies. She would put them in their place.

She drew herself up to her full, considerable height and regarded them coolly. "No. I refuse to believe that my husband is the man. Such a report is too terrible to discuss. *Of course it's untrue.* My husband was with me in Palm Beach. He left here Sunday a week ago for Philadelphia." As soon as she said the date, she wished she hadn't.

"So was he here on March 15? The night of the murder?"

"Um . . ." Mind racing, she desperately tried to remember. She realized she didn't even know today's date. What day *had* Jack left? Surely, he'd still been here the fifteenth! *Surely!*

The boys exchanged another look. "Well, did you know Mr. Marshall was alleged to be, uh, an 'admirer' of Miss King?"

"Admirer" was, of course, a thinly veiled code for "lover." Frances yearned to slap his insulting face and go back inside. But that wouldn't do at all. Instead of teaching them a lesson, it would only give them more fodder for the front page. "I know nothing at all about it," she said, trying to look bored. She fluttered her hand in a vague gesture of disinterest.

"Well, did you know that while calling himself Mr. Marshall, your husband gave Miss King over $10,000 in cash and another $10,000 in jewels over the last year?"

Frances's brain raced. *Could this be?* Of course it was *financially* feasible. She didn't handle the money. She was a *lady*! How could she notice its absence in their household accounts? How would one even begin to know? She couldn't very well say that to these reporters. She had to make it all sound terribly dull.

"How interesting," Frances said sarcastically with what she hoped was a bored and pitying smile.

The young men exchanged uneasy glances. One licked his lips and looked up at her warily. "Um . . . Dot King's mother, Mrs. Keenan, told the police that Mr. Marshall had promised to divorce his wife and marry Dot in Paris. Do you have any comment?"

Once, when Frances was a girl, she'd been wading in the ocean at their summer cottage in Bar Harbor. A wave had caught her unawares— at the last moment, it had swelled up unexpectedly high and crashed over her. The strength of it had knocked her over. For a terrifying moment, she hadn't been able to find her footing. She'd flailed wildly, unable to orient which was earth and which was sky, hadn't been able to stand up, hadn't been able to find air.

Cold, salty, briny sea had gushed violently into her mouth and up her nose and she'd choked and coughed and spluttered as her arms and legs thrashed, searching for the rocky bottom so she could stand.

Frances felt the same sensation now. She couldn't find her footing, couldn't find the ground. Her mind flailed for something—anything!— to say. "Talk of divorce is perfectly ridiculous!" she finally managed. She wanted to scream: *This entire situation is ridiculous!* She itched again to slap their insolent faces and order them off the property.

"Will you go to Mr. Mitchell in Philadelphia?" the first reporter asked her.

"Of course I will," she said hotly, simultaneously furious yet desperate to be at his side.

They would embrace and he would repeat that this was all a terrible misunderstanding. The thought was reassuring. Why, she'd leave at once—they all would!—to fight this insanity side by side, the best of chums.

"When are you leaving, ma'am?"

"As soon as I know whether there is any truth in this report." The words were out before she could control them. She regretted it instantly.

"So you don't know if it's true or not?" the one boy said.

Too many thoughts assaulted her at once, but one thing was clear: if she delayed or denied going to Philadelphia, it would validate this insanity. "I-I have entire confidence in Mr. Mitchell," she said woodenly, trying to keep her tone even. She reminded herself that she was a loyal and trusting wife. "But as for the report itself, I know nothing."

She knew she sounded confusing at best and contradicted herself at worst. They probably thought her foolish. She didn't care. Her head throbbed. Her stomach churned. The sun-warmed breezes, usually so soothing, now seemed nauseating.

She scrabbled for the doorknob behind her back, desperate to escape. She could turn and run back in the house, but how would that look? What would they print in their vile paper? She needed to keep up appearances. She had to speak to Jack and her father. "I'm so sorry, I must go now. I have a . . ." Frances trailed off, trying to think of something important enough to curtail this miserable interaction.

"Wait! Please! One last question!" the taller one interjected, scribbling notes. "Have you been following the case, ma'am?"

"I haven't read anything of that case." She watched them exchange another pointed look, as though they were embarrassed for her. They knew she was lying or stonewalling or maybe so out of touch, protected here in her ivory tower of wealth, that she simply didn't know what was happening in the rest of the world.

"Ferdinand Pecora, chief assistant district attorney, has been protecting Mr. Mitchell's identity as he called himself Mr. Marshall for the past nine days, even though by his own admission, he was the last person to see Miss King alive," the shorter one said slowly. Perhaps they pitied her, but neither of them backed down.

She looked toward the sky as though casually searching her memory. "Oh yes. Now I vaguely remember that there was a girl in New York named Dot who was supposed to have been murdered." She shrugged as though it were no concern of hers.

They exchanged another long look. The silence lengthened. One cleared his throat. "Is your father here, ma'am? May we speak to him?"

The request was a dagger. She closed her eyes, picturing her father, who said little but noticed everything. He couldn't take fending off an ugly, vicious rumor like this. "Please," she said as calmly as she could. "Don't speak to my father yet. I want this report to come from me. If anyone is to be bothered about this, let it be me. He knows nothing. This is the first I myself am hearing of it."

The taller one nodded. "Very well. We won't talk to him."

She felt her shoulders go slack at the small kindness. "Thank you."

They closed their notebooks and made to leave. "Thank you for your time, Mrs. Mitchell."

She smiled and shrugged as though it were nothing, nothing at all. She was again a hostess, and these boys guests on her stoop.

She watched them head back to their newspaper office to do their job: write the news. The sensational, scandalous, toe-curling news, Frances realized, that she guiltily enjoyed reading. Yes, it was utterly trivial, and space that could be used for more important articles, but wasn't the mindless indulgence what made it so delicious?

But now the rest of the world would soon feast on this scandal as *their* mindless indulgence, while her world shattered.

It took every ounce of her strength not to double over and vomit. She held her stomach, concentrated on breathing in and out. She tried to wrap her mind around the fact that she—Frances Stotesbury Mitchell, wife, mother, daughter, sister, member of society and the very best clubs on the East Coast—could ever be involved in something so very awful.

And Jack! Her husband. The father of her children. Supposed to play golf with the president of the United States and half the cabinet just days from now!

She grasped the doorknob with one hand and the wall with the other. Tears flooded her eyes. She took another deep breath, and tremors ran through her. Her father would make them print a retraction. But first they would need to get to Jack and speak in person. He would assure her that *of course* he wasn't involved in this case—he couldn't possibly be!

And yet, deep down, something wasn't right—every bone in her body said that.

She stumbled back inside. The shocked looks on the servants' faces said they'd heard.

"Call Mr. Mitchell," she said hoarsely. "Try everywhere—his office, Red Rose, the town house . . . just . . . find him."

The butler nodded, already rushing from the room. "Of course."

Emily came to her side. "Do you wish to rest, madame?"

Rest? Who could rest at a time like this? Frances shook her head. "I must speak to my father—have a car brought 'round. And tell the staff to start packing the house. We're going home. And call my doctor. I'm not well. Have him come to El Mirasol as soon as possible. I need a nerve tonic."

"Oui, madame." Emily's face—mortified, horrified—surely mirrored her own.

Frances collapsed onto the nearest chair, the room spinning. What had Jack done?

"Madame—"

"Call my father, goddammit, and get me a driver!" Frances ordered, hating that it sounded more like a helpless wail.

Emily, pale and terrified, nodded and ran from the room.

Chapter 29

Fresh off the chase that had taken her halfway around the city before losing Marshall and Wilson in the Times Square subway station, Julia hurried into the criminal courts building. The pressroom percolated with an undeniable air of excitement. Typewriters clattered, phones jangled, and what seemed like a hundred conversations bubbled up around her as Julia made her way to her typewriter.

"Marshall is *J. K. Mitchell*?"

"But they said the guy was from Boston!"

"Whaddya expect? Lawyers are always liars!"

"So he forks over *ten grand in cash*, plus *jewels*, *furs*, and *two* cars and his wife doesn't notice a thing? Imagine having that kind of sugar!"

The sick realization dawned that she'd missed something big. "What's going on?" she asked nobody in particular.

"The *Evening Journal* just put out a special edition revealing Marshall's identity," one of the guys called out.

She'd been scooped. While she'd been fruitlessly chasing the man, some other reporter—cleverer, faster, better—had discovered his identity. Julia sank into her chair as waves of panic and defeat washed over her. "Who is he?"

"John Kearsley Mitchell III, CEO of the Philadelphia Rubber Works, millionaire, and all-around respectable family man . . . except he was also the heavy sugar daddy for Manhattan's most infamous murdered model," George from the *Brooklyn Daily Eagle* told her.

Julia frowned. "Mitchell?" The name wasn't familiar.

"You'd know him better as Mr. Frances Stotesbury," George said.

"No!" Julia exclaimed. "Marshall's wife is a *Stotesbury?*"

"Yep. Son-in-law of E. T. Stotesbury," George added. "J.P. Morgan's Philadelphia partner, lord of the Versailles of America, maker of $100 million, pillar of the Republican party, loyal supporter of both Harding and Daugherty, and that ain't all. Turns out, *quite* the letter writer. It seems he wrote Dot King all sorts of peculiar mush about how he wanted to 'kiss her pretty pink toes.'"

"No!" Julia said again. This couldn't have been juicier if Sarah Bernhardt had been revealed as the toe-kissing "Marshall" and the whole deathbed act merely a plot.

"My darling Dottie, I miss you oh so much and cannot wait to kiss your pretty pink toes!" the guy next to George trilled in a singsong voice.

"How'd he get discovered? And who's the lucky devil?" Julia asked.

"The *Evening Journal* takes the cake. Seems he found out Marshall was staying at the Ritz, got a hold of the operator call logs, and traced which room called Dot King. Pretty smart, if you ask me."

"Very smart," Julia agreed, mentally kicking herself for not thinking of it. "But how did we find out about his pink toe fixation?"

"An anonymous source called it in, and needless to say, it spread like wildfire: how the old fella had a fixation on Dot King's toes. How he just couldn't wait to kiss her pretty pink toes, how he'd rather be with her, kissing her feet, than with the princess Old Man Stotesbury was hosting—"

"I see your point," Julia interrupted. Her first instinct was to call Westbrook and pour out her frustration. He also understood the stakes of the newspaper realm and the devastation of getting scooped better than anyone. But that would have to wait. She had a story to get first.

She grabbed the phone and asked for long distance to Philadelphia. Once connected, she asked the local operator for the Mitchell residence. "Locust 557, please hold." A moment later, the operator came back. "I'm sorry, that line is off the hook."

Julia hung up. *Locust 557.* Locusts were predatory, destructive, voracious, a plague.

She had first learned of the creatures, as a girl, from the book of Exodus in the Torah. In it, God threatened to send a swarm of locusts to darken the sky and destroy all the crops, forcing the Egyptians to face famine and starvation unless the pharaoh freed the Jews.

Julia had had nightmares of skies black with predatory bugs, their sharp little teeth descending to devour everything living, for months after that. Her mother's reassurances that God had done that to protect their people had done nothing to assuage Julia's fears.

Here now, she thought, was a modern-day locust who stood accused of killing a butterfly. Who had he been protecting—his wife?

Julia tapped her pencil. Didn't Frances Stotesbury Mitchell have a sister? She lifted her phone again and asked for an internal line to Daisy over on the society pages.

Daisy confirmed that there was another Stotesbury daughter: Frances's older sister, Edith, married to a pedigreed fellow by the name of Sydney Emlen Hutchinson, also in Philadelphia. Perhaps John Kearsley Mitchell and his team of lawyers hadn't had time to warn them yet. Julia clicked frantically for the long-distance operator again.

Two operators and another connection later, a cultured voice announced, "Hutchinson residence."

Julia affected what her mother would've called a snooty northern accent. "Yes, Mr. or Mrs. Hutchinson, and quickly. Tell them it's Julia Harpman, calling long distance from New York."

A moment later, another male voice, older and somehow more moneyed, came on the line. "Hello? Sydney Hutchinson here."

"This is Julia Harpman. I've just heard that Mr. Marshall of the Dot King case is really Mr. Mitchell. Is this true?"

"I can hardly believe it myself!" he replied. "I thought he was a New York or Boston man."

Julia's pulse picked up. "So you've heard the allegations?"

"Yes, of course!" Hutchinson said impatiently. "Edith and I were in Atlantic City the first week of March and also stayed at the Ritz-Carlton—same as the girl! So when we read of her murder and saw her picture in all the papers, we tried to think if we'd seen her in the lobby or on the boardwalk. But we hadn't."

"That's a startling coincidence!" Julia said, shocked the fellow was willing to speak to her. "And what of Mr. Mitchell? Do you know if he was in New York at the time of the murder?"

"I thought he was in Palm Beach," Mr. Hutchinson said.

"No," a female voice piped up from the background. "Frances was in Palm Beach with Papa and is still there. Oh, there must be some mistake! I cannot believe he would be that sort of rounder."

Julia's pulse picked up at the reference to "Papa." So this must be Frances's sister. "So you're shocked as well?" she asked, trying to steer the conversation around to more important aspects, but also keep the fragile thread of connection between them.

"Perhaps it's all a mistake," Mr. Hutchinson said more firmly to Julia.

"I always thought that he was more like we are," Edith Hutchinson continued, "the home-loving kind."

Julia raced to capture the society woman's exact words in her notes. Edith's blasé lack of loyalty shocked her. Julia had three brothers—two ran her father's tobacco business back in Memphis; one was in the army. She couldn't imagine being so clinical if their lives were crumbling. "So—" Julia began.

Mr. Hutchinson cut her off. "Wait a minute. Who did you say this was? Where are you calling from?"

Julia began to sweat. Her brain spun frantically, trying to get back to firmer ground . . . or at least get one more juicy quote. "I'm—"

"Hang up! Hang up!" his wife said urgently, and the line went dead.

Julia slowly replaced the earpiece and finished transcribing the conversation. Around her, there was friendly debate about the case. She ignored it, desperate to claw her way back from being scooped with a reputation-saving follow-up.

She'd just earned her byline two weeks ago, an honor that felt as fresh as it did fragile. None of the fellas around her, some who'd earned a byline, most of whom still labored in obscurity, seemed as burdened by the same worries.

"He wanted to *kiss* Dot King's *toes*? Depraved bastard."

"No—he wanted to kiss her 'pretty pink toes'—get it right."

"Say, where's all this 'toe-kissing' stuff coming from?" Julia asked. It was all anyone could talk about, but she had yet to hear about the source of the information.

"It's in Mitchell's mushy love letter," George said.

Julia looked around. "Right. But has anyone actually seen the letter? We're *hearing* about the letter. But who's actually seen it? Where did it come from? Who released it? Who has it now?"

"Who cares? It's hilarious," George said.

Laughter ricocheted around the group.

"Maybe Frances's toes aren't kissable," the fellow from one of the upstate papers ventured.

"Perhaps," Julia offered tartly, "Frances's toes are perfectly kissable and her husband nonetheless finds himself compelled to seek other toes. Or perhaps Frances adheres to the wholly reasonable theory that feet are for walking, not kissing."

This brought an abrupt end to the jocularity. "Jeez, lighten up, will ya?" someone grumbled.

Julia ignored him. Her job was to write the news, not be one of the boys. She focused on the task at hand: a rich, powerful, and predatory man had descended on a Broadway butterfly. Forces of evil had been unleashed, and Dot King had been left slain. Julia tapped her pencil. The question was, what was she going to do about it?

Chapter 30

Frances lay in bed, staring up at the ceiling, teeth clenched. She had not slept. Not even for a moment.

She'd been unable to reach Jack, even though she'd given orders for the staff to call his office, the town house, and Red Rose unceasingly. His secretary had said he was traveling, but did not know where. The servants at both houses thought he was at work, which was clearly a lie, but she could not let them know that.

She'd paced and fretted for the rest of the day to no avail. Finally, desperate, she'd gone back to El Mirasol and told Eva and her father the whole terrible thing. Her father had furrowed his brow, but was reassuringly certain that Jack must be the victim of salacious gossip. Eva had agreed, chiming in that the tawdry tabloids were well known to say anything in order to sell papers. As the hour grew later, they had even considered the possibility of a political ploy by Harding's enemies to undermine the presidential party's alliance building and fundraising in Florida. With no information and Jack missing, anything and everything seemed possible. Her father had dispatched his private detectives in Philadelphia to find out what was going on.

The hours had passed in a nightmarish limbo. They'd politely tried to talk of other things while picking at dinner, but the questions hung heavy over them: Where on earth was Jack? What was going on?

Then the final blow: late into the night, still with no information, her father had decided they had to cancel Harding's visit, and had set in motion the long line of dominoes required to halt an event of this size and importance. She could scarcely breathe when she thought of it. The dress and jewelry she would not wear, the conversations she would not have, the chance to preside at an event of this magnitude . . . the most important event of her life.

The loss of the social and political opportunity felt unbearable. Eva's forced bravery—her stoic insistence that there would be other visits—was nearly Frances's undoing. By then, she'd felt numb from the hours of shock and fear. She'd gone back to her cottage and taken a nerve tonic.

At some point very late in the night, a man named Neilson Olcott, apparently Jack's lawyer in New York, had called.

He'd informed her that Jack had returned from an interview with the police, for which he'd volunteered in order to assist with the case. Jack, the lawyer insisted, wasn't a suspect.

He didn't, however, explain how Jack had come to possess knowledge about the murdered vamp in order to be in such a position to assist, and Frances had been too embarrassed to ask.

The lawyer had told her to immediately return to Philadelphia, and had signed off with the chilling counsel that newspapermen and telephone operators were watching their homes and might be listening on any of their lines. She mustn't make any calls or speak to anyone.

Frances had dissolved in tears at that. Between sobs, she'd told this stranger issuing his high-handed orders that she wanted to speak to her husband! And this fellow Olcott had said, sounding annoyed, that wasn't possible. Then he'd hung up.

Frances hadn't followed his advice. She'd immediately called her father, who insisted on accompanying her back to Philadelphia. Packing and closing their houses for the season was no small feat, but was underway nonetheless. They would leave as soon as possible.

Her father's lawyers were readying possible libel and defamation-of-character suits against every lowly, loathsome paper that dared to print those obscene lies. "With our social position, we're an easy target, but there must be consequences," her father had said. "Why, that Marion Davies actress sued the *Daily News* last year for libel and won. They must learn not to hurl their filth at innocent people!"

Frances had desperately wanted to believe him. But the nerve-racking questions from the reporters—their calm certainty—made that harder. Still, she held on to the hope, in some small, hidden part of her heart, that the reporters were terribly wrong.

All night her thoughts had volleyed back and forth between these possibilities like a tennis match. Eventually, the shadows shifted into predawn light, and at 5:30 a.m., Frances decided it finally seemed a decent hour to ring for Emily.

"Madame?" Emily asked, arriving so quickly that she must've been up and waiting.

"I need the newspapers immediately," Frances said. A wave of bile surged. She was directly disregarding Jack's order not to read the news, but she didn't care.

"Yes, madame." Emily turned and hurried out.

When she returned a few minutes later, her face told Frances that she'd read whatever terrible news awaited, and that it was exactly as horrifying as Frances's worst fears. A heavy silence stretched as Emily placed the newspaper bag on the bed—mustn't get ink smudges on the linens!—and hurried from the room.

Frances took a deep breath and looked at the stack. It was Sunday, so the stack was high. This was her last chance to not know. There would be no going back. She hesitated, but knew whether she read them or not, everyone else would, and decided, therefore, she *must*. She reached for the top paper, heart galloping. And right there, on the front page, above the fold, a headline both sensational and stark screamed, J. Kearsley Mitchell Named as Marshall in Murder of Model.

The summary underneath, only slightly smaller, was just as bad. Prominent Philadelphian and Son-in-Law of E. T. Stotesbury Named by New York District Attorney Pecora as "Angel" of Dorothy Keenan, Who Visited Her on Night of Tragedy.

To the left, a huge picture of her husband, smiling and jolly in a tuxedo at the Bal Masque last year, the pinnacle of the Philadelphia social season. She had been next to him in that photograph, but the paper had cut her out of this reprint and instead run a photo of the now-dead girl shrugging prettily in a giant white fur coat. The headline above taunted, Dead Model and "Mr. Marshall."

Frances clawed the neckline of her nightgown, suddenly too tight. She heard a helpless, pitiful whimper. Then realized it had come from her. The room tilted.

"No. Noooo." These words, too, came from her.

The bottom of her stomach unhinged. She scrambled toward the bathroom, lost her footing, and fell—hard—on the floor. She tried to crawl, heaving, but her ankle-length white silk nightgown got in the way. She suddenly remembered reading that the murdered girl had been found in a yellow-and-black lace negligee that scarcely reached her knees. *She* wouldn't have tripped on her nightgown.

Frances lurched forward, grabbed a paper, and retched. Right there. On the pages. To preserve the beautiful Persian carpet. How much had it cost? Thousands? Frances's back arched and she heaved again and again.

She collapsed on her side, sobbing. She wiped at her nose and mouth with the sleeve of her nightgown, trying to rid herself of the acrid taste of vomit. Her cuff was wet with the yellow-green foulness.

An unwanted image of the dead blonde stranger sprawled across a messy, sin-laden bed, wearing an indecently short nightdress, flashed into her mind. Had her husband bought that *thing* for her? Frances tried not to think of what they had done while she wore it. The thought was too terrible.

Her fingers clawed at her bodice as if possessed. She wanted to tear her skin off. Wanted to claw this awfulness away. The sound of her sobs echoed in the beautiful room. And for the first time ever, Frances pitied herself.

Eventually, her sobs dribbled down to gasps and she rose to all fours. She folded the befouled pages and threw them away. Then drifted back to bed. She couldn't resist reaching for the rest of the paper.

It couldn't be true.

Though every ounce of pride begged her not to, she forced herself to read the terrible article. *It simply could not be true.* Not her Jack. Fourteen years of marriage. Two healthy children, three beautiful homes, all the clubs, the events, and their charity work added up to an utterly lovely, socially envied life. There was nothing she didn't know about him.

Or was there?

Before yesterday, she would've wagered her life upon it. She would've tied herself to a stake and demanded to be set on fire if this morning's story was true.

Now it felt like she *was* being burned alive.

Jack!

While she and the children stayed home, safe in their purity and their changed-twice-daily French linens, he'd traveled to New York under the pretext of business and *what*? Drunk bootlegged liquor with these . . . unsavory people? This *woman*? Gone to dark, secret places that respectable people didn't even know about?

She couldn't picture fifty-one-year-old Jack in these places. She couldn't even picture the places themselves!

This, she supposed, was a reflection of her virtue. Everyone knew that only certain kinds of women—flappers and vamps—also patronized saloons that neither Frances nor any decent member of polite society would ever dare go. It was indecent.

She forced herself to read on. It had to be done. Because it was printed for all the world to see in every newspaper in the country. Even here in sunny, beautiful Palm Beach! Even here, hundreds of miles away from Philadelphia, where all her friends—all of society—would see it.

And what of the yellow silk pajamas that supposedly belonged to her husband, which had been hurriedly stuffed under the couch by the maid he'd employed to care for his mistress? The maid later admitted she was trying to protect him because he had been generous to her during her lying-in, arranging private medical care, time off, and gifts for the baby.

Jack seemed oblivious to their servants—*their live-in servants*. She'd wager he didn't even know their names despite sharing a roof, yet he'd thought to provide for his mistress's maid's lying-in and gifts for her baby?

Who *was* this man she'd married?

Unbidden, details she'd read flashed through her mind of this bob-haired flapper, an alleged "model" whose jewel-box apartment, fine furs, jewels, and maid couldn't have been financed by a sporadic modeling career and who had, instead, been kept by her wealthy, mysterious patron. This young woman whose exquisite blonde beauty she'd been reading about in newspapers for nine days . . . this *whore*! Frances could scarcely make her mind form the word.

The images paraded on: this whore . . . kissing Jack! This . . . vamp entwined with *Jack*! Sweaty and twisted and her perfect bow-shaped red lips parted rapturously as she did things that Frances couldn't even imagine because they weren't fit for ladies to know about.

She closed her eyes to blot out the terrible thoughts. But what she saw instead was that filthy woman lying dead.

The only thing worse than being married to a publicly named adulterer was being married to a publicly named murderer. How had her perfect life come to *this*?

She wished for the oblivion of sleep, to stay in bed until she died. She would not return to Philadelphia. She would not receive visitors. She would walk into the sea and let herself sink.

She curled into herself, a primal urge for self-protection, but saw instead pictures of the children on the bedside table. Little Franny. Young Jack. She reached for the silver frame, bringing their sweet faces closer.

Her children! God, what would this do to her poor children?

The thought yanked her up to sitting. This wouldn't do at all. She was a *Stotesbury*! She was a mother! She was a member of *society*. Jack had said he'd made a mistake—he hadn't admitted to having an affair.

She wouldn't lie here and crumble into a thousand pitiful pieces. Surely, that was what everyone expected and simultaneously feared. Doing it was practically a confirmation of Jack's guilt.

He'd warned her that stories would come out this morning. But he'd asked her not to read them. A wave of hope glimmered. He'd *said* this was all a terrible mistake! She would prove his innocence, she decided. She would stand by his side and they would fight this together!

In the meantime, she would have tea and mentally brace herself to greet the children. They must never know that anything at all was amiss. They must think it was merely time to go home.

Chapter 31

10:00 a.m. Manhattan. 43 West 127th Street.

Ella Bradford was never one to skip church. Sitting with James and June as the word of God was preached was the closest to home she ever felt all the way up north in this big, cold city.

Sunday was always her day off (unless Miss Dottie needed her), and church the only time she could sit back and just be and count on not seein' white folk. Even when they was nice, white folk still felt like work.

She'd missed church only when June had come, and it was understood a woman would miss a Sunday service or two after a baby. But now if she missed services, tongues would wag even more than they already were.

When they'd walked into church last Sunday, it felt like every head in Harlem turned to look. She'd wanted to run right back out. But James had taken her hand, and marched to the pew where they always sat. He'd stared back at each gawker and greeted them like a challenge. Nobody had had the guts to refuse him a reply.

But on the way out, Ella had felt the stares and caught the whispers, the meanest glad she'd been knocked down a peg: "Miss Thinks She's Something, but there's no fancy Midtown job now." And "Don't matter how light, she still ain't white!"

She knew she had to go back to make the talk stop. But she couldn't go today. Then the papers would come out tomorrow, and everyone would know where she'd been instead: called down to police headquarters again. The real Christians would be worried for her. The others would set to gossip.

Ella swallowed nervously and hoisted June higher.

What more could they want to know about Miss Dottie? And what more could she say? She'd already told Inspector Coughlin about the letters.

◆ ◆ ◆

John Thomas sat alone in the waiting room, empty except for the white policeman on guard. Mr. Thomas was wearing a suit—probably his Sunday best, like her. It felt wrong to see him out of his uniform, as though she'd been caught where she shouldn't be.

"So they brought you back, too, huh, Mr. Thomas?" she asked, and took the chair next to him.

"Sure 'nuff." Mr. Thomas sounded none too pleased. He looked older and tired today. The bags under his eyes sagged into soft folds. His white hair was close-cropped, like cotton fuzz still on the boll. "This your boy?"

She turned Junebug's sweet little face toward the older man. "Yes, sir." With James on the brunch shift, she'd had no choice but to bring him.

Mr. Thomas nodded. "Fine young man."

"Yes, sir," she said. She looked over at the policeman again and lowered her voice. "So why'd they bring you back down here?"

John Thomas stared at the floor and shook his head. "Lord knows. Just keep on asking the same damn questions and I keep telling 'em the same damn thing: I *didn't* take Mr. Marshall back down that night, and I would've remembered if I had. Especially if he gave me a two-dollar tip. Dragging me back in here time and time again, pesterin' me, them policemen followin' me, standing outside work and home ain't gonna change that. Facts is facts."

The paper she'd bought from the newsie last week had said the police believed Mr. Marshall and that John Thomas had changed his story—first he'd remembered taking Mr. Marshall down after all, then that his memory was "unreliable." Fear cut through her, left her short of breath and sick to her stomach. Couldn't he see what was happening? Didn't he know what the police were doing? "You gotta tell 'em—"

"No talkin'!" the policeman barked. June startled at the sharp, loud rebuke, and Ella cuddled him closer so he wouldn't cry.

She took him to mean don't talk about *that*. "Yes, sir."

The policeman marched over to glare down at her. He was too close. Her knees brushed the blue wool of his uniform trousers. Real slow so he didn't notice, she pulled away, tucked smaller back into herself. June whimpered a protest, maybe from being squeezed too tight, maybe from the stiffness of her arms, frozen and afraid.

The policeman looked, beady eyed, back and forth between them. "Guess I'll have to separate you two. Shove over."

She kept her eyes down, shifted June to her other arm, farther from the officer, and obediently moved one seat over. He plopped down between them and huffed like he was put out at the trouble. She clamped her elbows in tighter so she didn't brush his arm, but didn't dare move farther, lest she offend him.

She gently jiggled June and stared at the floor. Mr. Thomas would do well not to boast about who he took up and down that night. Bein' stubborn was only gonna make his row harder to hoe. If he kept this up, he'd keep gettin' called back here. It was clear this many times in, they wanted to hear what they already told the papers: that Mr. Thomas *had* taken Mr. Marshall down after all. How come she knew this and he didn't when he must be more'n twice her age anyhow?

She tried to catch his eye, so that she could shake her head, to tell him, "No! Stay quiet!" But he avoided her gaze.

June began to fuss and she tried to shush him, but the fuss became a wail.

The policeman gave her a look.

She stood. "I'll just take him out," she said apologetically, and half ran to the hall as the wails became shrieks. "Shhh, buddy, shhh, it's all right," she crooned in his ear.

"Billie!" The surprise in the voice and the voice itself stopped her cold.

She spun around and there he was. "Mr. Marshall!"

It didn't seem right to see him here at the police station. It'd been just eleven days since he'd come to call, arms full of gifts. It embarrassed her to see him powerless now.

He looked at her sadly. "Oh, Billie, why didn't you tell me? We all could've been spared this terrible thing."

She knew that he meant tell him the truth about Miss Dottie. And the reminder of her deceit, when he'd only ever been kind to her and June, made her feel sick. Then she took his meaning and it just about knocked the breath out of her. *Was that true?* Could she have prevented this? "I . . . I'm so sorry," she finally managed to choke out. "I wish—*I wish with all my heart*—things had been different." And Lord almighty, did she ever. She wished Miss Dottie had been different, that that low-down, no-good Albert Guimares had never come 'round, that Miss Dottie had listened to her and stayed away from the gigolo, that Mr. Marshall had kept his word to divorce his wife and take her and Miss Dottie to Paris so he could marry her after all.

"Sir." One of the four men with him, his lawyers, she assumed, cleared his throat. "It's time we went in."

Mr. Marshall nodded and turned back to her. "How will you get home?"

She tried to speak around the lump in her throat. "The—the subway, sir."

He reached for his pocket, a gesture so familiar it fresh broke her heart. "Take a cab," he said gently.

She felt the stares of the other men, with their judgment and assumptions of who she was and who Miss Dottie'd been. Well, she'd show them! She lifted her chin, held June tighter. "Thank you kindly, but we just fine."

He withdrew a few crisp twenties, folded them, tucked them between her gloved hand and June's back. "Get home safely," he said, "please, with the baby."

Tears sprang and she blinked them away. The words "thank you" stuck in her throat. She didn't have the heart to tell him this would be grocery money, not taxi money.

"There he is!" a voice yelled, and the lawyers bustled Mr. Marshall away as a herd of newspapermen stampeded down the hall.

Ella shoved the money in her pocket and headed miserably back to the waiting room, the questions heavy on her heart: *Could* they all have been spared? *Would* Miss Dottie still be alive? If only . . . if only she'd told?

Chapter 32

March 26, 4:35 p.m. Manhattan. Criminal Courts Building.

ARREST NEAR. John Kearsley Mitchell, the millionaire Philadelphian who used part of his fortune to drape the shapely form of Dot King with furs and jewels and silken gowns . . .

Julia was grateful her story had captured a front-page spot and pleased with her turn of phrase. But now nobody could find the millionaire in question. Reporters were camped outside his Manhattan bachelor pad, all his lawyers' homes and offices, and the Ritz, in case he returned to the luxe hotel where he'd placed the calls that had later been traced back to him and unraveled his true identity, but the man seemed to have vanished.

She turned to Hellinger. "Where on earth do you suppose Mitchell's hiding?"

Hellinger snorted. "Hiding? Try *hunting* for new toes to kiss. The guy's got needs, Harpman. He can't go toeless for long."

Julia smothered her laughter, even as she shook her head. Who could've anticipated a depraved toe-kisser would enter in the case? She turned back to the list of homes the Stotesbury family had in Philadelphia. Frances Stotesbury Mitchell, her children, her father and stepmother, and a small fleet of servants were making their way up the East Coast in her father's private train car. When they arrived in Philadelphia, they'd have to go somewhere, and the *News*, along with every other major paper, had men camped out at every single one of their mansions for the chance of a photo, a question, a glimpse of the famous family. Julia tapped her pencil and considered her next move.

"Well, if it isn't Mr. Harpman!" Hellinger joked.

Julia twisted around as Westbrook, handsome as ever, strolled into the pressroom.

"Hello, all!" Westbrook said, beaming his magazine-perfect smile around the room.

Julia schooled herself to be studiously casual. "Hello."

A chorus of "Aww, lovebirds! Ain't they cute!" sounded around the room and Julia flushed.

"Whatcha doing here, Pegler? Is there a boxing match we don't know about?" George from the *Brooklyn Daily Eagle* joked.

"Yeah, slow day for sports, Peg?" Hellinger teased.

"You didn't hear?" Westbrook asked without missing a beat. "Pecora's gonna referee a fight to the death between Goldsmith and Olcott. Says it's the only way to settle this mess."

Amid the laughter, Westbrook made his way across the room, carefully far from her. They had a purely professional policy at work. It was a far cry from home, where she never passed him without an embrace, and he never missed a chance to say he loved her.

"Anyone see this?" he asked, holding up a copy of the *Tribune*. Their colleague, who covered crime for the paper, was not there yet. Necks craned to get a glimpse. "You only brought *one?*" George asked. "We supposed to share?"

"I suppose I should've wasted more of my sugar getting everyone a copy?" Westbrook retorted.

"Nah, that'd mean less flowers and chocolates for Harpman," Hellinger said. "We wouldn't want that, would we, boys?"

Westbrook cleared his throat and gave the paper a vigorous, wholly unnecessary shake.

"*Anyway*, it says Major Draper Daugherty, only son of Attorney General Harry Daugherty, is yet another 'friend' of Dot King's. And—*get this*—he's *also* being blackmailed for it."

A shocked silence fell over the group.

Westbrook began reading. "Draper said, 'I was a friend of Dot King. I knew her well and I liked her. I have been a guest in her apartment, but I had no intimate association with her.'"

Julia refrained—*barely*—from uttering a disbelieving and distinctly unladylike snort. Others were not as successful.

Westbrook continued, "If the blackmailers had sought to hold me up or extort money from me, as they probably intended to extort money from Mr. Mitchell, I'd have filled them full of lead."

Hoots echoed around the room: "Tough guy, eh?" and "Go get 'em, Draper!" "Pump 'em full of lead!"

"Fellas, please!" Julia interjected. "I wanna hear this! *Another* blackmail victim? What are the odds?"

Westbrook continued. "Draper is quoted as saying, 'I'm willing to go to the authorities and tell everything I know about poor Dot King—a girl who was more sinned against than sinning,' that he knew her for more than a year, but they were never more than friends—"

"Yeah right, and if you believe that one, I got a nice bridge I'd like to sell ya over in Brooklyn," Hellinger said.

"Also very odd he's quoting *King Lear*," Julia said. The entire thing—from his involvement with the world's most famous murder victim, to his bluster and bravado—teetered precariously between preposterous and hilarious.

Westbrook continued, "He says he got a call last Thursday from someone threatening to blackmail him about his relationship with Miss King. Get this, fellas—his reply? 'Well, I'm Harry Daugherty's son. I haven't any more quit in me than he has. Distasteful as this whole situation is to me, I'll face the music.'"

"And yet, they shared *no intimate association*," Julia said.

"Indeed," Westbrook said, raising a skeptical brow. "He claims he gave Miss King a check last year for a purchase, insured her two automobiles, and employed her younger brother as a collector in his insurance business—all at her request, of course."

"Quite the *friend*," Julia deadpanned.

Westbrook raised his brows. "The best part is that Daugherty claims he told the blackmailer, 'Why, you dirty little dog; come here to see me, and I'll break you in two.'"

Julia rolled her eyes at the male braggadocio. Was it possible Draper Daugherty was a blackmail victim? And did he truly intend to fight his blackmailer? Or was the grandstanding an attempt to garner public favor? The men in the room did not seem to notice. Applause and laughter punctuated the news, followed by volleying opinions. "Aw, come on! I ain't buying it! This is the stuff of cheap detective novels."

"He's a war hero! He wouldn't make this up."

"Oh, wouldn't he? Like father, like son."

"Well, we all know the *Tribune* might."

"Watch it, pal!"

Westbrook refolded the paper. "Who'd have thought someone more famous than the Stotesburys would be wrapped up in this case? Guess I picked a good day to work the crime beat."

"You always did have all the luck," the guy from the *Times* said.

Westbrook's gaze rested appreciatively on Julia. "I certainly do."

She smiled, bashful, besotted. For a moment, it was just the two of them and nothing else mattered.

"Aw, jeez. I'm gonna be sick," Hellinger said, breaking the spell.

"Yeah, good thing you don't write that slop for the sports column," George teased.

Julia stood. "Anyway, I don't know about the rest of you, but I'm getting to work."

In the ensuing commotion of the other guys diving into their stories, reaching for phones, grabbing their hats, and heading out to chase various angles on the breaking story, Westbrook casually edged closer—just two colleagues, chatting at work. "So what do you suppose gives?"

"Yeah, something's fishy, all right. That 'interview' couldn't have felt more staged," Julia said, glancing around to make sure nobody was monitoring them. She was proud to be Westbrook's wife and was happy to take ribbing for it, but she'd spent her whole career struggling to be taken seriously, and there was no need to provide extra grist for the mill. "But even the *Tribune* wouldn't be foolish enough to take aim at the attorney general's son and put themselves at risk of a libel suit if it wasn't true."

"It just doesn't add up," Westbrook agreed, keeping a respectable distance, doing his part to keep everything aboveboard. "And the strangest thing is, it seems Draper's gone missing. He checked out of the Elks Club this morning. And the word on the street is he's gone to Atlantic City."

Julia frowned. "The same place Dot King went twice the week before she was killed? Surely *nobody* likes the Jersey shore in March that much."

Westbrook shrugged. "Allegedly, he stepped forward so as to destroy the blackmailer's plot to extort him. Says outing himself was the only way to ruin the plan."

"But why disappear then? And why Atlantic City?" she asked.

"Exactly," Westbrook said. "Heading out?"

"Sure." She grabbed her coat, purse, and notebook, and they headed down the stairs side by side. "If Draper Daugherty truly stepped forward voluntarily, so be it. But the attorney general must be fuming, having just announced Harding will run again. Draper's involvement is a major embarrassment and distraction to the campaign."

"Maybe Draper's tired of living in his father's shadow?" Peg offered. "His first wife *was* a Gibson Girl, and his current wife is a senator's daughter."

"I don't know," Julia said. "But I just can't shake the feeling that something's really wrong."

Chapter 33

Frances stared dismally at the Oriental carpet on her father's train car. They were bound for Washington, DC, where Jack planned to join them. Then they'd continue on to Philadelphia. Jack's lawyer felt it presented a united front to arrive home together. Her father had agreed. Nobody had asked what she thought.

She'd been hiding in the guest bedroom to avoid small talk with her father and Eva in the sitting room. The children were with the governess down the hall. The luxuriously appointed car was comfortable as always, but it felt like a gilded prison, and she, a prisoner, being taken to her execution. They ought to be at El Mirasol preparing to host the president and his cabinet. But instead, she was now grudgingly headed home to see her husband, ostensibly a philanderer, who was also being investigated for murder.

It was shocking. *Unimaginable.*

And yet, an ember of hope still glimmered it wasn't true. She hadn't been able to speak to Jack. Meanwhile, the story had swelled unimaginably after the revelation that Jack was Mr. Marshall. Rumor had it phone operators were being offered a year's salary in exchange for anything they overheard—*or claimed to overhear*—on phone lines. And so, with Jack 1,500 miles away, the most she could do was stiffly exchange messages about travel arrangements with his lawyer.

She tried—ineffectually—to swallow the sharp lump in her throat as they chugged steadily closer to Washington. She tried to imagine seeing Jack, two weeks and another life since he'd been with them in Palm Beach, and the sudden, hysterical urge struck to run out to the observation deck, under the fluttering red awning, and hurl herself off.

She did not want to be here or deal with any of this—not with the gaggles of reporters and busybodies clustered at every station, peering in the windows, shouting offensive questions; not with her friends and their pity; and not even with Jack himself. She was being asked to shove down the embarrassment, shock, and betrayal; hold her head high; and present a united front.

"United front" indeed. She wanted to kill him, just like he'd probably killed that filthy girl.

The thought stopped her cold. It hadn't actually occurred to her as a real possibility: *Jack* might've *killed the girl.*

What if, instead of only being married to a philandering louse, she was actually married to a *murderer*? Frances froze, unable to breathe.

"Ready, dear?"

Frances startled, turning to find Eva in the doorway. "You scared me to death!" she exclaimed. Guilt made her voice sharp.

Eva looked at her with a kindly pity. "We're nearing Washington."

Frances wanted to say no, she was not ready. That she'd never be ready. That no woman was ever ready to face a husband who'd stepped out on her, but at least most women didn't have to make a show of it in a train station in front of a horde of reporters and gawkers.

She wanted to curl into a very small ball on the train floor and cry. She wished her mother were there to hold her. She felt exhausted and weak.

But she couldn't say or do any of that. She was a lady. She was a mother herself. She was a pillar of Philadelphia society and the Palm Beach Colony, a Stotesbury daughter and a Mitchell wife, though now more so than ever, she wished to be purely a Stotesbury. If only the title of Mrs. John Kearsley Mitchell could be amputated like the gangrenous appendage Jack had made it.

She suddenly wished that when her father had suggested it was time to marry nearly fourteen years ago, and that Jack Mitchell, newly widowed, would make a most suitable match, she'd simply said no. How different life would be now.

It had never occurred to her to simply remain a Stotesbury—a spinster, enjoying her glorious solitude, wholly in control of her destiny. It had always seemed a woman's highest pinnacle of success and happiness was to marry well and raise a family. Spinsters were to be pitied.

But spinsters were unencumbered by foolish husbands who dragged them into the fiery clutches of hell. Frances closed her eyes and wished briefly but with all her heart that it was she who was dead.

"Franny?" Eva asked again.

"I'm ready," Frances said simply, blinking back tears. She'd cried so much that even tears hurt now. She was shocked there were any left.

"We'll be by your side every step of the way," Eva promised. "Your family, your friends, the clubs, your father and I. We'll take care of this . . . ridiculous misunderstanding."

Frances nodded, grateful for Eva's kindness, though in the face of the news, it was also starting to seem like willful ignorance.

She trailed after Eva to the Lynnewood's sitting room. A servant huddled nervously in the hall.

"Draw the curtains," Eva ordered. "We don't need strangers peering in." The servant leaped to do so.

The rest of the staff would be in their quarters beyond the dining room and kitchen at the other end of the car. Frances perched on a green velvet chair and prayed for a stay of execution. For a miracle. For the train to run out of steam. For a tree to fall across the tracks. For this to be a dream and, for the love of God and all that was holy, that she'd wake up back in the little gray cottage by the beach.

But even with curtains drawn, Frances knew exactly when the train pulled into the cavernous station, the bright sunlight slanting under the curtains extinguished.

"Right," her father said, ever calm. "Not a word in front of the press. This is a family matter." When Frances nodded, he continued. "I'll go out first. I'll shake his hand. Then you take his arm, we'll reboard, then we'll divert the press from there."

Eva nodded encouragingly. Frances barely heard him. All she could think about was seeing Jack. She both wanted, and was terrified, to see him. But why—*why*—must they meet in public?

There was a last blast of steam from under the car, a tremor under her feet, then a tap at the door, guarded by her father's detectives and several burly porters.

Her father rose. "Let's go."

Frances took a deep breath—or at least as deep as her corset, cinched tighter than on her wedding day in some humiliating attempt to look slender and graceful for both Jack and the press, would allow—and somehow, she made her legs move. Her father—never one for affection—squeezed her arm, nodded grimly, and stepped out.

There was an explosion of camera flashes and a din of questions. About thirty yards away, a sea of reporters—at least fifty in all—surged forward. Policemen blew whistles and shoved them back.

Her father moved forward with the determination of a tugboat heading out to sea: small but unrelenting.

She looked beyond him. And there was Jack. Standing alone. Looking stoic. Regretful. Embarrassed.

And she suddenly knew, with fresh certainty, that he'd cheated on her. Until this moment, in some small, secret corner of her heart, she'd held out real hope that Eva was right: this really *was* a terrible misunderstanding. But it was all there, written on his face: her sweet Jack, her best chum, had been carrying on with that filthy Broadway girl.

Something within her fractured in a way that would never fully heal.

Her mind raced. *My God*—if Jack was capable of that once-unthinkable thing, was he also capable of *murder*?

Amid the din, in front of everyone, her father and Jack shook hands. She could tell from the tense set of her father's shoulders that he wore a stern, indomitable expression.

Every inch of her screamed to turn and run, but she forced herself to disregard that primal instinct and instead follow social protocol. She saw herself move, as though watching a film.

She extended her hand, limp and lifeless, and at Jack's foppish look of gratitude, pure, razor-edged rage sliced through her. In that moment, she hated him with a force the magnitude of which she hadn't known herself capable.

He took her hand, and she longed to retract it and slap him across the face—to hear the satisfying crack, to see the resulting red mark. Instead, she allowed him to tuck it under his elbow and automatically hunched to make herself smaller. He fell into step beside her, the way that couples do.

That he'd betrayed that familiarity was an additional wound. But there wasn't time to digest that. They were moving back toward the train car together. She suddenly understood he'd engineered this for the press. He was the contrite husband, she the dignified, forgiving wife. Together, they were a stoic front. The height of dignity and decorum. Of all that was right and good in their world. These rules felt far more oppressive and constricting than the laces of any corset. She felt foolish now—as though a minimally smaller waist meant or changed anything. Jack probably hadn't even noticed. She hated him and she hated herself.

Burly detectives bustled them back onto the train. Eva's eager smile wilted when she saw them. Frances looked away, bit her lip, and failed to hold back tears. Outside, the reporters waited like a swarm of bees.

One of the detectives, who looked to be made more of steel than muscle, cleared his throat. "Sir, we've got to move quickly." He addressed only her father.

Her father nodded. "Franny, these men will keep you safe."

"But—" she began.

The detective towered over her, a pistol holstered to his hip. Without a word, he took her elbow and propelled her back off the train. The children and governess trailed behind.

"Is Daddy coming?" Little Franny asked.

Frances had no answer. Her father and Jack had not included her in the plan. A cold detachment bled into fury at the realization.

Reporters shouted a deluge of questions from behind the police line. The detective plowed them forward toward another train, this one an ordinary Pullman. On board, Frances blinked, looked around. It was clean and serviceable enough. The detective pointed toward a sofa and she sat. Emily, the governess, and the children followed suit. The other detectives fanned out to search for stowaway pressmen.

She stared out the window, disembodied. A private train car pulled alongside them. "SCHWAB" was painted in giant, ornate gold lettering. Her father's friend was here? Before she could ask, Jack and her father boarded Schwab's car, and a moment later, the trains chugged out of the station.

Chapter 34

Julia winced at every detail coming in about Frances Stotesbury Mitchell's journey home. The curious combination of agonizing heartbreak and compelling voyeurism was the singular life of a reporter on the crime beat. As a newlywed—married seven months tomorrow, and still in the heart-fluttering phase of counting each month—it was unbearable to watch a woman suffer such betrayal, let alone betrayal bandied about on the front page of every newspaper in the country. But as a reporter covering the murder of J. K. Mitchell's mistress, Julia had a job to do. If the *News* didn't cover the nation's most scandalous story, they wouldn't sell copies and she would have to answer for it. She also recognized newspaper gold when she saw it.

Next to her, Hellinger grabbed his phone. "Another thrilling day of detailing Harding's golf and lunch schedule."

Julia reread the latest telegram. "You know, the one thing I'm stuck on is why Marshall—I mean, *Mitchell*—went down to Washington to meet his wife."

Hellinger clicked the lever for the operator, then turned back to Julia as he waited to be connected. "Whaddya mean?"

"Mitchell left their home in Philadelphia to go down to Washington and meet his wife's train, only to head straight back to Philadelphia.

And he's not even traveling with Frances—he's on another train with his father-in-law."

"So?" Hellinger said.

"Well, why didn't he just wait for them at home? Or if he was looking for neutral territory, her dad's castle, 'the Versailles of America'? He could've spared them all the drama of a public meeting in Union Station."

Hellinger rolled his eyes. "You kiddin' me? The guy was just caught havin' an affair with a blonde half his age who turns up dead, his toe perversions are publicly revealed, the world is laughing at him and feels bad for his wife. And you think he doesn't want to show E. T. Stotesbury what a good guy he is? If your father-in-law just so happens to be one of the richest and most powerful men in the *world*, you go the extra mile—*literally*. Not exactly a head-scratcher."

"The extra mile isn't Washington," Julia said. "If Mitchell really wanted to make a good-faith showing, he would've gone all the way down to Palm Beach."

"It's never enough for you dames," Hellinger said. "A guy goes to Washington for ya, but no, *you* want him to go to *Florida*."

Julia rolled her eyes. "Yeah, all us dames are exactly the same—me, Frances Stotesbury Mitchell, Dot King—three peas in a pod."

"You ain't a dame, you're a newspaperman," Hellinger said, chomping a toothpick.

Julia wasn't sure if she was flattered or offended. "I'm telling you, it feels wrong."

Hellinger, still waiting to be connected, ignored her. "Geez, you'd think I was phonin' the moon over here."

Julia decided to make a few calls herself. She grabbed her phone and asked the operator for Frederick Goldsmith's law office. As she waited to be connected to Guimares's lawyer, she flipped to a new page and scribbled:

Mitchell: Why DC?

The line clicked and an operator purred, "Mr. Goldsmith for you. Go ahead, please."

"Good afternoon," Julia began, pen poised over paper. "I'm calling to see if Albert Guimares would like to comment on the alleged blackmail plots against J. K. Mitchell and Draper Daugherty?"

"My client doesn't know anything about that," the answer came, immediate and defensive.

"Well, Pecora claims he's received secret information about a scheme that was in the works and that's why he called Mitchell back for further questioning. Given that your client was already leaching off Mitchell through Miss King—" Julia pointed out.

"Guimares is absolutely innocent," Goldsmith interrupted. "He's not a blackmailer or a thief. And he lavished just as much jewelry and money on Dot King as Mitchell did."

"Oh, come on," Julia said. "The Stotesbury-Mitchell fortune is one of the biggest in the world."

Goldsmith cut in. "Guimares liked good times just as much as Mitchell, and he paid just as much for them."

Julia couldn't even summon a response. Why was Guimares's lawyer so focused on spending? There was no way on God's green earth that Albert Guimares, twenty-seven-year-old gigolo, could compete with a millionaire, but clearly his lawyer wasn't budging on his strategy. She decided to change tack. "Pecora and Coughlin say Guimares has been missing since being discharged from jail. Coughlin has detailed detectives to try to locate him and thus far hasn't been able to. Do you know where your client is?"

"Guimares doesn't like these insinuations by Mr. Pecora—these veiled threats and dark thrusts," Goldsmith said heatedly. "*And as far as Mr. Coughlin is concerned*, he doesn't have to send out detectives for Guimares—I'll produce him on a telephone call. And by the way, my client was in my office for five hours today, and there was no sign of any police looking for him."

Julia straightened. "So Guimares was with you today?"

"He was. Listen, Pecora and Coughlin are barking up the wrong tree. Ask yourself why they aren't looking more at Mitchell. I don't like how they're throwing up a smoke screen to protect that guy. Mitchell may not be a New York resident, but he can still be placed under bond and made to appear as a material witness and potential suspect. So why hasn't he, huh?"

Julia could guess why. She could also guess why Goldsmith was complaining about it. Goldsmith, after all, had a very real vested interest. "Pecora says Mitchell's given his word to appear—" she began.

Goldsmith cut her off. "A DA has no right to take *the word* of a material witness or his attorney that he'll show up. Once a witness is out of New York, he can't be subpoenaed. And I don't need to remind you that there's *only one law*—not one for the rich and another for those less fortunate. My client today is practically destitute, except for the fur coat about which there has been so much talk—and he couldn't hock that for thirty bucks."

Julia arched a brow. "A minute ago you claimed he spent as much as Mitchell on gifts for Dot King. Now he's *destitute*?"

"You're missing the point," Goldsmith snapped.

"Perhaps that's not the point you want me to focus on, but it *is* an important one," Julia shot back. "I don't work for you. My job isn't to curry public favor for your client."

"Listen, let's talk about what really matters here . . . to your readers and justice," Goldsmith said, softening his voice. "If Coughlin and Pecora truly believe my client's guilty of blackmail or murder, they shouldn't allow him to roam the streets of New York without being arrested. But they don't arrest him, do they? They just keep issuing veiled threats to distract from the fact they're holding pink teas for Mitchell. How come I'm not a guest at some of these functions?"

"I wouldn't know," Julia said. But she suddenly *did*. Having grown up Jewish in Memphis, Julia understood all too well: a Jewish criminal defense lawyer and his Puerto Rican client yearned to be part of spaces that didn't want them. Some things never changed.

"Dig deeper," the lawyer said, and hung up.

Julia added the conversation to her notes and considered her next move. The last three people confirmed to have seen Dot King alive were Ella Bradford, John Kearsley Mitchell, and Mitchell's personal attorney and companion, John Jackson . . . plus, of course, the killer. *If the killer wasn't Mitchell.*

Julia flipped through her notes and potential sources. Hilda Ferguson had provided valuable clues the first time they met. Could she reveal something even more valuable now?

Chapter 35

During the day, Broadway was just a busy street. But at night, the electric streetlights, marquees, and billboards combined to create an incandescence surely visible from the moon, thus earning Broadway its moniker, "the Great White Way."

As the lights sparkled against the gathering dusk, Julia emerged from the Times Square subway station, where just days ago, the craziest car chase of her career had culminated in J. K. Mitchell, then still masquerading as Mr. Marshall, escaping. Now she hurried up Broadway, past Frederick Goldsmith's law office, and down 45th Street. She passed the Morosco and the Lyceum before reaching the Music Box Theatre. Built four years ago specifically for Irving Berlin's Music Box Revue, this was where Hilda Ferguson hula-shimmied every night.

Julia walked past the golden front doors and entered the small, unassuming stage door instead. Some theaters had their stage entrance in the back, where the alleys stank of rotting fruit, stale urine, and stagnant water. It was a small blessing to avoid that today.

If Draper Daugherty was to be believed, the AG's son hadn't been intimately involved with Dot King. Yes, he'd covered her bills. Yes, he'd arranged insuring her cars. Yes, he'd visited her so-called love nest on West 57th. *But they were still just friends*—an assertion that had the entire city sharing a collective eye roll.

After the man about town had finally found time in his busy social calendar to show up for a chat with the authorities, their official story had changed: Draper Daugherty had never met—*indeed wasn't even aware of the existence of*—Mitchell or Guimares. Which then begged the question: Who in Dot King's life had known of *Draper's* existence?

Inside the theater, a stagehand in a pageboy hat whistled as he untangled ropes. He glanced up and nodded at her, then returned to the task at hand.

"Dressing room?" she asked.

Without missing a note, he jerked his thumb toward a set of stairs.

Julia wound her way into the bowels of the theater until she reached a door marked CHORUS. Inside, the bare-bones communal space was jammed with girls jockeying for the mirror.

Julia dug in her bag for her notebook. "Anybody seen Hilda?"

"Down the back," a blonde replied, vigorously massaging red blotches of rouge into her cheeks.

"Thanks," Julia said, catching a glimpse of her own reflection. She looked starkly plain in contrast; her face, bare; her hair, as always, a pouf of riotous, unruly curls; and her skirt and blouse modest under her trench coat.

"Present yourself seriously and you'll be taken seriously," her mother had always said. "A painted face cannot distract from a muddled mind. We were born to be writers, not show ponies."

Down the end, as alone as one could be in the commotion, Hilda sat hunched. She puffed sullenly on a cigarette, the cloud of smoke a melancholy outcry.

"Hilda?" Julia said.

Hilda twisted toward her, and Julia couldn't help but notice her costume—or what there was of it. Her breasts were barely concealed under two sequined cups, the wispy skirt more of a suggestion. She looked up at Julia in a mix of suspicion, resentment, and exhaustion. "You again," she stated gracelessly, taking another puff off the stump of her cigarette. Her nails, still painted a screaming red, were filed into pointed daggers.

"I have a few more questions about Dottie, if that's all right," Julia said, intentionally using the murder victim's most familiar nickname in an attempt to align herself with the showgirl. "Draper Daugherty went to see the DA today. Do you know him?"

"D'you have any ciggies?" Hilda asked, stamping hers out in a nearby ceramic dish.

Julia reached in her handbag and held out the case. Hilda took her time removing one and lighting it. She shook the match out and tossed it, uncaring or perhaps unaware when it missed the ashtray.

"Dottie had a platinum case with the letter *K* set in rose diamonds from Mr. Marshall," Hilda said absentmindedly. "It was beautiful."

Julia's fingers almost twitched with the effort of not reaching out and placing the extinguished match in the ashtray, where it belonged. She replaced her own modest case in her bag. "Yes, well, a reporter's salary doesn't yet allow for platinum cases and rose diamonds."

"That's too bad," Hilda said, blowing twin plumes of smoke from her nostrils. "Anyway, sure, I met Draper a few times. He's a nice enough fella. Used to call on Dottie to discuss business."

"What sort of business?" Julia asked.

Hilda shrugged in a way that might've meant she didn't know or didn't care.

Julia touched Hilda's arm. The contrast of Julia's fingertips, hidden under navy-blue gloves, not terribly expensive but well made, and Hilda's fair skin was stark. "The one we discussed before? With her landlord? Did she introduce Draper to Arnold Rothstein?" Julia asked, lowering her voice.

Hilda shook her head. "You got it all wrong. Draper Daugherty introduced *her* to Rothstein."

Julia froze. "What?"

"Yeah. Dottie met Draper at the World Series in '21. Like every other fella with a pulse, he was charmed. Started hangin' around. Then when Marshall gave her those cars—the roadster and the other one—she asked Draper to take care of insuring them for her."

Julia shook her head. Nothing made sense. "But what's that got to do with Arnold Rothstein?" she asked.

Hilda rolled her eyes. "It was *Rothstein's* insurance company. Draper just ran the thing for him."

Whatever Julia had expected to hear, it wasn't that. *"Are you sure?"*

Hilda took an indifferent drag on her cigarette. "Sure I'm sure. Draper counted Rothstein as his best friend in New York. Apparently used to sit up with him all night at Lindy's till Harding won and his pops put a stop to it. But Rothstein still owns that insurance business, Draper's still involved, *and*"—Hilda gave a half smile—"Dottie got Draper to give her brother a job, as a collector, for Rothstein."

Each strange tidbit sifted into Julia's brain like puzzle pieces: Arnold Rothstein, New York's most notorious gangster, drug kingpin, and bootlegger, owned an *insurance company*? Where he employed Draper Daugherty, only son of the US attorney general? Draper was *friends* with Dot King? So she got her brother a job as a collector for the drug kingpin / insurance man?

The world couldn't possibly be so small and interconnected . . . could it?

If this was true, it not only connected New York's drug and bootlegging kingpin, Rothstein, to Dot King again, it connected them all directly to the White House. Corruption was always dangerous. But when corruption went all the way to the seat of power in politics, it could be deadly.

Julia looked around, as though they were being watched, and wondered if Inspector Coughlin had also managed to unearth this information. Was he hiding it from the press? Or was it still hidden from him?

"Five minutes, girls!" a man yelled from the door. A frenzied scramble of last-minute preparations ensued: lipstick swiped on, powder dabbed on noses, cigarettes frantically puffed and stubbed out, buttons fastened, headdresses straightened, shoes laced up.

Hilda looked nervously around them. "I've already said too much. Now stop poking around and don't come back here. You're gonna get us both killed." In a flurry of feathers and sequins, she merged with the scantily costumed showgirls streaming out of the room and was gone.

Julia hurried out of the theater. She would hold the Rothstein-Daugherty accusation for now. Blowing the lid off a story like that required concrete investigative proof. But it was clear this was no longer simply an unsolved murder of a scandalous flapper: it was the revelation of a web of power and corruption stretching between politics, society, and the underworld. If the attorney general's son was involved, it would affect the presidential election. As she stepped out into the night, under the lights of Broadway, Julia realized this might very well be the biggest story of her career.

Chapter 36

Frances stood at the window of the Adams guest room. How very strange to be an adult living with one's father. Though it wasn't so much living as hiding.

Of Whitemarsh's 147 rooms, Eva always put married guests in the much-larger Portico guest room, where they could enjoy views of the perfectly manicured promenade unfurling like a lush emerald-green carpet toward the front gate two miles away. Whitemarsh was renowned for its grounds, adorned with statuary and fountains, cared for by a staff of seventy gardeners.

The views usually gave Frances a pleasing sense of calm. But with "the events," as she'd come to think of them, the gates were now guarded by a fleet of detectives and state policemen, and it seemed the Portico's two beds mocked her. So Frances had chosen the smaller Adams room at the back of the house.

She trailed her fingertips along the delicate desk that Eva had had custom-made for this room. It was stocked with the usual thoughtful touches—note cards, breakfast menu cards, chauffeur cards, departure-transportation cards, and a sheaf of stationery engraved with "Adams Guest Room, Whitemarsh Hall" so guests might keep up with their correspondence. Each color-coordinated with the room's decor. Every morning, Frances's breakfast tray arrived—though she still could tolerate only toast—with a flower from the gardens, also color-coordinated.

This was the sort of meticulous care that had earned Eva a reputation as one of society's best hostesses. It should have made Frances feel cared for. Instead, it made her feel weary.

She wandered past the reading chair upholstered in matching brushed silk, past two little tables—one holding a geisha lamp, the other a book Eva had personally selected from her renowned library with a note that she hoped Frances might enjoy it—and sank onto the elaborately carved sleigh bed.

The only things Frances read now were newspapers. Emily fetched them each day—the *Philadelphia Inquirer*, the *New York Times*, and the *New York Daily News*, which seemed intent on vigorously earning its slogan as the "picture paper," and she devoured them all. Every salacious, horrifying detail was nauseating, but she couldn't stop the punishing practice.

The need to examine every single photograph of Jack's whore possessed her. Who was this woman who wielded the beauty and charm to lure her husband away? Frances was simultaneously fascinated and repulsed by every vulgar, tawdry detail, from the girl's bleached, bobbed hair to her painted, bow-shaped lips.

As she came to know the faces and stories of this girl and her family—an unseemly bunch—her breath grew short and her stomach bilious. And yet, Frances read on, inhaling fact and rumor with equal voracity. *In fact*, her husband was not faithful. *In fact*, her family was roasting on the spit of public scandal. *In fact*, Jack *was* the last-known person to see his mistress alive. He may, *in fact*, have killed her. *In fact*, she, Frances, could now be married to a murderer. *In fact*, they were hovering on social ruin.

The *truth* was: Jack had dealt a heartless blow to the bull's-eye of their lives. From there, fissures had spidered across her existence, shattering every illusion she'd counted as fact and truth.

Frances grasped the back of the chair and closed her eyes, forcing the nausea down.

Today, a most unflattering photo of her was plastered across the top of page 3 next to a photograph of Jack and that tramp, part of a trio she'd sooner die than be in. The caption was even worse:

> Philandering by middle-aged married men, who have scorned the love of their unattractive wives for beautiful young women, has twice in the past six months been followed by tragedy for the "other woman."

Below that, a brief, tantalizing synopsis of the case and the byline "Julia Harpman," followed by a lengthy article with the latest details of the case. One would hope a woman would possess better ethics. But this Miss Harpman was capitalizing on their family's humiliation, as though it were a tawdry novel.

> John Kearsley Mitchell, the millionaire Philadelphian who used part of his fortune to drape the shapely form of Dot King with furs and jewels and silken gowns . . .

Frances viciously tore the paper and hurled it, but it merely drifted to the floor. She fell back on the bed, her mind like a phonograph player going round and round: Why had Jack strayed? Had he really intended to run away to Paris to seek a divorce?

Then the even more incomprehensible thought: Had Jack harmed the girl? The idea of round-faced, cheery Jack asphyxiating anyone was impossible. Then again, five days ago, she would've sworn Jack wasn't even capable of stepping out on her.

The headlines were a daily reminder that the previously unimaginable was now her reality.

There was the gentlest tap at the door. "Your father is waiting," Eva said.

Reluctantly, Frances rose and followed her stepmother into the Gallery Hall. She made to ring for the east elevator, but Eva touched her elbow with a small smile. "Let's walk to the west."

Frances didn't have the strength to question or refuse. She obediently trailed along down the hall, past the grand staircase, past the other guest suites—descriptively named Blue, Apricot, Lacquer, and Portico—until they finally reached the west elevator, which took them to the first floor. Eva led the way through the west rotunda and into her father's sitting room.

Her father, dressed as always in a three-piece suit, nodded slightly. It was the silent communication of the well-married couple. Eva moved to take her place in the chair flanking his desk. They, at least, were a united front. Frances felt more like a target than part of a team.

Her father held a sheaf of typed pages. Frances did her best to read the upside-down top sheet—surely it had to be about this—but could only tell that it looked to be some sort of report. Her father put the pages in a folder and brought his gaze to rest on her. "Frances," he began, "this has been an unfortunate turn of events, but it's being handled."

"Handled?" Frances echoed. "Everyone's reading every sordid detail in the papers! Who will ever receive us? We're ruined!"

"You mustn't be histrionic," her father said, shooting a startled, concerned glance at Eva. "This unfortunate incident will pass."

"It'll never pass," Frances said, daring to oppose him in her bitterness and anger.

"You'll go to Europe," Eva suggested, and both the way she said it and the timing told Frances this had already been spoken about and agreed upon.

"Europe?" Frances echoed, trying to take it all in.

Eva smiled a small, calm smile that was probably meant to be encouraging. "Yes, as soon as the incident is closed, you'll go to Europe for the season, or perhaps for a lovely sail down the Nile. You, Jack, and the children. And when you return, this will all have blown over. Some other scandal will consume everyone's attention."

"But—" Frances looked between them, their calm, set expressions, the already-decided, plans-underway manner. Had she tumbled down the rabbit hole and landed in Wonderland?

Her father tapped the stack of papers. "Jack has met with our friends in Washington, and I've retained a fleet of private detectives to learn everything we can. I've also placed a few calls to the appropriate channels to express my enthusiasm for things being wrapped up expeditiously."

"But—" Frances began again.

"When you're back from Europe, we'll give little Franny a dance here at Whitemarsh," Eva said. "Just a little something before her debut, to keep society focused on happy news."

Her father nodded. "Very good." The Nedeva, as the couple were jokingly referred to and had since named their beloved yacht, were in full swing.

"And what if your detectives discover the very worst about Jack?" Frances dared to venture.

Her father blanched. "I'm sure that won't be the case. This is *Jack* we're talking about."

Frances shook her head. "A week ago I would've bet my life on Jack's loyalty—or at least his discretion. Yet here we are with our names and pictures in every paper in the world, Jack accused of adultery and murder. So . . . what if he *is* guilty of . . . both?" She couldn't seem to make herself form the word "murder" again.

"Frances!" her father protested.

She pressed on undeterred. "Will you share your findings with the New York district attorney's office and advise them to press charges? Will you advise *me* to divorce him? Or will you expect me to keep up appearances no matter what?"

"Frances!" Her father was shocked. "How can you doubt I've always had your best interests at heart?"

She wanted to say Jack's betrayal made her doubt everyone and everything. She wanted to say she was afraid her father would put business and reputation first. But instead she said, "I'm sorry."

"Never mind." Her father wouldn't look at her. "This is all . . . very difficult. We've just got to march forward."

Frances felt herself slump, as though her spine lacked the strength to hold her up. "Fine." She didn't care anymore. She just wanted to go back to her room and sleep.

"Tomorrow you'll talk with Jack before he goes back to New York."

She felt as though he'd slapped her. "New York? Why would he go *there?*"

Her father hesitated. "He's been called back for further questions."

"Further questions," Frances echoed. This was the polite substitution for words like "subpoena" and "interrogation."

"Yes—regrettable, certainly, but we'll persevere. I'm certain everything will seem better after you talk with him tomorrow."

Frances looked back and forth between them again. "You won't be here?" she finally managed to ask her father.

"No. I've got other business to attend to," he said. "I've already called for the Lynnewood. I leave this afternoon."

She wanted to ask what "business" could possibly be so important as to warrant leaving her here to deal with this, but instead, swallowing her bitterness and growing resentment, said nothing.

He stood. "We'll talk more when I'm back."

Eva also rose. "Very good, dear."

As Eva ushered Frances back to the Adams room, she clucked, "There, there. Your father will take care of everything."

"No," Frances said, more sharply than she meant to, as she tried to extricate her arm without seeming rude. "I *cannot* go to Europe with Jack. I can't bear to see him."

"You can and you must," Eva said, closing the bedroom door behind them.

Frances finally wrested her arm free. "But *how* can I? How can I live alongside a man who kept this harlot in New York and might even be guilty of"—she lowered her voice and nearly choked on the word—"*murder*! Am I supposed to just go on? Eva, have you ever considered that my own life may very well be in danger?"

Eva trilled a small, slightly forced laugh. "Frances, dear, you're hysterical. Jack isn't a *murderer*."

"Even if he isn't a murderer, he *is* an adulterer," Frances said steadily. "This man is a liar and a cheat, and he shamed me and the children in front of our friends, society . . . the whole world!"

"This *man* of whom you speak so distantly is your *husband* and the father of your children," Eva said sternly. "And while *he* may have temporarily disregarded your marriage vows, *you* haven't. *You* can save your family, Franny."

"But how can I ever forgive him?"

Eva's face softened. "Oh, my darling girl. Women are the moral compass of society. We exert our good influences on our marriages, our children, the circles in which we move, and the communities in which we exist. Without us, the moral structure of society would disintegrate, and with that, society itself. So we forgive, even when our hearts are broken. We hold our heads up and march on when we feel as though we might die—because we're *women* and we're *wives*. It's the bravest and best thing we can do—and our worlds, and the world at large, are far better for it."

Frances summoned the will to try but found only depleted exhaustion. "I can't," she said thickly.

"You *can*," Eva said firmly. Her round face, usually so cheery, had taken on a stony determination. "I defied my father's wishes and married the son of his sworn enemy for my first marriage."

Frances blinked, as confused by the startling confession as she was by the unyielding stranger who stood before her. Did she know her stepmother at all? Who *was* this woman? "Sorry—what?"

"When I made my choice, I hadn't yet taken marriage vows. I didn't yet hold the futures of my children in my hands. You *do*. When you take on the role of wife and mother, you choose to renounce whatever individual liberty you previously enjoyed," Eva said, her voice calm, her face placid.

Frances felt herself grow heavier under the yoke of responsibilities. "I've striven to live up to my roles until Jack ruined everything."

Eva shook her head. "You still have *everything*—your social position, Jack's name, your children, your homes, your lovely life. Never mind that girl. She was nothing—just a terrible, terrible mistake."

The vague awareness that she would forever be linked to this Broadway girl, this "terrible mistake," in more ways than she cared to acknowledge, prickled. They'd shared Jack's bed, attention, and gifts—and now they shared the burdensome outcome of his choices. Her social position was wounded, and her affection for him was dead. But that girl was *actually* dead.

"You must do the very best you can—even when the cost seems too great or the pain too much," Eva added. "Your sacrifice will be your salvation, yours and your family's." She squeezed Frances's arm and was gone.

Alone, Frances's gaze fell to the *Daily News*. There, in two jagged, uneven pieces, was the photo of herself. When she'd ripped that filthy paper apart, she'd inadvertently torn herself in half.

Chapter 37

Julia drummed her fingers on the desk, trying to figure out her next move. E. T. Stotesbury's private train car had been moved from the rail yard in Philadelphia, suddenly and mysteriously, without the usual routing paperwork. Rumor placed both the train and its famous occupant in New York late last night, but without the paperwork, from which Stotesbury, as chairman of the board of the Philadelphia and Reading railroad, was exempt, it was impossible to know.

The obvious reason for Mr. Stotesbury to come to New York was to meet with Pecora—to exert pressure on the DA to close the investigation involving his son-in-law. Pecora, naturally, had gone out of his way to deny any such meeting.

Her phone rang, startling her, and she quickly reached for it. "City desk. Julia Harpman."

"Is this the girl reporter who's been covering the Dot King case?" The voice was female.

Julia reached for her notebook. "Yes, ma'am."

"My name is Louise Bybee. I live in the female artist colony on West 56th, directly behind Dot King's apartment."

It was not every day Julia got calls from female artist colonies, but the address grabbed her attention even more. "Yes?"

"I wanted to let you know that on the night of the murder, I heard a man leaving down her back stairs at 2:15 a.m. And well, I just thought you oughtta know."

Julia sat up straighter. Footsteps on the stairs at the time that John Kearsley Mitchell insisted he'd left *by elevator*. This woman's claim aligned with John Thomas's account that Mitchell must've taken the stairs—and undercut Mitchell's own testimony. But why hadn't she come forward before now?

Julia reached for a fresh sheet of paper. She would proceed cautiously. "How could you hear anything?"

"You know how it is in the city: the alley's probably only seven to ten feet across. And I . . . uh, happened to be up, and I also happened to have the window open. And I thought to myself, 'That's strange this guy's up late too.'"

"What made you think it was a male?" Julia asked, wary of whether she could trust this source.

"The footsteps were heavy and big," Miss Bybee, of the female artist colony, said. "No lady walks like that. Even if she's larger—she wouldn't have big, clunky, rubber-soled shoes like that. I'm absolutely sure it was a man and he was coming from the top floor, because that's where I live, and I heard him going all the way down."

"I see," Julia said. "And may I ask what required you to both be awake so late and have the windows open on such a cold night?"

"I'd rather not say."

Julia leaned back. "Listen, I appreciate the call, but without something more concrete, I'm afraid I can't use this."

"I'm just trying to help," Miss Bybee snapped. "I figure it could've been me so we women gotta stick together."

That same nagging awareness had weighed on Julia since she started investigating the case. Until a year ago, Julia had also lived alone. It *could've* been her. It *still* could be, given how much Westbrook traveled for sports events.

She tapped her pencil absently. "I want to help you, and I want to help solve Dot King's case—really, I do. But I need something more. Believe it or not, some people just want to see their name in the paper."

A loud, resigned sigh came over the line. "Well, I don't want to be in the paper at all. Just keep me anonymous. But if you must know, I was in the bathroom. I was doctorin' myself. My stomach was upset and I was in there *a very long time*. And well, at some point, I needed to open the window, if you know what I mean."

"I see," Julia said, biting her lip to make sure she didn't laugh. "But why haven't you told the police?"

"I did!" Miss Bybee said. "I called and told them right away, and they sent a detective over and everything. I showed him how close our buildings are and how you can hear everything with the window open. He took my statement, but they haven't done anything about it. So that's why I called *you*. I figured a woman would actually get something done."

Julia rang off. This woman, the downstairs neighbor who'd smelled chloroform, John Thomas . . . three witnesses had provided testimony that aligned about the night's events, and stood in stark contradiction to Mitchell's. Coughlin was known for his ability and commitment to uncovering information and ferreting out the truth. So the questions remained: Why were the authorities ignoring and burying these witnesses with their information? And what was she, Julia Harpman, going to do about it?

Chapter 38

March 31, 8:45 p.m. Manhattan. Criminal Courts Building.

Coughlin made his way toward Pecora's office, exhausted and resentful. It had been another long day of questioning everyone remotely associated with Dot King—an utterly useless theatrical performance Pecora had offered up in hopes of distracting the press. Anything to keep them from asking about those pesky rumors about E. T. Stotesbury's rumored trip to New York for a secret meeting with the DA and a $500,000 bribe to clog the wheels of justice. Rumors of bribes and blackmail were like wildfire—quick to spread and impossible to put out.

It had taken them two days to locate the elusive Draper Daugherty, who'd managed to leave his mistress's love nest and skip town as the entire city watched the mockery this case had become. And when they finally tracked Daugherty down, he'd admitted his blackmailer was none other than Dot King's snot-nosed little brother, who Coughlin had first encountered at the crime scene. Enraged, he'd hauled the kid in, where the twenty-one-year-old broke down and admitted he'd threatened to reveal Daugherty's involvement with his sister, but unlike Guimares, who'd wanted to extort $100,000 out of Mitchell, Francis Keenan wanted only to nab a job at the DOJ. For all the hubbub about a second blackmail plot, the only thing Coughlin had learned was that Dot King's family was trash.

Meanwhile, Julia Harpman had continued to be a thorn in his side. Her articles had included the rumors, how the "pink-toe letter" remained missing, how members of the Keenan family had been called back and questioned for six additional hours, and anything else she could get her eyes, ears, or hands on. She had an uncanny knack for homing in on every unresolved lead or loose thread that made the authorities look like buffoons. Pecora had made it a thousand times worse, prattling away any chance he got and constantly contradicting himself.

The press had been waiting for updates on their interrogations, and all Coughlin planned to say was that nothing new had come to light. Of course, nobody could squeak a headline out of that, so there would be an onslaught of questions.

Julia Harpman certainly wasn't going to waste any time or take any prisoners. Like every other muckraker in the city, she continued to milk every angle of the story for all it was worth; unlike every other muckraker, she led each article with a "Summary of the King Murder Mystery" that rivaled any dime-store detective novel.

Her sensationalizing his investigation set his teeth on edge. But the *News*'s two million other readers seemed to disagree. They loved it. They loved *her*. And even Coughlin had to acknowledge that, theatrical lead-ins aside, her reporting was more thorough and more thoughtful than any other paper's in the city.

"Well?" Coughlin demanded, stomping into Pecora's office to prepare for the press conference.

Pecora tossed a sheaf of papers on his scarred desk. "I'm dropping the case."

Coughlin's jaw slackened. "Is this a goddamn joke?"

Pecora put his hands up, like he was helpless. "What more d'ya want from me? I just questioned Mitchell and Jackson for another five and a half hours and they acquitted themselves with ease."

"I didn't know persons of interest could acquit *themselves*," Coughlin snapped.

"Fine, *I* acquitted them," Pecora said, as though Coughlin was merely quibbling over details. "Both men were perfectly frank in their answers."

Coughlin raised his brows. "You sure you're asking the right questions?"

"You want new questions, get me new information," Pecora volleyed back. "We've gone over every move they made on the night of the murder on three separate occasions. All of which is to say: nothing new was discovered. These two men are innocent. Their only crime is associating with the wrong kind of girl."

Coughlin studied the DA. "I'm not sure that's their *only* crime."

Pecora snorted. "Don't tell me you actually think Mitchell killed the girl! Jesus Christ, the man has no motive, and the most strenuous thing he does is play tennis!"

"I'm not exactly sure how, but I still think he's involved in my investigation somehow, even if it's just helping to bring it to a *speedier conclusion*," Coughlin said testily.

Pecora shoved his chair back and leaped up. "Just what're you saying?"

"Whaddya think?" Coughlin slammed his palms on the desk, his frustration bubbling over.

Pecora shook his head. "I don't have the resources or men that you do, and I can't just keep questioning people over and over and not getting anywhere. You failed to bring me new leads or suspects, so I'm moving on."

"You think *I've* got endless resources and men?" Coughlin demanded.

Pecora gaped at him. "You've got *twelve hundred men* under you!"

Coughlin decided then and there the DA deserved a slug in the face. "I got more men because I got more to deal with! You know how many calls we get every goddamn *hour*? How many murders, assaults, robberies—"

Pecora cut him off. "Spare me. The bottom line is, your office is more equipped to handle this investigation."

"I'd like to remind you," Coughlin barely managed to grind out, "that you involved *yourself* in this investigation."

"If it wasn't for me *involving* myself, you'd still be out there looking for the ellusive *Mr. Marshall!*" Pecora snapped.

Coughlin ignored the cheap shot. "You should've told your old pal Olcott to piss off with his special conditions! But no—instead you kissed his ass, agreeing to protect Mitchell's identity and give him special consideration. You turned the whole city against us! And for what?" Coughlin realized he was yelling only when he paused and the office fell oddly silent. He cleared his throat, lowering his voice. "You could've referred Olcott and his rich client to my office just like any other person of interest, and we both know you *should* have."

Pecora met his gaze stonily, and a long silence stretched between them. "In hindsight, I wish I had. *But* when a former colleague, someone you worked shoulder to shoulder with for *years*, calls with information about a case—*of which he's entirely innocent*—you don't just turn your back—"

"Olcott might be your former colleague, but now he's just a run-of-the-mill defense attorney with a rich client who claims he's innocent," Coughlin shot back. "A client, by the way, who's been parading all over the city under a fake name with a girl half his age that ain't his wife, who turned up dead. Oh, and this guy just so happens to be tucked behind the House of Morgan and the DOJ and *now* you're droppin' the case? But I'm sure that's just a coincidence."

"Easy, friend," Pecora warned.

"You're no friend to anyone!" Coughlin said hotly. "You made our lives hell agreeing to this guy's special conditions, and now Guimares's loudmouthed lawyer won't stop yapping about how we have two different justice systems for the rich and the poor."

"A bone you should pick with the esteemed Mr. Goldsmith," Pecora said snootily.

Coughlin lunged across the desk. "You arrogant bastard!"

Pecora dodged sideways and smoothed back his hair. "Easy, fella."

"Oh, right," Coughlin said, straightening himself. "You wouldn't wanna have a shiner for your next front-page photo with Mitchell."

Pecora reddened. "I didn't ask for that," he muttered.

"Maybe not," Coughlin said. "But your mug was still all over the front page of the *Daily News*, cozied up with a murder victim's sugar daddy. And don't tell me that's not a paid placement . . ."

Pecora stiffened. "What's *that* supposed to mean?"

"C'mon, guy. You gonna stand there and tell me a certain, shall we say, *gift* from the house of Stotesbury-Mitchell didn't influence how you handled this whole thing?"

"How *dare* you!" Pecora said, taking a swipe at him.

They grappled, but Coughlin deflected, easily shoving the pint-size Italian off. "Careful, fella. You wouldn't want to get your precious hands dirty—any dirtier than they already are."

"Leave it to you to think everyone else is dirty!" Pecora shot back. "Everyone knows you paid to get promoted."

Rage bubbled up at Pecora's sucker-punch reference to the decades-old scandal that had alleged that every patrolman, including Coughlin, had had to leave $1,000 on the captain's desk on New Year's Eve in order to make lieutenant. "You son of a bitch," Coughlin sneered, barely resisting the urge to pummel the DA to a pulp. "Deflect and distract— that's your MO."

A tap at the door, and Pecora's secretary appeared. "There's a horde of reporters waiting. Ready to face the enemy, gentlemen?"

Coughlin brushed his sleeves off, as though he could brush away the stench of corruption that the public and the press were so fired up about. "I'm not sure who the enemy is anymore."

Chapter 39

It was Julia's first Passover as a Catholic, and she was spending it where she'd spent far too many holidays: in a pressroom.

Converting to Catholicism had been a formality—a box to check, in order to marry her bashert. She'd never been religious—too practical for it—but even if she had been, it still would've been worth it. *Peg* was worth it. Their life *together* was worth it.

Still, she'd thought about it more than she'd expected during Rosh Hashanah and Yom Kippur, a sad, hollow little tug at her heart that felt like something was missing, though it was so tangled up with being home-sick for family and Tennessee, it was hard to parse out each "missing-ness," and the business of newspaper life soon swept away the fleeting vestiges of hollowness anyway.

The pressroom was thick with smoke. A few guys played cards. Others dozed, hat brims pulled low. Hellinger, the only other one in the room who should've been attending a seder, nodded off. She nudged him and he jerked upright. She glanced at the clock and calculated she had just enough time to run downstairs to the ladies' restroom.

She hurried to get back to the pressroom and was just reaching for the doorknob when she saw a familiar knot of well-dressed, older men heading down the hall toward her. She yanked open the door. "Hellinger? Could you come out here?"

"Hellinger?" one echoed in a high-pitched falsetto. "Could you hold my skirt while I wee?"

Snickers ricocheted around the room. Hellinger looked like he wanted to throttle her as he stomped out. "Whaddya—"

"That's our man!" she hissed urgently, relieved he still had the camera. Mitchell, looking shell-shocked and weary, was surrounded by three tall men, gray-haired lawyers from the day of the chase. "Mr. Mitchell!" she called. "Did anything new come to light? Will you be called back for further questions?"

At his name, the man in question turned to look at her.

"No questions!" one of the lawyers snarled.

Hellinger had already hoisted the camera. Bam! The flash popped.

"Hey!" a policeman shouted at Hellinger. "No photos!"

Hellinger shook his head with something like wonder. "Cheese and crackers! You have the best luck!"

"Quick! Back inside!" Julia said, shoving Hellinger toward the door. "We just got an exclusive shot."

They hadn't even retaken their seats when Pecora, Coughlin, and Carey came in and the press conference began.

Pecora spoke first. "After additional thorough investigation—Mr. Jackson for one and a half hours, and Mr. Mitchell for three and a half hours—I've found them to be *completely* above suspicion. These two gentlemen presented their statements clearly and with the utmost frankness. To my mind, there's nothing to indicate they had anything to do with the murder."

Hands shot up, every reporter calling out questions. Julia, determined not to be left out, shouted louder than anyone else.

Pecora nodded to her. The rest of the crowd quieted.

"Are you saying Mitchell and Jackson are completely innocent?" she asked.

"I can't discuss the details," Pecora said firmly.

A man to her right jumped in. "Can you comment on your next plan of action?"

Pecora glanced at Coughlin, whose mouth was a thin, tight line, then at Carey, who looked away. "Tonight's examinations will be my last in this case unless the police bring me new evidence," he said, turning back to the crowd. "Otherwise, I'll resume my routine duties Monday."

Julia was taken aback. It was scarcely two weeks into one of the most active, high-profile investigations the city had seen. Every single day, new figures entered the case, new information came to light, new sources stepped forward. But now the DA was dropping the case? This was all wrong.

All around her, a moment of stunned silence greeted the announcement, followed by a frantic clamor of questions.

"Fellas!" The DA held up his hands for silence. "The case now rests in the hands of the police."

A reporter from the back of the room shouted, "Is it true that serious friction has developed between you and the police?"

"That's categorically untrue," Pecora said flatly. "There's no friction between myself and the police. Our offices will continue to collaborate."

Julia spoke up. "There's a story in an evening paper that the district attorney's office is impeding the police investigation. Can you comment?"

"That's absolutely without foundation," Pecora snapped.

"Inspector Coughlin? Can *you* comment?" she pressed.

Coughlin set his jaw, stared straight ahead, said nothing.

Captain Carey glanced between his two colleagues and cleared his throat. "All's well between the offices of the police and the district attorney," he said.

Pecora looked annoyed. "Fellas, I want to remind you that this is a *police investigation*. I was only brought into it at this unique stage because Mr. Mitchell's attorney requested that his client be questioned somewhere besides police headquarters."

If the DA hoped to remind everyone that he was just lending a helping hand, it had the opposite effect.

"Right," Julia said. "Because Mitchell's one of the wealthiest men in America. So he should be questioned wherever he wants."

A chorus of agreement rippled through the room.

Pecora glowered. "The police and I hold information about this case that we simply cannot reveal at this time. We intend to catch and prosecute the murderer to the fullest extent of the law, and we will update you on our progress when it's appropriate."

"'Appropriate' according to who?" someone called out.

Pecora gave a bitter laugh. "That's enough for tonight. It's been a long and tiresome day."

The newspapermen swelled forward, shouting a barrage of questions. The three officials turned to leave, Coughlin's face tight with rage.

Julia's thoughts returned to the bribery rumors. Pecora dropping the case certainly didn't look good. *Could they actually be true?*

Everything about Pecora's conduct felt wrong: his early involvement in the case, his concealment of Mitchell's identity, and now his abrupt and premature resignation from the investigation, *a scant four days* after Draper Daugherty entered the melee.

If the rumors were true, Mitchell—or his father-in-law—had bought his way off the flypaper.

Julia caught Hellinger's eye and gestured at the door. Public opinion about Pecora would surely plummet. But it seemed that public opinion was not the DA's top priority. Could the rumors of a $500,000 bribe be true? And who could afford that cost?

There were three obvious possibilities: Harry Daugherty, who wanted to spare himself further public embarrassment and prevent his son's involvement from diverting attention away from Harding's reelection; Rothstein, who certainly didn't want any publicity about his association with the murdered girl; and John Kearsley Mitchell, and his father-in-law, E. T. Stotesbury, who had the greatest motivation to hasten the conclusion of the case and end the international rampage of social humiliation.

Mitchell had also made that completely unexplained—and highly illogical—trip to Washington a few days ago. What could possibly have brought him down there, only to turn around and go straight back to Philadelphia?

All these men had the motivation and means to pressure the case to a premature conclusion. But even stranger were the interconnections between the three disparate powerhouses. Draper Daugherty, who claimed Rothstein was one of his closest friends in New York, and formerly his associate in the insurance business, was now in the spotlight for his association with Dot King. The attorney general had already been under scrutiny for protecting the interests of the House of Morgan, and Mr. Stotesbury had been a generous campaign donor and former treasurer of the Republican National Committee, so it wasn't a far leap to consider their interests in the King case entwined.

The maze of social, political, and financial connections was an intricate jumble, layer upon layer of favors and funding, debts owed and paid, more menacing for all that was unseen and unknown. Despite her questionable choices in terms of both associates and activities, in the end, the Broadway Butterfly had been more of a hapless fly who'd found herself fatally caught in that web.

Chapter 40

Time was running out. Ever since Pecora had dropped the case, each tick of the clock was a winch tightening around Coughlin's neck, demanding he work faster, drive his men harder, produce new leads, wrap up the damn investigation or surrender, admitting it would never be solved.

Inspector John D. Coughlin did not surrender.

Pecora's careless—or maybe calculated—withdrawal from the investigation was enraging; Julia Harpman's front-page coverage of the event was equally annoying. But with the DA finally out of his way, Coughlin figured, at least he could finally—*finally!*—run this investigation right. Soon he'd have an arrest. Let the papers cover *that*.

He had men working around the clock, chasing down leads in New York, Philadelphia, and Atlantic City and searching every pawnshop and pharmacy for the missing jewelry or the unusual-size chloroform bottle.

Something had to turn up. But so far, Dot King's former romance with Nucky Johnson hadn't led to any further discoveries, even though it was well known by those who needed to know that Arnold Rothstein and Nucky ran booze together. It made for nice expansion for Nucky, who'd practically leveraged bootlegging, gambling, and prostitution into Jersey shore tourist attractions.

Only rookies and fools thought crime could be eradicated, and John D. Coughlin was neither. He was, however, known as a man with friends in high places on both sides of the fence. On the legitimate side, his friends went up as high as Mayor Hylan, and that friendship allowed the mayor to share certain things he ordinarily wouldn't. This morning, Hylan had shared a copy of a letter he'd written to Enright, noting that talk of "so-called fixers who claimed to hold sway over public officials in influencing the outcome of the King investigation" had reached such prominence in the public and press that it had now gone as far as his own desk. He demanded Enright give the matter his full attention.

On the illegitimate side, there was Rothstein. Coughlin first met "the Brain" when he was promoted from a patrolman in the tenderloin district to the racetracks, where he was assigned to catch pickpockets. A certain level of awareness, if not mutual respect, had grown between the two. Both were unusually good at their jobs, minded their own business, and accepted the other's existence.

Coughlin had uncovered that Dot King lived in Rothstein's building. And just to add another layer to the tangled web, Draper Daugherty, recently outed as another close "friend" of Dot King's, also counted Rothstein as his closest friend in New York.

It didn't take a genius to connect the dots. Draper Daugherty rode on his father's untouchable coattails—nobody was going to mess with the attorney general's son. Rothstein sat on a throne of ill-gotten gains and underworld power. The wild card was Dot King. How was she involved? Was she running drugs for the operation? And was her murder somehow related?

But chloroforming a dame in her bed wasn't Rothstein's style. The gangster world had its own justice system. The only reason Rothstein had someone taken out was because they'd stolen from or betrayed him. Those "crimes" warranted capital punishment in the underworld, and it was always public and showy.

A knock interrupted his thoughts. "Yes?"

A deputy held out a folder thick with papers. "This was just messengered over from the DA's office, but doesn't say who the sender is. It seems they investigated a so-called brokerage firm named King and Scott with extremely murky investment practices last summer. Dot King was a financial backer and named partner. Guess who the other guy was?"

Coughlin didn't need to guess. "Albert Guimares."

Chapter 41

Coughlin's private line was already ringing when he got to work the next morning. It was Enright's secretary; the commissioner wanted to see him immediately.

Enright, plopped behind his desk, was scribbling away. No doubt hard at work on his next fictional detective story, which everyone knew he spent city-funded time writing.

"You wanted to see me?" Coughlin said, closing the door.

Enright glanced up. "Phase out the King investigation."

"But Pecora just got out of my way. I can finally run this thing the way it shoulda been run all along," Coughlin said.

"I *said* drop it," Enright said louder.

"Because of Pecora?" Coughlin practically spat the name.

The commissioner snorted like only a fool would think it was that runt. "No."

"Then why?"

"Why? 'Cause you've had fifty men on it for twenty days and ain't got squat to show for it. Because crime in this city hasn't stopped. Because this lemon of a case ain't never gonna get solved."

"But—" Coughlin began.

"No announcements," Enright said. "Nothin' official, understand? Just put your men on other cases and tell the press the trail went cold, there's no leads . . . the usual."

Enright wouldn't know a cold trail if he tripped over it. He was putting a stake in the ground and Coughlin on notice: fall in line.

Coughlin looked down. He oughtta go back to his desk and get to work on the other cases piling up on his desk. The system wasn't gonna change. It was just as he'd told rookies a thousand times: only fools thought things could change or they'd be the ones to change them.

He wasn't a rookie or a fool. But there was something about this case. "Gimme a week. I can close this."

The commissioner tapped his pen impatiently. "You hard of hearing?"

"C'mon. I'll owe you one." Coughlin swallowed. Asking Idiot Enright for a favor would cost him mightily.

Enright's bleary eyes flashed, calculating. "Two days—that's it."

Coughlin nodded and went back to his office. The pressure was on. A lot of things annoyed him, but three had the power to instantly enrage him: bullies who hurt women, arrogant bastards who thought they could outsmart everyone else, and swindlers who cheated honest, hardworking folks. And Albert Guimares, it seemed, was all three.

Coughlin read through the files about Guimares and Dot King's phony brokerage firm one last time before he went down to Interrogation Room 4 for another round with the gigolo. The ploy was buying oil stocks for twenty to forty cents a share, then turning around and selling them to so-called suckers for ten to one hundred times the original purchase price. Coughlin's outrage shot through the roof. He was furious at Pecora, who hadn't shared this information with him, but more so at Guimares, the arrogant sonofabitch who'd hoodwinked honest folks out of their hard-earned savings.

Nobody got away with withholding information from him. *Nobody.*

Coughlin had hollered for someone to haul the gigolo in again as soon as he read the file.

Now Coughlin would let Guimares stew in the interrogation room a good while. He'd given orders: nobody was to go in, and Guimares wasn't to be let out—not even for the toilet. Let the rat sit and wait until he ran out of cigarettes or pissed himself. A suspect's own fear and anticipation were more effective in an interrogation than almost anything a cop could do or say.

He'd had it with Guimares. The guy was clearly guilty. He *had* to be.

This was not a random act of violence. Like so many crimes, Dot King had been killed by someone she knew. Coughlin would stake his life on it. And it wasn't just that there was no forced entry . . . and it wasn't just that chloroforming someone required being intimately close to the victim. It was that Dot King had *opened* the door for her murderer . . . and she had been killed in her *bed*. That was deeply personal.

There was also Guimares's ever-shifting and still-unsubstantiated alibi and the bite marks and scratches on his hand. But ever since Guimares had made bail, and it remained a mystery who'd fronted the money for him, he'd been mighty hard to reach. As was that loud-mouthed lawyer of his, who was too busy running his mouth to the newspapers about how poorly his client had been treated while John Kearsley Mitchell ran free.

Mitchell wasn't a person of interest for killing Dot King, Coughlin tightly reminded anyone who was stupid enough to ask. Mr. Moneybags didn't even draw his own bath. His unnervingly doughy-soft hands were manicured. The guy didn't have the mental fortitude or physical strength for a crime like this.

Meanwhile, this wily gigolo thought he could outsmart him and had wasted his men's time disproving his various alibis. Well, Coughlin didn't have time or patience for the runaround, especially from a crook. Today the extradition-dodging bum was gonna come clean.

Coughlin threw open the door to Interrogation Room 4. Guimares was alone. "Didn't bring your lawyer today?"

"I don't need Goldsmith to sit here, billin' every goddamn minute, while I tell you—yet again—how I didn't do nothin'," Guimares said.

Coughlin eyed him. "Oh, I think you've done a lot, pal. And now we're gonna have a little talk about how you swindle honest, hardworkin' folks out of money they don't have with your fake stock schemes—first up in Boston and then down here."

Guimares blanched.

"That's right," Coughlin said. "I know about King and Scott. You should know I always find *everything*, son. But the more you waste my time playin' games, the harder you're makin' it on yourself. See how it works?"

"You never asked me about my businesses," Guimares said smoothly.

"I asked how you made your sugar, you know, back when you claimed you spent as much money as your girl's sugar papa, showerin' her with just as many gifts as the millionaire, and you said you worked in stocks. But you neglected to mention it was fake stocks in fraudulent schemes."

Guimares shrugged. "I assumed your pals over at the DA's office shared what they knew, since you're one big team. No trouble between you, I hope?"

A hot prong of anger surged through Coughlin. He shoved it down and pressed forward. Julia Harpman had already referenced the question someone had asked at the last press update about tension between their offices and Carey's awkward, utterly unsuccessful attempt to put the rumor to rest. The last thing he needed was Guimares and Goldsmith stirring that up again for the *Daily News* to feast on.

"So Dot King was financially backing your so-called firm with sugar she siphoned off Mitchell, so you could swindle people out of their savings."

Guimares snorted. "I never swindled nobody. There's no guarantees in investing. Stocks go up and down. Everybody knows that."

Coughlin tossed the stack of files on the table. "Well, what *everybody* didn't know is that yours always went up and theirs always went down."

"I facilitated trades," Guimares said evenly.

"You swindled people who couldn't afford it!" Coughlin ground out. "You knew full well those grossly inflated rates would never pan out! That $75,000 you claimed you made last year? That's all off their hardworking backs. But you don't give that a thought. You beat Dot King black and blue—and I bet she ain't the first or the last. You're still fightin' extradition for what you did up in Boston, *and* you're squirming like a lily-livered coward on this murder charge. I *know* it was you, and I'm gonna nail you for it before we're done."

Guimares didn't flinch. "There's a sucker born every minute. If you can't afford to lose, don't belly up to the table. And as for Dot, I told you, I didn't touch her. You're just trying to pin it on me because I'm Puerto Rican and as soon as you see dark skin, you think 'guilty.'"

"No," Coughlin said tightly. "I see a career criminal with a history of swindling, known for a violent temper, who likes to beat women."

"Right. My darker skin's got nothin' to do with this," Guimares said sarcastically. "*Please.* This whole town's prejudiced and you don't even know it. We even had to name the firm 'King and Scott,' because nobody would invest with a Puerto Rican manager. Nobody'd invest in a firm called 'King and Guimares.'"

"Jesus H. Christ—you want me to feel *bad* for you because you couldn't use your *real* name for your *fake* firm? Do I need to remind you that Dot King wasn't her real name either? You know what? You both should've used your real names—Keenan and Guimares. Then maybe some of your investors, or as you like to call them, *suckers*, would still have their money. But you're too fond of cheating people out of their savings and beating up those smaller and weaker than you. You know what? You make me sick. You're the worst sort of man: you're a bully and a coward."

"I never hit any woman," Guimares insisted. "You're just pinnin' it on me 'cause you can't find the real killer. Or maybe you found him but he threw enough sugar at you to make you forget him again."

Coughlin lunged across the table, grabbed the guy by his lapels, and yanked him close. "Why, you ignorant whelp! Say something like that again and I'll send you back to Boston in a goddamn pine box. Answer me or I'll bring the fellas in and we'll see if the third degree refreshes your memory."

This was an empty threat and they both knew it. Guimares was a murder suspect and a confirmed crook. But he also had friends with dough to bail him out and a loudmouthed lawyer who never shut his yap about the raw deal his client got.

Coughlin shoved him away, and Guimares fell back in his chair. They eyed each other like boxers circling in the ring.

"I'm sick and tired of you jerkin' me around," Coughlin said. "Just come clean and it'll go easier on you in court."

Guimares lit a cigarette and blew the smoke out his nose in twin spirals. "I'm innocent."

Coughlin opened the folder and took his time looking at the papers within. He let Guimares wonder what was there to be read. "Here's the thing, pal. You got no alibi. It's not good enough that you claim you were home if nobody else can corroborate it."

"You're just trying to force my hand," Guimares said.

"I'm trying to get to the truth," Coughlin corrected.

"I told you McBryan's girl stayed with him that night and had breakfast with us that morning."

Coughlin shook his head. "And I told you, I'm not gonna take your word that some little tart sneakin' around with McBryan saw you come in."

"She's no tart—she's a society dame," Guimares said tightly. "And if her name gets dragged into this, it'll destroy her."

"Right, and worryin' about her reputation is keepin' you up at night," Coughlin said sarcastically. "What's a society dame doing hanging around with riffraff like you and McBryan anyway?"

Guimares shrugged. "Who can understand a woman's heart?"

"You got some nerve trying to change your alibi yet again. But I ain't buying this phony-baloney," Coughlin said, pinning the man with his gaze.

Guimares shook his head. "I don't know what else I can tell you, Detective. It feels like you're hell-bent on nailing me for this, no matter how much evidence or what alibi I have."

The guy was too cocky, too sure. Which meant something was afoot. Coughlin shoved paper and pen across the table. "Her name and address—now."

"Seems you've left me no choice," Guimares said, taking his time to write it down.

Coughlin grabbed it and stomped out. "Get a car," he ordered the nearest deputy. "We've got another witness to question."

Chapter 42

Aurelia Fischer. Aurelia Fischer. Aurelia Fischer. The name chased circles in Coughlin's mind during the drive up the coast. Who was she? And if she was indeed a society dame, what the hell was she doing mixed up with bums like Guimares and McBryan? It didn't add up.

He touched on each fact from the case like working through the rosary beads his mother used to carry.

Both Mitchell and Guimares were motivated to get the pink-toe letters—Guimares as a blackmail tool, Mitchell to prevent himself from being blackmailed—and neither had a solid, substantiated alibi.

Mitchell was the last-known person to see Dot King alive, but the guy was soft. He'd also called the next day to take Miss King to lunch, voluntarily revealed his identity to the victim's mother when she'd answered the phone, then hired a PI to learn what happened after hearing his mistress was dead. Finally, he'd had his lawyer call Pecora with his offer to come forward and share all he knew about the victim. These were hardly the actions of a murderer.

Guimares had *not* come forward. And when they'd tracked him down, he'd tried to hide the incriminating scratches and bite marks on his hand. The guy also had a solid history of being a woman-beating crook. It wasn't hard to imagine that when Dot King had refused to give the pink-toe letter to him, he'd taken it by force. Maybe he hadn't *meant* to kill her; a blackmail scheme didn't work so well with a dead sugar baby. He could've been trying to knock her out so he could search for the letters without her raising a ruckus. That could also explain why her bedside telephone had been stretched out to the living room, beyond her reach. He might've expected her to wake up and wouldn't have wanted her groggily calling for help.

All that stood between Coughlin and justice was the dame giving him an eleventh-hour alibi.

Coughlin looked around as they pulled up to Aurelia Fischer's address. It seemed money and Connecticut got you two things: space and swanky houses. It was a stark contrast to Yorkville, the Upper East Side neighborhood abutting Harlem where he'd grown up—apartments crammed together without a sliver of space between them, their occupants crammed in even tighter.

He took in the manicured gardens, the big old trees, the quiet. He wasn't meant for the country, but it was a relief to be in a place where the streets meant nothing, and his encyclopedic knowledge of crimes could neither plague nor inform him.

A housekeeper answered the bell, looked them up and down, frowned. "Yes?"

"We're looking for Aurelia Fischer."

"Miss Fischer isn't available," she said, already starting to close the door.

Coughlin blocked it with his shoe, flashed his badge. "I think she is. What's more, I don't think you want me askin' all your neighbors."

The woman shifted nervously. "Wait here." She closed the door.

Coughlin waited several minutes and was about to ring again—and this time he wouldn't be so polite—when the door opened again and a real beauty of a girl came out.

She smiled shyly up at him. "May I help you?"

Whatever he'd been expecting, it wasn't this timid wisp of a thing. She was slender, delicate, blonde. Everything about her said refinement.

Everything except the company she kept, of course, Coughlin reminded himself. "Uh, Miss Fischer, I'd like to have a word."

She gestured to a set of chairs at the end of the porch. "Shall we sit?"

Coughlin feared the wicker would collapse under him. "Do you know Edmund McBryan and Albert Guimares?"

She glanced around, as though afraid to be overheard. "Why, yes. We're friends." Her blush said different.

"How'd you meet these *friends*?" Coughlin asked.

She turned redder. "We met last year while I was driving in Manhattan. Mr. McBryan stopped alongside me at a red light, and we started chatting. He invited me to a dance."

Coughlin shook his head. Women out driving alone. Such a thing never would've happened twenty years ago. It was safer then. Cars brought a whole new set of problems. Suffrage and flappers and women's rights brought even more. And it all landed on his desk.

"And where were you the night of March 14?"

She dropped her eyes and lowered her voice. "Why, I . . . I stayed in Mr. McBryan and Mr. Guimares's suite at the Hotel Embassy." The words seemed to be wrestled out of her. "We'd been out quite late, and Mr. McBryan didn't think it was safe for me to drive all the way home when I was so . . . tired."

The way she hesitated over the word made him think she'd been more drunk than tired. "When'd you leave?"

"The three of us had breakfast together at 8:30 the next morning, and I left shortly after." The answer was quick, pat.

"And the night before? Was Guimares with you?"

"No. I . . . I only saw him at breakfast, but I think I heard him come in at midnight."

Coughlin narrowed his eyes. The silence stretched.

"Yes, midnight," she said.

Coughlin crossed his arms. "Miss Fischer, do you read the papers?"

She looked confused. "Of course—every day."

"Then you're aware that Dot King was murdered early on the morning of March 15?"

She nodded. "Yes, it was terrible."

"So you're aware your 'friend' Guimares is under investigation for the murder?" When she nodded again, looking more wretched by the second, he continued: "So if you heard him come in around midnight, which gives him an alibi, why'd you wait for us to track you down? Why didn't you step forward?"

She shifted. "I can't have my name in the papers. This case is on the front page of every newspaper in the country. I . . . I've felt terrible seeing him in trouble, but what would my family think if they found out? I'd be ruined! My whole *family* would be ruined."

"How'd they pay for breakfast?" he asked.

Her brows knit together. "I'm sorry?"

"How did Guimares and McBryan pay for breakfast?" he repeated. "Together? Separate? Cash? Credit?"

She straightened primly. "Oh, I couldn't say. A lady never concerns herself with money."

Coughlin bit back a warning about ladies staying in hotels with men who weren't their husbands. "Miss Fischer, I'm here as the head of the New York City Police detective squad, to question you about your *friends*, one of whom is facing murder charges, and all you can say is, 'A lady never concerns herself with money'?"

She jerked back as though he'd slapped her. Her fingers fluttered to her chest. "Why, I—"

Coughlin leaned forward. "Perjury is a crime—understand? That means if you lie about anything—any part of this—you'll be guilty of protecting a *murderer*. And if you're caught perjuring yourself, you'll go to *prison*. Do you know what it's like locked up in a cell with the lowliest, dirtiest women on earth?"

Her big blue eyes grew bigger and somehow bluer as they started to fill with tears. She probably thought it was brave that she tried to hold them back. Coughlin pressed on relentlessly. "Prostitutes, thieves, even some female murderers—they'll make mincemeat out of a girl like you. You'll work alongside them all day and sleep alongside them at night. You'll eat a bowl of gruel in a basement room that stinks of boiled cabbage. Your family and friends will pretend they don't know you. You'll be nothing but a bit of gossip whispered about at parties. You'll freeze in the winter and sweat in your own filth in the summer until you finally take ill and die. Then *that'll* be in all the papers. I can make that happen. Do you understand?"

She stared at him in horror. "Please, please no!"

He took a breath, softened his voice. "If you help me, I'll protect you. Tell me what really happened, and nobody will ever know you were there or what you did, I promise. Now stop cryin' and start talkin'."

She looked up helplessly. "I . . . I . . ."

Years of experience on the force told him this was it—she was teetering. He pressed his advantage. "Nobody ever has to know you were there. Just tell me the truth. Did you *really* hear Guimares come in?"

She clutched the arms of her chair, as though they alone held her up. She sniffed in jagged breaths. Her big, sad eyes begged to be let go.

He didn't back off. "Well?"

"Yes," she finally said in a fragile but oddly defiant way. "Yes, I heard him come in around midnight. And we all had breakfast the next morning."

"Goddammit! Why are you lying to protect this guy?" Coughlin leaped up, the wicker chair scraping harshly across the porch. He turned his back to her, slammed his palms on the railing, and looked out over the fancy lawn.

She rushed over, put a small, pale hand on his arm, all woebegone and helpless. "Please—don't send me to prison!"

He shook her off angrily. "McBryan doesn't care about you. He'll toss you in a second. Don't be a fool. Come clean."

She shook her head, still crying. "No. Please!"

He stormed back to the squad car. The girl was lying—surely, she *had* to be!—but there was nothing he could do about it. He couldn't disprove her testimony, and at trial, if it ever came to that, Pecora would ask the question he himself couldn't answer: Why would a girl like this ruin her reputation and her family's name unless she was trying to save an innocent man?

He slammed the car door. This was the end of the line. Guimares would walk and Mitchell remained untouchable. It was only a matter of time—hours, he guessed—until Enright closed the investigation.

Coughlin pounded the door with a closed fist and welcomed the hurt. It was going to be a long drive back to New York.

Chapter 43

April 9, 4:12 p.m. Manhattan. New York Daily News.

Coughlin was stonewalling her. When she showed up at his office, he was "out"; when she called, he was "busy"; when she asked for an update, some assistant gave her some baloney about the trail going cold. She hadn't been able to gather enough to cobble together an article in days.

Ever since a well-heeled woman known only as "McBryan's Blonde" had come forward with an alibi for Guimares a few days ago, it seemed any hope of justice for Dot King had gone out the window.

Julia keenly felt the weight of obtaining justice for the murdered model. There was also the small matter of her own career. As always, she felt the pressure to maintain her standing at the paper and in an all-male field.

Philip walked by and dropped an accusatory finger on page 8, where her last article, one inch of coverage about McBryan's Blonde's eleventh-hour alibi, had been relegated. "You're grasping at straws."

"Perhaps you're confusing me with the police," she returned.

He laughed. "I like you sassy, Harpman."

"The public wants to know every detail about the Broadway Butterfly we can dig up," she insisted. "They won't rest until there's justice."

"They won't or you won't?" Philip asked.

She wasn't sure she could tell the difference anymore. "The story's still got legs—I can feel it."

"You know the drill," Philip said, already walking away. "If you wanna stay up front, I need sizzle! I need bite! Grannies fainting, ladies blushing, fellas arguing about it at the shoeshine stand, the whole city debating it over dinner. We're the *Daily News*! Find a hook or find a new story." Philip had gotten his start as a preliminary boy in a cheap fight club, earning peanuts as a minor-league reporter. But apparently, the fight had never left him.

"Get ze hook!" Hellinger called from mere feet away, cupping his hands around his mouth like a vaudeville heckler.

Julia glared at him. "Thanks a heap!"

"What? I was just kidding!"

She turned away, tapping her pen against her desk with unwarranted ferocity, and decided to try Coughlin again. Time was running out.

"It's urgent," she told the guy who answered the phone. "I'm running my story with or without a quote from Inspector Coughlin—and trust me, he'll want the chance."

He put her on hold, until finally Coughlin's voice came on the line. "Miss Harpman? I'm very busy."

"I won't take much of your time," Julia promised. "I'm just puzzled how the King case has gone to *no new leads*?"

The detective didn't hide his annoyance. "You've been on the beat long enough to know sometimes the trail goes cold."

Julia wondered just how impertinent she dared to be. "But if a rich, white, married society woman was killed, the trail wouldn't go cold. The nation wouldn't rest until the killer was caught. But an Irish Catholic, divorced, Broadway sugar baby is murdered and you run out of leads two weeks later? I'd hate to think what would happen if Ella Bradford died."

Coughlin issued a long-suffering sigh. "Miss Harpman, this has nothing to do with anything other than a murder. A crime was committed, like crimes are every day. As the chief inspector of the detectives' division, I assign my men to investigate these crimes. If the trail goes cold, I can't keep fifty men on it, spinning our wheels. I've got a foot-high stack of files on my desk of other cases. What about *those* families, who want answers about *their* loved ones?"

Julia squirmed, thinking of that tall stack of also-worthy cases waiting for police and press attention. He raised a good point. And perhaps it was wishful thinking, but she could almost swear he sounded just as frustrated as she felt.

"I won't pretend to know what's best," Julia said finally. "But I do know if you drop the Dot King case, a killer will go free. He'll literally get away with *murder*."

"Miss Harpman—" Coughlin started.

But Julia hurried on, "I've reported on every case you've worked on—"

"Reporting that leaves room for improvement," he cut in.

She continued, softening her tone. "Listen, you've always given newspapermen and . . . me a fair shake. I *know* you. You're a good detective. You *must* want justice."

"Oh, justice will be served," Coughlin said. "I always get my man."

"But how? When? It doesn't seem like the police are still working on the case at all," she said, knowing that with each day that passed, the likelihood of the killer being caught decreased exponentially.

"When I have enough evidence to charge him," Coughlin snapped. "It's not just about an arrest. It's about ensuring a mountain of information to last all the way through trial to conviction, *which you should know*. And now I have to get back to work." *Click.*

Julia slowly replaced the earpiece. She cranked a fresh sheet of paper into her typewriter and pounded out a headline. Time's Dust Falls Over the King Case.

She flicked the return lever twice, and her fingers flew over the keys:

Dot King's murder has been consigned to that ash heap of police investigations where are also the discarded inquiries into the killing of Joseph Elwell, Reim Hoxy, and other crimes which had their day in public interest and are now officially forgotten. With the revelation that John Kearsley Mitchell, son-in-law of E. T. Stotesbury, Philadelphia financier, was Dot King's benefactor, the mystery lost its spice. Assistant District Attorney Ferdinand Pecora turned the entire investigation over to the police more than a week ago. Inspector Coughlin declared no progress has been made by the police.

She ripped the paper out with a satisfying zip and called for a copy boy. If Coughlin thought she'd be kind enough not to mention the investigation being curtailed, he was wrong. This article, he would soon learn, was just the beginning. He wasn't the only one who "always got his man." This case meant something to her too. And she wasn't ready to quit.

Chapter 44

Julia rang Westbrook at the *United News*. "Got time for a coffee?" she asked.

Ten minutes later they were at their favorite diner. The lunch buzz, long gone, had settled into a predinner lull. A busboy wiped down the counters while a waiter refilled the saltshakers and a deliveryman finished off a slice of pie.

They took two stools at the counter and ordered two coffees. Julia took off her gloves and rested her hand on his. "Peg, I know this will sound crazy."

Westbrook raised a knowing eyebrow. "You know I like crazy. Spill."

She smiled. "This whole thing just doesn't add up. So I started thinking: Who has the most to lose from Draper Daugherty getting pulled into the King case? The attorney general, of course. And who has the most to gain? Guimares and Mitchell, because finally the heat is off them. Because the AG doesn't want the embarrassment and distraction from the election, he's motivated—*very motivated*—to bring about a quick conclusion of the investigation. So here's my far-fetched theory of the day: the Stotesbury-Mitchells leaked the story about Draper Daugherty."

Westbrook's eyebrows shot skyward. "That's quite a theory!"

"I know it's far-fetched—" Julia began.

"No," Westbrook said. "Give me a minute. I'm just thinking—Draper's involvement has catapulted the case *more* into the spotlight, which is exactly what the Stotesbury-Mitchells and the AG *don't* want, right?"

Julia held up a finger. "That's what I thought at first—and it's true. *But* it throws the heat from Mitchell onto Draper Daugherty, and—here's the really crazy part—it incontrovertibly involves the attorney general in this case, which is *exactly* what Mitchell wants."

Westbrook frowned. "But why on earth?"

"Because if Harry Daugherty has skin in the game, with a personal stake in the case like the Stotesburys do, he is that much *more* motivated to make this whole thing go away. Think about it: Mitchell tried to handle this on his own. He struck some sort of deal with Pecora to hide his identity. But the case still had legs and he got outed. Then Old Man Stotesbury brings in the big guns, hires a fleet of PIs, moves his private train secretly out of Philly. Rumor places him in New York, where Pecora volunteers the information that the millionaire definitely did *not* come to meet with him. Only to then drop the case twenty-four hours later. It's too perfect."

Westbrook took her arm, a cloud of worry settling over him. "Julia, you have to be very, *very* careful," he warned. "Guys like this with stakes like this? They'll stop at nothing."

"Of course," she promised lightly. "I will."

"No," he said. "I mean it. You're all I've got."

She squeezed his hand. "You're all I've got too."

As she walked back to the *News*, Julia went over her options. She *had* to get this story. Philip didn't care about Dot King; he cared about selling copies and keeping advertisers. But if she could align both interests, she could get justice for Dot and circulation for the paper.

And she would. She was Julia Harpman—the lead crime newspaperman in New York.

Chapter 45

April 26, 3:15 p.m. Manhattan. New York Daily News.

"Julia!" Hellinger's excited shout cut across the newsroom. "Julia!" He was clutching a telegram.

Julia, having just broken an exclusive that morning on the year-old Ward murder case whose premature closure was now being investigated for corruption, was still in high spirits and pounding out her latest update. It had been more than two weeks with nary a peep about the Dot King case. As soon as she wrapped up her Ward case exposé on how the accused murderer had paid off a source, sending the girl and her family on an all-expenses-paid trip to Europe, she would turn her attention back to Dot King. She didn't bother to lift her fingers off the keys. "What? A dancer twisted her ankle?"

Hellinger held the telegram aloft victoriously. "Ha-ha-*hardly*! Draper Daugherty's been committed to a sanitarium!"

A respectful hush spread across the newsroom. Julia did a double take. "A *sanitarium*? Why, that's *crazy*!"

"No, *he's* crazy, and that's why he went to a sanitarium," Hellinger corrected and was promptly rewarded with a smattering of laughter from the ten or so men around the room.

Julia ignored it. "Last time I checked, being the victim of a blackmail scheme and friends with a murder victim wasn't grounds for being committed."

Hellinger scanned the sheet. "Dr. Robertson, superintendent of the sanitarium, says Draper's in a rather debilitated condition. It seems he needs a nice long rest."

"Night-night, Draper," Joe joked. "Sweet dreams!"

Julia shook her head. "Fellas, I'm serious. This isn't right," she insisted.

"Aww. Sorry, Harpman. Your story ain't comin' back if Chatty Draper's sent to sit in a corner," Hellinger said.

"It's not about *my* story!" Julia insisted.

"Careful!" Joe warned, only half joking. "If Philip hears you, you'll be out on the street!"

Julia rolled her eyes. "OK, fine—it's about the story. But it's also about social class, and right from wrong, and the fact that justice shouldn't be for sale. And in case any of you jokers didn't notice, I happen to care about all those things."

"Well, you'll get at least one article out of the fact that the attorney general put his son away in a sanitarium, but beyond that, I think it means the King case is officially kaput," Joe added.

"But that's what I mean!" Julia said. "There have always been dark forces affecting this case that shouldn't have been. Putting Draper away works awfully nicely in terms of shutting the case down and letting Papa Daugherty focus on Harding's reelection."

Hellinger hesitated, clutching the message. "Well, it says he went voluntarily, but proceedings to have him formally committed by his family are underway."

Julia raised her brows. "So Draper's happily living his life when he finds himself thrust unceremoniously into the national spotlight due to his *friendship* with Dot King. He gives interviews to the press, tells the police everything he knows, seems fine as can be. And today his family forcibly commits him to a sanitarium? It doesn't make sense."

"Yet here it is nonetheless!" Hellinger said, holding it out.

"Here it is," Julia echoed.

The newsroom din churned around her, but Julia stared at the message, unable to shake the feeling that the attorney general was tying up loose ends, clearing any distractions and potential obstructions to the reelection campaign.

She wished she could speak privately with Draper and that he would somehow feel comfortable speaking frankly with her. But, of course, that was impossible. She was dealing with the most powerful law enforcement officer in the land. His official power was nearly unlimited, which was intimidating enough. But now he'd committed his only son to a sanitarium because Draper had been inconveniently, distractingly linked to a murdered model?

What might the AG do to silence a reporter who *inconveniently, distractingly* refused to stop reporting on Dot King? She had a feeling whatever it was would make the sanitarium look like a vacation.

Julia steeled herself. She would bide her time and be careful. But she wasn't done yet.

Chapter 46

May 4, 2:10 p.m. Manhattan. New York Daily News.

It had been nearly two months since Dot King had been murdered, five weeks since J. K. Mitchell had gone to DC and Pecora had swiftly thereafter dropped the case, two weeks since the attorney general of the United States had stuck his son in a sanitarium, and exactly zero seconds since Julia had stopped thinking about it all.

The police investigation had ceased, though no officials would admit this. Coughlin and Carey had turned their respective attentions to other cases. Julia called Coughlin weekly to inquire if any new clues had come to light, and each time he rotely insisted a few men were still investigating, but no new leads had turned up, no witnesses had been questioned, and absolutely no progress had been made. Pecora had kept his head carefully down.

If someone didn't do something, a killer was literally going to get away with the murder of Dot King. It was time, Julia decided, to crank up the heat, and she knew just how to do it.

She took a deep breath, re-tucked her blouse, and attempted to smooth her riotous curls. She would brave one of the most feared and simultaneously revered locales of any newspaper: that oasis of femininity, cosmetics, and beauty—the place where the delicate and refined lady writers resided, safely tucked away from the indelicate chaos of the city desk. There, ensconced in the scent of perfumes press agents provided gratis, the lady writers tapped out their advice for the lovelorn, recipes for housewives (and aspiring housewives), and astrological predictions for the mystically minded under the iron rule of Antoinette Donnelly.

Toni had been at the paper since it launched in 1919, penning the Dear Doris and astrological columns. She arrived at 6:45 a.m. and smoked, downed coffee, and worked until 7:00 p.m. every single day. She had three girls just to handle her fan mail and had once received ten thousand letters in one week.

Julia respected Toni's fortitude, work ethic, and results but didn't appreciate her constant proselytizing that a woman's place was in the home. Of course, it was fine if that's what a woman wanted, but it was downright duplicitous when written by a woman with a demanding career who barely went home to her kids.

Julia took a deep breath and headed in. "I've got a story for Debutante," she announced to the room. The women swiveled as one toward Toni, stationed, as always, behind her typewriter at the head of the room, cigarette in her left hand. Toni nodded her permission and gestured with the cigarette-bearing hand toward Daisy, the young woman who occasionally wandered over to the city desk to make eyes at Hellinger.

Julia moved toward Daisy and lowered her voice. "I'm thinking, 'Dot King's slaying leads to social oblivion for the Stotesbury-Mitchells.' They've been in hiding for a month and a half—*that's* a story."

Daisy glanced away toward Toni. "I don't know. That seems awfully . . . aggressive?"

Julia continued, resolute. She was playing with fire, but it was the only way. "Nobody's covering the story anymore. We can call the Stotesburys at Whitemarsh Hall and the Mitchells at Red Rose Manor and ask the uncomfortable questions. We need to smoke them out. Do you want me to write it?"

"No, I'll do it," Daisy said after a brief hesitation.

Julia nodded. "Thank you." There was a pecking order at the paper in terms of both seniority and subject matter. Julia won on both counts, but she tried not to take advantage of her position.

She couldn't get back to the city desk fast enough. Years spent surrounded by newspapermen and the tipsters, press agents, and flimflams who loved them, had made her into a lady who no longer fit in with other ladies, but neither did she fully fit in with men. The only place she truly belonged was the desk itself. And now that she'd set that first domino in motion, she'd wait there while the rest fell.

Chapter 47

May 5, 12:30 p.m. Wyndmoor, PA. Whitemarsh Hall.

Frances's life had grown very small. They'd been socially exiled for nearly a month and a half now, safely tucked away from prying eyes and the press. Her only interactions were with the servants, the children, and Jack, whom she meticulously avoided. Her anger, at first a volcanic eruption, had now hardened into something unyielding and cold, a scab of ashen lava between them.

Her only outings were to see Eva and her father, and only then at Whitemarsh Hall. There were too many curious eyes in the city. Their town house remained shuttered and closed. She didn't have the will to return calls to friends, to put up a brave front.

Today, she was taking tea with Eva in Eva's private dining room. Her stepmother had suggested a walk through the gardens afterward. This was what they spoke of now: the gardens and the weather. Everything else had become too dangerous. She still hadn't forgiven Edith for her callous, thoughtless comments to the *Daily News*—how *dare* her sister pontificate about the sanctity of her marriage, calling Jack a "rounder"? But they didn't speak of that either.

Frances sipped her tea and allowed herself to hope that everything really would be all right. Things—she wouldn't let herself use the words "the investigation"—hadn't been officially closed in New York, but they were *quiet*. She let herself think of a tour of Europe, or down the Nile, a change of scene.

Mrs. Mac, Eva's social secretary, appeared, her expression peculiar and tense and pitying. "Phone call, ma'am."

"Can't it wait?" Eva asked.

Mrs. Mac bent close to Eva's ear. "It's a reporter."

She'd spoken so quietly Frances *almost* couldn't hear. Immediately, her stomach twisted, the familiar sick fear flooding back.

"Oh, very well then," Eva said irritably, dabbing the corners of her mouth with a napkin. "Why don't you head down to the sunken gardens?"

"But I—" Frances protested.

"I'll be right down, dear." Eva's tone brooked no argument. And then she and Mrs. Mac were gone.

How could she be expected to enjoy the gardens knowing a reporter was calling? There was no reason to call except Jack: no guest list for a dinner or dance they were hosting, no menus for upcoming luncheons. But she had been dismissed and that was that.

Frances marched through the house and outside, resenting Eva's high-handedness. This was about *her* husband. She had a right to know! She strode through the terrace garden, barely glancing over at the arcade loggia that ran the length of it and showcased the four giant statues symbolizing the seasons.

Today, all the grandeur grated on her. Her mother had neither wanted nor lived in this level of opulence, even though her father could've afforded it then as well. Eva's fondness for luxury was nearly incomprehensible to Frances. When Eva went out, she would have her personal maid select the correct wrap for the event, then bring it to the top of the grand staircase and present it to the footman, who would, in turn, carry it down and provide it to the butler, who would then hand it to Frances's father, who would help his wife into the garment. The theatricality of it all was excessive and absurd.

She stomped between the parterre fountains, where sprite statues streamed arcs of water. Off to the right, stairs led up to the west belvedere. The towering stone rotunda with its pink Tennessee marble had always been her favorite; the wise, feminine face carved into the center of the towering arch and the hand-carved stone pineapples that stood sentry at each corner of the roof—symbols of welcome—were comforting in their reliability.

She made her way down to the long, curving staircase that led to the grotto fountain and the sunken gardens. Two gardeners, brushes in hand, knelt and scrubbed the stairs. "Careful, miss, it's very slippery," one warned, leaning back on his heels as she passed.

"Thank you," she said, taking extra care in her low heels—always low for a woman born ungracefully tall and married to a shorter man.

At the bottom, two white stone statues—one male, one female—lounged against a shared old-fashioned stone jug that gurgled forth water. The male statue's chiseled muscles bulged, his bearded face gazing adoringly down at his delicate stone lady. Frances turned away.

How many times had she diminished herself to make Jack feel big? Not just physically, hunching her way through life, but in her social efforts? She was known as an exceptionally graceful hostess, generous in her charity work. But how often had she consciously and unconsciously shrunk from the spotlight, scaled back her efforts, so as to put Jack forward? And for what?

New licks of rage swept through her. So that he could cheat on her? *Humiliate* her in front of the world? And now, just when it had seemed the whole ugly ordeal had passed, another reporter was calling. *What could they possibly want? Would this never end?*

"Franny!"

Frances turned to see her stepmother hurrying down the steps, the hem of her skirt fluttering.

"Careful, ma'am! Slippery!" the gardener called out.

"Careful!" Frances shouted.

But it was too late. Eva Stotesbury screamed as she lost her footing and tumbled headfirst down the wet marble stairs.

Chapter 48

May 14, 4:44 p.m. Manhattan. New York Daily News.

Two Society Thrones Fall in Shadow of Slain Dot King—Oblivion for Stotesburys and Mitchells

Julia looked at the one-page spread in the Sunday *News* with grim satisfaction. Daisy had done as she'd asked: written a searing piece on the seclusion and social isolation of the Mitchells and Stotesburys, wondering in ink how Mrs. Mitchell could bear to live with her cheat of a husband.

It was surely as painful as it was unwarranted for Frances Stotesbury Mitchell. But pressuring the powerful family who had exerted such undue influence over the case to once again push for action was the only way Julia could see to light a fire under the authorities. It was unfair but there was no other choice.

The paper had run separate photos of Frances and John Kearsley Mitchell to emphasize the marital schism. In one square, Frances sat, alone in her finery, looking forlorn, staring off in the distance. It was an old shot, since nobody could get anywhere near the family now, and Julia wondered what the society matron had been ruminating on.

Frances Stotesbury Mitchell didn't deserve any of this. She was, indeed, *more* innocent than Dot King, Julia reasoned, as Dot was having an affair with a married man, running a fraudulent brokerage firm, and doing heaven only knew what to earn those enormous bank deposits.

A shadow fell over her desk. Julia looked up to see Daisy. "Eva Stotesbury fell down a flight of stairs Saturday afternoon," the girl said flatly.

Julia pushed a quiver of guilt away. "Is she all right?"

Daisy's brow furrowed. "No. She broke her arm and was badly cut and bruised. She's in a state of severe shock. The doctor has ordered total isolation and rest. She's canceled all her social engagements."

"Thank goodness it's only that," Julia said.

"She fell after I called." Daisy's voice was sharp, accusatory. "She was probably upset and distracted by all the questions—*my questions*. She could've *died*."

"You don't know that," Julia said automatically, stubbornly.

"Well, I know she fell after I called and asked hard questions," Daisy insisted. "And I . . . I feel awful. She's an old lady who hasn't done anything wrong."

Julia squirmed, resenting the implication. "She's going to be all right—that's the important thing," she said almost mutinously, even as a very small, very ugly part of her couldn't help but recognize that if Eva Stotesbury had fallen to her death, the case would be back on the front page and the ensuing attention would reinvigorate the investigation.

Almost as though she could read Julia's dark thoughts, something shifted in Daisy's eyes—a condemnation. It made Julia feel dirty.

"Listen," Julia said, her voice growing testier. "We do what we have to do. We work in *news*."

"This isn't news," Daisy muttered, backing away, as though it might be catching. "It's a vendetta."

"Yeah—*a vendetta for justice!*" Julia called as the girl fled.

"Girl trouble?" Hellinger teased, walking in.

"Oh, why don't you shut up?" Julia snapped.

Hellinger blanched. "Sorry! Jeez."

Julia slumped. "No, I'm sorry. I shouldn't—" Her phone cut her off. "City desk. Harpman."

"Miss Harpman? This is Ella Bradford. I need to speak with you. It's about Dot King."

Chapter 49

May 16, 12:52 p.m. Manhattan. 43 West 127th Street.

"Why didn't you tell me? We all could've been spared this terrible thing."

What Mr. Marshall had said at the Criminal Courts Building haunted Ella, gnawed at her through the days, kept her awake at night. Was it true? *Could* she have saved Miss Dottie? She'd thought of little else these past weeks.

Then in church Sunday, the first sign had come. The preacher spoke on John 8:32: "And you shall know the truth, and the truth shall set you free." The hair on the back of Ella's neck had risen. She'd known it was for her.

After church, they'd walked home and she'd fried up pork belly and eggs.

"You're awful quiet," James had said.

Later still, they read the papers while June napped. James read the *Age*; she read the *News*. And right there, for the first time in weeks, was a big picture of Miss Dottie and Mr. Marshall, and in the middle of the page, his wife. She'd known then what to do.

She'd told Inspector Coughlin the last time they'd called her in and he hadn't listened, even when she'd told him she had information, even the last bit, the part she'd held back until the end. There was only one thing left to do.

The answer was right there on page 20 of the *Daily News*.

James didn't agree. "This is white-folk business."

Well, maybe it was. But Miss Dottie had trusted her more than anyone else in that sad, crazy life of hers. And Miss Dottie'd always done right by her.

The way Ella saw it, there was white-folk business and there was doing-right business. And it wasn't right how Miss Dottie's body was still over in the mortuary, on account of how that penny-pinching mother of hers still hadn't paid for her burial, while Guimares was out there, Lord knew where, just as free as he liked.

It wasn't fair. The lady reporter would care and maybe could do right by it.

I can do all things through Him, who gives me strength. Philippians 4:13.

And now she straightened the couch pillows again and pushed the window up a bit more to try to catch a breeze while she waited.

At one o'clock exactly, the bell rang. And there she was, just as she'd promised. She was white, of course—that much was to be expected. The rest, well, Ella didn't know too many white ladies, but this one didn't keep herself up like Miss Dottie or Miss Hilda or any of the showgirls they ran around with.

This woman was plainer. She was fresh-faced, no hint of powder or lipstick. Her navy skirt looked bought off the rack and hadn't been tailored.

She stuck out her gloved hand—navy, worn at the fingertips—looked Ella straight in the eyes, and shook harder than a lady should.

"Mrs. Bradford?" she said. "Nice to meet you. Thank you for calling."

"Yes, ma'am. Come in." Ella's stomach fluttered. The newspaperwoman's handshake, the way she stared, her serious, manly sort of demeanor, made this official and definite, which was even scarier. James was probably right. This was a mistake. Hadn't she had her fill of white-folk questions from police, lawyers, reporters? She should've let well enough alone. But it was too late now. Better to get her inside before the neighbors saw.

As Ella showed her in, she thought of Miss Dottie, and a ball of courage formed in her belly.

Ella poured coffee on the good tray with the good china, then sat as far away as she could, even as she reminded herself the newspaper-woman was here at her invitation and on her side. They both wanted Miss Dottie's killer put away.

Julia Harpman looked around in a way that made Ella fidget. "More cream?" Ella offered.

"No, thank you. It's perfect."

The newspaperwoman's voice was gentle and had a hint of south-ern in it. Ella wondered where she'd come from—it wasn't Georgia or Florida by the sounds of it. Back home, a lot of whites still treated Negro folk some sort of way—seemed to think it was still plantation times. But clearly they'd both come north and the news lady wanted to put her at ease.

Ella cleared her throat. It was now or never. "Mr. Marshall didn't do this. That I know."

Miss Harpman nodded, kept quiet. Those big, serious eyes didn't look away.

Ella kept her voice steady. "But they had words the day she died. He was . . . upset."

Julia Harpman didn't look surprised. "Do you know what about?"

Ella nodded. "Yes. She—Miss Dottie—didn't want to wait on him anymore. Mr. Marshall promised to get a divorce in Paris, then send for us and they'd get married there."

"So it was true then," the news lady said.

"Yes," Ella replied, thinking of how Mrs. Keenan wouldn't shut her mouth back in March.

The newswoman looked down at a list in her notebook, then back up. "You know, one thing I never understood," she said in her calm, quiet way, "is her will. The police said they found copies—that she was in fear of her life, but never signed it. Who was she afraid of? And why didn't she sign it?"

Ella nodded. "'Round about January, she got fearful. Said she felt the walls closing in. And she wasn't much wrong."

The news lady looked like she was about to ask more questions—questions Ella didn't want to answer, so she kept on. "Miss Dottie knew some tough characters. Once she got herself mixed up with Atlantic City, then it was a whole other bushel of trouble."

"You mean with Arnold Rothstein? And Draper Daugherty?"

Only one other person had that information. "Miss Hilda?" Ella asked.

"Well, I guessed the truth and she confirmed it," Miss Harpman said. "But she didn't tell me anything else, and to be honest, I still can't piece it all together."

It was a surprise Miss Hilda had learned to keep her mouth shut. "Miss Dottie was involved with Nucky Johnson way back," Ella said. "By the time I came along, he was just a friend. Kept a room for her at his hotel when she went down the shore. But Guimares had to be the one who killed her. He couldn't stand that she wouldn't give him those letters to blackmail Mr. Marshall. And I figure Guimares is the one who told the papers about them too when it came out who Mr. Marshall really was. When Guimares found himself in the hot seat, he wanted to make it look like Mr. Marshall had something to hide that was worth killing over."

"The infamous 'pink-toe' letter?" Julia Harpman asked.

Ella nodded, got up, fussed with the window. She didn't like to talk about all that. What was private between the couple should've stayed private. She'd told Inspector Coughlin because staying quiet had protected Guimares, literally let him get away with murder. She never thought Mr. Marshall's true identity would come out.

Ella sighed. She didn't want to say the next part, didn't want to make Miss Dottie look bad or tell on Mr. Marshall. But with no justice and the case shut down, there was no other choice. "For about a year and a half, Mr. Marshall promised he was gonna marry her. He'd talk all about going to Paris to get a divorce. But then, as time wore on, and he didn't . . . well, her faith was tested."

"She didn't believe he actually intended to divorce his wife," Julia Harpman said. And Ella heard in her tone a woman who understood.

"Yes. And Miss Dottie wasn't gonna just let herself be strung along forever. So she finally told him, 'You gotta marry me or settle up with me.'"

Miss Harpman nodded. "And what'd he say?"

"Well, he was . . . plain shocked. Said he couldn't believe this was really her. Said it over and over—just couldn't believe it. But by then . . . ," Ella said, and shook her head, then sighed. "Miss Dottie was stubborn. I told her to let him come around in his own time. But she said she wasn't gonna wait and let him make a fool of her."

Julia Harpman knit her brows and considered.

Ella stiffened. If this lady spoke a word—a single word!—against Miss Dottie, she'd find herself right back out on the sidewalk.

But the news lady didn't. Instead, she asked, "What'd she mean—'settle up with me'?"

"I couldn't say," Ella said, even though she *could*. But she'd take the specifics to her grave for Miss Dottie.

"And when was this?" Julia Harpman asked.

Ella looked her right in her eyes. "That afternoon."

"You mean . . . ?"

"Yes, ma'am," Ella said. "The night she was killed."

The news lady took that in, blinked, and drew a very slow, very deep breath.

And suddenly Ella remembered back when she was little—how they used to stay out past dark on summer nights to chase after lightning bugs. How the night was warm and alive with the sounds of crickets and cicadas, when the air was still close but didn't swelter so much after the sun went down.

Dusk was the best time to fish, and she'd run around under the weeping willows while her brothers threw lines in the mill pond to try to catch sunnies to fry up for breakfast after church.

But one time, the night had bedeviled her, as summer nights can, and she'd picked up the biggest rock her skinny little arms could lift and thrown it with all her might into the pond. There was a ker-splash; then the waves rippled out as the cicadas pulsed and crickets cheeped. Her brothers had hollered that she'd scared off all the fish, took their buckets, and left. There'd been no fried sunnies for breakfast the next day. She'd ruined it all.

Now, all these years later, this felt the same. What she knew would cause a splash, would send ripples out, disrupt the calm, still waters on top, stir up the mud underneath. But she'd gone and done it—thrown it in, ruined the stillness. And now all that was left to do was to watch and wait.

The news lady wrote her notes and looked up again. "Did she see anyone else that afternoon between this . . . conversation and when they went out to dinner later?"

Ella closed her eyes and returned to that day—that awful day—in her mind. She knew every single minute by heart. "Her masseuse, Bobbie Ellis, came over for her massage appointment later that afternoon."

Julia Harpman's eyebrows shot up. "A massage? Are you sure? This is the first I'm hearing of it."

Ella held her gaze firmly. "Well, ma'am, that's what happened. Bobbie Ellis was supposed to come back the next morning for another session. But then . . . you know."

"The morning of the *murder*?" Miss Harpman asked in her serious, quiet way. "Mrs. Bradford, may I ask? Why didn't you tell the police about the massage and the conversation between Miss King and Mr. Marshall?"

And here it was: the very heart of it—what chased around in her head every night when sleep wouldn't come. It was now or never—cast her stone for Miss Dottie or stay silent and let regret hang heavy on her shoulders. She took a deep breath. "Oh, I did," Ella said. "I told the police back in March."

Chapter 50

1:47 p.m. Manhattan. 43 West 127th Street.

Julia looked up and down the street, her arm raised to hail a cab at the corner of 127th and Lenox. She'd been followed before, and it was always the same: a man—*of course always a man*—in a parked car, or standing in a studiously casual way, perhaps making a show of reading a paper. Whether it was a gangster or an undercover fed, the dead giveaway was their watchful gaze, which zinged like electric current between predator and prey, making the back of her neck prickle even before she saw them.

Julia now knew the stakes were higher, the danger exponentially greater. Mrs. Bradford had already known, and she'd still called. She didn't have newspapers to sell or Philip breathing down her neck. Her intentions were pure.

In a world that ignored and devalued her, Ella Bradford's power lay in what she knew and what she did with that knowledge. And today, she'd aimed her slingshot at Goliath, drawn it back with all her might, and fired.

Ella Bradford had done more than anyone had a right to expect. She'd carried the burden of her secret, which held the power of truth and the danger of consequence, long enough. She'd handed the baton to Julia, and now it was up to her to run the final lap.

Julia could only hope she was up to the task.

The police knew that Ella Bradford knew these explosive secrets. But they didn't know Julia knew. Whoever had shut down the investigation wouldn't want a newspaper reporter learning this secret.

She had the cabbie drop her at Columbus and West 69th, ducked into a store to make sure she wasn't being followed, then hurried the last block home.

That Ella Bradford had it in her to risk everything—her own safety—to try to get justice for a white woman displayed a sort of courage, a depth of loyalty, Julia had never seen before in anyone. If Mrs. Bradford could do that for Dot King—with everything to lose and nothing to gain—Julia would redouble her own efforts. She owed that to both women.

She said hello to her doorman and took the elevator up to the fourth floor, thinking of how, nearly two months ago, Ella Bradford had walked into an apartment twelve blocks south of here and found herself in the middle of a crime scene. Julia twisted the Yale lock on her door shut, looked around the small, tidy living room, tidier perhaps because she and Peg worked so much they were never home, and called Philip.

As she waited to be connected, she made a list of outstanding questions and unresolved issues. She now knew that Dot King had pressured Mitchell to "marry her or settle up with her" hours before she was murdered. This didn't look good for the millionaire. And what of this masseuse? What had she seen or heard in her time with Dot King the day of the murder?

Meanwhile, she still had yet to discover why Mitchell had taken that very strange trip to DC. There had to be an urgent reason he'd made the trip, supposedly to meet his wife in the middle of Union Station, which they surely must have known would be swarming with reporters and curious onlookers, only to hop on a train *with his father-in-law* and go straight back to Philly. Could it be connected in some way to prematurely ending the investigation?

Julia looked back through her notes. At that very same time, the attorney general, also based in DC, just so happened to have had his son publicly exposed as being involved in the same case.

There was just one problem: Harry Daugherty had been in Florida with the presidential vacation tour when Mitchell went to DC.

So who *had* Mitchell gone to meet?

In the shadows of her mind, another suspicion began to form. Julia scanned the dates again. It was especially odd a "friend" of Draper Daugherty's had spoken for him, only to then have Draper himself disappear, and when he resurfaced, insist that he wasn't Dot King's lover, hadn't seen her in months, and had nothing to offer the investigation. And why had this "friend" gone to the press instead of the police?

Since Draper had been no help, it seemed the only purpose of publicly revealing his involvement with the case was the revelation itself. So the question then became: *Who benefited from Draper being pulled into the case?*

Julia drew an arrow in her notebook beside Draper's name, followed by a question mark.

Shortly after Draper Daugherty got involved, Pecora had dropped the case. Certainly, both Guimares and Mitchell would have been relieved by that development. The attorney general, publicly humiliated and furious at the distraction from his announcement about Harding's renomination, had then stashed his son in a sanitarium.

Philip's voice came through the line. "Payne."

"I need to go to Washington," Julia said. She hadn't put everything together yet, but she knew the next step.

"Care to elaborate?" he asked drolly.

"Who would Mitchell meet with there if the attorney general was away?"

There was a pause as Philip considered the question. "Hold on."

She knew him so thoroughly that she could picture him reaching into his second desk drawer on the left, pulling out his address book—a career's worth of contacts, priceless and irreplaceable.

He rattled off a number. "Tell him I sent you and burn it afterward. These guys aren't to be trifled with. And then hurry up and get me an exclusive. I'm already seeing a headline: 'What's Happened to Justice?'"

They hung up and she clicked for an operator and requested the number. She wondered who she was calling. A warning pulsed through her body.

"Yeah?" a gruff male voice answered.

"Philip Payne gave me this number. I need some information."

"Yeah?" he said impatiently.

"If Harry Daugherty was away, who would a very prominent Philadelphia society man meet with about a very, very large favor in a criminal case with national attention on it?"

There was a long pause. "You sure you wanna know?"

Julia's stomach did a sick little flip. She suddenly wasn't sure at all—but there was no going back. She couldn't unknow. "Y-yes."

"Jesse Smith," came the immediate reply. "If you want to get to Daugherty, you have to go through Smith."

"Who?" Julia asked.

"Jesse Smith, Daugherty's closest friend, most trusted adviser, and business partner," the man said. "They go way back. Smith owns a successful store in Ohio but came to Washington with Daugherty when Harding took office. And starting last summer, he's been the target of business and political gossip."

"What sort?" Julia asked.

"Well, he has an office in the Department of Justice but no official position," he replied. "He's Daugherty's constant companion and right-hand man while all these rumors about corruption bubble up, not to mention the impeachment proceedings."

"So a secret lieutenant then? Managing Daugherty's dirty work?" Julia asked, taking notes.

"Yes, but there's something else." He hesitated. "They keep three homes together. The so-called Little Green House on K Street, which they rent from Ned McLean." When she didn't react, he added, "The publisher of the *Washington Post*."

Of course she knew who owned the *Post*—newspapers were her business. What she hadn't known was that McLean was so close—and financially entangled—with the attorney general.

"That's where they throw their infamous parties—where you'd go if you wanted to grease the wheels and buy yourself a judgeship . . . or a criminal pardon."

The enormity of what this guy was casually rattling off began to sink in.

"They also keep a suite in the Wardman Park Hotel." The man paused, letting his meaning carry across the line. "They travel together, work together, room together. They're . . . *intimate friends.*"

Julia's pen froze on the word "friends."

"I see," she said. "And how do they . . . manage that?"

"How's anyone do anything? Friends in high places and surface-level respectability. Daugherty's *the attorney general.* Smith's close friends with the president and especially Mrs. Harding, squires her all over town, advises her on fashion, orders her gloves. The AG's married, though his wife is frequently ailing. Smith's divorced from a showgirl called Roxy Stinson, but they remain close friends. It all works—so long as you don't look too closely."

"And if Smith was with Daugherty in Florida, who'd my guy meet with in Washington?"

"Warren F. Martin," he replied. "Daugherty's 'special assistant,' does whatever the big guy wants. Plus, he's from Philly. If your guy's from Philly, they'd know each other."

Julia wrote the name down. "Got it. Thanks."

"Be careful," he warned. "Daugherty took that sick wife of his back to Ohio, and Jesse Smith followed shortly thereafter to visit and 'do some shopping.' But he's back and running things as usual now. So if you're going anywhere *near* this, you better make damn sure it's worth it, and you'd better know what the hell you're doing. These guys have eyes and ears everywhere, ya hear me? And they'll do *what they have to* in order to keep things quiet. I may not have a name, but you do. If you kick the hornet's nest, you can't run fast or far enough."

The line went dead. Julia slowly replaced the earpiece in the cradle. She glanced around, as though someone might be watching her right that very moment. But of course the apartment was empty.

She shook it off and called Westbrook.

"Just promise to be careful," he said when she told him her plan.

"Of course," she said lightly. "You know me." And it was true. He *knew* her. Knew this was what she did. Knew she'd gone poking into dangerous stories before. "What're you working on?" she asked to get them back on firmer ground.

"Oh, the usual assortment—baseball, wrestling, Delmonico's closing," he said.

"Not Delmonico's!" she said, only half joking.

"A New York institution," Westbrook agreed. "I've gotta go talk to some devastated waiter about how it's the end of an era."

"Go get 'em, honey!" she said, fiercely proud of him as always, not only because he was a talented newspaperman but also because he was man enough to marry a fellow reporter, especially one who was known as the best on her beat, supported her desire to continue to work, and cheered for her success. "I love you."

"I love *you*. Just remember, men have killed over far less."

She went into the kitchen, lit a burner. She watched the number catch flame and the black ash crumble onto the stove top.

Westbrook was right. But she was made of tougher stuff—she was a *newspaperman*.

Chapter 51

Julia stepped off the overnight train from New York and let the crowd carry her toward the exit. She'd been able to grab a few hours of sleep and, after a bracing cup of coffee in the dining car coupled with the excitement pulsing through her veins, was ready to infiltrate the Department of Justice.

People swirled around her, businessmen rushing to board their trains, travelers bidding farewell to family, porters shoving dollies piled high with suitcases, and conductors announcing departures. As she walked through the station, Julia marveled again that John Kearsley Mitchell had chosen this as the spot for a reunion with his beleaguered wife.

It seemed cruel to have subjected Frances to this further indignity. But then John Kearsley Mitchell did not seem especially concerned about subjecting his wife to embarrassment. Unbidden, the memory of Daisy's horror at the role they had played in Frances Stotesbury Mitchell's continued public humiliation, not to mention Eva Stotesbury's life-threatening tumble down the stairs, flashed into her mind. Perhaps Mitchell wasn't the only one causing or prolonging Frances Stotesbury Mitchell's public disgrace.

Julia shook the unwelcome thoughts off, reminding herself this was the cost of attaining justice for a murder victim.

It was a quick trip by taxi to the DOJ Building on K Street. "Excuse me, sir?" she said to the front desk attendant, letting her Tennessee creep in good and strong. "Where do maids go?"

The man barely glanced up from his newspaper, pointing toward an unmarked wooden door. "Basement."

While she fought to be seen in every room as a reporter, she could flip the forces that usually worked *against* her to work *for* her while she was undercover: if a woman was in the DOJ, surely she must be a maid.

Julia made her way down to the basement; found the women's locker room; stashed her coat, hat, and purse; then grabbed a bucket and mop. She took the elevator to the second floor. She would take her time establishing her presence as a cleaner before finding Warren's office.

It was a completely unremarkable Thursday morning in May, but as she mopped for the next few hours, the hallways began to buzz with the intensity of a swarming beehive. Every office had more desks and suit-clad men jammed in it than seemed possible (or advisable), and all of them seemed to be packing. By 11:30, the halls streamed with men in overalls carrying boxes, pushing carts piled with more.

"You there!" a man bellowed.

Julia froze, then slowly turned to face the music. Had they discovered her? Would they call the police? Interrogate her? They were the Department of Justice, for heaven's sake—their power had no limits.

A skinny man in an ill-fitting suit hurried toward her. "The floor of the men's restroom . . . uh . . . flooded."

Waves of relief washed over her. Her shoulders slumped. "Yessir," she said obediently, heading where he'd pointed, the bucket knocking against her leg.

It was only when she knocked on the restroom door, received no answer, and tentatively pushed it open that a secondary wave—this time of distaste—crept in. The vague smell of stale urine and fusty air was far worse than any ladies' restroom she'd been in, even the one she'd used at the women's prison after interviewing an accused murderess.

She propped open the door—the last thing she needed was some man coming in to relieve himself—and got to work.

After she finished mopping up the fetid puddle, she emptied the bucket, refilled it with fresh water from the utility closet, and went in search of Warren F. Martin, special assistant to the attorney general.

It was almost noon. Lunch would be the optimal time to catch the office unoccupied.

She found his secretary's desk outside unattended. Inside, a man with overly brilliantined hair and a close-cropped mustache was hunched by the phone, muttering into it urgently.

She tapped on the doorframe. "Need cleanin', sir?"

He scowled at the interruption and covered the mouthpiece with his palm. "The windows—I called days ago," he said, annoyed.

"Yessir." She dragged her supplies inside and began to wash the windows, working as slowly as possible.

He went back to his call. She was unremarkable to him, cloaked by both her gender and her role.

A few minutes later, she heard a knock. "You ready?"

"One minute, Jess," Martin said.

Could this be Jesse Smith? Julia risked a glance at the rotund man, who plopped down in a guest chair and began marking up a sheaf of papers. He cut an unusual and somewhat awkward personage. He was tall—she barely came up to his shoulders—with a potbelly protruding insistently from his unbuttoned jacket. He had a close-cropped mustache (she was grateful Westbrook was clean-shaven), and a double chin that no amount of proper "head-up" posture would assuage. He wore an immaculately cut pinstripe suit with a bright purple pocket square.

"Very good. I'll attend to it," Martin assured whoever was on the line, and hung up. He came around the desk and offered a handshake to his guest. "Ready for lunch? I'm famished."

Jess paused writing and rose. He reached for the handshake, forgetting that he was still holding a pen. He nicked Warren's palm with the nib.

"Ow!" Warren said, withdrawing his hand.

"Ah! Sorry!" Jess Smith, flushed and flustered, tried to put the pen in his other hand, and lost his grip on the sheaf of papers.

Both men bent to pick them up. "Sorry, sorry!" Jess repeated.

"It's OK, pal. Take it easy," Warren said, patting the larger man on the back. "You all right?"

"Yeah, yeah, I'm fine. Just . . . a lot on my mind. Let's go."

Warren, seeming to remember her presence, turned. "Don't forget the trash."

"Yessir," she said again. She rubbed at the glass, the panes squeaking under her ministrations. Then they were gone. It was almost too easy.

In case anyone was watching, she began mopping—swish-swishing her way over to the door. Then *swish*, the mop thunked into the door, knocking it mostly closed. Her privacy ensured, she clicked the stopwatch function at the top of her watch. The second hand began to tick frantically. She figured an hour was a fairly average lunch for men of this ilk. But to be safe, she would try to take less than ten minutes.

She dropped any pretense of cleaning and ran to the desk. Quickly, she began riffling through the stacks of papers covering the entire surface. Tick-tick-tick-tick.

Already one minute gone.

Hands shaking, heart beating nearly as fast as the frantically ticking stopwatch, she shuffled through letters, memorandums, meeting requests, meeting summaries, a Department of Justice Appropriations Report that was at least several hundred pages . . . all useless.

Two minutes down. She had to move faster! She shuffled through more useless reports and notes, not sure what she was looking for. She lifted a bound report and froze. Underneath was a stack of newspaper clippings. The headline from the front-page article screamed up at her: Hunt Blackmailers in Death of Model—Special to the Washington Post.

The fine hairs on the back of her neck tingled menacingly.

John Kearsley Mitchell, the millionaire Philadelphian
who used part of his fortune to drape the shapely form of
Dot King with furs and jewels and silken gowns . . .

She knew each word by heart. They were hers.

She scanned the next paragraphs—down to the mortifying part
she'd penned about the Stotesbury-Mitchells: It was known that Mitchell,
who has admitted his identity as the mysterious Mr. Marshall, the last-
known person to see the girl alive, had written letters to Dottie, in which
he expressed his desire to be with her; his preference for her society
over that of the Princess Anastasia, who was then being entertained by
Mr. and Mrs. E. T. Stotesbury, Mitchell's in-laws, at their winter home, El
Mirasol, in Palm Beach; his consuming wish to "kiss your pretty pink toes."

Tick-tick-tick . . .

She scanned the stack. How many of her stories had they reprinted?
And had they ever given her a byline? Were Daugherty, Smith, and
Martin aware of her identity?

And now, dear God, she was in Martin's office! These men had been
in here with her just moments ago!

Tick-tick-tick-tick. Five minutes down.

Panic escalating, she paged through the stack. Every single clipping
was about the King case. She flipped faster. Sure, every newspaper in
America had run articles about Dot King . . . but these were *hers*, and
these were from March, and Warren F. Martin, Harry Daugherty's special assistant, had not only read them but meticulously cut them out
and saved them. *Why?*

The phone rang and she nearly leaped out of her skin. The insistent
brrrrrrrrrring was a crucial reminder: time was limited and running out
fast. *Six minutes gone.* She dropped the papers and yanked open the top
right drawer. Inside, pens, paper, notes—"Call S," "Deposit WCH,"
"Roxy 4/1," "Sinco confirm!"—but nothing immediately decipherable.

The middle drawer was similarly stuffed. She kept rummaging, trying to get a sense of its contents, then trying to reassemble it exactly as it had been, so Martin wouldn't know she'd riffled through his things.

It was a fruitless endeavor—there were too many papers, and she didn't even know what she was searching for. How was she supposed to find anything under these conditions? What was she even doing here?

Tick-tick-tick-tick. Nine minutes down.

She looked around, scanning hurriedly for a clue—*any clue!*

Two men walked by, their rumble of conversation a sickening reminder that she wasn't alone. She knelt to examine the desk more closely. There was a shallow middle drawer with a keyhole—it didn't even have a handle, rather an under-drawer fingertip pull.

She pulled. It was locked. She knelt, running her fingers frantically under the drawers. *Where would he hide the key?* Desperation escalated. The safest place was on his person. Of course he'd taken it with him. Dejected, she sat back on her heels.

Tick-tick-tick-tick . . . ten minutes.

A coat-tree behind the door held a few hats and one wool blazer. She thought about the handkerchiefs and keys Westbrook left in his pockets. She ran over, rummaged through the pockets. In the shallow waist pocket, the heavens smiled upon her: one tiny key.

She rushed to the desk, jammed the key in, turned it. The locked desk drawer opened. There, in plain view, was an appointment diary.

Tick-tick-tick-tick. Eleven minutes down.

Sweating, she looked at the door. How much longer would Smith and Martin be gone?

She thumbed backward through the pages, each day organized by time slots from 8:00 a.m. until 8:00 p.m., each line filled with names.

She flipped back through the weeks of May, then April, frantic to get to the one day she'd come for: March 27. The day that Frances Stotesbury Mitchell had traveled north with her children, father, and stepmother on a private train car full of servants. The day that her philandering cheat of a husband, John Kearsley Mitchell, had inexplicably traveled to Washington, DC, to meet them.

The day that someone had mysteriously thrust a seemingly reluctant Draper Daugherty into the case.

April 15. April 5. March 31. March 30. Tick-tick-tick-tick . . . thirteen minutes.

The same question that had plagued Julia ever since rang with renewed force through her brain: Why had the recently revealed, freshly embarrassed "Mr. Marshall" traveled to DC to meet his wife, only to immediately turn around and go back to Philadelphia?

March 29. Tick-tick-tick-tick.

John Kearsley Mitchell had tried to deal with the case himself for nine days and failed to hush it up or shut it down.

March 28. Tick-tick-tick-tick.

Why hadn't he waited for them at home? Why hadn't he made a truly grand gesture of traveling all the way to Palm Beach? She flipped one final page.

March 27.

She ran her finger down the page.

8:00 a.m. Sinco

9:00 a.m. Doheney

10:00 a.m. J. K. Mitchell

Everything froze. She could hear each breath. Here it was, right in front of her eyes, the smoking gun—a definitive tie between the Stotesbury-Mitchell empire and the corrupt Daugherty-Smith political machine.

Mitchell had come to Washington, DC, to meet Warren F. Martin, his fellow Philadelphian and Daugherty's special assistant, in person, just as she'd suspected! Just four days before Pecora publicly withdrew from the investigation, thus effectively ending it. It was all right here!

The immediate elation of her victory was tempered by wondering: *Now what?* Should she rip the page out? Without context, it was worthless. Steal the entire diary? That was a crime—a crime that would probably get her killed. Could she try to get back in with a camera? *Impossible!*

Footsteps came closer in the hall. She slammed the appointment book back in its drawer, and leaped toward the bucket. She was mopping the floor convincingly when a man appeared.

He was holding a sheaf of papers and looked surprised to see her. "Uh, where's Mr. Martin?"

"Lunch, I reckon," Julia said with a forced shrug.

"Ah, I see." He blinked, looking around as though she might be concealing Mr. Martin.

He stood there—watching, waiting—as she mopped. She tried desperately not to shake, or give herself away, or panic. But why was he still here? Did he suspect?

He was blocking the door. He could call security. She couldn't push past him. And even if she could, the exit was halfway down the hall. She'd never make it.

She kept her eyes down and tried to rein in her racing thoughts. He had no reason to suspect her, let alone chase her. She swished the mop in the bucket and told herself to keep mopping. Cleaning, like all "women's work," was an excellent way to be ignored. But could he hear the stopwatch? She started to hum to cover it up.

Perhaps she was imagining his extra attention. Perhaps he just wanted to know when to come back. He looked young. She could get rid of him. She swished the mop too close to his shoes. "Scuse me please, sir."

He leaped out of the way, not wanting his leather to get sloshed by the filthy mop. "I guess I'll come back later."

She nodded. "Yessir."

He looked at the papers in his hand, like he was still undecided.

She told herself to move slow and tired—the most important thing was to get out of here undetected and safely back to New York. She just had to stay calm and act the role.

Finally, after one more look around, he left.

She closed the door behind him, went back to the desk, and, hands still shaking, relocked it. She put the key back in Martin's jacket pocket and took a deep breath.

She clicked the stopwatch, and the frantic ticking ceased. Out in the hall, she made herself mop slowly toward the exit. *Slow and tired, one step at a time.*

Swish-swish. Halfway there. *Don't rush. Plunge the mop in the water, clean the floor.*

Male voices echoed down the hall and she jumped. It was Smith and Martin. Some deep part of her—the primal part—screamed to turn and run. But she made herself grip the mop tighter and keep working. *Head down, another step closer to safety.*

The men drew closer, arguing, it seemed.

Swish-swish. *Don't look up.* Four steps more.

They blew past her, as though she didn't exist, immersed in their disagreement, went in Martin's office, slammed the door.

"You're a fool!" Martin bellowed.

Swish-swish. Two steps closer. Then, finally, the door.

She grabbed the bucket and ran down the stairs toward freedom.

Chapter 52

4:30 p.m. Northeast Corridor Train Route.

The train ride back to New York seemed endless. Every station announcement, stop, and shuffling passenger slowly boarding or leaving was another infuriating delay in Julia getting to her typewriter. The facts of the case restlessly circled in her brain. She took to staring out the window, trying to corral the sprawling case into a story.

She thought of her mother. Josie Harpmann had never dealt with a murder case, by virtue of her choice to work on the society pages instead of the court beat. But it often seemed to Julia that social events were no less perilous. Josie's advice, no matter the story, was to sit down and start at the beginning.

Pen in hand, Julia closed her eyes and thought back to where the case had begun. On March 15, Ella Bradford had discovered Dot King, murdered. Here they were two months later: the investigation shut down, no arrests. Julia opened her eyes and wrote, What Has Happened to Justice?

As the train chugged north back to New York, the reporter's alchemy of facts and words intermingled and poured forth an article.

Justice slept late on the morning of March 15, 1923, she wrote . . .

When Justice awoke and followed the trail that led from the murdered Dot King's butterfly nest to the realm of millions and the office of the attorney general of the United States, she went back to bed again.

She read her words, and a shiver sliced through her belly. It was all true, of course. But printing it for the world to read was the sort of thing that could get a reporter sued for libel . . . or worse.

Was she really going to do this?

Philip would be thrilled, of course. With a lead-in like this, and pictures of the startlingly beautiful Broadway Butterfly, copies would *fly* off the stands.

It was all true—but would the house of Stotesbury-Mitchell send its lawyers anyway? Those used to wealth and the privileges it afforded didn't take kindly to unflattering accusations.

And what of Harry Daugherty? Was she *actually* going to put an indirect accusation against the attorney general of the United States *in print* in the largest morning circulation in the country?

She had the power to do that. But she'd also reap the consequences. Both were dizzying, terrifying, irrevocable. She had to be careful. And she *was*. She wouldn't—*couldn't*—write what Ella Bradford had told her; nor would she reveal what she'd found in Martin's office.

But she could tell the story without those details, and still get the point across.

Julia Harpman was always up for a challenge. She took a last, furtive look around and wrote.

◆ ◆ ◆

It was after 9:00 p.m. by the time she returned to the city desk. She'd never been so happy to be back in her chair, surrounded by the guys. She was home. She was safe. And, most importantly, she had gotten the story.

She hurriedly typed up the piece from her notes and took it straight to Philip, who paced as he read. Finally, he looked at her over his glasses. "You got chutzpah, Harpman, chutzpah! This part about Rothstein? 'Now it chanced that Daugherty, on his own word, found his best friend in New York in Arnold Rothstein, insurance and real estate operator. What business he had with the former gambler, one cannot say.' This is fantastic!"

She plopped down in his guest chair. "That's the part I'm worried about. I don't want to get slapped with an accusation of libel."

"Let me worry about that," he said, though he worried very little about that, even after having faced a libel suit himself. Philip Payne saw the world only in terms of potential copies sold.

Julia was sure she'd die of shame if ever faced with the ugly accusation, but Philip would probably parlay it into an even bigger story.

He kept reading. "This ending is pure gold. 'The doors of the sanitarium closed on Daugherty. Mitchell went back to Philadelphia to his family. The gems of Dot King have not been found. WHO ROBBED DOT KING? Therein lies the story of her death in all human probability. Justice does not know. For justice lost wind when the avenue of the inquiry had the banking house of Morgan and Co. at one end and the nation's chief law agent at the other.' Whoa, boy! Somebody call the fire department because these pages are burning up!"

Julia couldn't help but laugh. "I'm glad you like it."

"I don't *like* it," Philip corrected. "I *love* it!" He snatched up one of the phones on his desk and called for a copyboy. "Remind me to sock Westbrook Pegler right in the beak next time I see him. That bastard snagged the best gal in town."

Julia cleared her throat. "One more thing. I think we better skip my byline."

Philip nodded. "I didn't want to say it, but I agree."

She was disappointed, even though it had been her idea. She'd worked ten times harder than any of the men to get that byline, and now it would be gone as quickly as that.

Gone for my protection, and just for this piece, she reminded herself. And even without her byline, anyone worth his salt would know it was her. She would be stripped of the honor she'd earned and still possibly face danger. That was the price of working on big stories. But it was worth it: the satisfaction of knowing she'd done what she could in pursuit of justice for Dot King, and to stay as safe as possible.

"Then it's decided," she said matter-of-factly.

"It'll run Sunday, with daily teasers till then," Philip promised. "But listen, you have to be careful. This ain't the minor leagues. This is dangerous stuff."

The warning packed a punch coming from a guy who had once volunteered to drive a rattletrap Ford filled with one hundred thousand cigarettes from war-torn Paris to the front lines in the middle of the night so the soldiers would have smokes.

She met his gaze squarely. "Oh, I know."

Chapter 53

Frances paced rabidly between the boudoir's windows, desperate to see the car's headlamps coming up the drive. Where on earth was Jack? She'd reached her limit, by God. How much could she be expected to endure?

Copies of the last two Sunday editions of the *New York Daily News* taunted her from their perch on the desk. She tried—mightily—to resist reading them yet again. But if the will to refrain from the self-punishing task existed in a stronger woman, she'd never know. The first headline trumpeted her humiliation: Two Society Thrones Fall in Shadow of Slain Dot King—Oblivion for Stotesburys and Mitchells. The next, a week later, had read: What Has Happened to Justice?

Frances threw them aside, bitterness and rage rising biliously in her throat. *Oblivion? How dare they!* How dare they poke gleefully into the most private and painful moments of her life! *And as for justice . . .* Well, she wouldn't let herself think of that.

All the other papers had moved on from regurgitating every nauseating detail about the filthy whore who'd captivated her husband, then turned up dead. Frances had *almost* begun to not think of it every single second. She'd even dared to hope for the future. But now the *Daily News* was stirring everything up again—first, calling Eva and upsetting her so much she'd fallen down the stairs, then continuing their campaign of harassment. The so-called picture paper had even run photographs of her, Jack, and that girl *next to each other*—trotting out every detail for public dissection.

For the past two months, she'd tried to be a dignified wife, a devoted mother. But really, how many times could she be expected to be humiliated?

Rage and bitterness threatened to overtake her. Where on earth was Jack? She stared out the window at the empty road, and the two hundred acres stretching out in every direction, as though she could make him appear. In a house full of servants, the children already in bed, she was utterly alone waiting and wondering.

After the police stopped finding leads, the forty to sixty reporters stationed outside their town house had decamped. The calls to their homes had dwindled to a trickle, then dried up altogether. The mudslingers had moved on.

Except for one: the stubbornly persistent Julia Harpman at the *Daily News* still called their houses, family, and friends. Leave it to a woman to remain undistracted. Leave it to a woman to be so hateful.

The servants had their instructions to deflect: *"Mr. Mitchell is out of town on an indefinite stay, Mrs. Mitchell is unavailable, but they are still very much married and living under the same roof."* Say no more and hang up.

Frances had come to loathe this Miss Harpman and dread the butlers' reports of her weekly inquiries. And thanks to her father's corps of private detectives, she knew exactly who to hate: the detectives had returned photos and details of everyone associated with the case. Frances had memorized every detail about the serious-looking girl standing outside New York's City Hall at the edge of a crowd of men. Miss Harpman was attractive, if bookish, with a head of hair that would've benefited from a conditioning treatment and proper dressing by a maid. In fact, *all* of Miss Harpman would've benefited from proper dressing.

But the newspaper girl was apparently too busy writing venomous articles to take any care with her appearance. Why, Eva had broken her arm when she'd fallen. *She could've died.* Yet the paper, undeterred, had had the audacity to print a full-page spread sneering about their social oblivion, rehashing the whole ugly thing. And then, the following week, a *two-page* spread under the accusatory headline: WHAT HAS HAPPENED TO JUSTICE? That piece had pictures of Jack, her father, and her at the boardwalk—a happy memory from happier times—on the very same page as Draper Daugherty and some scantily clad showgirl. The opposite page had featured a huge photo of her husband's mistress pouting saucily.

And worst of all, that unspeakably offensive, humiliating last paragraph: WHO ROBBED DOT KING? There lies the story of her death, in all human probability. Justice does not know, for Justice lost wind when the avenue of inquiry had the banking house of Morgan and Co. at one end and the nation's chief law agent at the other.

How dare they!

The district attorney had turned the case over to the police, whose skeleton crew had blessedly turned up nothing. This had provided a month and a half of welcome, if uneasy, quiet. But now, in black and white for New York and *all the world* to see, the *Daily News* and its wretched newspaper girl were directly accusing them and Harry Daugherty of thwarting the investigation. And who needed to thwart an investigation? *Only the guilty.*

Surely this must be libel! How dare that trashy tabloid print such things? They mustn't be allowed to get away with it. She wouldn't stand for it! Her father wouldn't stand for it!

And yet if, as the article had said, Morgan and Co. loomed at one end of the avenue with the attorney general at the other, why *was* the case still open?

The police still hadn't *officially* closed their investigation, without any explanation for the delay, forcing her family to wait in limbo—neither condemned nor free, their town houses and social calendars mortifyingly empty. Her father and Eva were similarly exiled to Whitemarsh Hall.

She'd left word with the butler to send Jack up as soon as he arrived from the office. She knew from his manner at dinner every night—a deep sort of weariness mixed with a cautious watchfulness around her—that he fought similar battles, but she withheld the kindness of inquiry or sympathy. Whatever suffering he endured was his own fault. This entire thing was all his fault. He deserved to suffer.

But the blisteringly unfair bit was that he'd consigned her and the children to the same fate. The injustice of this slashed a welt of anger deep within her that would never fully recede.

Finally, twin headlamps, tiny stars, far off down the dark road, appeared. Her heart sped up, and she steeled herself for the scene ahead. She sat at her desk and waited for his car to arrive, the chauffeur to open his door, his feet to crunch on the gravel, the butler to deliver the message, take his coat and briefcase, and Jack to climb the stairs. Eventually, his knock sounded.

"Yes?" She tried to keep her voice moderate.

He was, as always, wearing a three-piece suit but looked particularly drained tonight. "You wanted to see me?"

"These articles, Jack." She gestured vaguely, standing. "Is there any word on . . . things?"

He sighed. "There's no developments and no news. But it seems they haven't closed it either."

They both avoided the word "investigation."

"Well, what do you suppose is taking so long?" she asked, sharp-edged impatience creeping into her voice.

He started to answer, but she quickly held up her hand, terrified he'd say something like, "Well, Franny, a girl has been *murdered*, after all."

"Jack—"

He plowed on, speaking over her. "It seems they still haven't found the culprit, or haven't been able to gather enough evidence against that Spanish brute to press charges. And because it's in the spotlight, measures must be taken to ensure a thorough and exhaustive process. The public . . . and the . . . uh . . . family demand it."

Her stomach heaved at the mention of that creature's family. "Well, Jack, *you* have a family too. This matter must conclude so that we can return to our lives."

His face, still placid, hardened a fraction, as though her request irritated him. "Your father and I are doing everything we can to make that possible—*everything*."

She turned away. He should be groveling, apologetic. They were circling around an argument like boxers, waiting to see who would throw the first punch, or if, indeed, a fight could be avoided. "Yes, but how much longer?"

He sighed. "I don't know, darling. I wish I did."

She tensed at the endearment. He didn't deserve to use it. "Well, surely there's something *more* you can do? The children and I . . . we can't bear it!"

She didn't know what the children could bear. They didn't read the papers and were insulated out here from other children whose parents might not be so careful. But they couldn't stay in Villanova forever.

"Well, Franny, I'm doing all I can," he said, his voice growing sharp.

"Perhaps we should ask my father," she ventured, knowing full well the effect the barb would have, and issuing it anyway.

Predictably, he stiffened. "You already did," he said bitterly.

"Well, you left me no choice!" she flared. "You'd been found out—dragging us all into this nightmare. The publicity will stain us for the rest of our lives. We *needed* my father's help!"

"No, we didn't," he snapped. "I was handling it. I didn't need the world-famous E. T. Stotesbury bailing me out."

Frances was horrified by both his arrogance and ignorance. "How can you be so vile? So ungrateful! And wrong! You had time to *handle it*, and you failed to do so. So don't blame my father. He's only ever tried to do *everything* to help us succeed!" She took a breath, anger making her bold, giving voice to all the things that had simmered inside for years. "You knew who I was and who my father was when you asked me to marry you. I thought you'd *appreciate* how my family's social standing has helped you!"

He looked as though he'd flare up again, but instead looked down in a shamefaced misery that made her both pity and hate him. "I thought I would too," he finally said. "But you've got to understand what it's like to be a man, the man of the house. I'm the CEO of a successful company, for God's sake! But no matter how much I do and no matter how successful I am—and I *am* successful, goddammit—there's always this monolith of your father's greater success towering over me. No matter what I do, or what I can provide for you and the children, it pales in comparison to what he can."

Frances looked down. There was nothing to say. It was true.

"And I realized that on our wedding day," Jack continued quietly, bitterness lacing his words with an acidity that she felt might actually cut her, "when he presented you with that check...and the diamonds... and the pearls and even this estate, for God's sake!"

She flushed. "I thought you loved it here as much as I do. I thought you appreciated my father's generosity! I won't let you twist it into something ugly."

"I'm not trying to!" he practically wailed. "I *do* appreciate it! I feel like a heel for complaining. But how much charity can one man be expected to take before he starts to feel unmanned? Like some sort of goddamn Dickensian charity case! 'Please, sir, may I have some more?'" he said, lifting his hands like the supplicant in *Oliver Twist*.

The red-hot rage that jolted through her was a surprise. And where before she'd always tried to be sympathetic, had, in fact, spent years treading oh-so-carefully around the issue, pretending she didn't notice the disparity, even downplaying her father's wedding gifts—the diamond tiara, ropes of pearls, and $1 million check—to protect Jack's tender ego, now she pressed directly on the bruise. "How *dare* you! My father is a *real* man. He came from nothing—a stock boy—and *worked* his way up to being Mr. Morgan's partner. And he never once stepped out on my mother or Eva. If your response to his sharing his hard-earned fortune with us is to go out and find some street tramp—some uneducated whore who thinks every thought you have and every word you say is utterly brilliant and fascinating—so you can feel like a big man next to my father, then maybe it's not me or my father making you feel small. Maybe you just *are* small!"

"Frances!" He blanched, shocked.

She'd gone too far. Some things couldn't be unsaid or apologized for later. Jack looked so devastated she almost wished she could take it back. "I'm—"

"That's enough!" he said, drawing up to his full height, which was, regrettably, still not equal to hers. "And . . . I'm sorry, Franny, truly I am."

"If you were truly sorry, you'd find a way to end this!" Frances wailed. "I don't care what you have to do or how it's done. Only that it's done swiftly so life can get back to normal."

They locked gazes, and he gave the very briefest of nods. Then he was gone. Her shoulders sagged with shame and relief. But solitude was preferable to his company.

She hadn't invited him to share her bed since this happened—couldn't imagine she would ever do so again, even if he succeeded in closing the case and putting a stop to the publicity, which, it pained her to note, he'd failed to do.

His reference to that . . . vamp's . . . *family* struck her again, almost like a physical blow. He'd failed to protect his family, and family was everything. It was still unfathomable to think of Jack—*her Jack!*—knowing such people. Worse, that horrid laundrywoman *continued* claiming that Jack had promised to go to Paris, obtain a divorce, and marry her daughter!

Frances could only imagine the horrified pity of the Philadelphia 400 reading that.

Had Jack actually wanted to leave their enviable life behind and marry that scandalous, filthy girl half his age? The daughter of a *laundress*? A Catholic divorcée who'd been bedding at least two other lovers, including a Puerto Rican gigolo and the attorney general's wayward son?

Frances slumped weakly. It had to go away. And if, as a consequence, that wicked girl's death went unsolved, well, that was necessary collateral to her bad choices.

So why did she feel a sickening wave of guilt?

For one fleeting moment, the girl's mother flashed into her mind, and the devastation of one's daughter dying—murdered, no less—rose nauseatingly. Frances reminded herself that nothing would bring that woman's daughter back. One couldn't expect such a wicked, wayward girl could come to a good end.

She tried to focus on her own children. Jackie would soon be off to St. Paul's, followed by Princeton, while Franny would be presented to society and have her choice of suitors.

Frances tried to imagine the wedding . . . adjusting her daughter's veil, dabbing a tear as Jack walked her down the aisle. And when that day came, Frances prayed she wouldn't look at him and wonder: *Could he have been capable of killing someone else's daughter?*

Frances's breath caught, and she physically recoiled at the horrific question that had floated, unbidden, to the top of her mind. She stumbled to the window and stared out into the darkness, shoving the terrible thought away and down, where it would stay buried.

Chapter 54

Coughlin stormed into Carey's office, a rolled-up copy of the *Daily News* clenched in his fist. The paper had had the audacity to run the offensive "What Has Happened to Justice?" spread about the Dot King case for the second Sunday in a row. He was going to blow a gasket.

"'What has happened to justice?' I'll goddamn tell you what happened: Idiot Enright and his merry band of incompetents happened."

Carey raised his brows. "Another glorious day at police headquarters, I see."

Coughlin smacked the paper against his palm. "So I'm supposed to just stand here while the entire city throws rotten tomatoes at me, and Enright gets off the hook? All cozy in his office, hard at work on his next detective novel? Jesus Christ!" He plunked into a chair, the weight of it all, the unfairness of it all, too heavy for even his broad shoulders. "If people only knew."

Carey snorted. "They'll never know."

"Well, this can't stand. I won't allow it," Coughlin said.

"So what's your next move?" Carey asked, always practical.

Coughlin had his answer ready. It had been percolating for weeks, ever since Aurelia Fischer had given that son of a bitch Guimares an alibi. "Word came from on high that we had to drop it. But they didn't say I had to drop Guimares."

Carey frowned. "But that *is* . . . I don't get it."

"They wanted the Dot King investigation closed and buried. Things hushed up. Everyone move along. But they didn't say I couldn't get Guimares."

"But that's the very definition of stirring things back up, of *not* letting it die down," Carey said.

Coughlin pointed, victorious. "Not if I make sure he's nailed on charges unrelated to the King case. Which brings me to Pecora."

"But I thought that's what . . . sorry, pal . . . I'm lost," Carey said, holding his hands up in surrender. He forced a nervous chuckle, as though he were trapped in a room with someone who'd gone batty. Hell, maybe he was.

Coughlin stayed razor-focused. "Pecora thought he got the last laugh when he had those files anonymously messengered over about the King and Scott investigation. It was *his office's* investigation, but he didn't follow through with charging Guimares or Dot King with anything . . . and then just dumped the whole goddamn mess on me! Well, now I'm going to turn the tables on that two-timing little bitch. Guimares didn't just swindle investors; he sent them fake statements by mail. That makes it a federal crime."

Carey's eyes lit up. "Hell *yes*! That's brilliant!"

"Nobody muzzles John D. Coughlin. Guimares won't do twenty-five to life for murder, and that's a goddamn crime in itself. But at least I can make sure that bastard does a nickel in the federal pen. He won't get off scot-free, at any rate." Coughlin leaned back. "One way or another, I *always* get my man."

Chapter 55

The phone jangled, jolting Julia out of a deep sleep. She shrugged into her robe and made her way into the living room.

Westbrook, already up, answered. "Yes?" He paused to listen to the response, and the quiet grew more ominous the longer it stretched.

Westbrook held out the phone. "It's Philip."

The certainty that something terrible was afoot lodged itself in her belly. "Hello?"

"I've just received word: Jesse Smith, the attorney general's right-hand man, is dead." Philip's voice was grave, urgent—and this was a man who had spent his career on the front lines of the news, sifting reports of every misfortune and marshaling them into stories.

"What? How?" The memory of the large, jittery man who'd come to Warren Martin's office, dropped the sheaf of papers, then accidentally jabbed Martin's hand with a pen flashed into her mind.

"Shot himself," Philip informed her. "He was found with his head in a waste bin and the pistol in his hand, in the suite he and the attorney general shared at the Wardman Park Hotel."

"I'll head in," she said, hanging up. The fact was, Smith's connection to the attorney general in the wake of their "What Has Happened to Justice?" piece might even give the story wings.

Westbrook poured her a cup of coffee and she took a bracing sip, her brain stumbling toward the promise of wakefulness. "Peg, I met him. I was in Warren Martin's office and Jesse Smith came in . . . I was *there* with him . . . and now he's dead."

She touched the gold band on his ring finger, grateful that she had found him, grateful that he was hers. They hadn't even been married for a year yet. "You never know how much time any of us has."

"No," Westbrook agreed. "But being involved with powerful, corrupt men certainly doesn't seem to extend anyone's life expectancy."

◆ ◆ ◆

There were five telegrams on her desk when she got to the newsroom. She picked up the first.

Jesse Smith had been found dead at 6:30 a.m. The report said he'd shot himself with an automatic pistol. The bullet had exited his right temple and been found lodged in the doorframe.

Julia froze. The bullet had exited his right temple and been found lodged in the doorframe.

Exited his right temple.

Which meant the bullet had *entered* his left temple.

She looked up. "Oh my God."

Like the majority of people, Jesse Smith had been right-handed. She'd seen him taking notes with his right hand as he waited for Warren Martin to go to lunch. She clearly remembered the proffered handshake that turned into the awkward pen-stabbing-palm incident. But this article clearly said the bullet entered Smith's left temple and exited his right.

Julia tried holding her pen in her left hand. It felt foreign. *Impossibly foreign.*

Around the newsroom, the skeleton staff who was in that early went about their business: typing, talking, making calls. The room was still waking up. She sat in the middle of it all, having read the same missive that Philip, the telegram operators, and who knew how many others had read, and yet nobody else seemed to have noticed. To be fair, nobody else had recently been in the same room as Jesse Smith. Most people didn't know he was right-handed.

But in that moment Julia knew Jesse Smith had been murdered. He'd been *murdered*, and nobody had even noticed.

She read through the other telegrams, most with only minor updates. She skimmed the last and froze. Then picked up the phone and called Westbrook. Keeping her voice low even though Hellinger, Joe, and most of the other city desk staff hadn't arrived yet, she told him her suspicions based on the bullet exiting Smith's right side. "And that's not all. When I went to Washington, I learned Smith and Daugherty had three homes together there—the so-called Little Green House on K Street and a suite at the Wardman Park Hotel where Smith was found dead this morning. But here's the real kicker—the attorney general wasn't at either one of them last night. No, *he* was spending the night at the White House."

"What?" Westbrook's shock radiated over the line. "The attorney general spent the night at the White House the same night his lover was murdered in their own home?"

"Yes!" Julia said. "Talk about a rock-solid alibi."

"Jesus Christ," Westbrook said.

"Wait, there's more," Julia said, looking around nervously. "Daugherty was away, but Warren F. Martin was *there*. At the suite. With Smith."

"*What?*" Westbrook's shock was validating, somehow an anchor in this storm.

"Yes!" Julia said again. "I mean, it was one thing when they put Draper in a sanitarium—putting your own flesh and blood away in a *sanitarium!* *That* was sobering. But this? Peg, they *killed* him. *They killed him!*"

Westbrook drew a sharp intake of air. "I can't believe we're watching this happen."

Julia rubbed her forehead. If Jesse Smith, the attorney general's right-hand man, lover, and literal partner in crime, had been murdered, surely she wasn't safe. She remembered the stack of her articles in Martin's office and shuddered. And what of Westbrook? Panic laced with terror, a nauseating emotional cocktail. *Dear God.* What had she gotten them into? "I can't believe I got us into this," she said.

"It's not your fault!" Westbrook said instantly. "Who could've imagined that Dot King's murder would lead *here?*"

"Definitely not me," Julia said. She took a deep breath. "I think the best way forward is to write about it. There's safety in public revelation."

"Please, just be careful," Westbrook said. "These people will stop at nothing to get what they want. They don't care if you're a so-called friend or family member. And you, my darling, are nothing to them and everything to me."

She spun her wedding ring with her thumb. "I will," she promised. "You're everything to me too."

They rang off, and she clicked again for an operator.

"Go ahead, please," a pleasant female voice said.

"Police Headquarters, Inspector Coughlin, please," Julia said.

As she waited to be connected, she remembered the last conversation she'd had with the imposing detective. What would he say when she presented this unsubstantiated evidence?

And how would she explain that she knew Smith was right-handed? *Because I met him while I was undercover as a maid at the DOJ? So I could write an article accusing you of throwing the case?* That was bound to go over well.

Julia hung up before the connection went through. She was alone in her quest for justice. She just had to think.

The story was Jesse Smith. She needed a source. She drummed her fingers. And then she remembered what Philip's secret contact had told her: Jesse Smith was divorced but still close with his showgirl ex-wife, one Miss Roxy Stinson.

Julia reached for the phone again. This time, she asked for long distance to Ohio.

Chapter 56

It seemed an hour passed as she waited for the long-distance connection. Finally, an operator carelessly announced, "Your party," followed by a quiet, hoarse "Hello?"

That there was any answer at all was nearly too good to be true. "Miss Stinson?"

"Yes?"

Julia leaned forward, heart racing. "This is Julia Harpman at the *New York Daily News*. I met Jesse recently. I was shocked when I heard the news. I'm so sorry."

"Yeah, well, I'm heartbroken, but I ain't shocked." Roxy Stinson's voice, jagged with grief, was bitter. "He always watched out for me. He did everything for the Daughertys—everything! And he wasn't afraid to stand up to them either. He knew his own mind. When I got the news, it's what I've always feared." She trailed off with a sniffle.

"You feared he'd take his own life?" Julia asked carefully.

"He'd never take his own life!" Roxy snapped. "Jess was terrified of guns. He wouldn't even go hunting with the president's party. He couldn't even bear the sight of guns. No, this was anything but suicide. You see, he's had tortures of pressure brought on him."

"By whom?" Julia asked.

"All sorts of different people trying to betray Harry Daugherty, which Jess would never do. But now that Jess is gone, I won't have Harry Daugherty hiding behind Jess Smith's skirts."

"What do you mean?" Julia asked.

"Whaddya think?" Roxy snapped, a fault line of anger bubbling to the surface. "They were in constant touch. They lived together. They were most intimate friends, and Jess adored him. He wanted to shield Harry in every possible way. Jess lived for Harry; he loved him. Why, Jess hadn't been in Washington more than three or four months when he told me, 'I'm not made for this. This intrigue is setting me crazy. If only I could just come home, but I'm in it now and I have to stand by Harry.' And now look! It's cost him his life!"

Julia considered. "I'm so sorry. Do you know . . . was there trouble between them?"

"Oh please! Why do ya think Harry wasn't there?" Roxy Stinson burst out. "Harry Daugherty did this."

"Any idea why?"

"Because Jess knew too much," Roxy said bitterly. "He knew everything there was to know about Harry Daugherty and the president and all of them. Jess would've stayed loyal—he was the most loyal guy out there. But Harry didn't want any loose ends because he can't believe that everyone isn't as rotten as he is."

"But why *now*?" Julia pressed.

"That I don't know," Roxy said. "But he's been terribly scared lately. Nervous and paranoid. He came to visit and took me out to dinner and they sat us in the middle of the restaurant and Jess couldn't stand it. He said he couldn't see *them* coming from there. The maître d' had to reseat us so he could sit with his back against the wall. He kept saying, 'They're closing in. It's all closing in.'"

"But *who or what* was closing in?" Julia pressed.

"I don't know!" Roxy declared. "I don't know the half of what they were involved in. A few months ago, he showed up with $50,000 strapped to his torso under his shirt. I didn't ask, but I heard Harry was selling appointments, pardons, confiscated liquor, getting friends off the flypaper. And that's not even the half of it!"

Julia remembered the notation in Jess's calendar: *March 27: 10:00 a.m. J. K. Mitchell.* "Did Jess ever talk to you about a John Kears—"

A man's voice rumbled, low and urgent, on the other end of the line.

"I gotta go," Roxy said.

"Wait!" Julia pleaded, but the woman was gone.

Chapter 57

It was late when Julia called Westbrook and told him she was heading out.

"Why don't you grab a taxi?" he suggested. "I'll finish up and see you at home."

Just the sound of his voice made her smile. "Can't wait," she said.

Outside, the street was fairly empty. Suerkins, the restaurant next door, and Woolworths across the street, had closed hours before. She lifted her hand to hail a cab, even as she wondered whether it would be better to take the subway. But she was tired, and it would be nice not to walk to the station and wait for a train, plus, of course, it was safer.

A taxi immediately pulled forward, as though it'd been waiting for her. "Must be my lucky night," she said, sliding in. "West 69th and—"

A man hunched against the opposite corner. His eyes seemed to bore holes in her.

"Oh, I'm sorry! I thought this was empty!" She reached for the handle. But even as she moved to leave, a warning screamed at her. He watched her like a predator.

"Don't," he said. Streetlight glinted off the barrel of a gun.

The cab lurched forward and cut into traffic too fast, throwing her off-balance. Her shoulder rammed the door. Horns blared. "I—" she began, looking at the driver and realizing he was in on this, whatever *this* was. She swallowed, trying to make her rising panic recede. She had to stay calm. She steeled her voice. "What do you want?"

"I wanna talk, *Julia Harpman*." His voice was quiet, menacing. His fedora was pulled low. She couldn't make out his face. "I know what you're doing, because it's my business to know. And I've come to make sure you stop."

"What do you mean?" she asked, though she knew *exactly* what he meant.

"Stop poking your nose into things that don't concern you or you'll get hurt. Understand?"

Julia swallowed. "My husband and editor know where I am. They have all my notes." She was lying, but if this guy believed there were copies of her notes out there, he might let her go. Why hurt someone who wasn't the only leak?

He snorted derisively. "You have no idea who and what you're up against."

The car jerked to a stop, and she calculated the odds of being able to yank the handle, jump out, and run to safety. They weren't good. He'd shoot first.

"You will immediately stop working on this story. You'll tell Philip Payne, Westbrook Pegler, and anyone else who asks that the trail went cold. You will drop all efforts to prove otherwise. You'll keep your head down and your mouth shut. Got it?"

She couldn't see him well in the dim interior, but he was sturdy and strong. "Yes," she said calmly—anything for a chance to escape. The farther they took her, the less chance she had of survival. She had to make her attempt soon.

The car slowed and she yanked at the handle, even though they were still moving. But she didn't even get the door open. The man lunged across the seat. He slammed her head into the window once, twice. The pain reverberated through her skull. He curled his hands around her neck as she slid down the seat. "I don't think you do. But you will." His weight bore down on her, crushing her. His grip, impossibly strong, tightened, choking her.

A strangled, painful sob escaped her. She grabbed at his hands, trying fruitlessly to tear them away.

He tightened his grip, his fingers digging into her throat until she couldn't breathe at all. "I *will* kill you," he said.

She made strangled gasps for air. Black spots appeared in her vision. She tugged ineffectively at his wrists, but he was just so heavy, so strong.

Suddenly, inexplicably, he released her. He reared back to his side of the cab and she scrambled to sit up, cowering away from him in the small space. She heaved in breaths, rubbing her throat, which felt bruised. Tears pricked her eyes and she looked down, ashamed and humiliated that this monster should see her cry.

The car stopped. She looked out blindly. She had no idea where they were. "Dot King isn't worth dying for. And if you keep doing what you're doing, it *will* cost you your life. We're watching *you* and we're watching *everything*. Understand?"

Tears blurred her vision. "Yes."

"Get out. And don't make me come back." The threat was chilling.

She hastened to obey, fumbling for the door handle, frantically spilling out of the car, tripping on the curb. She caught herself, regained her footing, and ran.

Chapter 58

It had been two months since the man in the car attacked her. Julia had done as he'd demanded and dropped the story. She had, however, dared to disregard his demand not to tell anyone and had confided in Philip and Westbrook, knowing they would keep her secret. Their understanding—a knowing look, a small nod, a hug from Westbrook at the end of the day—was infinitely healing.

She'd thought of Dot King every single day, the injustice of it all nagging at her like a toothache. But the fear of being attacked again woke her up gasping for air in the middle of the night. The fear sometimes reduced her to tears in the bath. The fear haunted her. And yet, she went on. Because she was a newspaperman, because she was a woman, and because the essence of human spirit is resilience. She went to work, she and Westbrook went out to dinner and saw friends, she covered other stories.

And there was no shortage of other stories to cover. Crime never stopped in the city that didn't sleep. Murder and mayhem filled her days. She was currently covering a cop-killer case. The killer remained on the loose. The entire city was desperate to catch him. The *Daily News* had offered a reward and to fund the defendant's legal counsel if he came forward. But so far, nobody had.

It was midnight when Philip got the call. The city desk was relatively quiet. Julia had turned in her article. Most of her fellow reporters were working various angles about Harding's recuperation from food poisoning, which had taken down the presidential party on the cross-country "Journey of Understanding" tour. Apparently, the entire cabinet was confined to their toilets after eating improperly canned crabmeat. Why *anyone* would eat canned crabmeat was another mystery. Julia may have converted to Catholicism, but this reaffirmed her decision to abstain from shellfish—canned or otherwise.

Though weak, the president was improving, as the *News* had reported in what Julia deemed to be unnecessarily exacting detail today, including his regular and satisfactory "eliminations."

So when Philip shouted, "Fellas!" she barely noticed. Working in the newsroom had taught her nothing if not how to tune everything out. "Harding's dead!"

The clatter of typing ceased; conversations halted midsentence; Hellinger, walking across the room, froze.

"But I thought he was improving!" Julia pointed at the day's issue.

Philip glanced at the giant clock hanging above them. "He was—until he died an hour and a half ago."

"Of what?" Hellinger asked.

"Apoplexy stroke," Philip said. "The First Lady was reading to him. Two nurses were present. He seemed fine, but then he shuddered and was gone."

Julia blinked, trying to take that in. The president of the United States was dead. Her phone rang. And then, like dominoes, every phone in the room began to ring.

"We've got work to do!" Philip called over the discordant symphony of jangles. "Pull the front page. We're redoing the issue."

The team came to attention. The linotype had already been set and now would have to be recast. Stacks of papers had already been printed, perhaps even bound and loaded on trucks to be delivered to newsies around the city. But the president was *dead*. New articles would have to be written, laid out, and printed. It would make for a long night ahead, but such was the newspaper business.

Philip kicked into action. "OK, let's get all the angles: Harding's last words, his last meal, the doctors who declared him dead, the grief-stricken First Lady sobbing her farewell, where the body is right now and where it's going. Start pulling pictures. I want one shot where he looks half-dead next to one where he's never looked better."

Julia answered her still-ringing phone.

"Have you heard?" It was Westbrook.

Julia lowered her voice. "Yes. We're pulling the entire front page and lead stories."

"Same over here," Westbrook said. "Looks like we'll both be working late."

"Seems that way," Julia agreed, and in spite of the sleepless night ahead, smiled. At least they were in it together. "Talk in a few hours?"

"Oh, I'll be here," he said.

She turned back to her typewriter, ripped the page out, and cranked a new one in. The headline was a skipping record in her brain: President Warren Harding Dead. All the patter around all the scandals, his corrupt cabinet, this cross-country, morale-boosting trip, fundraising for his reelection . . . it was all for naught.

Everything was for naught. Realization dawned and took shape. With Harding dead, Daugherty had no reelection to run, no campaign to protect, no motive to hush her up, and probably very soon, no power to wield.

She flashed back to the attorney general's announcement that Harding would run again just as the King case was heating up; the calendar entry denoting Mitchell had met with Daugherty's "special assistant," Warren F. Martin; and how just four days later, Pecora had dropped the case, exactly as someone moving the chess pieces of this investigation had intended.

Corruption was rampant. Money and power ruled politics. This was neither news nor surprising. But watching Draper Daugherty get locked away and left to rot and Jesse Smith shot and killed shortly thereafter was a level of vicious ambition Julia hadn't seen before. Even Evalyn Walsh McLean, the DC heiress whose husband owned the *Washington Post*, had publicly questioned why there'd been no autopsy.

And then, of course, there was the attack. Julia reflexively touched her throat. She'd swung hard at the powers that be when she'd dared to write that justice "went back to bed" after following the trail from Dot King's butterfly nest to the realms of millions and the attorney general's office. And the powers that be had swung back. Julia shivered, remembering how that predator had choked her nearly to unconsciousness.

She didn't know who he was, who he worked for, or who had orchestrated the assault. Perhaps it had been at the hand of the Stotesbury-Mitchell empire. But with Harding dead, Daugherty's gangrenous reign would end. Whatever threat he'd posed would be gone at least. Perhaps there could be justice for Dot King after all.

A furious movement caught her eye, and Julia turned to see a mouse scurrying along the wall, weaving around balled-up drafts and used Dixie Cups, toward the crust of a cheese sandwich. It felt fitting. It would not be long before the political rats went scurrying for scraps and then ran for cover. Daugherty would surely try to tie up the loose ends of all his misdeeds before Coolidge replaced him. Officially closing the King case would be on his list.

The time had come: she'd waited and watched for two months, but now would launch her own private investigation and write an exposé. It was a last-ditch effort, but it was all she had left.

Chapter 59

Over the weekend, even more swiftly than Julia had predicted, the police officially closed their investigation into the murder of Dot King and gave the story to a guy at the *World* who was known not to ask too many questions.

Nobody could deny that Philip Payne was an excitable fellow. But Julia had never seen him quite so thrilled as when she pitched him her idea. "Weeklong exposé! Now we're talkin'!" he'd shouted.

Julia had returned to her desk and begun her work. There was nowhere to start except the beginning. The case had begun, as all cases do, with a body. And the body had been correctly diagnosed as murdered by George Petit LeBrun.

A traffic-filled cab ride later, she was at the ME's office, winding her way past a desk where a staff member had once found himself the unknowing caretaker for a snake when a former reporter asked if he could leave a suitcase for an hour and the suitcase started hissing. That reporter now worked as the herpetologist at the Bronx Zoo, and the only reptiles the ME's office had seen since were the human kind.

LeBrun was waiting at his door. After exchanging pleasantries, she found herself sitting across from the tall Frenchman once again, with all that had happened and all that was said and unsaid hanging between them.

Julia tugged off her gloves. "The Dot King case has been officially closed."

"Yes, I wondered how long until you'd come," the Frenchman said.

"And here I am," she said, opening her notebook. "I'd like to go over the entire case again. There are so many unanswered questions and I'm trying to get some clarity . . ."

He let a moment of silence stretch. "And you're doing this because . . . ?"

She raised her brows. An understanding passed between them— her silence was his protection. This way, if anyone ever asked what he knew, he could honestly say nothing. She pressed on. "I've always had the feeling that there's more to know. I'm hoping you can point me in the right direction."

LeBrun slowly removed a cigarette from a silver case on his desk. He reached for a matching silver lighter, flipped the arm up, scratched the spark twice before the flame caught. He leaned back and exhaled twin tendrils of smoke. "Well, I can tell you where *I* would start. But I'm not sure this is information you'll want to know."

"I want to know," Julia said again, more determinedly this time.

He shook his head. "You're a very brave woman, Miss Harpman."

She didn't feel brave. She felt scared. She'd worn the bruises around her neck for weeks after the attack. It could happen again, or worse next time. But it wouldn't do to say that . . . especially when she was asking for dangerous information.

LeBrun sighed, then leaned forward and tapped the tip of his cigarette into a crystal ashtray. The French were known to like fine things. "I can speak only in general terms, you understand, not about any particular case and *not* on the record."

Julia nodded. "Of course."

"Start with the time of death," he said. "Everything flows from there. The police originally stated Miss King was killed between 5:00 and 7:00 a.m., based on Ella Bradford finding her feet very cold but her chest still warm when she arrived at 11:30. Now they claim it was definitely 7:00 a.m. But the truth is, a layperson such as Mrs. Bradford, especially under duress, when, say, finding their employer murdered upon arriving for work, would not be able to distinguish the difference in temperature between a victim who'd been killed at 5:00 or 7:00 a.m., versus, say, at 2:00 a.m."

"That is, of course, the time that Mitchell admits he was still there," Julia said carefully.

"Yes," LeBrun said, his voice devoid of judgment. "Many factors account for how quickly a body cools: if the victim is robust or emaciated. Environmental temperature—outdoors or in. What the victim was wearing. If she's covered. So let's imagine the victim was a healthy, slender twenty-seven-year-old female, found in a negligee on her bed. General guidelines are a body loses 1.6 degrees per hour, making the difference between 2:00 a.m. and 5:00 a.m. approximately 4.8 degrees, depending on the temperature of the room."

"OK," Julia said. "So you're saying Ella Bradford's testimony doesn't support the time of death being at 7:00 a.m.?"

LeBrun blew twin lines of smoke out his nostrils and did not so much as blink. "Almost certainly not."

Julia exhaled and only then realized she'd been holding her breath. "So it's possible that Dot King *was* killed at 2:00 a.m., when Mitchell admits he was still there."

LeBrun didn't change expressions. "Yes, medically, it's . . . quite possible. In fact, Mrs. Bradford saying she found the body quite cold more strongly supports the time of death at 2:00 a.m. If the murder had taken place closer to her arrival, the body would've been warmer."

A sick little feeling rose within her, the way it always did when she unearthed something dark and dangerous. Julia looked down, away from the intensity of the Frenchman's stare, until she could steady herself and continue. "Back in March, you told me chloroform is used as a medical anesthetic by doctors and dentists, sold as a sleeping aid at pharmacies, and also used in some industrial processes."

"Correct," LeBrun said. "It's used as an extraction agent for fats, greases, gums, adhesives, resins, floor waxes, as a chemical solvent in dissolving rubber . . . many things."

Julia added this to her notes. "The toxicologist reported that he'd never seen a brain so soaked with chloroform, and the police had said the bottle was a very unusual size that had never been sold in pharmacies."

LeBrun nodded. "The issue number had also been scratched off."

Julia considered. "Scratching off the identifying number seems to indicate premeditation. But the unusual size also seems noteworthy. Who would go to the trouble of procuring such an unusual bottle instead of just going to the drugstore and getting a regular one?"

"Anyone planning to commit a crime, I suppose," the Frenchman deadpanned.

"Or the police made a huge mistake in not pursuing the source of the bottle," Julia suggested.

The Frenchman raised his brows and inclined his chin. "Indeed."

The knowledge pressed down, its presence heavy and toxic. Probably not unlike the chloroform-soaked brain of Dot King. Julia looked at the clock ticking relentlessly forward.

"What should we do?" she asked quietly.

LeBrun flicked ash from his half-finished cigarette. "I've been wondering the same thing," he confessed. "To be completely candid, I've asked Dr. Norris to open an inquisition, which is not only well within his rights as the chief medical examiner, but also his moral, ethical, and professional obligation, but he won't."

Julia felt hope rise and fall within the span of a moment. "But why?" she demanded.

"Long-standing political forces. He feels his hands are tied. He doesn't want to make waves. He insists on refraining from the politics of his position. I understand why . . . and yet, I'd make a very different choice. This case could absolutely be solved if he chose."

"So with the police as they are, and Dr. Norris as he is, the case stays unsolved, and a killer goes free?" It was unfathomable to say it.

LeBrun hesitated, then spoke. "It seems the police know the identity of the killer, but don't feel they have sufficient evidence for an arrest or eventual conviction."

"Well, why don't they gather that evidence?" Julia asked.

LeBrun leaned forward. "I spoke with Mrs. Keenan at the crime scene, and she told me that three days before the murder, her daughter was considering having one of her admirers arrested on two complaints. First: beating her on many occasions. Second: seeking by threat and intimidation to compel her to be part of a blackmail scheme against one of her wealthy suitors. Mrs. Keenan provided the name of this man to police."

"Guimares!" Julia said instantly. "But if he killed Dot King, what *possible* reason can there be to delay arresting him? He's not a Stotesbury . . . or married to one. His isn't a politician or a rich man's son. He's nobody."

LeBrun lifted his eyebrows. "Is he?"

If it was possible to be even more flummoxed, Julia was. "He has none of the advantages that have protected Mitchell."

LeBrun shrugged. "While it's true Guimares wasn't born to wealth or power, through pure luck, his future is now happily tied to some of the most powerful people in the country—on the right side of the law and not. Even *if* Guimares was indisputably the killer, and even *if* the police had enough evidence to prosecute him, a trial would keep this case in the news. Which is exactly where the Mitchell, Stotesbury, Daugherty, and Rothstein empires *don't* want to be. So Guimares rides free on their coattails.

"What I'm *trying* to say is that there's plenty of evidence—pointing at both Guimares and Mitchell—to warrant continued investigation. I've strongly recommended Dr. Norris open his own. However, the political intricacies of the New York City justice system prevent that. And since Dr. Norris is the way he is . . ." LeBrun trailed off.

"But—" Julia protested.

"Trust me, I've tried," LeBrun said. And something in his voice—stern, defeated—made it clear he had.

Julia scowled. "So . . . these political *intricacies* mean a murderer goes free? So much for faith in the justice system."

LeBrun shrugged. "I ask myself the same thing. But in the end, I know that I am but one man. All I can do is my job to the very best of my ability. I greatly admire what you're doing, and I respect that you want to tell this story. But you must understand and respect that for me, the time to tell has not yet come."

"So where does that leave me?" Julia asked.

LeBrun took a final drag and ground his cigarette out in the tray. "If I were you, Miss Harpman, I would go straight home and forget we ever had this conversation. I wouldn't pursue this line of questioning. And I most certainly wouldn't write about it."

Chapter 60

4:35 p.m. Manhattan. Office of the Medical Examiner, Bellevue Hospital.

For months, Coughlin had known the day would come, but that hadn't made it any easier when it finally did. One of Enright's minions had called him at home early Saturday morning and told him to get down to headquarters, where he was to pick a reporter "known to be a friend to us" and inform them the King investigation was officially closed.

Coughlin had received the order with weary resignation laced with bitterness. It tasted, he decided, like coffee left on the burner too long and gone acidic. But he did as he was told, called the fellow at the *World*, made the bullshit statement, and got on with his day.

The only thing that had kept him going since then was knowing that his plan to nail Guimares on federal charges was in the works. It was only a matter of time until his pal at the feds called with news of the bust.

Coughlin headed straight up to the ME's office on the second floor. He was there to meet with Dr. Norris about his latest case.

Julia Harpman had continued her campaign of public humiliation by making "What Has Happened to Justice?" an ongoing column. Every Sunday, there it was, a two-page spread with the accusatory headline trumpeting his department's failure to solve some crime or other. After the Dot King case, she'd turned to digging up cold cases; last week's was four years before he'd taken over as chief of detectives (though it still rankled).

Though there was some natural distrust between the police and the medical examiner's office—inherent since theirs had the ability to launch their own investigation should his "fail"—Coughlin hoped they could find ways to increase their solve rate. Then the newspapers could feast on good news for once.

He reached the second floor, more out of breath than he cared to admit, and stopped dead in his tracks. As though he'd conjured her, Julia Harpman was walking out of the ME's office. She saw him at the same moment and froze.

He was the first to recover and scowled. "Miss Harpman."

She flushed guiltily but had the courage to meet his eyes. "Inspector."

He marched closer, towering over her. "Dare I ask what you're doing here?"

"I was meeting with someone," she said, looking away.

"Digging up another cold case? Something for your next 'big' justice exposé on Sunday, perhaps?" He hoped his sarcasm would take her down a peg, but as her eyebrows shot up, he cursed himself, immediately regretting revealing that he read her column. *Dammit.*

"I didn't know you were a fan of my—" she started.

"Or perhaps honing your knowledge of coroner's work? A second career analyzing bodies?" he hurried on, lamely, louder.

She gave him a small smile that was clearly more of a kindness than genuine amusement. "No, no, nothing like that," she assured him. "I'm just a humble girl reporter. I leave the forensics to the doctors."

He snorted. "Right. And when have you ever left anything to the experts?"

She looked up at him then with a calm frankness. "You know, if you appreciate my work ethic, I would've appreciated getting a call when you officially closed the King case."

He blanched, caught off-guard by her directness. He still felt unsettled by the impossible role he'd been forced to play to keep his job. "I—" he began.

"And now I'll get out of your way," she said, every inch the southern lady. "I'm sure you have important business to attend to."

With that, she stepped around him and made her way down the stairs.

He watched her go, not fooled for a second by her meek "I'm just a humble girl reporter" routine. He'd seen her hold her own in the seething scrum of the pressroom, shouting questions at him, Carey, Pecora, Norris, and whoever else was giving a press update. She worked harder than anyone else—throwing herself into each case as though her *own* life depended on it. But she was also a relentless pain in the ass. He wished she would trust the process . . . trust the authorities . . . trust *him*, goddammit.

He hurried in, where the usual bespectacled fellow was at the front desk. "Who was Julia Harpman meeting with?" he asked.

The fellow scowled up at him. "Who's Julia Harpman?" he asked.

"That woman who just left!" Coughlin said impatiently. "The one with the blue hat and the curly hair. She just passed by a second ago."

The guy, who'd never bothered to hide the fact that he wasn't a fan of Coughlin, or the police for that matter, shrugged. "Sorry. Didn't see her."

Coughlin stomped past him. "Tell Norris I'm here," he snapped over his shoulder.

Julia Harpman was up to something. He just didn't know what it was.

Chapter 61

It was another sweltering summer day. The sun bore down on Park Place, and New Yorkers, the fastest walkers in the world in the fastest city in the world, learned what folks down south always knew: it was best to move a little slower in the summer—there was no besting the heat. Westbrook kissed Julia's cheek outside the *Daily News* and headed on toward his office at the *United News*. Julia watched until he reached the corner, looking back to wave once more, before she lost sight of him.

She reached for the door but, thinking of the strange chloroform bottle, decided to head to the nearest pharmacy instead. She made her way past the mahogany cabinets displaying tins and tinctures for everything from constipation to hair loss; past the soda fountain, which was already doing a brisk business; past the candy counter, where a cluster of mothers with young children waited to fill paper bags with scoops of treats; and to the pharmacist's office at the back.

A young apprentice, neatly dressed and wearing a white apron, looked up. "Help you, miss?" he asked. Behind him, an older man funneled pills into bottles.

"Yes please, I have some questions for the pharmacist," she said, and watched as the boy went to fetch him.

The man, well into his sixties, finished filling a bottle, corked it, and came over. "Yes, miss? How can I help?"

Julia introduced herself and explained she was looking into the Dot King case now that the police had closed the investigation. "I understand that the chloroform bottle they found beside the body was one hundred milliliters, which was never sold in pharmacies," she said.

The man's gray brows shot up. "That's right—I've never seen that size. You sure it was a hundred milliliters?"

Julia double-checked her notes, even though she knew them by heart. "Yes, quite sure," she said.

"Do you know the manufacturer?" he asked.

"E. R. Squibb and Sons," she said.

The pharmacist took a pad and pencil from his apron. "Give me your office phone number and I'll look through my records. I'll call my fellow at Squibb and double-check if they ever made that size for anyone. Might take me a couple days. But I've been in this business a long time, and I'm sure I've never seen anything like it."

◆ ◆ ◆

Back in the newsroom, Julia tossed her summer hat on her desk and finger-combed her curls, which had bloomed into a frizzy halo courtesy of the August humidity. The bob, barely chin-length when pulled straight, would've been unthinkable a few years ago. Even now, it was considered a statement. But why did it matter if women wanted to cut their hair? Why did societies feel the need to govern women down to the length of their hair, while refusing them any rights to govern, including, until three years ago, the right to vote? A right, Julia noted grimly, still withheld from colored women, in spite of the National Association of Colored Women organizing in 1896 and advocating for access to the ballot box still today.

Julia switched on the electric fan she shared with Hellinger, who of course hadn't arrived yet. She let the breeze blow over her as she read her notes from LeBrun. It was infuriating that Dr. Norris wouldn't budge, even though LeBrun said there was enough evidence to warrant continued investigation. Thankfully, as a reporter, she wasn't similarly constrained.

She turned to her mail, quickly opening the few envelopes on her desk. Most were letters from readers suggesting unsolved cases for future What Has Happened to Justice? columns. One was in a small envelope, marked "To Julia Harpman, City Desk." With no stamp or return address, the sender must've hand-delivered it. She looked around the always-crowded, chaotic room nervously. Was the person still here . . . watching? But no, it seemed only the usual cast of characters was present.

She took a breath and ripped it open. Inside was a small clipping from an unidentified newspaper. The sender hadn't included the masthead.

The headline read: Keenan Murder Still a Mystery: Hilda Ferguson, Model's Friend, Can't Aid Probers After Trip.

Julia quickly read the two paragraphs: Hilda had returned from a two-month trip to Europe Monday and had already told police that she could "shed no light on the slaying."

A two-month trip to Europe? This was eerily similar to the Ward murder case Julia had obtained an exclusive on during her hiatus on the King case. There too a pesky witness had been exiled to Europe on an all-expenses-paid trip until things blew over.

Julia had last seen Hilda Ferguson backstage in April. Hilda had warned her not to return. But Hilda hadn't said not to call. Julia reached for her phone and asked the operator to connect her. A moment later, a coquettish voice purred, "Hellllloooo?"

Julia smiled. It could only be the dancer. "Hilda, it's Julia Harpman—from the *Daily News?*"

"You again," Hilda said, all coquetry gone. "Well, I ain't got nothin' to say. Goodbye."

"Wait!" Julia said. "I heard you just returned from a trip to Europe? That must've been wonderful!"

"Paris," Hilda corrected. "I did my hula shimmy in a cabaret, and I got four encores a night in the same costume that was banned on

Broadway—bunch of prudes. *Plus,* I met a man on the ship, and we're just mad for each other. He works in shoes and had never seen size two, triple-A feet before. He's having platinum mesh shoes studded with diamonds handmade just for me."

Diamond-studded shoes? Hilda should run as far and fast as her disturbingly tiny feet could carry her. "I'm surprised you didn't stay in Paris," Julia said.

"Well, the news is so international now that everyone was all, 'Dot King's roommate! Dot King's roommate!' same as New York. So I stayed the whole two months and then came home—I missed my daughter."

"What do you mean you 'stayed the whole two months'?" Julia asked, at the same time trying to imagine the hula-shimmying showgirl as a mother.

"I . . . I . . . meant I stayed for two months!" Hilda stammered.

Julia held the phone tighter. "Hilda, did someone arrange to send you to Paris for two months?"

"No!" Hilda said too quickly. "I already told the police I don't know nothin', and nobody paid me to go!"

"Listen—" Julia began.

"Why you always stirrin' up trouble?" Hilda demanded. "Can't a girl get a break? Don't call me again!"

"Wait," Julia said again. "Any idea where I can find Guimares?"

"Last I heard he was over on East 38th—38 East 38th as a matter of fact, cuddled up with that tall blonde troll. And if I never see him again, it'll be a day too soon." Click. Hilda was gone.

Julia slowly replaced the receiver. If someone *had* arranged for Hilda Ferguson to leave the country for two months, it was because they wanted the showgirl out of the New York spotlight. And like the Ward case, this party had to have enough sugar to shell out for such a trip. Unlike the Ward case, Hilda had also wanted a showgirl gig, which must have presented an interesting, if not comical, challenge.

Julia bit back a chuckle as she imagined one of the attorney general's lackeys, or perhaps an associate of Neilson Olcott's, bellowing into a transatlantic call to Paris, "She does the hula shimmy! *I* said *hula shimmy!* Do you have any chorus-girl spots?"

Julia looked at her notes and turned serious. The truth, it seemed, was that Hilda had been sent away, and now the case was closed and Hilda was back. The question was: Who was trying to tie up loose ends?

Chapter 62

As Coughlin headed out to lunch, he couldn't shake the feeling that Julia Harpman was up to something. He supposed he'd have to wait for her next What Has Happened to Justice column to see what she had up her sleeve. He briefly considered going somewhere new—perhaps an automat, where he could eat fast and get back to his desk—but it was too hot to wander far, and he was a creature of habit. So he headed instead to his favorite luncheonette and took his favorite stool, farthest from the door.

It was hotter inside. The air was not moving and the smell of fried onions mingled with the stench of body odor. Coughlin felt the sweat run ticklishly down his spine. Back here, it was impossible to catch even a hint of a breeze from the front door or open windows, but at least he was unlikely to be disturbed by other customers. He didn't take off his suit jacket. It wouldn't do for anyone to see the sweat patches. He would instead deal with the discomfort of his shirt clinging to his skin.

It was a busy day and people soon packed in around him, raising the sweltering temperature even more. He scowled, hoping the loud-mouthed guys next to him—Wrigley's chewing gum salesmen, if the catalogs they'd slapped on the counter, coupled with their aggressive chomping of the product they peddled, were anything to go by—would take the hint to leave him alone.

The one closest to Coughlin fanned himself with the menu. "Phew! Hot enough for ya?"

Coughlin ignored him, but realized he was talking to his friend and not looking for a response anyway. Another trail of sweat chased down Coughlin's back as he tried to get the waiter's attention, but the fellow was taking orders from the customers on the other side of the U-shaped counter.

"You figure the mayor's gonna solve the bus shutdown?" the salesman closest to Coughlin asked his colleague.

"Who knows? Gonna be hard to get to work if he don't," the other said, in a gratingly nasal voice.

"Feels like city officials can't find their way out of a brown paper bag. Did you see the police officially closed the Dot King investigation? I'm shocked," the first said, his tone heavy with sarcasm.

Coughlin stiffened. Annoyance bled into anger.

"There was never gonna be any justice for that poor dame—not with the most corrupt police force in the country at the wheel," the second lamented, like he was some sort of expert.

Coughlin glared at them, but before he could say anything, the idiots prattled on.

The first one snapped his gum. "Now they're sayin' the murder was at the hands of a thief who did it for the clothes and jewels. What do they take us for—fools?"

"Yeah, and I suppose it's got nothin' to do with the fact that E. T. Stotesbury's son-in-law was bonking her," the second one said around another wet smack of his gum.

"Oh sure," the first one said. "And it's definitely unrelated to the attorney general's son bein' her close personal *friend* too." They both laughed, an ugly, insulting sound.

Coughlin shot to his feet. "Why don't you two shut your traps?"

The pair froze, shocked, it seemed, to realize that anyone was listening to them. The rest of the customers at the counter didn't seem to hear Coughlin, drowned out by the noise of the lunch crowd. The nasal-voiced salesman recovered first.

"Why don't *you* butt out of our conversation?" he flared back, jabbing his finger at Coughlin emphatically, even though he was much smaller and slighter.

"Yeah," his friend added. "What are you, an eavesdropper?"

Rage pulsed through Coughlin, and he forgot the heat and the noise and the crowd. "I'm head of the New York City Police Detectives Unit, and I suggest you shut your fool mouth, before I shut it for you!"

The pair, practically back-bending over the counter as Coughlin towered over them, exchanged a nervous glance.

Realizing that his mood and meal were ruined—how could he be expected to keep sitting next to them, let alone eat?—Coughlin stormed out.

The midday sun blazed down but it was a relief compared to the stifling air inside the diner. Coughlin began walking back toward headquarters. The only thing worse than being forced to overhear the idiotic ramblings of those two upstarts was knowing that the rest of the city probably felt the same.

He would call his pal in the federal office as soon as he got back to his desk and demand an update on Guimares's arrest.

Chapter 63

Julia arrived on West 57th Street as the late-summer light softened into pre-sunset. She stepped out of the cab, notebook in hand, her shadow cast like a sundial on the sidewalk. She'd wanted to come here ever since Ella Bradford had revealed that on the day of the murder, Dot King had issued an ultimatum to Mitchell to marry her or settle up, while Guimares was leaning on her to blackmail the millionaire, had threatened to "toss" her, and, just hours before she was killed, had screamed so loudly at her on the phone that Ella could hear him across the room. Then a masseuse named Bobbie Ellis had arrived to give Dot King a massage.

For months, Julia had wondered what the women had talked about. Finally, here was her chance. She'd booked an appointment for herself and would use the opportunity to discover what the masseuse knew.

The beauty parlor, sandwiched between a Garland Stove store and the Somerset Laundry, had tall glass windows and a cheerful striped awning. A sculpture of a foot hung over the sidewalk, advertising chiropodist services. John Kearsley Mitchell's now-infamous desire to kiss Dot's "pretty pink toes" sprang to mind. Hours later, those toes had gone stiff with rigor mortis.

Shaking off that morbid thought, Julia went in. She'd never had the time, money, or inclination to seek out a massage. Beauty parlor treatments were for women of leisure—women who wanted to be pampered and petted. Women who idled and preened as they waited for marriage, wearing high heels that couldn't carry them through sixteen-hour days chasing stories around the city.

A notably beautiful woman in a white dress and cap reminiscent of a nurse's uniform showed Julia to a treatment room, and then waited outside as she undressed and slid under the sheet.

"I'm your masseuse, Bobbie," she said. "How are you today?"

Julia briefly considered answering honestly: *Oh, just fine except for stirring up a bushel of trouble with a secret murder investigation.* "I'm well, thank you," she said instead.

The masseuse began to firmly knead the soles of her feet. "Your muscles are very tight. You must spend a lot of time standing."

"I'm afraid so," Julia admitted.

"You should take warm baths every night." Bobbie Ellis was stronger than she looked. Her ministrations were somewhat painful.

"Good idea—thanks." Julia cleared her throat. "So I understand you were Dot King's masseuse."

Bobbie paused her ministrations abruptly, then continued. "That's right." Her voice was suddenly guarded.

"I covered the case for the *Daily News,*" Julia said.

"You're a *reporter?*" Bobbie Ellis sounded the usual amount of skeptical.

"Yes, ma'am," Julia said, letting some hints of Tennessee sneak in, which usually seemed to put folks at ease. "And I'm working on a weeklong series about it again now. The more I can keep it in the news, the more likely it is to be solved. But in order to do that, I need help from people who *knew* her, people who know the *truth.* You were one of the last people to see her before she died, so I came to ask if there's anything you can tell me about that night?"

"There's nothing to tell," Bobbie Ellis said, working her way up a calf.

It was awkward to be naked while trying to get information. "A woman was murdered and the case has been officially closed," Julia said. "If you cared about her at all, anything would be helpful."

For a long moment, there was silence. Then finally the masseuse spoke, her voice quiet. "I went over to her apartment around 5:00 p.m. and gave her a massage. She told me she was going out to dinner. Billie was there and everything seemed fine. I . . . I was shocked to see the news the next day."

"And what about her mood?" Julia asked. "Did she seem afraid of anything . . . or *anyone*?"

Bobbie paused again. "I shouldn't be talking about this," she whispered.

"Did someone tell you not to?" Julia asked, lowering her own voice.

"No! Nothing like that!" Bobbie Ellis said too quickly. And then, as though to prove Julia wrong, continued, "She wasn't in fear of anyone. She was in good spirits and looking forward to the evening. She made an appointment to have me call the next morning and I left."

"Did you go the next morning?" Julia asked, her heart speeding up.

"Yes," Bobbie said. "I went over shortly before 11:00 a.m., as we'd arranged, but there was no answer when I rang the doorbell. Miss King usually left her key in the elevator, and if she or Billie didn't answer, I'd get the key from the elevator man, let myself in, and just sit and read until she woke up. But on that morning, for some unaccountable reason, when nobody answered, I just left." She took a jagged breath. "I've asked myself why a thousand times. I'll never forgive myself."

"It's not your fault," Julia said. "By the time you arrived, she'd already been dead for many hours. The only person who could've saved her is the man who killed her. The best thing you can do now is to help bring that man to justice."

Bobbie hesitated, but finally nodded as she moved up to work on Julia's hand, which felt as though it were permanently curled around a pen or pounding at a typewriter.

"What did you do after nobody answered?" Julia asked.

Bobbie started digging in harder. Julia's muscles screamed in response. Massage, it seemed, was an interesting combination of pain and torture.

"I came back to work and then telephoned over there at 1:00 p.m., but there was still no answer," Bobbie said. "Then I tried again at 5:00 p.m. and Billie answered and said, 'Something's happened to Miss King.' And then she told me . . ."

"What about the night before, did she say anything—*anything at all*—that seemed strange?" Julia asked.

"I . . . I can't," the woman whispered.

Julia half sat up, clutching the sheet to her chest. "It's the only way," she said urgently. "If you want justice for her. If you want to make sure her killer doesn't get away with it. You can trust me."

There was no denying the fear in the masseuse's eyes, but she took a shuddering breath, glanced around, and spoke. "She told me she'd rather die than have her daddy blackmailed." The words came out in a rush. "I'm sorry. I . . . I can't talk about this!" Bobbie Ellis turned and practically raced from the room.

Julia watched her go, her mind spinning. Was Bobbie Ellis right? Had Dot King died protecting her sugar daddy? Or had her sugar daddy snuffed her out over her ultimatum?

Chapter 64

Julia felt like she was making solid progress. She'd gathered a few juicy revelations, which made for a strong foundation. But what was she missing?

The fellas, not yet privy to the secrets Bobbie Ellis had spilled, had ribbed her about getting a massage treatment—one guy yelling across the newsroom, "Hey, Philip! Wanna pay for my hot shave?"—but as long as she kept digging up gems for the exposé, she knew she could do as she pleased.

She drummed her pencil against her desk, a frantic beat, as she paged through her notes—her chat with LeBrun, the new information about Dot's time of death, his advice to drop the case.

She still hadn't heard from the pharmacist. She reached for her phone and waited as the operator connected the call, then waited while the apprentice went to fetch him.

"Miss Harpman? I've been meaning to call." The pharmacist's familiar voice finally came over the line. "It turned into quite a little project, but I finally heard back from the fellow at Squibb. So it seems they did make the one-hundred-milliliter size but haven't since 1917, and it was never distributed in pharmacies."

Julia began taking notes. "So where was it distributed? Hospitals?"

"No," came the surprising answer. "Two batches of fifty thousand bottles each were created for the army, for the American Expeditionary Forces, and almost all of it was shipped to France."

"France?" Julia echoed.

"But then it gets even stranger," the pharmacist said, and Julia's heart sped up. "A small portion of the batches was held here in the States, and that surplus stock was just recently placed on sale by the army."

Julia clutched the phone harder. *At last! A breakthrough!*

"And then it gets even stranger," the man said again, and Julia hardly dared hope. "Squibb is a good company—takes real care in the manufacturing process. But they realized about a year ago that improper storage and extended age of the product can cause a dangerous decomposition, resulting in it being far more potent and unpredictable when used as an anesthetic. So they issued a warning notice to the public and explicit instructions not to use it in that capacity and put the remaining cases they had up for sale for nonmedical uses only. If the issue number is legible, it should be easy enough to trace."

Julia's hopes plummeted. "Unfortunately, it was scratched off," she said. "Is there any other way to trace it?"

"Afraid not," the gentleman said. "The only other thing I can tell you is the stock was mostly sold in Fort Dix, New Jersey, and Philadelphia. That mean anything to you?"

Philadelphia was the domain of the Stotesbury-Mitchell empire, but that didn't equate with buying surplus chloroform. "No," Julia said reluctantly, "I'm afraid not. But this has been very helpful. Thank you."

She replaced the phone and tried to think of other ways into the story.

"Say, fellas, anybody got a source for the rubber shortage?" Joe asked.

"Yeah—there's a severe shortage now that everybody's got a car," Hellinger said.

"I said I need a *source*, not reiteration of the problem, wise guy," Joe said irritably.

Something plucked at Julia's memory. She flipped back to when she'd first talked to LeBrun in March. Had she missed something?

Hellinger smirked. "How about J. K. Mitchell? Harpman's probably got his private line by now."

"Oh sure, we talk daily, and he'd be delighted to comment—can't get enough of his name in the papers," Julia said, still scanning her notes.

"Maybe he'd cut me a deal on a new set of tires," Hellinger joked.

"What's it to ya, kid?" Joe volleyed back. "You ain't even got a car!"

"Say—why are you goons always pickin' on me?" Hellinger demanded. "If I *did* have a car, Harpman would get *me* tires before any of you guys. Right, Julia?"

"Oh sure," Julia said. "Tires for everyone." Something clicked and she sat bolt upright. "Oh my God!"

"See?" Hellinger said to the guys, then looked at her sharply. "You all right?"

Julia felt like she could scarcely breathe. "Mitchell isn't in the tire business!"

"You gone soft or something?" Hellinger chuckled warily, like she was pulling his leg. "Of course he is! He's the head of the Philadelphia Rubber Works."

Julia shook her head. "No! That's just it! He's not in the rubber business at all! Mitchell's in the rubber-*reclamation* business."

"That's still the rubber business," Hellinger said.

Julia tapped her notes excitedly. "No. It's different, don't you see? He's not *manufacturing* rubber. He's *reclaiming* it. He's taking old tires and making new products. But how d'ya think that happens?"

Hellinger looked like a kid who hadn't studied and found himself called on by the teacher. "Um . . . by getting old tires?"

"No, by dissolving old rubber! Which requires a chemical solvent!" she said, slapping her desk victoriously. "You need a solvent to *dissolve* the original rubber product. And George Petit LeBrun told me chloroform has three uses." She began to read from her notes. "As a medical anesthetic, a sleeping aid, and as a chemical solvent in many industrial practices, including rubber. The Philadelphia Rubber Works must need huge vats of it! And guess where the army surplus stock was just sold? *Philadelphia!* Where the Rubber Works could've scooped up barrels of it. *Plus*, I just learned the batch had deteriorated, making it dangerously potent . . . and that much easier to accidentally overdose a Broadway sugar baby!"

Hellinger raised his brows appreciatively. "Say! That's pretty good!"

Julia lifted the earpiece of her phone once again. "Operator, get me New York University, Chemistry Department. It's urgent."

The chemistry professor confirmed it: chloroform, combined with acetone, was a key part of the rubber-reclamation process. If the Philadelphia Rubber Works, meeting the nonmedical usage requirement, had acquired the Squibb army surplus, it could explain the bottle found next to Dot King, in that very special size made only for the army and just recently sold.

It also opened up new complexities of the investigation. The first and most stunning implication of all was that if Mitchell had administered the deadly dose, it was definitively premeditated. He would've had to snag a bottle and bring it from Philly in order to chloroform his "Darling Dottie." That was first-degree murder.

Chapter 65

At twelve stories tall, made of white brick and sandstone, with accompanying flourishes, and no fewer than three grand entrances, the Hotel Embassy, which Guimares had called home at the time Dot King was killed, immediately declared its importance to all from both outside and in. Julia pushed through the revolving doors of the entrance, then hurried down the three shallow steps and across the modern black-and-white-tiled lobby to the reception desk, dodging aggressive or disapproving looks from other guests. Like all nice hotels, unaccompanied women, assumed to be prostitutes, were not allowed.

She was two weeks into her reinvestigation—ironically just about as long as the police had spent investigating the murder back in March—and she was here to speak to the hotel manager, J. C. LaVin. When she'd called to tell him that she was running a private investigation for the *News*, he'd eagerly agreed to see her. She hoped that he or his staff might have seen something the night of the murder.

"Miss Harpman? This way, please." A slender, bespectacled gentleman led her to LaVin's office.

The hotel had been designed to impress, as a place for people who had acceded to a certain level of success—or, in Guimares's case at least, wanted others to think they had. It had opened in winter 1921, just as Julia had moved to New York. Mr. LaVin, she'd learned through researching him in advance of this meeting, was a nationally known hotelier. He'd taken out ads in all the papers promoting the guest rooms, each with a private bath, as well as the restaurant, which featured unparalleled French cuisine. While it certainly sounded nice, a meal there was far above a reporter's means.

LaVin rose as she entered his plush private office and extended his hand. "Miss Harpman, a pleasure. How may I assist?"

Julia crossed her ankles, right over left, just as her mother had taught her. "Thank you for seeing me. I'll cut straight to the point. I understand that Albert Guimares was a guest here at the time of Dot King's murder, and I was wondering if you or your staff might have any information that could be useful in our investigation."

He nodded. "Yes, I took matters into my own hands and questioned him myself. I couldn't have the hotel's reputation, or my own, be compromised by one errant guest."

"So Mr. Guimares is *errant*, then?" Julia said with a small smile.

"*Most* errant," LaVin agreed, and smiled as well.

"And what did you learn from questioning him?" she asked.

He made a dismissing gesture with his hand. "I'm not a detective, of course, but I have to admit I've been curious as to why the police didn't release one particular detail."

Julia leaned forward. "Yes?"

"He was reluctant to shake my hand. At first I thought he was just rude. But then I noticed he was hiding his right hand either under his left if they were stacked on his lap, or in his coat pocket in a very awkward way—like this." He positioned his hands awkwardly on his legs. "When I asked him to hand me a receipt, he did so very grudgingly. But when he did, I saw deep red scratches over his knuckles, and bite marks here." LaVin pointed to the webbed, fleshy triangle between his thumb and forefinger.

"*Bite marks?*" Julia echoed.

LaVin nodded. "Yes. And not just one or two little marks that could be anything: a perfect full set of teeth marks. It's certain that someone had bitten his hand."

Both the information and the fact that she'd never heard it were equally startling. "Did you point this out to the police?" she asked.

The hotelier threw his hands up. "Of course! They said they'd checked up on it and he'd gotten into a fight at some cabaret."

Julia remembered the alleged fight. "I suppose that *could've* been it."

LaVin raised his brows and snorted. "Because that's how grown men usually fight—*biting each other*? No. When Guimares wasn't arrested for this murder, I was the most amazed man in New York City."

Julia was shocked but had to agree—the evidence was compelling. Worry that she'd made a mistake started to spiral. She looked down at her notes to try to gather herself. Bite marks on Guimares's hand were so incriminating that she had to wonder if perhaps she'd missed other clues. Had she committed a cardinal sin of reporting—becoming so biased toward Mitchell's guilt that she'd lost objectivity and unconsciously realigned facts to fit her own theory?

One thing was clear. She had to interview Guimares.

She took a breath. "Just to play devil's advocate, the police arrested Guimares on the flimsy Sullivan-law violation, kept him in jail for days longer than they should have, set his bail outrageously high, and questioned him so many times I lost count. Which seemed to indicate that they were gunning to find him guilty. In fact, they seemed so set on putting Guimares away that both the public and press even accused them of being biased. So if he actually *is* guilty—*and bite marks on his hand are pretty incriminating*—why didn't they share this important clue?"

She was aware that the police had every right to withhold any clues or information they wished. If it would help solve the case to keep it secret, it was their *responsibility* to withhold it. Their priority was solving crimes. But it seemed beyond odd to have withheld this particular bit of evidence about this particular suspect, when they'd shared everything else that made him look guilty.

LaVin looked at her so hard she felt as though he were looking straight through her. "Perhaps, Miss Harpman, that's the greater mystery."

As Julia left the hotel, LeBrun's theory that Guimares, if guilty, had benefited from powerful people wanting the case shut down at any cost played in her ears. Perhaps it wasn't a mystery after all.

Julia sighed. For every piece of evidence that pointed to Mitchell, another pointed back to Guimares, and vice versa, until the entire investigation felt as though it were being rabidly volleyed back and forth like in a tennis match. In the absence of the evidence pointing to one of the suspects, the case against the other would seem completely incriminating. The existence of the competing evidence against both, however, made the case a seemingly impenetrable jumble. She knew it was because someone had obstructed the investigation, and she hoped her weeklong exposé would bring it to light and force some action on behalf of Dot King.

LeBrun had been sure this case could be solved, if only the ME would launch his own investigation. LeBrun gained nothing from this and therefore had no motivation to lie. Resolution was possible. This wasn't the work of mystical forces. It was a puzzle, and she just had to figure it out.

Chapter 66

August 21, 4:15 p.m. Manhattan. New York Daily News.

To get to the bottom of things, Julia needed a very particular kind of source: someone embedded with the police, high enough up to know what was really going on, and disgruntled enough to spill it to a reporter.

Only one person would be able to ferret out such a fellow.

Julia found Hellinger at his desk. "I need a police insider," she said. She had, of course, considered going to Coughlin, putting all her cards on the table, and seeing what the chief inspector had to say. But it had always been clear something was rotten in this investigation—had been wrong from the start—and she wasn't sure whether she could trust the man. Their run-in at the ME's office hadn't warmed things up.

"Ever heard of a guy by the name of J. C. Hackett?" Hellinger asked.

Julia pulled a face. "No. What rat are you about to drag out of the nearest drainpipe?"

"No rat," Hellinger said. "Hackett's a special deputy to the police commissioner, works directly under Enright. Enright's an idiot who can't tell his ass from his elbow, so Hackett's pretty much the only one who gets things done in that office."

Special deputy? This was better than she'd expected. "Now we're talking," Julia said. "Why hasn't he been on my radar before?"

Hellinger shrugged. "Eh—he's not exactly clean as a whistle."

With Hellinger that could mean anything. "Care to elaborate? Underground gambling? Offing little old ladies?"

Hellinger smirked. "You got a vivid imagination. Nah, a few years ago, he was forced to resign as Enright's secretary over an accusation that he protected some old creep who took a sixteen-year-old girl to his apartment. When the police showed up to question the creep, Hackett distracted them while the old guy slipped out the back. That was back in '19, way before you were in New York."

Julia lifted a brow. "And before you were in big-boy pants?"

"You crack me up, Harpman," he deadpanned.

"So how is it that Hackett, onetime protector of old creeps, finds himself back on the force and Enright's top guy?" Julia asked.

Hellinger shrugged. "Once you're a friend to the powers that be, the powers that be protect you. Enright hired him back to officially work under some deputy—and on the deputy's private payroll too. Doesn't even work on the city's dime."

"Where can I find this bastion of morality?" Julia asked.

"He frequents a watering hole I know," Hellinger said, twirling his hat on his finger. "I could take you there tonight."

◆　◆　◆

True to his word, Hellinger gained easy entrance to a speakeasy and led the way through the dim space toward the bar, where a middle-aged guy sat alone.

"Well, if it isn't my old pal," Hellinger said, slapping the man congenially on the back.

"Should've known I'd run into you today," Hackett muttered.

"I'll take that as a compliment," Hellinger said, undaunted. "Listen, I brought someone you'll wanna meet—Julia Harpman, lead crime reporter in the city. She's running a private investigation into Dot King's murder for the paper."

Hackett straightened. "Girl reporter, huh?"

"*Crime* reporter," Julia corrected, "but yes."

"Harpman's the best we have," Hellinger said. "I told her you were the guy to help."

Hackett turned his attention back to his drink. "Well, you got your work cut out for you. What happened wasn't right. But in this city, right and wrong don't matter as much as rich and powerful."

Hellinger signaled the bartender for a round as Julia settled in. Years on the beat had taught her that some sources needed prompting, while others needed time and space. Hackett was the latter.

In the far corner, a jazz trio played something melancholy, and Hackett stared at his drink like it held all the answers. "When I started on the force, you had to have integrity," he muttered. "Sure, there were always a few on the take. But now everything's for sale. And if a murderer goes free, well, a soul's a small price to pay."

The bartender put three teacups of bourbon in front of them. There was always the risk of a raid, and even though the Prohis weren't likely to be fooled by jag juice served in a teacup instead of a cocktail glass, speakeasies did what they could to stay in business.

Hackett took a ponderous sip. "A few weeks back, Enright handed me a confidential report on the King case. He signed the Third Endorsement, meaning it'll go to the Crime Committee of the Executive Board. Then he looked me straight in the eye and said, 'That fellow Mitchell is as guilty as hell. Pecora got $500,000 for turning him loose and is now making a fool of himself, uptown in Washington Heights.'"

Julia froze. This was it: everything she'd suspected. All the incongruities. The subterfuge. Pecora's bizarre contradictions throughout the rushed sham of an investigation. She let it all sift through her brain. "So the going rate to hush up a murder case is $500,000," she finally said, and downed her bourbon in one swallow.

Hackett raised an appreciative brow.

"Told ya she's all right," Hellinger said.

Julia signaled for another round and slid a generous tip across the bar when it arrived. "So what'd you do then?" she asked.

"I read the report and put it back on his desk," Hackett said.

"You just left it?" Hellinger said, his disbelief mirroring her own.

Hackett scowled. "You know how it is. The rich and powerful run this town, and there's nothing anyone can do about it."

"Well, I can do something about it. I intend to print the truth," Julia said, emboldened, perhaps, by the bourbon.

"You can't," Hackett said. "If you do, you won't stay on your paper. You'll never get police sources again. You won't have access to press conferences. No cop, or DA, or anyone they control will ever talk to you again. Sure, it's New York and 1923, but might just as well be some feudal kingdom in the Dark Ages. Money wins out. Rich beats poor. A murderer goes free. Just another day in New York City." He downed the last of his drink, stood, and shrugged into his coat. "Our time will come. But it isn't now." Then he turned and slowly walked away.

"Well, there you have it," Hellinger said. "Life ain't fair."

She rolled her eyes. "And when has life ever been fair? You know that as well as I do."

Hellinger shrugged. "So whaddya gonna do?"

Julia swirled her drink. "Learn everything I can and print the truth. But I won't include what Hackett said about Coughlin and Pecora . . . Even I'm not *that* crazy."

Hellinger considered it. "You're still gonna cross an awful lot of people: Old Man Stotesbury; Mitchell, who may be a murderer; Guimares, yet *another* potential murderer, and also a violent brute to women; Rothstein, New York's most notorious gangster. Let's see, am I forgetting anyone? Oh yeah—and Harry Daugherty, the highest lawman in the country." Hellinger whistled. "You've basically got a who's-who list of enemies gunnin' for your hide."

"Yes, I'm aware," Julia said dryly. "But nobody should get away with murder." She raised her teacup. "To justice."

Hellinger clinked her cup. "I'd get an extra lock for your front door."

Julia downed her last sip. "You're tellin' me."

Chapter 67

Julia looked up at the unassuming building. This was where Hilda Ferguson, Dot King's former roommate, had told her Guimares was holed up. Could the gigolo lover—*and possibly killer*—be inside? This was the last lead she wanted to investigate before turning to the task of writing.

Julia took a deep breath and scanned the nameplate. No Guimares. Had Hilda been wrong? Just then, an older woman came out, pinning her hat.

Julia smiled. "Excuse me, ma'am? I'm looking for Albert Guimares—does he live here?"

The woman eyed her beadily. "Nobody here by that name."

Julia nodded, disappointed. "Thank you anyway. Have a good day now."

She was about to turn when the woman called after her. "And I don't hold with young ladies visiting men unaccompanied."

Julia smiled. "Oh, I'm not calling on him socially, ma'am. I'm the crime reporter at the *Daily News*, and I'm here to question him about Dot King's murder."

The woman's thin white eyebrows shot up into her wrinkled forehead. "Well, now!" Julia braced for an even sterner disapproving cluck. "Well, in that case, there's no Albert Guimares here, but there *was* an

Albert Santos here in June—Latin fella, livin' in sin with a very tall blonde. Her name was . . . let me see . . . oh yes, Betty. Then the two of them left in the middle of the night. Ran out on the rent and a sky-high phone bill. We don't hold with that kind of behavior. We're good folks here."

Julia reached in her bag, pulled out an old issue of the paper with a picture of Guimares. "Is this the man?"

"That's him, all right," the woman said.

"And do you know anything about the blonde?" Julia asked, remembering Hilda had referred to her as "the tall blonde troll." Interesting he was already living with his new girl by June.

The woman shrugged. "She went by the name of Betty Piermont—very tall girl. Said she was an actress, but I never saw her in any shows. And with her face all bruised up the way it was so often, I'm not sure how she could've been."

"You're sure?" Julia asked.

"Oh, I'm sure, all right. The neighbors all talked of it—we felt terrible for the poor girl. She had bruises more than half the time, and once she had the most terrible black eye."

Julia looked down as a bitter sort of rage settled in, wondering how many women Guimares had beaten before Dot, and after Dot, and how if Dot hadn't died, he'd probably still be beating her.

The woman adjusted her hat again. "Well, I'm off. You take care, young lady."

"Yes, ma'am. Thank you." Julia headed down 38th toward Park Avenue, wondering where Guimares and Betty might be hiding out now. If they were smart, far away and under new names.

At the corner, Julia realized she was just two short blocks from John Kearsley Mitchell's residence. She quickly headed down that way, and took a right onto 36th Street. There, she stood in front of the luxurious, but clearly deserted, carriage house turned bachelor pad that served as Mitchell's Manhattan home.

How strange to think that *this* was where he'd returned the night Dot King was murdered . . . perhaps after he'd killed her.

She slowly turned. Behind her, she found herself dwarfed by the imposing grandeur of J.P. Morgan's colossal mansion. Morgan had been one of the richest and most powerful men in the world, and the firm he'd left behind, his namesake, continued to thrive as one of the largest banking houses in existence, ten years after his death. Mitchell's father-in-law, E. T. Stotesbury, was Morgan's Philadelphia partner.

The reach of these men and their corporations stretched all the way to the White House. Their influence had shut down the King case and enabled a murderer to go free. Their power stood unchecked.

But not anymore. Julia squared her shoulders and walked out of the shadow of the enormous mansion. *Not anymore.*

Chapter 68

For the first time in a long time, Coughlin was having a good day. The call had finally come from his pal in the federal office: Albert Guimares would be arrested today on federal charges of using the mail to defraud investors. Coughlin was welcome to be there as a professional courtesy.

But he had declined the invitation. If he wasn't leading the charge to make the arrest, he wasn't just going to watch. He'd leave it to the tourists to stand around and gawk. But he *had* asked to have a few minutes alone with the suspect. He wanted Guimares to know this had been at his hand.

He nodded to the guard and stepped into the holding cell where Guimares, who looked gaunt and tired but otherwise the same as when he'd last questioned him, sat alone.

"I should've known," Guimares said bitterly.

Coughlin, smug, victorious, didn't bother to deny it. "Yeah, you should've." It was, perhaps, the only thing they would agree on. He yanked the metal chair out and sat down. "Seems you're a tough man to find, what with fake names, movin' around so much, and runnin' out on the rent all around the city."

Guimares narrowed his eyes. "Why don't you leave me alone?"

Coughlin ignored that. "Where's that bigmouth lawyer of yours?"

"On his way," Guimares said. "Call me crazy, but like every other innocent, average American citizen, I don't have a lawyer sittin' with me all hours of the day waitin' for the next phony arrest from you people."

"Well, maybe you should," Coughlin countered, "seein' how you're *not* an innocent, average, everyday American citizen. You and I both know you snuffed out Dot King, and you cheated a lot of hardworkin' folks out of their life savings, and now you're gonna go to prison for at least one of those things."

Guimares shook his head. "You never quit, do ya?"

"Nope, never," Coughlin said, and while the gigolo had meant it as a dig, Coughlin threw it back at him as a badge of pride. "I actually give a shit about justice, and even though a few years in the federal pen isn't a tenth what you *should've* gotten for murder, it's still gonna give you a nice long time to think about all the bad things you've done."

"You seem to be forgetting I'm entitled to a fair trial," Guimares said.

"Oh, I'll be watching the trial," Coughlin assured him. "And I'll also be watching as the feds pull out every single bullshit statement and solicitation you sent to the folks you robbed blind. Because every time you dropped one in a mailbox, it was a federal crime. So while you're waitin' for that lawyer of yours, why don't you think about how many times you did that . . . and then multiply it by how many years you're gonna serve."

Guimares tried mightily to hide the dread that washed over him, but couldn't conceal it altogether.

Coughlin leaned forward and jabbed a finger toward the prisoner. "And every single day you're in there, remember I'm the one who put the feds onto you. And that the day you get out and every day after that, I'll be watching you. And if you so much as jaywalk, I'll be waiting."

"This is harassment. It should be illegal," Guimares said, his voice shaking.

Coughlin rose. "You still don't get it, do you, son? Guys like you never do. You always think *you're* the victim. But what *you* did was illegal. You hurt a lot of folks with your swindles, and you hurt a lot of women, *and* you killed Dot King. This isn't harassment—this is *justice*. Maybe you'll finally realize that when you're inside, or maybe you won't and we'll get to do this again."

And with that, Detective John D. Coughlin left the holding cell. It wasn't perfect by a long shot, but he would rest easier tonight knowing at least some measure of justice would be served.

Chapter 69

Julia took a deep breath, clutching the file she'd typed tracing the trail of the army surplus–stock chloroform, and marched into Inspector Coughlin's office at the appointed time. She knew the chief detective appreciated punctuality.

"Thank you for agreeing to see me," she said. "I won't take long. I just wanted to let you know we're planning to run a weeklong series on the King case."

If the detective was surprised, he hid it well. "Slow news day, Miss Harpman?"

She ignored the gibe. "You've always given me a square deal, treated me like one of the fellas, taken my questions and my calls as much as anyone else, so I wanted to give you the respect of letting you know," she said. She didn't tell him the second half, that she was afraid that even with the courtesy of advance warning, he and his cronies might cut off her access to future press conferences, comments, and quotes.

He didn't change expressions. "And just what do you think you'll get out of something like this?"

She had her answer ready. "You know, Inspector, I've thought long and hard about that. I'm almost the same age as Dot King; we were both single girls trying to make it in this big ol' city, albeit in very different ways. And for no particular reason, I find myself in a unique position to be able to say something and have people listen. At the end of the day, I want to be able to sleep at night, knowing I've done all I can. I know you can understand that."

He looked like he was weighing something. "What if I told you I've set forces in motion to ensure justice is served?"

"You're reopening the investigation?" Julia asked, simultaneously thrilled there might finally—*finally*—be justice for Dot King and panicked her monthlong investigation and planned exposé might be for naught.

Coughlin frowned and she knew she'd stepped wrong. "No."

"But what . . . how then? If the investigation stays closed, how can there ever be justice for her? Someone is out there, walking around, literally having gotten away with *murder*."

Coughlin gave away nothing. "As you know, I always get my man."

Julia considered. The chief inspector had only ever been focused—stubbornly, she'd felt—on one man. Although, he'd known about the bite marks and who knew how much more damning evidence she wasn't privy to. "Guimares? But how will you get your man if you don't reopen the investigation?" she asked.

"By opening another investigation," Coughlin said calmly. "I couldn't get that bastard on murder. But at least we'll get him on something. White-collar crime, this time. Using the mails to defraud."

"But . . . that's only a handful of years," Julia protested. "Homicide is twenty-five to life. The death penalty if it was premeditated!"

"I'm aware of the penal code," Coughlin snapped.

"I didn't mean—" she began.

"I know what you *meant*," he said.

She took a deep breath, began again. "I'm sorry. I just meant, a handful of years for a white-collar crime doesn't seem enough for murder."

"It's not just about an arrest, Miss Harpman. It's about ensuring a conviction. We were unable to get Guimares on homicide. But the feds have enough to get him on something. Now wouldn't you rather have him locked away for *something* than not locked up at all?"

"Yes," she said, picking her words very carefully. "I'd rather have Dot King's killer put away."

"Well, then," Coughlin said. "You should be happy."

Julia wondered how much she dared to push him. "But what if it's not Guimares?"

He threw his hands up. "Jesus Christ! This again? You should try writing pulp detective stories—or better yet, the actual news and not some cheap-thrill version designed to sell copies in spite of the truth—and leave the criminal investigations to the real detectives."

She steeled herself not to flinch, not to even blink. She'd been through worse, after all. "You've always been so sure it's Guimares. I just wonder if that sort of focus doesn't blind you to other possibilities." She didn't add that she was worried she'd been guilty of the same thing about Mitchell.

"I'm a cop who's been on the beat for twenty-seven years—as long as that little creep's been alive—and when you live and breathe crime all day every single day for more than half your life, when your sole job is to get information and catch the bad guys, and when you're leading an investigation and have access to *all* the evidence, you can be goddamn sure of your conclusions."

"But what about Mitchell being the last person to see Dot King alive—by his own admission? And how John Thomas said he never took him down?" Julia asked. While what the detective said was true about his job, his unblinking focus on Guimares made her remind him of the equally incriminating evidence pointing toward the millionaire.

"Miss Harpman, do you really think that a man of his age and stature who had his ass wiped for him his whole life, who has a manservant run his bath for him, is capable of holding the victim, who, by the way, was a young, strong woman in her twenties, down for an estimated five minutes while she flailed and fought for her life? You think he's got that gumption? Mentally *or* physically?"

Julia blanched as she remembered flailing and fighting for her own life in the back of the cab three months ago. Coughlin—big, strong, male—could never know what it was to be a woman and attacked by someone so much larger than oneself. But she wasn't going to bring that up. She would stick to his language: facts and evidence. "Well, how do you propose Guimares got in? Past John Thomas?"

"I *propose* you leave the investigating to the detectives," Coughlin said.

Julia tried to gather herself. She felt foolish, and sure she was skating on treacherously thin ice. But this was her chance—*her one chance, her last chance, and therefore Dot King's last chance*—so she would persevere. "The odd-size chloroform bottle always bothered me, so I took it upon myself to dig around a bit, and I found something I hope might be of some service to you." She held the file out tentatively— an offering, an apology—and was relieved when he took it. "It turns out Squibb manufactured that size last in 1917 and recently sold the remaining surplus stock, primarily in New Jersey and Philadelphia. I thought you might find that noteworthy . . . especially since chloroform is a necessary chemical component in the rubber-reclamation process."

Coughlin tossed the file on his desk, unopened. "I'll have my men look into it. But without being able to tie this further to Mitchell or his company, this just isn't enough for me to make an arrest. The chloroform was sold in Jersey or Philly? Big deal. Do you know how many people live there? Whoever bought this bottle and killed Dot King was in the tristate area. We never thought he came from Idaho. With the issue number scratched off, it'll be nearly impossible to prove who bought it."

Julia's stubbornness rooted and her mettle rose. "The fact that Dot King gave Mitchell an ultimatum to settle up with her or marry her the afternoon she was killed, and the fact that, by his own admission, he was the last-known person with her that night means nothing? Plus, John

Thomas's testimony that he never left his post and nobody else came in or out is pretty compelling from where I sit."

"*Where you sit* is not in the detectives' unit," Coughlin reminded her tightly. "And while I'm sure you enjoy playing amateur detective, and your millions of readers fork over their two pennies to read along every day, over here at the *police department*, we actually have to produce evidence to support charging and convicting a suspect. And this ain't it."

"Well," Julia said hotly, "even if we disagree on these points, it's indisputable that Dot King was harmed twice. First by the man who took her life, of course, and second, because whether or not John Kearsley Mitchell III was that man or not, he deployed every single point of power at his disposal to interfere with and clog the wheels of justice. And in doing so, Dot King's killer will not be charged with, stand trial for, be judged by a jury of his peers, or serve time for the crime that he committed."

"Well, at least he'll do time for *a* crime that he committed!" Coughlin flared, still intent, it seemed, on steering the conversation back to Guimares.

"*If* it's Guimares, then maybe he'll serve a handful of years for *a* crime that didn't take anyone's life and therefore isn't the twenty-five to life—or the death sentence!—he should get."

"It's better than nothing!" Coughlin said.

Julia nodded. "I suppose the question then becomes, is *better than nothing* good enough for you?"

Coughlin flushed a deep, angry red. "We're done here."

Julia stood, her legs wobbly. "Thank you for your time, Inspector. I've always admired and respected you as an agent of the law. And if you can't further investigate, charge, or convict Dot King's killer, I'll know it wasn't at your hand and you did your best."

"Guimares will serve time at my hand!" Coughlin bellowed after her. "Sometimes it's just as simple as the thug did it! That may not sell as many papers, but some things are more important than selling papers! Like truth and justice!"

She paused at the door; the well-aimed dig hurt, but she couldn't deny it. "I want justice for Dot King too," she said quietly. "I'm just not sure Albert Guimares doing a few years for some minor infraction is it."

Chapter 70

August 27, 5:23 p.m. Manhattan. New York Daily News.

Julia cranked a fresh sheet of paper into her typewriter. The crisp white edge dived under the platen and rose in front like a cresting wave. It was time to write this story.

Her fingers rested on the well-loved keys. *ASDF ;LKJ*—the poem she knew best, the random alphabet song of her soul. She closed her eyes, inviting the article.

All the evidence she'd uncovered and all the information she'd gleaned formed a tangible presence, waiting for her to find the words, waiting for her to strike key to paper, waiting to be turned into a story, waiting to reveal the truth.

And yet . . . she hesitated, looking down at the blank sheet. This was a precipice. In a situation in which nearly every woman involved had little power and limited choice, she held extreme power and *the* choice. But the choice had consequences that affected an awful lot of people in myriad ways.

If she wrote this exposé and launched the series, she could rest easy knowing she'd truly done everything she could do for Dot King, supporting the pursuit of justice for one woman's murder. But she'd also know she'd *personally* set in motion a domino effect for *everyone involved*. Could she be at peace with *that*?

Yes, it would turn up the heat on Coughlin, and even on Pecora, despite how he was painstakingly ignoring the case, a necessary, desperately needed consequence if there was ever going be justice for the murdered model. It would also make the city officials look like buffoons, which would make it a whole lot harder for her to get access, quotes, and comments from the police or DA on future cases.

Julia was willing to take that risk. But what would it mean for Ella Bradford, who'd done nothing but work for a scandalous white woman, and had her life turned upside down for it in return? What would it mean for Hilda Ferguson, who'd been exiled to Europe for two months, an ocean and three thousand miles away from her daughter? *Will Hilda and Ella be threatened? Harmed? Sent away again?*

What would it mean for Frances Stotesbury Mitchell, whose only crime was inadvertently marrying a philanderer? Was it fair she should suffer as she continued to be socially ostracized? Should she be pilloried with ongoing nationwide speculation, gleefully dissecting her husband's betrayal?

Julia flexed her fingers. The blank sheet waited.

What would it mean for *her*? For *Westbrook*? She'd already been attacked. What was this story worth to her? What was the price of justice, and was she willing to pay it?

What of Dot King's family, who'd been denied justice for their daughter/sister/aunt? And what of Dot King herself, slain, her life extinguished too soon, while her killer still roamed free?

Julia's action would affect everyone, but her silence benefited only the murderer.

Julia shoved back from the desk, went to the window, crossed her arms, stared out. She had to make a choice. If she went forward with this series, she'd have to live with the collateral risk and whatever ramifications befell Frances Stotesbury Mitchell, Ella Bradford, Hilda Ferguson, and herself.

The women, as always, would pay the price.

Coughlin remained unflagging in his focus on Guimares. It wasn't the first time she'd seen the police become fixated on a particular suspect and bend the facts to fit their narrative. Maybe it was willful blindness, ignorance, or foolishness . . . or maybe he had information and evidence she didn't. Certainly, corruption was afoot, though she was not sure if the rot had spread to Coughlin or merely Pecora. But the fact remained: the detective continued to ignore the evidence that pointed toward Mitchell, possibly as the killer and almost certainly as an unfairly interfering force.

Julia stood at a crossroads. She could walk away, stay silent, not poke at those very powerful people, not risk her life again.

Or she could write the series, reveal the truth, and live with the knowledge that while she hadn't uncovered the killer, she'd done all she could do to spur the authorities, holding them publicly accountable, fulfilling her duty as a journalist to uphold and support the pursuit of justice.

It was a choice, and yet really, no choice at all.

She was Julia Harpman, newspaperwoman, proud member of the fourth estate, daughter of Josephine Bush Harpmann, granddaughter of Julia Bush. She was proud to be a link in the Jewish tradition of carrying a grandparent's name and admirable qualities forward. Writing was in her mother's blood. Perhaps, courage was in their lineage as well. She took a deep breath and began.

Dot King, beautiful woman of Broadway, was murdered in her apartment in the rear of 144 West 57th Street on the morning of March 15.

The police have officially stated that their investigation of the crime has ended.

John Kearsley Mitchell, Philadelphia millionaire and son-in-law of E. T. Stotesbury, the last person known to have seen Dot alive, was questioned by the police, but he was not arrested.

Albert E. Guimares, sweetheart of the dead girl and the person who profited most from her Broadway saunterings, was arrested on a flimsy charge but was released.

Why the mystery was never solved, the *News* does not pretend to know. It was recently charged that $500,000 had been used to clog the wheels of justice in this particular case.

The *News* has conducted an exhaustive private investigation into the life and death of John Kearsley Mitchell's heavy sugar baby, the results of which it will publish. No attempt will be made to direct suspicion toward anyone. No conclusions will be drawn. But the facts will be printed fully.

The *News* will publish, for the first time, the true story behind the cruel murder of the "Broadway Butterfly." This is the first story of the series.

Chapter 71

It was just past noon when the knock came. Ella Bradford, at the sink while the pork belly fried, turned the stove down, wiped her fingers on her apron, and hurried to answer before they knocked again. She'd just gotten June down and needed to keep him down so she could search the want ads.

She pulled the door open and came face-to-face with two white policemen. She quickly stepped back. She should've asked who it was first—that's what big-city folk did. Back home, you never had to ask who'd come to call 'cause usually it was warm enough so as you'd be out on the porch to see 'em coming anyhow, but because the doorbell hadn't rung, she'd assumed it was a neighbor within the building.

"Billie Bradford?"

She reached for the neck of her dress, pulled it tighter, and tried not to think about the articles in the *Daily News* all week. "Yes, sir. Can I help you, officers?" She kept her voice small and waited nervously—what for, she couldn't say exactly.

"The Dot King case has been closed," he said.

She looked at first one, then the other, surprised. She'd seen that small notice a month ago in the *World. So why'd they come now? Why today?* Must be Miss Harpman's articles stirred things up again.

After she'd told the news lady what she had back in May, she'd checked the papers every day, and every day she'd expected to see . . . well, *something* . . . but there'd been nothing for months. The futility of it all threatened to swallow her, powerless, hopeless. She'd come north for a better chance, and a lot of things might be better up here than back home, but some things were the same. If you were poor, Negro, or a scandalous white lady, you'd get treated as less. Poor white folk might get some sort of a police investigation but, in the end, no justice. Negroes didn't even get that.

It wasn't new, but the days felt a little heavier, a little harder, after that. She'd asked herself what else she'd expected and ignored the little corner of her heart that had dared to hope for more.

Then out of the blue, three months after Ella had done her part, Julia Harpman finally did hers. The *Daily News* started those tell-alls last week. And all of a sudden, her name was back in the papers, and it was all anyone could talk about all over again. This time, there was no name at the top of the articles, but Ella knew it was Miss Harpman, the only other person who cared about justice for Miss Dottie.

Surely, *now* there'd be new leads, new clues, Guimares finally charged with *murder* instead of just mail fraud. But these police had come to say it was over. She felt the powerless, hopelessness of it land heavy on her heart.

The first spoke again. "It'd be best if you went away for a while."

Fear fell over her like a blanket, dark and choking. "But why? Where?"

"Maybe you oughtta go back where you came from," the second one, meaner than a polecat, sneered.

A chill ran down her spine, even though the day was warm, and Ella tightened her hold on the neckline of her dress. It was modest and high, but she pulled it tighter anyhow. She didn't want their eyes on so much as her throat.

Would they drive her out of New York? Force her to go back to Jacksonville? Though she'd never told a soul, she'd thought of it sometimes herself—when New York was too fast and hard, or in the long, cold winters that froze a body down to the bones. On those days, she'd close her eyes and summon the smell of hominy grits and pole beans simmered in salt pork, the lull of warm Sunday afternoons after church, of people who *knew* her and sounded like *home* in a way Harlem folk never would. Where the air was clean and the days slow. Where you could step outside and pick an orange and eat it still warm from the sun. A place where everyone wasn't always in such an all-fired hurry.

On those days, she almost ached with it: *home*. But home was just a daydream—she couldn't ever *really* go back south.

She thought of James, so smart and fine in his suit. What were his chances? A job at the pencil factory? Sharecropper? No sir, not when it was barely one step out of slavery. They'd both come north for more.

Questions and fears swarmed around her head like bees. She took a deep breath. First things first: she had to get these two gone.

The first one, the nicer one, spoke again. "You don't have to go that far. Just not *here*. Not this building, this apartment, this street, you understand? Maybe take a different name—that'll be better for you, anyway. Make it easier to get another job and not be so noticed."

"Yeah, we don't want you getting hurt," the mean one said, but he sounded like he did—like maybe he'd like to do the hurting himself.

She remembered then what it was to be hated for no particular reason. She settled her eyes on the floor as anger and bitterness churned deep inside.

It isn't fair. She bit those words back, shoved them down, where they burned. "Yes, sir. I understand," she said, even though she didn't—anything to get them gone.

"Don't talk about Miss King. Don't talk about Mr. Mitchell or even Guimares. Don't talk about any part of this case to anyone. Just make yourself scarce and keep quiet. It's for your own good, you understand?"

"Yes, sir," she said. "You won't have no trouble with me."

The first one nodded and settled his hat down on his head. "I know we won't."

They turned to go, and she closed the door and locked it. Her hands shook and her knees felt weak. She slid to the floor next to the little table where they kept the mail and keys. A hot tear slid down her cheek and she swiped it away angrily.

It isn't fair!

She should've known better than to think any white policemen would ever come all the way up to Harlem just to tell her what happened. The rage boiled up and the tears ran faster now. Her hand flailed for the key bowl, and she was just about to throw it when she saw the bumblebee painted in the bottom.

Miss Dottie.

She'd come into work one day and found a box on the coffee table tied up with a pink satin ribbon, the bowl inside. "'Cause you're the bee's knees, Billie," Miss Dottie had said, and winked.

Miss Dottie had been murdered in her bed, tossed out like she wasn't a full person with a life to live, like she didn't even matter. And now it was official: the police would never put her killer away . . . and not because they couldn't find him.

The memory of finding Miss Dottie, cold and dead, rose again, as it often did in the quiet moments.

June stirred in his crib and she went to get him. She was lucky to be *alive*, to be a mama to her boy. How many didn't even have that? She was free, as free as a Negro woman could be. She'd had her own job, made her own money—*good money*—and would again.

"Mama's here, Junebug," she murmured, his solid weight a comfort. These would be her last tears on this. She had her husband and her son, and that was most important.

She'd brace up and do what had to be done. This was how it had to be for now. There was no other choice about it.

Chapter 72

For the first time in his forty-nine years, Inspector John D. Coughlin, chief of detectives, stayed home from work. Through his closed door, he heard the usual morning bustle—his father heading off to swap stories with other retired cops whose wives or daughters kicked them out from underfoot, Samuel heading out for his shift at the fire station, William leaving for school, and once she'd gotten everyone fed and out, Mamie clanking around before she left to do the shopping.

Usually, he was part of the fray—rushing down to headquarters, already going over the day's cases, already feeling behind.

But now the house sank into a deep stillness. The bed creaked as he pushed himself up. He shuffled down the hall to the bathroom. Today, there was no jostling for a turn.

Julia Harpman had come through with her weeklong series, just as she'd warned. Every article carefully referenced an "independent investigation undertaken by the *News*." There was no byline, but he knew it was her.

This series—*this goddamn series.* It was just like back in May, when she'd run that other goddamn article—also no byline, also definitely her—which had accused the police and DA's office of throwing the case. Her words were still seared into his brain: "Justice slept late on the morning of March 15, 1923. When Justice awoke and followed the trail that led from the murdered Dot King's butterfly nest to the realm of millions and the office of the attorney general of the United States, she went back to bed again."

Even now, the accusation made the tic in his jaw twitch to life and rage flow hot through his veins. Who the hell did she think she was? There was a time when there was such a thing as respect for the authorities. And there was also a time when a girl reporter was unthinkable. Apparently, not anymore.

Julia Harpman had been on the crime beat for years now, doggedly covering every case he investigated. She was thorough. She was merciless. He shouldn't have been surprised at the vicious right hooks she'd laced through each article.

And yet . . . he had been.

Like the rest of New York, every morning, he'd rushed to get his copy, yanked the paper open, devoured every word, then waited for the next day's installment. Unlike the rest of the city, every article stuck in his craw.

Each had carefully promised no conclusion would be drawn. And yet . . . the conclusion was inescapably drawn. He and the entire detectives' division looked like clowns.

What made him angriest was that nobody had listened—not Pecora, when he'd warned the DA this would happen. And not Julia Harpman, when he'd told her Guimares was the man and he would stand trial on other charges.

Coughlin stomped back to bed.

He'd told his division he had the flu, but he was really just sick of the bullshit.

All he wanted to do was his goddamn job. He wanted to investigate crimes, extract information, put bad guys away, and be left alone. It was pretty simple—or at least, it should've been.

But interoffice politics and corruption were never simple.

Everyone else had fallen in line. Even Carey hadn't been immune—
that last conversation still haunted him: *"Well, isn't that what you
wanted?"*

No! What he'd wanted was for everyone to get out of the way and
let him run his investigation.

If he'd just been allowed to do his job, he could've nailed Guimares
on homicide charges.

Coughlin sat down on the bed, elbows on knees, hands on head.
God, he was tired.

It wasn't fair. But it had always been like this. It would always be
like this.

He thought fleetingly—longingly—of escape. He could go into
private work and make three times the pittance the city called a salary.
Firms would pay handsomely to have New York's chief of detectives
as their head of security. But deep down, he knew he'd never leave the
force. It was in his blood. It was all he knew, all he had.

Long ago, there'd been friendly prodding that he oughtta get married. "Big handsome fella like you? You'd make some lucky girl a good
husband!" Only Mamie knew enough to never ask.

The prodding had petered out as he edged toward forty. Now, a
year out from fifty, nobody asked. His only prospects were spinsters and
widows. The whole idea of it—courting some dried-up old biddy, the
forced conversation, her expectations—was grotesque.

He was happy—or as happy as he could be—with Mamie and her
family and their father. Samuel was a good brother-in-law, William a
good nephew, and Mamie kept an orderly house. It was enough.

But it was only enough because being the chief of detectives had
always been *everything*.

Was it, though? He was worn down, worn out, bone-tired. The
unending assault on his conscience—immersed in the filth of humanity
day in and day out—could tarnish any soul, slowly draining the life out
of anyone.

After he'd been shot in the line of duty in 1918, he'd received the departmental Medal of Valor. He'd received two commendations for excellent work in 1912, an honorable mention in '13 for a capture in which he'd risked his life, and even a Congressional Medal for bravery for saving a young boy's life. It was good to be recognized. But the real satisfaction was in the work—the pursuit of justice was the pursuit of happiness in his book.

He glanced over at the Medal of Valor. It sat on his bureau next to the little statue of the Blessed Virgin his mother had given him when he joined the force. They were the only decorations in the room.

Being on the beat, in the scrum of people at their very worst—finding kids beaten to death and thrown out with the garbage, women raped and eviscerated and left to slowly bleed out in some putrid alley, men butchering each other over a few bucks or a bar fight, so many lives ruined and ended for no good reason—he could still believe he was doing God's work. He still had honor.

But being muzzled? Wasting his time handling the higher-ups and the DA's office? Having to be a goddamn Houdini to get around the ridiculous constraints they placed on him just to be able to put Guimares away for a few years on fraud charges when the mug should've been headed to the electric chair for first-degree murder . . . or at least doing twenty-five to life for second-degree charges? And now being called out in the papers for *not* doing his job? It was a kick in the gut after taking the fall for Pecora and Enright.

It was all Coughlin could do to climb heavily back into bed and pull the worn-soft cotton sheet up. Tomorrow, he'd go back to work.

But not today. Today, just as the impudent—*and, goddammit, right*—Julia Harpman had written about Justice: he would go back to sleep.

Chapter 73

September 22, 11:00 a.m. Manhattan. White Star Shipping Dock.

The ship, enormous, gray, hulked in the harbor. Frances Stotesbury Mitchell sat in the car with Jack and the children.

Her maid, Jack's valet, and their steamer trunks were in the other cars.

"Are you sure it can't sink, Mother?" Franny asked.

Frances shifted her gaze slowly from the window to her daughter's grave young face. "Quite sure."

"That's what they said about the *Titanic*!" young Jackie piped up.

"Listen to your mother," Jack admonished, taking her hand and lifting it to his lips. "She's a very wise woman."

She could manage only the barest hint of a smile for the children's sake, the corners of her mouth lifting, as though weighted with sandbags, before withdrawing her hand and turning back to the window. His attempts at levity meant nothing.

There had been no joy, no ease, no frivolity between them for months now. Nothing could be the same since March 24, the day that would be permanently, irrevocably seared into her memory for the rest of her life. The day that her perfect, beautiful life had shattered into a million irreparable pieces.

Things had been mercifully, blessedly, *officially* closed at the beginning of August. She'd dared to hope life might return to normal. But the exposé by that wretched girl at the *Daily News* had made it clear they must go far, far away. There had been no byline, but it had to be her . . . of course it did.

So finally, after five endless, hellish months in limbo—afraid every time the phone rang, afraid to read the newspapers each day lest their names be lurking shamefully in the pages—they were leaving. With the scandal still plaguing them, hanging over their heads like a horrid storm cloud, it was the only option. And so, just as Eva and her father had advised back in the spring, they would go abroad and wait. Europe had been decided upon, followed by a trip down the Nile.

Frances did not care to go touring around Europe, or sailing down the Nile. But what choice did she have? They remained, in effect, socially exiled.

It wasn't fair.

She was married to a philanderer, a consummate liar, and a possible murderer. Whether or not he'd been exonerated of this last charge was only part of the problem—a large part, of course, but only part. Her life was ruined regardless. Her marriage was a disaster. Her only reason for living was the children. Franny's future. Her debut in four years. Someday, her marriage. And little Jackie. While less worrying—he was male, after all—what of his schooling? His future? Their social standing had to be settled—in fact, firmly reinstated!—before then. And the only way to do so was to quiet the talk by staying with Jack, heads held high, and to sail straight through it side by side.

She was stuck with her rounder of a husband because without him, they were all lost. He was the anchor around her family's neck, and yet, he was also the anchor that would secure them in this social storm. It was bitterly, wretchedly, horribly unfair.

She sneaked a look at him and was instantly flooded with rage. There he sat, with his chubby face and gray, balding head, placidly looking out the window. How had this man, calmly sitting in their limousine with her and the children, cavorted behind her back for nearly two years with that filthy harlot?

Frances turned away and squeezed her eyes shut so that she wouldn't see even a hint of his reflection in the window.

There was a soft knock outside, startling her. Jack wound the window down an inch. "Yes?"

"First class may board now, sir."

"Very good." Jack rolled up the window. "Ready, everyone?" The children responded with an eager chorus. This was how they communicated now—through and for the children.

Frances said nothing. Jack opened the door and the children scrambled out. "Ready?" he asked again, offering a hand to help her from the car.

Defiantly, she refused it. She stepped from the car by herself and then followed Jack and the children through the crowd to the gangplank. Emily, Jack's valet, and the chauffeurs bearing the baggage trailed behind. The fracas—all the goodbyes, the searching, the throngs of people, the foul stench of cheap fried food from the vendors selling heaven knew what, the noise—threatened to give her a headache.

As first class boarded, the ship's staff ensured the economy-class passengers stayed behind ropes. Frances focused firmly on the ship. It would carry them away from this wretched ordeal to a fresh start.

It was what they needed, what she wanted. But as Jack moved aside to let her go first and she stepped from the dock onto the gangplank, her breath hitched and she stumbled.

Jack caught her elbow firmly. "Are you all right, darling?"

She yanked away from him and, grasping the railing, forced herself to walk up the gangplank even as her breath grew shorter and the world threatened to tilt and slide away. Jack trailed along with a resigned sigh—as though it were he who'd been put upon. She tried not to sway while he presented their tickets. She studiously avoided his solicitous, inquiring gaze as they followed a porter through the ship's hallways, past happier couples.

When they finally reached their suite, the porter opened the door and the children eagerly shoved ahead to find their rooms. Emily directed the bags to the master suite, and Jack made to go toward the lounge. "Coming?" he asked, holding out his left hand.

Frances, still standing just inside the door, stared down at it. His hand—once so dear and familiar, the gold ring resting reassuringly on his fourth finger—now looked alien. Had this hand strangled the life from his . . . lover's . . . body? Could he have . . . *had he . . . done that?*

She felt a sudden heave of sick rise in her throat. She shook her head frantically and stepped back. It wasn't fair!

"Franny?" he asked. "Do you want to lie down, darling? Shall I ring for the doctor?"

"No . . . no, I . . . I—" She stepped back again. "I need some air." She turned to go back the way they'd come.

"I'll go with you."

"No!" The word sounded sharp. She had only one frantic thought: *Escape!* And that did not include John Kearsley Mitchell III.

Jack frowned in concern, and she quickly adjusted her voice to be more measured. "I'll be fine. You have to manage the servants and departure. I'll go out alone." She attempted a small smile and then walked slowly, carefully away until she heard him close the suite door; then she quickened her pace until she was nearly running back along the hall they'd just come down. Her shoes made a tapping sound on the floor as she hurried as fast as her layers and long skirts would allow, until she burst out on the top deck.

She ran to the rail and held it tightly, gasping for air, gulping in breaths as desperately and deeply as her corset allowed. She wanted to cut the darned thing off. Cast it overboard and into the sea—be uncontained like that filthy whore Jack had kept and maybe killed. She would be damned if she'd stay, a corseted, confined, silent prisoner on this boat and with him!

She couldn't do it. She had thought she could, but she'd been wrong. Nothing was worth this. She'd told herself that she had to stay focused on the future, and that if anything truly awful had turned up, her father would've told her. But deep down she knew she'd been too terrified to ask. *But no more!*

She would stay here in the States and divorce Jack, and her family, friends, and society would have to deal with it.

She walked down the nearest stairwell to a lower deck, pushing against the tide of the crowd flowing on board, back toward the gangplank. She must catch the chauffeur before he left. She looked around frantically for him, searching a sea of unfamiliar faces, panic mounting.

What if she didn't find him? How would she get home? She suddenly realized she had nothing with her—no money, no passport, no papers. She never did. Jack or the servants managed all that.

"May I help you, madam?" the official with the clipboard asked, clearly startled by her reappearance and apparent intention to disrupt the flow of people boarding by *leaving* the ship.

"Yes, please get my chauffeur back—" The rest of the words stuck in her throat. There, at the bottom of the gangplank, that infernal girl reporter was standing with a male cohort holding a camera.

Frances froze. The whole world froze. All the clatter, the throngs of people, and the bustle fell away. Why she saw *that girl* in the shifting swarm of strangers, she'd never know. But there she was.

Frances stared at her. The girl stared back, with a calm, implacable look.

Frances swallowed hard and considered her options. She could secure her freedom or sleep next to a philanderer and possible murderer for the rest of her life. She could leave this ship, leave Jack, and effectively condemn him in the court of social opinion, but the price would be their reputations. She didn't care about his, of course. She would even take a certain visceral pleasure in securing his destruction. And she could probably bear living with the unfair collateral loss of her own. But the children—the children had done nothing and would pay everything.

In that moment, she saw that she had two choices and yet really no choice at all.

"Madam?" he prompted, looking concerned.

"I wanted something, but I suppose it's too late now."

"Perhaps it's not too late, madam. What is it you're looking for?"

Perhaps it wasn't too late. What *was* she looking for? Oh, if only he were right! Frances's thoughts raced. The warm harbor air gusted and she put a hand to her hat. Then she looked again and saw the girl reporter still waiting. It wasn't fair, but it *was* too late. And there was nothing this man could do. "My gloves."

They both looked down at her hands, encased, of course, in gloves. "Of course, madam. Your name, please?" Clearly, the man was accustomed to dealing with the whims of first-class passengers.

"Frances Stotesbury Mitchell."

He scanned the list. "I'm sorry, I don't see—"

"Mrs. John Kearsley Mitchell," she said, bitter at the reminder that she existed, as all wives did, primarily as an extension of her husband. Jack even had their passport, which listed "John Kearsley Mitchell and wife."

She waited for his response, and her heart sank a fraction more when it came—the dawning of awareness, the slight widening of his eyes, the careful shifting of his gaze, a polite attempt to show nothing. "Yes, uh, why yes, of course, madam. Shall I call for your chauffeur?"

"No." The word sealed her fate. It was over. She slumped with defeat.

"Are you sure, madam?"

No, she wasn't sure. She wasn't sure of anything anymore. But she knew now she wasn't getting off this ship. The fissure that had splintered her heart split deeper, until it felt as though she were being cleaved in half.

She said nothing. She just turned and walked very, very slowly back to her suite, back to her cheat of a husband, back to her innocent children, back to her life.

She would pay the price of Jack's sins for the rest of her life without ever knowing the extent of them. It wasn't fair, but life wasn't fair.

She wasn't free, but no woman was free. This was her life now, and she would accept it with courage and grace—her children deserved that, and her sacrifice could provide it for them.

Eva was right. Women were the guardians of life as they knew it. Her privilege came at a cost. And the cost was due today.

1929

Chapter 74

October 18, 9:00 p.m. Manhattan. New York Daily News.

Julia, now associate editor on the city desk, surveyed the newsroom from her new spot at the front. She circled the front-page leads for tomorrow's paper with a well-worn red pencil and began weaving her way through the desks. "Nicely done," she told Norma Abrams, the new sob sister, who also worked on fashion and features. Norma was covering the latest trials (literally) and tribulations of Harry Thaw, the violent millionaire who'd shot and killed architect Stanford White in front of hundreds of people at a show in Madison Square, stood trial for the crime twice, and yet somehow was back out in society while facing yet another trial—this time for the assault and battery of a woman, not his wife, in his hotel room.

Myriad other scandals—corrupt mayors caught rum-running as Prohibition raged on, the skull of a murdered seventeen-year-old girl found on a beach, a politician who'd persuaded his mistress to commit forgery—crowded the first three pages of the paper. There were no slow news days in New York, or at least not at the *Daily News*.

Julia gathered her things and reached for her coat. As always, the newsroom was an all-out assault on the senses: the smell of ink mingling with cigarette, cigar, and pipe smoke; the neat snicking of typewriter keys; phones incessantly ringing; and conversations—still almost entirely male—overlapping each other.

Julia felt at home in the chaos. She lived for long days fueled by the excitement of being on the front lines of the news in the greatest city in the world.

"All right, fellas. I'm heading out to grab a bite. See you in a bit," she said.

"Sneaking out, are we?" Joe joked, barely looking up from his typewriter.

"Got a hot date or something?" Hellinger chimed in.

She glanced down at her left hand and the gold band that now seemed to be as much a part of her as skin, bone, and muscle. "Yeah, don't tell Peg."

"Fine, he can read it in tomorrow's edition," Hellinger joked. "How do you spell 'Casanova'?"

"P-E-G-L-E-R," she said.

"Wise guy, huh?" Hellinger said.

One of her lines rang. She briefly considered not answering it, but this was the newspaper life, which meant the rest of life had to wait. "Harpman," she said.

"Julia Harpman?" a female voice asked.

"The one and only," Julia said. "What can I do for you?"

"Are you the one who covered the Dot King case?"

Julia stilled. The commotion of the newsroom fell away. Nobody had called about the King case for six years. They'd put out 2,236 issues since her exposé—every single one chock-full of broken hearts, broken heads, corruption, theft, rum rings, adultery, murder, and mayhem. And yet, in all that time and all those issues, there'd been no calls about Dot King.

In spite of her private investigation, weeklong series, and risk to herself and others to keep the case in the public eye, after a brief resurgence, it had joined the legions of other unsolved cases that languished in obscurity, gathering dust in some police filing cabinet. There had been no justice for Dot King and no punishment for the killer.

In the world of newspapermen, however, the case was still alive. She and Peg debated with friends over late-night bourbons: Who killed the Broadway Butterfly? Guimares the gigolo, determined to blackmail Mitchell over the mortifying pink-toe letter, as Inspector Coughlin thought? Or sugar daddy Mitchell, determined to be neither blackmailed nor pressured to leave his wife, as many other reporters thought? The whodunit debates were passionate. But day in and day out, nothing new had come to light for six years.

Until now.

"Yes, ma'am, that was me," Julia said, reaching for a notepad and pen.

"I need to speak with you," the voice said.

The old shimmer of curiosity and excitement began to thrum through her veins. Who was this woman and why was she calling . . . today of all days? "Yes? How can I help?"

"I can't say over the phone, but please, you're the only one I can talk to," the voice said, a bit more desperately.

"Why me?" Julia asked.

"Because even when everyone else had moved on, you didn't give up. You did more for her than anyone—far more than me, and I should've done more. Dottie deserved that." She said the last of this with the sort of raw grief and guilt that never fully heals. Whoever this woman was, she'd known the victim personally.

"Yes. I'll always do everything I can," Julia said simply.

There was a deep, shaky breath on the other end of the line. "My name is Aurelia Fischer Dreyfus. You'd know me as 'McBryan's Blonde.' I'm the one who gave Albert Guimares an alibi."

Julia's pulse surged. "McBryan's Blonde" was exactly how she'd written it. Memories flooded back of the mysterious woman who'd told police she'd heard Albert Guimares come home at midnight the night Dot King had been murdered and had breakfast with him the next day.

Surely there was only one thing that Aurelia could be calling about after all these years. "We should meet," Julia said. "I can get a cab—"

"No—I'm not in New York." Aurelia whispered desperately, as though afraid of being overheard. "I moved back to Washington a week ago. I thought that might help. But I've come to realize only one thing will give me peace, and that's telling the truth."

"And what's the truth?" Julia asked, holding her breath.

There was no reply—just a broken sobbing on the line. "I'm sorry. I shouldn't have called. God, I don't know what I'm doing."

"Wait, please!" Julia said, holding the phone so tightly it hurt. "I know you're under a lot of strain. I understand—*truly*, I do. But I can help you. I'll protect your identity, and I won't print anything you don't want me to. We can figure this out together."

The sobbing continued. "What I did is too terrible."

"I assure you I've heard worse," Julia said, slowly and calmly. "The things I've heard would curl your hair. I've interviewed murderers. Why, you might even bore me."

"No, it's awful, what I did. Everyone will hate me. And I deserve it." The sobs continued.

"I promise *I won't*," Julia said firmly.

Through the line, the sobs slowly dissipated into ragged breaths. "I . . . I perjured myself," Aurelia Fischer Dreyfus finally said, quickly, as though to get it out while she could. "And I cannot live with it anymore. I'm so sorry and . . . and . . . I'm scared . . . oh God, I'm so scared! But I have to come clean!"

Julia closed her eyes as the word ricocheted through her. *Perjury!* The only thing Aurelia had testified to was Guimares's alibi. This meant that Guimares was guilty . . . or at least now firmly without an alibi. Inspector Coughlin had been right all those years ago: sometimes it was just the thug. She forced her racing thoughts to return to the conversation at hand. She would sort the rest out later.

"OK. There, you did it. See? That wasn't so bad, was it?"

Aurelia expelled another shaky breath. "It's the hardest thing I've ever done."

"But you did it," Julia said. "The rest is a piece of cake. Now tell me when and where to meet you."

"Monday," Aurelia said so quickly Julia knew she'd planned it. "My family—we have an annual Autumnal Soiree at the Potomac Club this weekend, and I want to warn them this could come out in the papers. Of course, I hope you can write that I retract my alibi while protecting my identity," she added, "but I have to prepare for the possibility that I'll be revealed like Mr. Mitchell was. It would destroy my reputation and ruin my family. I mean, I *perjured* myself . . . and the reason I was in the position to give an alibi at all is because I stayed overnight with Mac before I was married, and then I . . . I married someone else six months later. And that isn't all." Aurelia drew a shaky breath. "I . . . I stepped out on my husband and we . . . divorced. It seems I just couldn't quit Mac."

Julia paused, her brain racing. "Everyone will be focused on Guimares—not you," she finally said. What she didn't say was that Aurelia Fischer Dreyfus was right: perjury was no small matter, and revelation of her premarital "relations" and extramarital affair would indeed mean social ruin.

"It's OK, Miss Harpman," Aurelia said, her voice taking on an edge. "I've had six long years to think about this. People will say *awful* things. That's what's kept me silent. But I just cannot live like this any longer. It haunts me every hour of every day. My reputation is safe, but I'm not free. There's only one path forward, and this is it. It must be done. I'm resolved."

Julia circled Monday on her calendar. "Listen, why don't we meet today? I could leave now and be in Washington in a few hours."

"No. I have to tell my family," Aurelia said. "And I want to come back to New York—it seems right to do it there. I'll meet you Monday and tell you everything."

Julia hesitated. Her gut said this was a bad idea. But what other choice was there? She couldn't force the woman to meet, and trying to push the issue could spook a source. "Very well," she agreed.

"I still have my apartment through the end of the month: 128 West 59th Street. Say, around 1:00 p.m.?" Aurelia asked.

"I'll be there," Julia promised, scribbling it down. "I'm so glad you called. A heavy conscience is too great a burden to bear for one's whole life. You deserve peace."

"Yes," Aurelia said, sounding a fraction relieved. "I just want everything to be OK."

Julia swallowed. She knew better than to promise that. This case had already proved that money and power trumped truth and justice. Some powers that be had shifted in the last six years—Harry Daugherty had been removed as attorney general in 1924 and gone on to stand trial twice, then twice evaded conviction. On the record, he'd returned to practicing law. Off the record, who knew? He was still connected, still powerful, still dangerous.

Arnold Rothstein had been shot and killed almost one year ago, yet another unsolved murder in the city, and the one that had finally cost Captain Carey and Inspector Coughlin their jobs. But the Stotesbury-Mitchells lived on, insulated as ever by their wealth. This woman's testimony seemed to exonerate Mitchell. So why had he spent a fortune and pulled every political lever at his disposal to ensure the case was prematurely closed? Had it really just been to avoid further embarrassment for his family?

Julia had gone up against every Goliath involved in the Dot King case six years ago and lost. Would three fewer players on the board change the outcome this time? She wouldn't know until she tried, but she knew she'd always keep trying.

"Just keep thinking of Dot," Julia finally said. "She deserves justice and you deserve peace."

"I assure you, I think of little else," Aurelia said. Then she was gone.

Julia slowly replaced the phone. Six years ago, she'd accused Inspector Coughlin of being so wholly and utterly focused on Guimares that he'd failed to consider all evidence to the contrary, including any evidence against Mitchell.

Now, all these years later, this woman's testimony undercut Guimares's alibi, reminding Julia of the damning evidence pointing to Guimares. The unsettling possibility that she'd been so fixated on Mitchell that she'd ignored the case for Guimares as the killer came rushing back. It was a distressing, disheartening possibility. And yet, perhaps the time had come for redemption: her own as well as Aurelia Fischer Dreyfus's. It was six years too late, but as the saying went, better late than never.

Chapter 75

It was Sunday and Julia was spending it in the newsroom, brushing up on everything about Dot King's murder in preparation for her meeting with Aurelia Fischer Dreyfus the next day. Julia had pulled all her old articles and notes and was making a list of questions. Only two mattered: *Where was Guimares the night of the murder? Did he kill Dot King?*

"Awful perky for a Sunday," Hellinger groused, finding his way to his desk. "What gives?"

"Oh, only the Dot King case," she said.

Hellinger gaped. "No, sir!"

"Yes!" she said, his disbelief fueling her giddiness. "McBryan's Blonde called out of the blue and confessed she perjured herself. I'm meeting her tomorrow: one Aurelia Fischer Dreyfus."

Hellinger let out a long, low whistle. "That's the scoop to end all scoops!"

"Fingers crossed," she said. She returned her attention to her notes and considered. "So it seems Coughlin was right: it was Guimares after all."

Hellinger tipped his hat back. "That guy always gave me the creeps."

"Oh, he was *definitely* a creep," Julia agreed. "My only question was whether he was a murdering creep or just your garden-variety woman-beating, stock-fraud-committing creep."

"Hmm, well, based on this whole perjury angle, I'm going with murdering creep," Hellinger said, and winked.

Julia rolled her eyes. "So do you charge for your detective work? Or do you just offer up dazzlingly clever insights after someone else has done all the legwork?"

Hellinger put his hands up in surrender. "I'm just kidding. Listen, in all seriousness, you did a bang-up job six years ago, and you'll do it again now. You're the best in the business, Harpman, and everybody knows it."

"I want to believe I did a good job," Julia said, "but this has me rattled. When I learned about the bite marks on Guimares's hand, I got worried. But there was still so much evidence—*legitimate evidence*—pointing toward Mitchell. But now? If Guimares has no alibi? I'll have to face the flaws in my reporting."

"Don't be too hard on yourself," Hellinger said, and his tone, almost always jocular, took on a serious bent. "Being a watchdog all day every day could drive anyone batty."

Julia rubbed her forehead. "Couldn't we say the same about Coughlin?"

"The difference is, you're jumping back in," Hellinger pointed out. "But can we say the same about the police? Will they reopen their investigation? Will the DA finally charge Guimares? Heck, is the guy even still alive?"

Julia paged through the stack of old articles she'd been digging through and held out one. "He got three years in the Atlanta federal pen for using the mail to defraud investors. But with this perjury angle, Guimares should be back on the chopping block—this time for murder."

"Sharpen your pencil—you're back on the crime beat," Hellinger said, rubbing his hands together.

Nearby, Pete, standing near the telegraph desk, froze. "Julia . . ."

His stillness—wholly unnatural stillness—and the horror on his face stopped her cold.

They locked eyes for an interminable moment as a sickly dread cut through her. "What is it?"

He looked down at the telegram in his hands as though he couldn't quite believe it. "Did you say Aurelia Fischer Dreyfus?"

The hairs at the back of Julia's neck rose. She knew then that the worst had happened but couldn't speak.

Pete handed her the message and she made herself read it: Aurelia Fischer Dreyfus Killed in Mysterious Fall.

> Aurelia Fischer Dreyfus, NY socialite, fell from bal-
> cony last night. Potomac Boat Club. Autumn Soiree.
> Washington, DC. Still alive on impact. Rushed to hos-
> pital. Succumbed to injuries. Last seen with Edmund J.
> McBryan.

Each shocking tidbit felt like a slap.

"Oh my God." Julia rose as the words, hollow, shocked, tumbled out.

Edmund J. McBryan had been Guimares's friend and roommate. The guy Aurelia had had relations and later an affair with. She'd stayed in his hotel room the night of the murder, which had enabled her to provide Guimares's alibi in the first place.

On Friday, Aurelia said she'd perjured herself. Now she was dead.

The room began to spin as Julia replayed how Aurelia had said she shouldn't have called, that it had been a mistake, and Julia had issued confidence-boosting platitudes about peace and justice. But now Aurelia was dead, and her escort for the evening had been McBryan.

"You all right?" Hellinger asked quietly.

She shook her head. She hadn't realized Aurelia was still with him. When Aurelia had said, "It seems I just couldn't quit Mac," Julia had assumed she meant back then, not now. *But the news clearly said Aurelia was last seen with McBryan.*

So why would McBryan push her?

Julia's brain raced. One thing she knew for sure: there were creeps and rats and cheating bastards. The world was chock-full of them—heck, this *case* was chock-full of them. And conversely, there were friends and best friends. But nobody—*nobody!*—murdered their girl-friend of seven years because she planned to retract her alibi for a friend.

There had to be more. But what? Why would McBryan do it?

Julia had covered thousands of murders over her many years on the beat. Unless it was a cold-blooded killing for hire, murders committed by men almost always stemmed from primal emotions: fear, rage, greed, jealousy.

What had motivated McBryan? Julia's brain raced with possibili-ties. *Could it be unrelated to the King case?* The timing made that seem implausible.

Had McBryan somehow been involved in Dot King's murder?

Julia flipped through her old articles, not even sure what she was looking for. Dot King had been found on her bed, her arm twisted back in a hammerlock grip so violently that her fingertips grazed the base of her skull. *Could one man do that?*

Or had Guimares had an accomplice?

Three days ago, Julia had promised Aurelia everything would be fine. But she hadn't counted on Edmund J. McBryan. She'd had no idea Aurelia was still with him, but even if she'd known, she never could've anticipated he'd be willing to shove his girl off a balcony.

Bottom line: she hadn't counted on McBryan being a murderer. But was he? Now twice over?

If so, what had been the Guimares-McBryan team's motive in kill-ing Dot King? Obtaining the pink-toe letter as a tool for blackmail? Had the small fortune in jewels and furs they'd taken merely been a bonus?

A chill shimmied down Julia's spine. The person most motivated to keep that letter hidden was John Kearsley Mitchell. She'd always found his need to peg his alibi on John Thomas odd, his desperation to close the case excessive, the lengths to which he'd gone to do so extreme—especially since, unless he'd killed Dot himself, the greatest damage to his reputation was already done the moment he'd been publicly revealed as Marshall, a philanderer and sugar daddy.

What was she missing?

She drummed her fingers on the desk. It just didn't make sense.

Another bit of evidence that had never sat right was that Guimares's lawyer, Frederick Goldsmith, had called Mitchell at his home in Philadelphia. It was unheard of for one primary suspect's lawyer to call the other primary suspect . . . *unless they had a reason. Like those letters.*

Dot King had told Bobbie Ellis she'd rather die than have her sugar daddy blackmailed hours before she'd been killed.

Julia's thoughts raced, trying to fit the pieces of the puzzle together. On her desk, an old issue featured a photo of Guimares—handsome, suave, arrogant even as he stood accused of murder—staring back in his infamous $700 coat. What if Guimares, working with McBryan, his roommate and partner-in-crime since the duo's Boston days, had already put the blackmail plan in action while Dot was still alive? He might've gone around Dot and contacted Mitchell himself. Then all he needed was that pink-toe letter.

Guimares knew his way around the building. Dot King would've opened her door for him. It all fit. Except that John Thomas had sworn *nobody else* had gone in or out that night after the newlyweds.

Nobody, including John Kearsley Mitchell.

"What if Mitchell left by the stairs, which aligns with John Thomas's testimony, and held the spring-locked door open for Guimares . . . and McBryan?"

"Wait . . . *what?*" Hellinger asked.

"If Mitchell left by the stairs—as John Thomas claimed he must've—he could've held the emergency door for Guimares. Which explains why John Thomas never saw Mitchell leave *and* how Guimares as the killer, if, indeed, Mitchell wasn't the killer, got in."

Hellinger shook his head. "You lost me."

Julia raced on. "If the three men were in cahoots, it also explains why Guimares's lawyer called Mitchell at his home in Philadelphia—to warn him Guimares wasn't going down for this alone. And if Mitchell was directly involved, it also explains the extraordinary lengths he went to in order to shut down the case."

She rose and began to pace. "All this time, I assumed Mitchell and the Stotesbury family were motivated to spare Frances, and of course himself, further embarrassment. *But what if it was actually something far more serious? What if Mitchell wanted to avoid being charged with blackmail and manslaughter?*"

"Wait . . . you think they all acted together?" Hellinger looked as dumbfounded as she felt.

Julia paused—did she? It sounded crazy out loud. It also left some things unexplained like the downstairs neighbor who'd claimed she heard a scream and smelled chloroform when Mitchell himself admitted to still being there. Most glaringly of all, why wouldn't Mitchell have chloroformed her himself to ensure he got his incriminating letter back?

On the other hand, it seemed utterly implausible that Guimares had sustained scratches and bite marks on his hand any way *except* chloroforming Dot King. Those injuries combined with his weak, ever-changing alibi were damning. And most damning of all: Aurelia Fischer Dreyfus confessed she'd perjured herself and turned up dead that weekend while in the company of Edmund J. McBryan.

Still clutching the telegram, Julia rubbed her forehead. It was all so confounding. Warring emotions—guilt, regret, sadness—crashed over her, but she made herself focus on what she knew best: getting the story.

If Aurelia had died to set the record straight and finally get justice for Dot, the very least she deserved was to have that effort carried out. Julia steeled herself, kicked into gear. She would not let another woman die in vain.

She turned to the room at large, raised her voice. "All right, who do we have in DC? I want quotes from the DA, the detectives, and any witnesses we can get our hands on. I want to know who saw her fall.

Someone find McBryan and get a quote, even a denial! Hellinger, find Inspector Coughlin at that private company where he works. Tell him he was right about Guimares all along and get some sort of quote about how revenge and justice are best served cold. Then dig Guimares out of whatever hole he's taken up residence in and see what he has to say. Find Aurelia's friends and family and interview them. I want to know if she told anyone else what she told me. Pull everything there is on the King case. And I want pictures—of Dot, Aurelia, Guimares, McBryan, Mitchell, Frances Stotesbury, and anyone else we have. Let's go, everyone—we've got a story to get!"

The men scrambled to action. Perhaps she could *finally* get justice for Dot King after all. Or perhaps Aurelia's death was just a tragic coincidence—yet another in this bizarre, twisted case. Perhaps Guimares had acted alone. Perhaps, in fact, John Kearsley Mitchell, lounging at one of his many estates, was the killer.

In the end, Julia realized, she might never know for sure who had killed the Broadway Butterfly.

Or perhaps their coverage of Aurelia's death would set the wheels in motion to finally solve Dot's murder. There was no telling until they tried.

Julia went to the window and watched the bustle of pedestrians, motorcars, and buses below. How strange to think she'd shared this city with Dot King until the murder . . . and stranger still to think that Dot's killer (or killers!) was still out there, moving among the public, as though he hadn't taken a life. The injustice of it all was unbearable.

The truth was, two wrongs had been done to Dot King: first a man had taken her life, and second several powerful men had pulled every lever within their reach to curtail the investigation into her murder, thus denying her justice. Julia had hoped to blow the lid off the case, revealing the culprit to the public and spurring the authorities to pursue justice. But wealth, power, and influence had won out. Justice was, after all, for sale in New York City.

Once again, Julia would pound out a story to reveal the truth. And while she had failed to solve the crime, she could rest easy in knowing she had done everything she possibly could to fell the powers that had dared to interfere with the sanctity of the pursuit of justice.

Just as life goes on in the wake of death, always bizarrely, it seems, to those grieving the loss, so too did the justice system, as the police and DA turned their attention and allocated resources to other cases, and the newspapers scrambled to cover them.

But Julia would always think of the Broadway Butterfly.

That was the life of a crime reporter: to bear witness to the ripple effects of tragedy, and to have one's own life irrevocably intertwined with the people involved. And then to pick up and move on—always onward—to the next case, the next story, the next unbelievable set of facts. And so she would.

But Dot King's story would stay nestled inside her, in the way that all stories live inside their tellers. And in that way, on the page and in her heart, Dot King would live on.

Epilogue

February 25, 1930.

On Thursday, October 24, 1929, just four days after Aurelia Fischer Dreyfus plummeted from the Potomac Club balcony to her death, the stock market, which had been teetering precariously since September, began to fail. Morgan Bank spearheaded a $750 million fund to buy stocks and restore market confidence, which briefly held back the tide. But by the following week, all hell broke loose in the financial markets. On Black Monday, October 28, and Black Tuesday, October 29, the market was down nearly 25 percent. In spite of some signs of potential recovery in the following months, bank failures and panic gripped the nation in late 1930, and further freefall ensued through July 1932, by which point the Dow had lost nearly 90 percent of its prior peak value.

With the financial market tumult of October 1929 serving as the starting gun for the Great Depression, the death of a beautiful, wealthy New York divorcée was eclipsed by the world's economy crumbling. Every industrialized nation was affected. Some of the wealthiest families of American society were wiped out, and the most vulnerable were more desperate and disenfranchised than ever before. The Roaring Twenties—hallmarked by postwar elation, carefree excess, illicit booze, sexual exuberance, and newly liberated social and gender freedom—were abruptly over.

After a coroner's jury ruled that Aurelia Fischer Dreyfus's death was accidental, her mother and sisters filed affidavits attesting Aurelia told them she had intended to admit perjuring herself in the Dot King case and that they'd witnessed McBryan threatening and striking her.

Aurelia initially survived the fall. While waiting for the ambulance to take her to the hospital, Aurelia's sister swore that McBryan told Aurelia she'd better not mention anything about New York or Dot King. A nurse at the hospital testified that before Aurelia died, she'd mumbled incoherently, except for the words "He never gave me a chance."

Aurelia's sisters and mother successfully pressed the DA to convene a grand jury. On February 25, 1930, after hearing the testimony of twenty-nine witnesses, the grand jury ruled that Aurelia Fischer Dreyfus's death was accidental. Edmund McBryan was never called to testify.

In spite of the grand jury outcome, Aurelia's family continued to assert that she'd been killed because she knew too much about the Dot King case.

Postscript
(Warning: Contains Spoilers)

Dot King was born to Irish immigrant parents John Keenan and Catherine (sometimes called Kate) Delia King on November 11, 1894. The family lived on Amsterdam Avenue on the Upper West Side of Manhattan. As of the 1905 and 1910 censuses, she was in school and her father worked as a chauffeur, then a clerk. He eventually became a night watchman at Wannamaker's. Quite extraordinarily for the time, her mother later opened her own business, a laundry.

On her seventeenth birthday, Dot married Eugene Oppel. She later left him and moved back home with her mother and (younger) brothers John and Francis. John, who became head of the house after their father died, objected to her independent ways. When she had the audacity to cut her hair in the new "bobbed" flapper style *and* color it blonde, he kicked her out of the house. She quickly found work as a model and plunged into the glamorous, intoxicating life of New York City in the Roaring Twenties. She made her own money . . . and made her own choices. She lived alone, went to cabarets, dated various men, had multiple lovers, owned and drove her own cars, and loved jewelry, nice clothes, and fur coats. She was legendarily generous—literally giving a woman she didn't know, who had a job interview and nothing to wear, the dress she herself was wearing, then went home wearing only her "step-ins" under her coat. She considered Ella Bradford her only friend and confidante. She would've turned twenty-nine the year she was killed, but she told everyone she was twenty-seven.

Julia Harpman met fellow reporter Westbrook Pegler while reporting on the Elwell murder in June 1920. They married August 28, 1922. In a shocking twist, given the times, Julia continued to have an incredibly successful career as a journalist, rising to become a leading reporter in New York City and eventually the assistant editor on the city desk of the *Daily News*. She covered additional murders, as well as famous cases such as the Lindbergh baby kidnapping, and landed an exclusive to cover the historic swim of Gertrude Ederle, the first woman to cross the English Channel. Julia was in the boat next to Ederle as she made her famous crossing. Known as a consummate editor, Julia later devoted herself to supporting Westbrook's career. They were happily married until 1955, when Julia died of a heart attack while traveling in Rome.

Westbrook Pegler worked as a war correspondent, sports writer, and most famously, political editorialist, notoriously criticizing President and Mrs. Roosevelt and the New Deal. He went on to win the Pulitzer Prize for journalism for exposing criminal racketeering in labor unions. After Julia passed, Westbrook remarried twice. He is buried next to Julia.

Ella Bradford knew Dot King better than anyone, and provided the police with more information to help solve the case than anyone else. Her first loyalty was always to her employer and friend. In spite of the rampant racism that plagued the time, both police and newspapers universally acknowledged her as a respectable woman, wife, and mother who kept a proper home. In this way, at least, she was more highly regarded than her infamous employer.

Ella was born Nellie Anderson in Jacksonville, Florida. According to J. C. Hackett, secretary to the police commissioner, corrupt men within the department acted in conjunction with the DA's office to strongly suggest that Ella change her name and go into semi-hiding. Because of this, despite extensive research, I was able to find very little about Ella. She was almost certainly justifiably afraid of repercussions if she didn't do as authorities asked. Six years later, a white cleaning woman at the Central Park Hotel who was a key witness to Arnold Rothstein's murder did not tell the police what they wanted, and was held in jail for three months in spite of not being a suspect. Ella, as a Black woman, would have been even more vulnerable to police injustice and wrongful, unfounded imprisonment. Ella and her husband, James, had a second child. After many years of research, I was able to find two photos of her, which you can see on my website: saradivello. com/behindthescenes.

Frances Stotesbury Mitchell set sail for Europe with Jack, their two children, and two servants shortly after Dot's investigation was quietly closed. They returned in May 1924—an event that was covered in the *Daily News* (article and photo are also on my website, listed above). She remained married to her famously philandering husband and managed to keep her name and her family away from further scandal. Frances died on October 14, 1950, at the age of sixty-nine.

John Kearsley Mitchell III sold the Philadelphia Rubber Works in 1929. His family escaped any suffering from the Great Depression. He died peacefully at the age of seventy-eight at Red Rose Manor on November 29, 1949. He caused no further scandals.

Hilda Ferguson had an extraordinary onstage career, joining the famous Ziegfeld Follies in September 1923. She was known as "The Body" and considered one of the most beautiful girls in New York City. On February 7, 1926, the *Philadelphia Inquirer* noted that she had "been awarded numerous trophies for her skill [as a dancer] . . . and she has frequently been a model for many important art creations." She commanded the front cover of *Theatre Magazine*, September 1925 issue (also on my website). The success and independence she earned in New York allowed her to return to Baltimore to seek a divorce from her husband, who, she testified, locked all her clothes away to keep her imprisoned. She was granted the divorce and sole custody of her daughter, Yolanda.

Hilda, like Dot King (and probably because of her), was also involved with infamous Atlantic City racketeer and politician Nucky Johnson (the protagonist of HBO's hit series *Boardwalk Empire*). During their yearslong relationship, he built the Silver Slipper Cabaret for her, where she headlined shows and also starred as the hostess. Nucky kept the ninth-floor suite at the Ritz for Hilda's use. Years later, she "quit Nucky" and opened her own speakeasy, off Broadway in New York. The gangster "Tough Willie McCabe" was another of her famous lovers. She was arrested with him during his most famous encounter with the police, though she claimed to have been in the powder room during the drama. She died, possibly of a heart attack or peritonitis, in a New York City hospital in 1933. She was twenty-nine years old. Her daughter changed her name to Hilda and went on to have a well-regarded theatrical career of her own.

Inspector John D. Coughlin joined the NYPD in 1896 and was asked to step down on December 19, 1928, by Police Commissioner Whalen, who was brought in following accusations of police "laxity" after an official investigation, led by Coughlin, failed to solve Arnold Rothstein's murder.

Commissioner Whalen, on his first full day in office, forced Coughlin and Chief Inspector William J. Lahey into retirement. Coughlin's rebuttal, that Commissioner Whalen had also failed to produce any leads, suspects, or arrests in the Rothstein case, was ignored. Coughlin became the chief investigator for the privately held Johns Manville corporation, a position he continued in until the age of seventy-five. He and his sister, Mary, nicknamed Mamie, moved back to Yorkville in 1949 and lived next door to each other. He died two years later, after a lengthy illness, less than two blocks from where he was born and raised. His obituary in the *New York Times* noted that he "was particularly known for his courage and crime detection."

Chief Assistant District Attorney Ferdinand Pecora, who, under the intense glare of national media attention for nine days, staunchly refused to reveal the identity of the infamous "Mr. Marshall," was also

Sara DiVello

rumored to be a serial philanderer. In 1929, the DA chose Pecora as his successor, but the nomination was unsupported by Tammany Hall, the powerful, notoriously corrupt political machine that unofficially ran New York City politics. This was rumored to be because the members of Tammany Hall, rife with malfeasance, feared his honesty. Pecora quit and went into private practice until 1933, when he was appointed as the chief counsel to the US Senate Committee on Banking and Currency. The Senate committee hearings he led investigated the cause of the 1929 crash and launched a major reform of the American financial system, including legislation that we still use today: the Glass-Steagall Act, the Securities Act of 1933, and the Securities Exchange Act of 1934. In this role, Pecora crossed paths with the House of Morgan again, this time as an adversary. Pecora's questioning of J.P. Morgan Jr. on the stand led to the revelation that the man and his partners hadn't paid any income tax in 1931 and 1932, the height of the Great Depression, and ripped open the contrast between the rich and the millions of Americans struggling in abject poverty.

Rumors of Pecora's mismanagement of—and potential bribery during—the investigation into Dot King's murder resurfaced later in his career. He rebutted them, claiming it was his political adversaries' attempt to undermine him.

He was later appointed as a New York Supreme Court judge. Like Captain Arthur Carey and Secretary to the Medical Examiner George Petit LeBrun, he wrote a memoir. Unlike both of the other men, he did not mention the Dot King case.

Albert Guimares lived openly with Betty Piermont following Dot King's death. She was noted for being exceptionally tall. It was later revealed he had been cheating on Dot with Betty. They were married August 1, 1923, four and a half months after Dot was killed. He continued to have a reputation as a brute and a batterer, with neighbors often seeing Betty Piermont with bruises on her face. In October, Guimares was found guilty of defrauding the mail system, and in December he was sentenced to three years in the federal penitentiary in Atlanta.

406

On March 28, 1924, one year and thirteen days after Dot King was murdered, Betty Piermont Guimares was arrested on charges of attempting to steal a bolt of fabric. She was wearing a sable coat that, police said, was similar to one allegedly stolen from Dot King's apartment.

After serving time in prison for defrauding the mails, Albert Guimares changed his name. In 1952, he was found dead of natural causes in the Hotel Madison, only a few blocks from Dot King's apartment.

Aurelia Fischer married Herbert Dreyfus, a wealthy stockbroker, on October 16, 1923; however, it appears she never stopped seeing Edmund McBryan. She traveled to Boston and stayed at the Copley Fairmont Hotel with McBryan for New Year's Eve 1923, where they told hotel staff they were on their honeymoon. Herbert filed for divorce in July 1924. In the proceedings, Aurelia claimed to have met and fallen in love with McBryan on 5th Avenue in 1922. Herbert said he found it "strange," then, that she'd married *him*. She replied she was sorry she had.

Philip A. Payne, renowned editor of the *New York Daily News*, nearsighted, partially deaf, and wild haired, possessed the soul of an entertainer. He had incredible instincts for story and showmanship, boundless energy, and a preternatural ability to turn any story into sizzling, sold-out, front-page news. He was unusual in that he not only gave female reporters a chance; he saw women as a potential advantage over his competitors. Tabloids were just budding, helped by the advent of photography, which made an exciting addition to otherwise word-dense pages of reporting at other papers. Nothing was too crazy to try. Under his crafty leadership—pulling stunts like trying to get a murder suspect to confess at a staged séance and resurrecting the same murder trial years after it had lost steam—the *News* became the largest distribution daily in the country. He died as theatrically as he'd lived—trying to make a transatlantic crossing in a tiny plane with two other men—in 1927. He left behind his second wife, Dorothy Hughes, an actress and the first Miss New York, who had also won the *News's* beauty contest in 1922.

Draper Daugherty turned up in Chicago after his successful escape from the Hartford sanitarium. In July 1928, he petitioned for divorce from his wife, Jean, daughter of West Virginia Congressman George Bowers. Draper was granted a divorce from the Mexican courts at Nogales and remarried almost immediately. He died in 1930 of complications from appendicitis at the age of forty-one. After his death, a pending lawsuit against him was revealed. In the lawsuit, actress Pearl Barremore claimed that she was the one who'd planned, engineered, and paid for Draper's dramatic escape from the sanitarium. They'd been secretly living together and in love. Her first attempt to free him had failed when the sanitarium employee she'd bribed disappeared with her money. She'd then hired two men to pretend their car was broken down. When Draper and his armed sanitarium escorts walked by, the two men asked for mechanical assistance. Draper jumped in the back; as the men raced off, the sanitarium security opened fire on the speeding getaway car, blowing out the tires. In spite of this, the men managed to get Draper to Pearl, waiting nearby in a sporty red roadster. Pearl and Draper made it to Chicago, where they continued living together while he promised to get a divorce. This continued for several years. Eventually, they split up. Pearl's lawsuit sought damages to the tune of thousands of dollars: reimbursement for the escape and then while supporting Draper in Chicago while he looked for work. They eventually parted ways, and she married Joseph P. Goodman, a stockbroker. She was never reimbursed by the Daugherty family.

Arnold Rothstein, consummate gambler, was also the largest drug kingpin and bootlegger in New York. He's credited with fixing the 1919 World Series and funneling organized crime into mechanized, efficient, corporate-like organization. Rothstein was shot in November 1928 at the Central Park Hotel after allegedly racking up $320,000 of debt in a poker game, which he promised to repay after the elections when he successfully backed President Hoover. He later died at a local hospital.

Even on his deathbed, he refused to name his killer. Like Dot King, his body was examined by Chief Medical Examiner Dr. Charles Norris. The case was investigated by Inspector Coughlin and Captain Carey and later used as grounds for their dismissal.

Homicide Squad Captain Arthur Carey continued to work on the force until December 1928, when Commissioner Whalen, who had been in office for three full days, asked him to step down. Whalen confronted Captain Carey with the statistics that while 228 murders had been committed between January and December 20 of that year, the homicide squad had made only two arrests. Whalen forced him into retirement on a captain's pension and dismantled the squad, moving from a centralized model to homicide squads for each borough. Captain Carey, who took only seventeen days of vacation during his fifteen-year tenure as captain of the squad, was said to be visibly devastated at the demotion—his voice quavered as he said goodbye to his team, and he was unable to give any statements to waiting newspapermen. Refusing retirement, Carey went to work as an investigator for the Westchester County DA for an additional two years.

Carey had seven children—three sons, two of whom became detectives, and four daughters. In 1930, he wrote *Memoirs of a Murder Man*. Although he estimated he'd worked on more than ten thousand cases, he devoted an entire chapter to the Dot King investigation. He wrote that he was keeping one important—and as of yet unshared—clue to himself in hopes that the murder would someday be solved. What that clue is, like the case itself, remains a mystery.

President Harding was a notorious adulterer. He carried on numerous affairs simultaneously, including with Carrie Fulton, his longtime friend James Fulton's wife, and Nan Britton, who was thirty-one years younger than him and became the mother of his only child, Elizabeth Ann Blaesing. The Harding family denied this claim and condemned Britton. Though Harding allegedly paid for Britton's personal, pregnancy, and child-support expenses, when he died unexpectedly, he left no provisions for his mistress and their daughter. Britton, suffering the stigma of being a single mother (and adulteress), wrote a book, *The President's Daughter*, to support them. No publisher would accept the book, so she published it through the Elizabeth Ann Guild, an organization she established to support children born out of wedlock. Politicians and the New York Society for the Suppression of Vice tried to prevent its printing and distribution, but the book was released. In 2014, the Library of Congress publicly released Harding's sexually explicit love letters to Fulton, and in 2015, DNA proved Elizabeth Ann was indeed Harding's daughter. Many speculate that the president was poisoned by his long-suffering wife, First Lady Florence Harding. Readers may wonder how Frances Stotesbury Mitchell received that news.

Attorney General Harry Daugherty became the subject of a US Senate investigation in March 1924. He was indicted in 1926 for misconduct, alleging that he had improperly received funds while serving as AG. The case went to trial twice. The first jury deadlocked—seven to five, in favor of conviction. During the second trial, only a single juror held out on conviction. Daugherty died peacefully in his sleep in 1941.

George Petit LeBrun continued working as secretary to the medical examiner until age forced him to retire. He estimates that, during his career, the ME's office investigated more than one hundred thousand deaths. In his hundredth year of life, he wrote a memoir, *It's Time to Tell*. In it, he says if the King investigation had been better handled and if Dr. Norris had overcome his fear and bias against opening his own investigation, the case could've been solved.

Mark Hellinger eventually left the world of journalism and produced the movie *The Naked City*, which won two Oscars and received praise as a film noir cult classic. The movie features a character and plot similar to Dot and her too-short life. Like Julia, he had a heart condition. *The Naked City* screenwriter Malvin Wald claimed that Hellinger knew Dot before she died.

In 1929, Hellinger judged a beauty contest sponsored by the *Daily News*. He later proposed to the winner, Gladys Glad, married her the next day, and the following day after that, wrote about it for the paper.

They divorced in 1932, then remarried one year later on their original wedding date (July 11). He died at forty-four of a heart attack.

Some unsolved cases stay with those who have worked on them for a lifetime. And some unsolved cases find, decades later, someone who will work on them again. In the notoriety of the case, in these pages, and in this teller, Dot King lives on. Which is perhaps exactly what this extraordinary young woman, whose time was unfairly and prematurely ended, would've hoped for.

THE BACKSTORY

I came to this story, and it came to me, in the most extraordinary and unexpected way, on what started out as a very ordinary day. I was fifty thousand words into writing another book when I went home to Philadelphia for Thanksgiving. I hunkered down at home on Black Friday and was sitting around eating leftovers with my aunts, uncles, and cousins when the conversation turned to reminiscing. My uncle Ed shared that when he and my uncle David were in high school, they used to walk over to the "Old Stotesbury Castle" to sneak cigarettes after class.

"Castle? What castle?" I asked, which led to the revelation that there used to be an enormous castle nearby . . . and there were still remnants standing.

Obviously, I needed to know more. We piled into cars and caravanned over. And there, five minutes away, in the middle of a very ordinary suburban housing development, between the Subarus and flower beds, stood six towering pillars, stretching fifty feet into the sky, that used to comprise the entrance to Whitemarsh Hall.

I was mesmerized. But that wasn't all. Throughout this field, on the original footprint of the estate, there was a stone staircase, a belvedere with carved stone faces, headless statues where a fountain had once gurgled. Scattered in people's yards and in the adjoining woods, pieces of stonework and statuary stood. I share photos I've taken on my website: saradivello.com/behindthescenes.

I felt like I was in Athens or Rome, among the remains of the Acropolis or Colosseum, but no, I was in suburban Philadelphia, and these were the last vestiges of "the Versailles of America." I went down the proverbial research rabbit hole and over the next several months learned everything I could about Whitemarsh Hall: it had 147 rooms, 28 bathrooms, 24 fireplaces, a ballroom, a gymnasium, a radio system, and a movie theater; a staff of 70 full-time gardeners to maintain the exquisitely kept grounds. President Harding was the first notable guest, before the family hosted a housewarming attended by eight hundred of their nearest and dearest friends.

I also learned about the family: E. T. Stotesbury, the wealthiest person in Pennsylvania; his second wife, Eva Cromwell; his daughters, Edith and Frances; and their husbands and children. I learned of their charitable work and summer homes.

But I knew I was meant to write something else. Eventually, I found a passing reference in a book about historical Philadelphia . . . Mr. Stotesbury's son-in-law had found himself in an uncomfortable position when his mistress, a young model in Manhattan, was discovered murdered.

My first thought was, *What about his wife? What must it have been like for* her?

I got goose bumps. This was my story. I had found it, and it had found me. I felt it with a deep visceral recognition that some people describe experiencing when they meet their soulmate.

Over the next nine years, I spent thousands of hours researching. I traveled to New York, Philadelphia, and other locations countless times. I applied for research passes to the University of Philadelphia Rare Books Collection, Columbia University Rare Books Collection, the Morgan Library and Museum's Reading Room, the Herbert Hoover Presidential Museum, and more.

I spent untold days in the New York City Public Library Microfilm Department, scrolling through rolls of microfiche and printing off Julia Harpman's articles.

I interviewed professors, detectives, forensic pathologists, and a psychic who works with the police and FBI to solve cold cases.

I ran into infuriating dead ends, and I experienced the addicting high of uncovering long-buried clues, including one of two copies still in existence in the world of J. C. Hackett's tell-all book.

The most magical moments came from feeling connected to these real-life people, having the honor of telling their stories, and feeling the privilege and responsibility of getting it right.

I have come to love and respect almost all of them, and even want to honor the accused murderers by telling the truth.

Most of all, I am grateful for the chance to tell this extraordinary true story about these extraordinary real people. They will live on within me . . . and now within you. Thank you for reading.

ACKNOWLEDGMENTS

It truly takes a village to bring a book into being, and I am so grateful to these incredible stewards of knowledge for sharing their expertise with me so that I could honor these real-life characters:

Professor David Witwer, PhD, for helping me understand Westbrook Pegler.

Professor Michael Perino, PhD, for helping me understand Ferdinand Pecora.

Professor John A. Morello, PhD, for his insights into the 1920 presidential election and Jazz Age politics.

Professor John Noakes, PhD, for helping me better understand this crime, criminal investigation, and murderous minds.

Professor Dina Pinsky, PhD, for her insights into Judaism, southern Judaism, Jewish feminism, and criminal justice.

Professor Mark Bauman at the Southern Jewish Historical Society, for helping me understand the history of the southern Jewish experience and what life would've been like for Julia and her family.

Professor Christopher Wilson, PhD, for helping me understand how policing in the 1920s was portrayed by the media.

Professor Marilynn Wilson, PhD, for helping me understand the history of police and police violence in New York City in the 1920s and beyond.

Professor Emeritus Martha Saxton, PhD, whose study of how gender, race, and socioeconomic factors impacted women at the turn of the century seemed like a custom-made godsend. Dr. Saxton not only added invaluable illumination to these characters and the time period but helped me understand my own experience as well.

Bernadine Nash-McClam, PhD, MBA, M-Div, MS, for her invaluable guidance, love, and support throughout the years, in helping me understand Coughlin and, especially, in helping me understand and portray Ella with honor, love, and authenticity.

Professor Piper Huguley, PhD, for helping me with Ella, Junebug, and sensitivity insights throughout.

Matthew Schaefer, archivist at the Herbert Hoover Presidential Library and Museum. Thank you for your help with Julia and Westbrook. Seeing their photos and papers was such a gift.

Maria Isabel Molestina-Kurlat, MLS, Librarian at the Morgan Museum.

John H. Pollack, Curator, Research Services, in the Kislak Center for Special Collections, Rare Books and Manuscripts at the University of Pennsylvania Libraries.

Rebecca Haggerty, research archivist at the New York Transit Museum. Thank you for all your help mapping 1923 commutes for all these folks and answering all my train, subway, and MTA questions.

To all the librarians in the Milstein Microform Reading Room at the New York Public Library, where I spent countless hours scrolling through rolls of microfiche and printing Julia's articles, thank you.

Melissa Boyd, for the clue that took this book in a whole new direction. After I stopped panic-screaming about the months of rewriting it would require, I knew it would be worth it.

Detective Bruce Coffin, Detective Jason Allison, Detective Mick Curley, and Captain Isabella Maldonado: thank you for helping me understand police work, the lives and mindsets of detectives, and the mindsets of perpetrators. Thank you, too, for your service in keeping your communities safe. Your work doesn't come without a cost to self and family. I see and appreciate you.

I am blessed to have the most incredible publishing team:

Jessica Tribble Wells: In the words of Chandler Bing, "Could you *be* any more amazing?" I'm so lucky to have found an editor who immediately *got* the magic of this story, and with whom I could communicate in *Friends*-ese with oblique references to episodes, dialogue, and the artful weaving of story! Thank you for your stewardship, support, and belief in this project.

Celia Blue-Johnson: You exceeded every hope and expectation I ever dared to have for an editor. Your gentle, extremely wise counsel elevated, polished, and honed this story in ways far beyond anything I could've done. You're the partner in crime I was seeking.

Kellie Osborne: I didn't know eagle eyes of this caliber existed. I'm slightly terrified . . . and incredibly impressed. (Also, is this grammatically correct? If there's a mistake, blame Celia.)

Richard Ljoenes: I got goose bumps when I saw the cover. It is so deep-down *right*. I have no idea how you homed in on the essence of this story and created something so beautiful, but I am grateful.

Tamara Arellano: Thank you for keeping the trains running and me on track!

Robin O'Dell: Thank you for your editing and care with this project.

Jill Schoenhaut: Thank you for your extremely careful proofreading and fact-checking.

Shuja Khan: Thank you for your sensitivity read.

Ashley Vanicek: Thank you for reading and believing in my work and cheering me on. You empower and uplift women and stories. It's a gift to have a collaborator turn into a friend like you.

Liza Fleissig: Thank you for your fierce advocacy, your belief in me, your innovation and hustle, your Mediterranean ways, your fondness of jackfruit tacos and oat-milk cappuccinos, and your indomitable determination. You *get* this story (and me!).

My family and friends are my fierce champions and my soft place to land.

Allen Nunnally: It can't be easy to live with a writer . . . from the research highs to the self-doubt lows (often before lunch! On a good day!), from the night-owl hours to the *A Beautiful Mind* decor (strangely, I hear not everyone would love giant Post-its all over their living-room walls!), you have tolerated, supported, and encouraged me. Thank you for your love, patience, belief in me and in this book, comfort when I (frequently) had doubts, and constant cheerleading.

Captain Hanna DiVello, ninja detective and investigator extraordinaire, who plucked the clue from Melissa while I bemoaned that we would *never, ever* find it. Somehow you did, which took me to UPenn's Rare Books collection and the last-known copy of the tell-all that changed everything.

Joan Lagan: my adoptive mother. When you told me that it would be OK even if this book took me ten years, I almost panicked. But as usual, you were right. I love you.

Lisa Genova, PhD: As Janice (née Hosenstein) Litman-Goralick says, "Oh . . . my . . . God." I am so blessed to have you in my world. Thank you for your love, support, and believing in this book (and me!). Your wise counsel and guidance on writing and editing, on finding balance and flow, and your excitement about this story has truly meant *the world* to me.

Caroline Leavitt: Your kindness, compassion, empowerment, and support of others is so beautiful and so heartfelt. You are the real deal and have the purest heart. Thank you for believing in me and for supporting me.

Lisa Unger: Your fullhearted, openhearted approach to writing and community is so inspiring. I'm so blessed to have you as a friend.

Lisa Sharkey: my owl-loving, bird-watching, Central Park–exploring, NYC-loving, yoga-doing, dog-loving soul sister. I love our walks and talks and I'm so grateful to have met you.

J.T. Ellison: Thank you for your support, wisdom, and advice. Whether it's your cats or my cat-size dog, it's such a joy to have met a fellow yogi and thrillerista.

Heather Gudenkauf: From one of the very first authors I interviewed to three years later, a friend and fellow dog mom, I so appreciate your support.

Kimberley Howe: Thank you so much for your support, invaluable insights, and advice. Your ability to listen deeply and hold space for others is so special, and your kindness and mentorship is a rare gift to the writer community.

Amy B. Scher: Without our daily texts alternately cheering and bemoaning (and sometimes crying) as we slogged through the process of creating our books, I would be lost. Somewhere between my fondness for details and your intolerance of them lies the golden land. We'll find it someday. Until then, we have Bloody Mary Fridays.

Judy Ginsberg-Sinsheimer: From lunches at Shun's as you listened to me endlessly drone on about minute research to calls, yoga, and texts. Thank you for your unending support and love.

Helen Klaebe, PhD: Thank you for reading, critiquing, supporting, and cheering for me. From Brisbane to Boston, from 1998 to now, you are my Aussie sister from another mister. I'm so blessed to have you in my corner!

Saumya, Jill, and Alicia: Thank you for being there with advice, support, camaraderie. The gift of your friendship is precious.

Christina Cook: Your deep love of books and your appreciation for story and storytellers is heartfelt. Stories are the song of your soul and your lifeblood. You are an incredible gift to the author and reader community. You have such a generous and good heart, and I am so grateful for you.

Marcie Ann Cagle: Queen of the Haus of Thrillers, rescuer of cat-size dogs. You showed up on New Year's night like some Xena Warrior Princess x guardian angel mashup. Your incredible generosity, support, and fierce advocacy is such a blessing, and I am so grateful for you.

My writing group: Karin Crompton, thank you for your incredible, careful editing and for *getting* this story. Katherine and Debs, queen of the roulette table, cheerleaders of spirit, thank you.

Andi: Thank you for listening to me vent and bemoan the trials and tribulations throughout this process. Someday I may even learn to purl. Until then, I'll keep on with the garter stitch and scarves while you whip up works of art.

Gonzali sisters (Reb and Sandy): Thank you for your support through two books, your readiness to leap behind the camera (Sandy) and your decisiveness on marketing options (Reb).

And finally to Pelu, who has walked, sat, and slept by my side as I've worked every single day, alternately guarding the window and soothing me with her meditative canine breathing: Thank you. Rescued is my favorite breed.

ABOUT THE AUTHOR

Photo © 2022 Lisa Schaffer Photography

Sara DiVello is a true-crime novelist and the creator/host of the Mystery and Thriller Mavens Author Interview Series. She also serves as the director of social media strategy for the International Thriller Writers association. Sara has appeared on CBS, ABC, and CNBC, as well as in the *New York Times*, *Forbes*, the *San Francisco Chronicle*, and more. Her articles have been published in *Marie Claire*, *Elle*, *Redbook*, *Cosmopolitan*, and *Woman's Day*, as well as in other outlets. In her spare time, Sara loves to cook (and eat!), garden, and go for leisurely walks with her husband and their beloved rescue mutt, Pelu.

She runs the Mystery and Thriller Mavens Facebook group, a free online book group where readers can continue the conversation. All are welcome. To learn more, and download book club questions, please visit www.saradivello.com.

Sara loves to connect on social media! Find her on all platforms:
Facebook.com/AuthorSaraDiVello
Instagram: @saradivello
Twitter: @SaraDiVello
TikTok: @saradivello